Traumatized in childhood by the tragic loss of her parents and then starved of love in an uncaring adoptive home, young Beth Morgan falls easy prey to the silk-tongued charms of handsome, dashing Kevin Brady. But from then her life is thrown into chaos and terror by him and his domineering family.

Finally, brutalized beyond endurance - emotionally by the horrific discoveries of her new husband's evil, covert activities and physically by her bullying brother-in-law - Beth is rescued from their clutches after Kevin's murder brings her to the abyss of insanity.

Brought into the loving care of two unlikely priests, one Catholic, the other Protestant, both sharing a calling and a gift for healing - not so much of the body as of the emotional and spiritual damage that trauma and despair can wreak upon their victims - Beth is gradually brought back from the edge and restored to wholeness, freed from the stranglehold of fear by experiences of the benign, loving, healing reality of the Holy Spirit.

Along the way to restoration brought about by these life-transforming events she finds a greater dimension of love, forgiveness and understanding which expunges the burdens of her troubled past, undertakes an act of selfless generosity toward the families of her evil-doing husband's victims and encounters a profound and abiding love with whom to share the new creation that she has become.

Tessa Charles was born in Birmingham, England in 1948 and moved to British Columbia, Canada with her family as a child. There she grew up and married, returning to England in 1970 to raise a family of 2 daughters. She and her husband now live in Gloucestershire.

Seeds of Redemption

Dedicated to Hope

Seeds of Redemption

Tessa Charles

THE
HONEST TO GOODNESS
PUBLISHING COMPANY

Gloucester, England

Published 1997 by
The Honest To Goodness Publishing Company
Gloucester, England

ISBN 0 9531396 0 3

Cover illustrations by Dee Washbrook
Cover design by Dan Lewis

Printed and bound in Great Britain by
Biddles Limited
Guildford

Seeds of Redemption

Bless the LORD, O my soul;
And all that is within me, *bless* His holy name!
Bless the LORD, O my soul,
And forget not all His benefits:
Who forgives all your iniquities,
Who heals all your diseases,
Who redeems your life from destruction,
Who crowns you with lovingkindness and tender mercies...

Psalm 103 vs 1-4
NKJV

Whirlwind

Fair laughs the morn, and soft the zephyr blows,
While proudly riding o'er the azure realm,
In gallant trim the gilded vessel goes;
Youth on the prow, and Pleasure at the helm;
Regardless of the sweeping whirlwind's sway,
That, hushed in grim repose, expects his evening prey.
Thomas Gray 1716 - 1771
'The Bard' (1757)

1

Beth hurried in from the street, through the large, imposing doors to O'Grady's Fine Art Emporium. She was almost late for work but that was hardly surprising on such a beautiful morning. It was the first really cold, crisp day of autumn, to her the very best time of year. The air was so clear, so cleansing after the stifling heat of the long summer. This was to be her second winter in Boston after moving down from Canada. She was really loving her life, her freedom, her part-time job at O'Grady's that adequately paid her rent and enabled her to spend as much time as possible on her real love - painting.

Beth was totally unaware of the picture she created as she swept into the large store. The cold air had brought a soft blush to her cheeks and a sparkle to her beautiful, dark eyes. Her short, black hair, feathered lightly about her face, gave her an elfin quality.

Her appearance did not go unobserved by the tall, dark-haired man who had been intently studying an elaborate porcelain figurine that he had noticed from the sidewalk, tantalisingly positioned on a small table near the window, successfully drawing him into the store. It would make a perfect gift to take home to his mother in Belfast at the end of his business trip. She would appreciate it even more that it had come from O'Grady's, for that had been her grandmother's name before she married Michael Kelly shortly before they emigrated to Boston. Their son, her father, had returned to Belfast as a young man to establish his family business now being managed by her own sons.

He looked after Beth as she hurried through to the staff rooms at the back of the store to remove her outer garments and begin work. Then he looked again at the figurine in his hand and knew a keen sense of disappointment. Suddenly it seemed almost tawdry. He hurriedly replaced it on the table, almost upsetting it in his haste to put it down. Who was this girl that she could affect him so immediately? She looked nothing like his usual preference in women - tall, blonde, leggy and with intelligence not a priority.

Sean O'Grady, the owner of the emporium, emerged from his office and hurried across as soon as he saw the young man, trying as he went to hide his anxiety.

"Kevin, my friend," he said. "This certainly is a surprise. I didn't expect to see you here this morning. I thought we had concluded all our business last evening. Has anything else come up? Everything seemed to be settled okay last night."

"Don't worry, old man," Kevin replied. "This is a purely personal visit. Just to browse around and maybe do some shopping to take home. I'm certainly impressed with the goods you have on display," he added rather pointedly as Beth returned to the display area. "Very intriguing."

"Can I leave you to look around on your own?" Sean sounded more relaxed now. "I have some phone calls to make and I've just had some new stock in that needs to be sorted out. Come and see me before you go. Ask Beth or Dick if you need any help." He waved his arm vaguely in the direction of his assistants, busy with their work.

Beth was arranging some silver pieces on the display shelves. She was struggling to place a small vase on the top shelf when it was suddenly taken from her hand and a voice behind her spoke in a deep Irish accent.

"You don't look like Dick so you must be Beth. Allow me," and the vase was placed neatly in the middle of the shelf.

Beth spun around and looked up in amazement into the handsome face of the man she had glimpsed examining the figurine as she arrived for work. She was so astounded that she could think of nothing to say. All she was aware of were his brilliant blue eyes laughing down at her, in such contrast to his intensely black hair.

"You'd better close your mouth, there's a Number 49 bus

coming," he teased.

"A 49 *what*!" Beth stammered.

"Sure, did you never say that when you were a child?" he laughed. "Or were you ever a child at all? Did the Little People not just bring you here as a gift for me, all wrapped in rosy cheeks and fine black feathers?" and he ruffled her hair.

Beth was suddenly angry and she took a step backwards and bumped into the display shelves, which made her even more angry because she also felt trapped.

"Don't touch me!" she snapped. "Who do you think you are? How dare you sneak up behind me and frighten me like that! Go away and let me get on with my work." She stepped forward, hoping he would move out of her way and let her escape but he stood his ground.

His eyes were now positively dancing with merriment. "Who do I think I am? Well now, I thought I was Prince Charming come to help a damsel in distress because she couldn't reach the top shelf, even standing on the tips of her dainty toes. But sure, I've been felled by love." His legs suddenly buckled under him as if he was about to fall to his knees.

"Don't you dare move!" hissed Beth. "Now go away and leave me alone."

"First you tell me to go away, then you tell me not to move and then you tell me to go away. Sure, you sound more Irish than I do meself." He was visibly shaking with suppressed laughter. "All right, all right, you win." He raised his arms in mock surrender. "I promise to behave myself if you will show me some of your finest treasures. After all, I am a paying customer and Sean said I was to ask you if I needed any help."

"Ask Dick!" snapped Beth.

"Oh, but Dick isn't nearly as pretty as you and I'm sure his eyes don't flash the way yours do when you're angry and besides, he's with someone else right now."

Beth glanced around quickly and saw to her dismay that Dick was indeed busy with another customer.

"I really am very busy," she said coldly. "Couldn't you just look around until Dick is free?"

"But you see, I have rather a lot of money to spend and I'm sure Sean would not be too happy if I was to spend it elsewhere because his staff were 'too busy' to assist me."

"Now you're being unfair. Emotional blackmail is very undignified and ungentlemanly."

"You're right, I am being unfair and I'm genuinely sorry that I teased you so much. I honestly didn't mean to upset you. Please show me that you forgive me by having lunch with me today."

Beth opened her mouth to refuse but to her horror found herself saying yes! "I don't even know your name," she added. "No. Really I can't. It wouldn't be right. I can't have lunch with a complete stranger. I really couldn't."

"But you have already said yes and you can't go back on your word. Besides, how can I be a complete stranger when we have known each other for ever? I, Kevin William Brady, and you, Beth - I don't know the rest - are one and have been one since the beginning of time."

"Elizabeth Madeline Morgan," whispered Beth.

"Well, Elizabeth Madeline Morgan, I wish to buy some gifts. Come and show me what is on offer." He turned away abruptly, breaking the spell and leaving Beth stunned.

She stumbled after him, thinking to herself, he is crazy. He has just *got* to be crazy!

2

What am I *doing* here? *Why* am I here? How did I even *get* here? I must be as crazy as he is! These thoughts tumbled through Beth's mind as she gazed, almost in disbelief, at Kevin sitting across the table from her in Luigi's.

Kevin was leaning back casually in his chair, chatting with Luigi as if they were lifelong friends instead of complete strangers. When Kevin and Beth had entered the restaurant, Luigi had come towards them immediately, as though drawn by a magnet.

Beth had been coming to Luigi's every working-day lunch-time for almost two years, as it was more convenient for her to have a proper cooked meal at midday so she was able to just grab a snack when she got home from work and then concentrate on her painting. By now she considered herself as one of the regulars at Luigi's and all the staff treated her as such, including Luigi, who always raised his hand to her and exchanged a few words of greeting. Never before had he escorted her to a table, yet here he was, actually taking their order personally. That sort of treatment was reserved for the very select few, those who had known Luigi for years and were usually fellow Italians.

What is it about this man? wondered Beth. What charm, what charisma does he possess? It is almost as if he has them all bewitched. *Bewitched*!

She remembered suddenly the thrill of seeing that programme on television when she was a young girl. The thrill was not so much in the programme itself, although it had been fun then, but in the fact that she was watching it illicitly. It was one of the many programmes that she was forbidden to watch but it was on T.V. on the night when Aunt Mildred and Uncle Douglas went to one of their many church meetings. Beth couldn't think of any other way in which she had defied her aunt and uncle but perhaps this act was a subconscious rebellion against their very strict regime.

They told her repeatedly that it was for her own good, that a frivolous nature only led to unhappiness and self-destruction. And it was well known, to their personal shame, that both her parents had been disastrously frivolous.

Mildred had been a plain, serious, friendless girl and an only child for many years. With what appeared to her to be alarming regularity, her mother began to get fat and would have to spend long hours each day resting. Although Mildred dutifully loved her mother, she came to resent these times of resting as she then had to do even more to help around the house. Her mother managed to do most of the cooking but the cleaning, housework and laundry were very hard work for a young girl and Mildred was often too exhausted to go to Sunday School, the only activity she had outside her home and school and the one thing for which she lived through each week.

Each spell of getting fat and resting always ended the same way, when her mother was mysteriously no longer fat but now spent all day in bed, crying silently to herself. Then Mildred had even more to do as her mother was incapable of doing any cooking. The family meals were very basic then, often burned or not fully cooked, as Mildred tried hard to cope with this new and quite frightening task.

When Mildred was twelve, her mother stayed fatter for much longer than usual. By now Mildred was so used to doing most of the housework that she hardly noticed, except that she had never seen her mother so fat before. The doctor came most days to visit and as her mother's stomach grew bigger and bigger, Mildred became quite frightened that there was something seriously wrong with her. Whenever she asked her father what was happening, she was simply told not to worry. No matter how hard she prayed, her mother's stomach kept on growing until one night Mildred was awakened by her father shaking her shoulder. He was holding her big winter coat and he helped her into it as she struggled sleepily from her warm bed. Without saying anything, he took her across the road to old Mrs Smythe who put her straight to bed in a made-up cot, telling her not to worry!

Several days passed, during which time Mildred lived with Mrs Smythe, going to and from school as usual, but for once having no housework to do. She spent long hours looking from the front window over to her own house. She could see no activity other than the doctor's daily visits. At Mrs Smythe's urging, she prayed even harder for her mother, but really didn't know what she was praying about.

Then one day her father came to fetch her home. Mildred felt a great sense of relief when she saw his smiling face. Surely all must be well if he was so happy. Maybe her mother would now be strong and Mildred wouldn't have to do so much around the house. However, when she got home she found that her mother was still in bed. Her father took her into their bedroom where her mother was sitting up in bed, smiling and looking a lot thinner. Mildred was puzzled that this time she was not crying.

Mildred then noticed that the old family cradle was standing by her mother's bed. She walked slowly over to it and looked in. To her utter astonishment she saw a tiny, dark-haired baby inside. This, apparently, was her new sister, Diana, who had been brought by the angels on the night when she, Mildred, had been dumped on old Mrs Smythe! *How dare they*! *How dare any of them*! And now she would have even *more* work to do because her mother needed all her time and energy for looking after the baby. *Diana*!! What a *stupid, frivolous* name! Mildred fled from the room to the sanctuary of her own room, which she would soon have to share with the interloper.

Over the years Mildred's dislike for Diana hardened into a bitter core of hatred, deep within her, known only to herself and God, may He forgive her, but what else did He expect considering the way in which she had been treated? To her disgust, Mildred eventually learned the true details of Diana's birth and vowed never to have children of her own.

Because Diana's birth was premature, she remained a tiny, frail child but unlike her plain, heavy-set sister, she was beautiful. As dark as Mildred was mousey-brown, as happy and carefree as Mildred was dour and put-upon.

When Mildred was twenty, Douglas Pratt asked her to marry him. Both were members of the local Unitarian church and had known each other all their lives. Like Mildred, Douglas was a dour, sombre man, not given to frivolities, his most redeeming feature in Mildred's eyes. By accepting his proposal of marriage, Mildred would have the perfect excuse to leave home and get away from that she-devil,

Diana, for surely she was not from the angels and therefore not from God. Nothing so frivolous could be a product of *her* God. *Her* God demanded discipline and duty, not laughter and merriment. That creature had turned their family upside down. But she, Mildred, was not fooled. She knew her duty.

When Douglas told her that after their wedding they were to move north because of his new job, Mildred almost wept for joy. Now there could be no calling her daily to come and help around the house or look after the brat. Now, at last, she had been vindicated.

Mildred and Douglas were married with the minimum of fuss and moved away to start their new life together. They chose not to make return visits to their old home town but maintained contact with infrequent letters, Christmas and birthday cards. True to her self-determined word, Mildred had no children. This did not appear to bother Douglas who did not seem to be either happy or unhappy but was accepting of and settled in his daily routine of work and church, with Mildred silently, almost stoically, by his side.

Just after their tenth wedding anniversary had passed, acknowledged by a quiet dinner for two at a local restaurant, they received an invitation to Diana's wedding. Mildred was shocked to realise that the little eight-year-old she had last seen was now eighteen and about to be married. She had never cast more than a cursory glance at the photographs their mother sent each year before they were put in an old shoe box, never to be looked at again. According to her mother's letter, Diana was marrying a David Morgan from Vancouver. He was twenty-eight, a pilot with his own small plane, doing private charter work. Typical Diana! Marrying someone flashy and flamboyant and very likely frivolous, too!

All the bitter resentment and hatred was rekindled in Mildred and she announced that nothing on earth would induce her to attend such a charade. Only when Douglas pointed out that it was their Christian duty to attend did Mildred relent and accept the invitation.

As she feared, it was, in her eyes, a mockery of a wedding. Diana was radiant with happiness and David was all Mildred had suspected: tall, dark, devastatingly handsome and utterly charming. *Flashy, flamboyant and frivolous.* Her bitterness was tinged with smugness. *They will come to grief!*

In her stark navy blue dress and jacket and navy lace-up shoes, Mildred looked more like a maiden aunt than the sister of the bride and the guests paid her as little attention as if she *were* a maiden aunt. Mildred didn't know whether to feel angry or triumphant at this behaviour. What did surprise her, even shock her, was Diana's obvious delight on seeing her again. For Diana truly loved her older sister and had missed her very much over the years. Mildred was outwardly pleasant to Diana, indeed to everyone with whom she had contact and nobody, not even Douglas, was aware of the bitter, angry resentment that roiled within her.

Mildred thought she had acquitted herself quite satisfactorily until after the newlyweds and all the guests had departed and she and Douglas were alone with her parents. She was so unprepared for the bombshell that they then dropped on her that at first it simply wouldn't register. It transpired that David was a Roman Catholic and their minister had been happy to allow the marriage in *their* Unitarian church. Mildred felt as though she herself had personally been defiled. But even worse than that, Diana was preparing to become a Catholic as well. Mildred's rage knew no bounds. She demanded that Douglas take her home immediately even though they were due to stay for another three days. She would not stay a moment longer in a house where such shameful things were allowed to happen. She had always known that Diana was a she-devil and now she had contaminated their parents with her wicked ideas and they had been weak enough to be swayed by her wiles. She, Mildred, would *never* return to such an ungodly place again.

3

From the infrequent letters sent by her mother over the next two years, Mildred learned that Diana and David were wonderfully happy. She often accompanied him on his various flying missions all over the country. Then came the news that Diana had given birth to a daughter, Elizabeth Madeline. Yet another frivolous name! Despite Diana's pleas, Mildred refused emphatically to attend the baby's christening. Nothing and no-one would ever induce her to set foot in a Roman Catholic church. That would be a fate worse than death itself.

When Elizabeth was a year old, Diana and David announced plans for a visit to Mildred and Douglas. At first Mildred was outraged and refused point-blank to allow them into her home but Douglas, for once asserting himself and speaking out against Mildred, put his foot down and reminded her, once again, of her 'Christian duty'. Mildred was so astounded at his quiet but determined show of authority that she relented and allowed the visit to take place.

Diana again was delighted to see her sister and told baby Beth, in front of all the family, that Mildred had been such a kind and caring sister to her that she wanted Beth to grow up knowing her auntie so that she, too, would learn what a wonderful person she was. Mildred was speechless! The child actually meant every word she was saying. She really believed that all the things Mildred had done for her as a child were done through love, not duty. She truly believed that Mildred was a very special person.

Diana's genuine love and Mildred's resultant confusion gradually brought about a partial transformation in Mildred. Whilst she would never forgive Diana for her religious defection and she would always be contemptuous of what she perceived as flamboyance and frivolity, Mildred actually began to look forward to the annual visits from Diana and her little family.

Beth was growing into a beautiful little girl, as dark as both her parents and as dainty as Diana. She was a gentle child and Mildred had to admit that she was very well behaved and actually found herself becoming quite fond of her, although she would never overtly show this to anyone.

During the Easter holidays, just before she turned ten, Beth went to stay with Aunt Mildred and Uncle Douglas on her own for a week. To celebrate David's fortieth birthday, he and Diana were going to fly out west and then down to Oregon, visiting friends and relatives along the way. They had been gone three days when news reached Mildred that their light plane had crashed in the mountains during a dreadful, freak storm. Both had been killed instantly. Mildred reminded Douglas that she had said they would come to grief but secretly, deep inside, she was the one who grieved.

Beth's world fell apart. As her parents had made no provisions and had also left very little money, it was decided amongst the various family members that the best course of action was for Beth to remain with Mildred and Douglas. They would become her legal guardians. Beth was so bereft that she really didn't care where she lived or with whom. Whoever they were, they were not her adored parents and could never replace them in any way.

As a concession to the tragic circumstances, Mildred agreed that Beth would continue at a Catholic school; there was apparently a very good one in their town. After all, the child had been brought up Catholic and had had enough changes lately; one more might just be too much.

Mildred and Douglas were dutiful guardians, kind but not particularly warm, very strict but not unfair. Beth adjusted to this new, strange way of life with resignation. She knew she could do nothing to change things back to the way they had been so she just had to accept the situation the way it was now. Only at night when she was alone in her room did she give in to her grief, weeping silently into her pillow. She didn't think she could possibly bear the pain of not seeing her parents again, not hearing her mother's delightful bubbling laughter, not feeling her father's strong hands on her as he swung her into the air each day when he came home, laughing with her as he caught her to himself in a huge bear-hug. They had been so happy, so complete, the three of them. Would she ever be happy and whole again? She doubted it. Aunt Mildred and Uncle Douglas were kind in their own way but they never touched her, never kissed or hugged her, never showed her any affection. How she hungered for affection!

Beth remained a quiet, withdrawn girl as she grew into her teens. She had a few friends at school but was never allowed to bring them home (one heathen in the house at a time was more than enough for Mildred!) and felt slightly guilty if she spent too long at their homes. The only time she was truly happy was when she was painting. One of the nuns at school had discovered that Beth had a definite talent and did all she could to develop and encourage this. When she was painting, Beth could be her true self, could find a release for all the emotions she had to keep suppressed in order to maintain the delicate equilibrium at home.

Mildred was not impressed with Beth's burgeoning talent as she considered art to be frivolous and not a worthy occupation for a decently raised girl. However, when she was in grade twelve, Beth won a scholarship to university to study art and so in September she packed all her belongings and headed south for Toronto. Mildred's work was finished. She had done her duty and raised her dead sister's daughter to be a decent, God-fearing young woman with no frills and fancies, no airs and graces. God knew her sacrifices and that she had done her best and now it was ended. But how she missed that little gentle soul around the house. Only she and God would ever know. No-one would hear it from her lips!

4

Luigi himself brought their meal to their table and opened the bottle of wine that Kevin had ordered. Beth gently shook her head in wonderment. This personal service for other than his closest friends was so rare for Luigi that his staff and some of the regulars were glancing over at them with questioning looks tinged with some degree of respect. Beth was starting to feel a little uncomfortable under such scrutiny. After pouring Kevin a glass of wine (Beth had refused any) and exhorting them to "Enjoy!", Luigi left them to their meal. Those around them turned back to their own meals and conversations and Beth began to feel less uneasy. To her surprise she became aware of herself relaxing and she certainly was enjoying her lunch - Luigi's mushroom fettucini was the very best!

"Can I persuade you to try a glass of this really excellent wine?" urged Kevin. "It will help you to unwind a bit. You've been looking as nervous as the proverbial cat on a hot tin roof, although in your case, it should be kitten."

"Thank you, but I never drink mid-day, especially when I'm working. Besides, I need all my wits about me to keep up with you. I just don't know what you're going to do or say next," replied Beth.

"Sure, I can't be that difficult to read, can I? I'm like an open book written in extra-large print for all the world to see. It must be as clear as the finest crystal that I have fallen deeply, completely, irrevocably and totally head-over-heels in love. God help me, but I'm totally done for. You will marry me, of course?"

Beth slowly put down her fork, drew herself up as tall as she could and looked up at Kevin across the table from her.

"Mr Brady," she began.

"Kevin."

"Mr Brady, this nonsense really has to stop. A joke is a joke and I enjoy a good laugh as much as the next person, but this is starting to not be funny at all. In fact, it is becoming embarrassing and I am not enjoying being the butt of such frivolity." (Oh my goodness, she thought with horror. I sound just like Aunt Mildred!)

"Oh Beth! Sweet Beth. Can you not see that I am deadly

serious? I promise you, there is nothing remotely frivolous about my feelings for you. I feel as though I've been struck by a bolt of lightning and I'm all turned upside down. I have never, ever felt like this in all my life. I know I've been teasing you and seem to be making light of all this but, honestly, I'm so taken aback by what has happened to me that I hardly know how to act. Please, *please* believe me. I'm in deadly earnest," he pleaded.

He had reached across the table to take Beth's hand and was now pressing it so hard that she winced. Before Beth could say anything, he realised what he had done, leaned forward and raised her hand to his lips. He kissed it gently several times and murmured, "Oh my sweet little darling. I'm so sorry, so very sorry. I wouldn't hurt you for all the world."

Then he looked up and said, "I promise you I will never, I *could* never, hurt you in any way, but please marry me, Beth. I don't think I could stand it if you were to say no. It would be the very end of me. My life would not be worth living. Oh, don't worry," he added hurriedly, when he saw the shocked expression on Beth's face. "I won't do anything silly but I might as well become a priest, for there would be nothing else for me to live for, I'm sure of it."

"And I'm sure that they wouldn't take you. And *I* can't take you seriously, either. I don't think I can believe anything you say. I've heard all about the famous Irish Blarney from Sean but this is verging on the ridiculous and if it continues then I shall leave right now and go back to work."

"Beth, I am serious," he said harshly and his grip tightened on Beth's hand so that she gasped. He relaxed his hold a little. "I'm sorry, but somehow I must make you see just how serious I really am. I love you, I want you, I need you to be my wife. No-one else will do. You are perfect for me and I swear I will make you happy and you will never for one moment regret being Mrs Kevin Brady. Oh Beth, please believe me," he implored.

"Kevin, I don't know what to think," said Beth gently as she tried unsuccessfully to extricate her hand from his. "I don't see how you can say I'm perfect for you when we don't even know each other."

"I *know* you, Beth! My *soul* knows you and I know that yours knows me! Can't you *feel* it? You *must* feel something!"

"I feel confused and not a little punch-drunk. I feel as though all the air has been knocked out of me and I'm having difficulty breathing properly."

"That's just how *I* feel! You see, we *do* feel the same. It's the power of our emotions that has taken our breath away."

"I didn't mean it quite like that," Beth said cautiously. "I don't know what has been going on today. I don't understand what I'm thinking or feeling. I only know that nothing like this has ever happened to me in all my life. I think it would be best if I now go quietly back to work and you go quietly back to Belfast and we both get on with our normal lives."

"When I go back to Belfast, Beth, you are coming with me, as my wife. I am not leaving Boston without you. You are now my life. I have no other without you."

"Kevin, please be reasonable," Beth implored softly. "I can't just give up my life here at the drop of a hat. I have my job, my friends, my painting, *here*. *This* is my life."

"And in Belfast you can have a job if you want one, although you won't need one. We have so many friends you could never need for more and you can paint to your heart's content. I am a very determined man, Beth. When I want something I will do all in my power to get it and we are a very powerful family. I want you more than I have ever wanted anything and I *will* marry you. Don't fight this, sweetheart. You know, deep down inside, that you want this as much as I do. I can see it in your eyes. I feel it coming from you. You, yourself, are the only thing standing between us and a wonderful life together or loneliness and unfulfilment. Come with me, Beth. Be happy with me. Find fulfilment with me."

His voice was soft, almost hypnotic. Beth felt herself being drawn towards him as if she were mesmerised. Was she being foolish in listening to him? Or would she be foolish in rejecting him out of hand? He appeared to be so earnest, so serious. Was this the chance of love and happiness that she had dreamed of for so many long, loveless years? Ever since her parents had died fourteen years ago she had craved love but had never known it. She had always believed, perhaps naïvely, that there would only be one true love for her, as there had been for her parents. Was this the love that Kevin was offering her now? She desperately wanted it to be so. If she rejected him now, would she live to regret it? Oh, how was she to know? What was she to do?

5

By the time Kevin had walked Beth across the street to O'Grady's she had made no commitment to him but had agreed to see him that evening. He was to collect her from her apartment at seven o'clock and take her out for dinner.

Beth could concentrate on nothing all afternoon and seemed to wander around in a stupor most of the time. Sean kept an anxious eye on her as she drifted aimlessly about the store. Fortunately for her, if not for him, it was a quiet afternoon with few people requiring assistance. He was almost relieved when three o'clock came and it was time for Beth to go home. He watched after her uneasily as she walked up the street to her bus stop. He sincerely hoped she wasn't getting involved with Kevin Brady. Sean had a nasty feeling that Kevin could be a very dangerous man if he was crossed in any way and Beth was such a little innocent. He had become very fond of her in the time she had been working for him and he felt a kind of paternal concern for her wellbeing.

Sean shrugged as he turned away from the window. What can I do about anything, he said to himself. She's a big girl. She knows her own mind, pray God. Why should I give my ulcers ulcers? I have enough grey hairs already and my blood pressure could do with a vacation, not a volcano. But he *was* seriously worried.

When Beth had first moved to Boston, she spent a long time looking for a place to live. It had to be just so. She was not the least interested in having the 'right address' or the most modern or trendy apartment. She needed somewhere where she could paint. Finally she found the perfect place. It was the third floor of a large old house in a neighbourhood that had seen better days. The bathroom and kitchenette were both tiny and old-fashioned but the two main rooms were spacious and airy.

When she moved in, Beth dragged the large old chesterfield and arm chair into the front bedroom to make a kind of bed-sitting room. She had no plans for lavish entertaining and so didn't need lots of space. By rearranging all the furniture she made herself a cosy, attractive room and by so doing had emptied the back room of nearly all its furniture which was just how she wanted it, for this room was her prize. This was the reason she had taken the lease on the apartment in the first place. Being up under the eaves, the room had a sharply sloping ceiling which was all one huge window, facing north. It was perfect for a studio. Here she could paint to her heart's content.

Normally when she returned from work, Beth would change from her work clothes, make herself a cup of tea and head straight for her studio. This day, though, she wandered aimlessly about the large room, almost as though she hadn't seen it before, picking up brushes and putting them down again as if she was completely unaware of what she was doing.

What am I doing?

It's only dinner.

It could be so much more.

It doesn't have to be.

He expects so much more.

That doesn't mean you have to go along with anything. Just go for dinner and have a good time. He *is* entertaining, if nothing else.

This two-way conversation seemed to be going on somewhere beyond Beth. She felt disconnected from herself as if she were floating off somewhere in another world - a world of daydreams and unreality. She was brought back to earth with a jolt as the shrilling of the telephone cut through her reverie.

She rushed into the front room and grabbed the receiver.

"Hello!" she gasped breathlessly.

"You sound as though you've run two marathons non-stop! Hi, Kid. How are things? I was wondering if you wanted to have a break from painting and take in a pizza and a movie tonight." It was Beth's best friend, Cathy.

"Oh Cathy, you don't know how much I would love to, but I really can't."

"If you want to that much then do it. Painting can wait. You sound really harassed and in need of a good night out."

"I will be having a night out, but I'm not sure just how good it will be. I actually have a date but I'm undecided about going. I don't know if I'm doing the right thing."

"Don't tell me you've given in to poor old Steve?" joked Cathy. "You've been putting him off for months. What made you change your mind?"

"No, it's not Steve," answered Beth. "I almost wish it was. Look, Cathy, I have to go and get ready. I've been mooning around here for ages and I've just noticed the time. He'll be here to get me in just over an hour and I haven't started to get ready yet."

"Who will be here - or there, to be precise?" enquired Cathy.

"Oh Cathy, I need to talk with you and soon. Can we meet for lunch tomorrow? *Please*!" Beth almost pleaded.

"Hey Kid, this sounds serious. Are you sure you're okay? Are you sure you should be going out with this guy, whoever he is? Do you want me to come over? If I'm there and you really don't want to go out with him when he gets there, I'll give you some excuse not to go."

"That's really sweet of you, but I'll be fine. He really is a nice guy - a bit different, but I will be perfectly safe with him. Just say we can meet tomorrow and don't worry so! I really have to go now."

"Luigi's at noon - and I'm worried already! Take care, Kid," Cathy added, as she hung up her phone.

Beth sat looking at her own receiver for some time, pondering on what Cathy had said. It was true that Cathy did worry about her. In so many ways Beth was very naïve. Having spent most of her life in a small town in the 'wilds' of Ontario, she had very little experience of city life. Even her four years in Toronto had been spent very much within the University environment. Her move to Boston had been almost like stepping into another world, it was so very different from anything she had known before.

Beth met Cathy during her first week in Boston. They were sitting at neighbouring tables in a café having morning coffee. Beth was trying to find accommodation with the help of the newspaper and a street map and was getting nowhere very fast. Cathy observed her efforts quietly for some time and then offered her help. It was to be the start of the most special friendship Beth had ever known. Boston born and bred, Cathy knew all there was to know about life in the city. She sensed instinctively that Beth was very

very unworldly, unsophisticated and felt very protective towards her, although she was two years younger than Beth, whom she nicknamed 'the Innocent' or 'the Kid'.

Unlike Beth, Cathy came from a large, close-knit family, but she was the only girl, with three older brothers and one younger. So she valued her friendship with Beth even more as she sometimes felt a bit alone within the family and had often longed for a sister. She had always been very popular with the girls at school (especially having three attractive older brothers) but had never had a really close friend until she met Beth.

Steve was Cathy's second eldest brother and he had fallen for Beth in a big way. Beth was fond of him but felt nothing more than that. He was a Physical Education teacher at a local high school and was totally sports-orientated. He knew nothing about art and Beth had no interest in sports. She had been to some ball games with Cathy and Steve and had enjoyed herself in their company (although she was utterly bemused by the game itself) but she had no inclination to date Steve, even though he had become quite persistent.

Cathy loved Beth like a sister and would have loved to have seen her paired up with Steve but she knew they weren't right for each other. Steve would eventually get the message that Beth wasn't seriously interested in him, they would remain friends and he would find himself another girlfriend in no time, Cathy was sure. But she wasn't so sure about Beth. Beth needed protecting. There was a kind of fragility about her that sometimes made Cathy uneasy - and she was concerned now.

6

At exactly seven o'clock Beth's doorbell rang. She was ready and went straight downstairs to meet Kevin. She did not want him coming up to her apartment, at least not yet. That was her haven and very few people were invited there and then only when Beth felt at ease with them. Kevin was definitely not amongst their number.

Kevin escorted Beth into a waiting taxi and they sped up town to the restaurant he had chosen. Neither of them spoke during the journey. Beth was far too nervous and Kevin appeared to be preoccupied. Actually, he was intently studying her reflection in the cab window, wondering yet again what it was about her that intrigued him so, that filled him with such intense longing. She was certainly beautiful, although she seemed unaware of just how beautiful she was. Her make-up was very discrete and her short, feathered hair cut was far from elaborate. She was wearing a very simple light wool dress in a most becoming, delicate shade of blue. Hardly provocative and yet immensely alluring, almost sensual.

Kevin felt an overwhelming desire to reach over and crush Beth to him and yet he wouldn't dare do such a thing. He wanted her so desperately but there was something elusive about her that he couldn't grasp. It was as though she were just beyond his reach and if he stretched out his hand towards her she would drift a little further away, always just that little beyond his range. He suddenly took a deep breath and gave himself a mental shake. He was becoming positively fanciful! What he needed was a very large Jameson's!

Beth heard Kevin's sharp intake of breath and turned anxiously towards him, not knowing what to say. However, at that moment the cab drew up in front of the restaurant and Kevin stepped out instantly to come around and open Beth's door.

As they entered the restaurant, the maître d'hotel turned towards them and his experienced eye flicked over Kevin in a split second, taking in his whole appearance and demeanour. He hesitated only fractionally and inclined his head, almost as though bowing with respect. Someone else has been bewitched, thought

Beth. But when she heard the deep, courteous voice bidding them 'Good evening and welcome' in a cultured English accent, Beth wondered if she was being a little unfair to Kevin. Perhaps it was merely the high standard of the *maître d'hotel*'s impeccable British manners that had suggested a touch of subservience.

The *maître d'hotel* turned to a waiter standing just to one side and spoke briefly and discreetly to him. The waiter immediately escorted Kevin and Beth to a quiet, secluded table, obviously one of the best in the restaurant. Perhaps it wasn't just good manners after all, mused Beth.

Kevin and Beth sat in silence whilst they waited for their drinks to be brought to them, a large Jameson's for Kevin and a mineral water for Beth - she definitely wanted her wits about her this evening.

When their drinks came, Kevin raised his glass to Beth. "*Slainte*," he said and took a sip. She raised her glass in acknowledgement but said nothing. She hadn't understood what Kevin had said and she didn't have the nerve to ask him to explain. The two sat in silence for a few moments, taking occasional sips from their drinks. Then Kevin reached across the table and took Beth's hand in his.

"Oh Beth, Beth," he said. "What are you doing to me? What am I to do with you? I know what I want to do. More than anything in the world I want to marry you and take you home with me to Ireland. I've never felt like this in my life. I want to sweep you off your feet and run away with you. And yet I'm frightened that if I make a sudden move I'll scare you off and you'll disappear. Help me to know what to do, Beth. I love you more than I've loved anything in all my life. I want to be with you always. I don't want to pressure you but I need to know. I need to know whether there is any hope, any chance of our being together. Do you like me, even a little? Do you think you could possibly come to love me? Tell me, Beth. *Please* tell me."

Beth was quite taken aback by this change in Kevin's attitude. Up until now he had been very forceful, domineering, persistent to the point of obsession. And now he was gentle, tender, pleading. She felt a stirring deep within, as tenderness for Kevin welled up inside her.

"Oh Kevin, I don't understand what's going on either.

Nothing like this has ever happened to me before. It's all so new, it's almost unreal. My emotions seem to have run from A to Z and back again and my mind is reeling. You are, by far, the most unusual man I have ever met. And yes, I do like you. I think I like you quite a lot, but I don't know whether I love you. I've had so little experience of love, I'm not sure if I would recognise it. All I do know for certain is that what I feel for you I have never felt before. Perhaps this is the beginning of love. I don't know for certain," she added, a little hesitantly, "but I think I want to find out."

Kevin raised Beth's hand to his lips and kissed her fingers gently, one at a time. "Beth, sweet Beth. You won't regret it, I promise. You will never regret marrying me."

He caught a quick breath and sat back in his chair quite suddenly. He looked at Beth intently, silently, his eyes absorbing every inch of her face, the tiniest details, how her long eyelashes cast soft shadows across her high cheek bones in the subdued lighting. He continued to study her, slowly shaking his head, with a slight smile curling up the corners of his mouth. He reached for his glass, raised it towards Beth and said softly, "To our beginning."

Then he sat forward suddenly, turning to catch the attention of their waiter who was hovering close by. "A bottle of Dom Perignon!" he ordered. "And no arguments!" This was to Beth as he swung back to face her. "Tonight is a night for celebration. Tonight is the beginning of our new life, yours and mine together, as it was always meant to be." His eyes, in the candle light, were sparkling, flashing with emotion. There was an aura of excitement emanating from him that crackled like electricity.

"Two weeks tomorrow, we fly home."

"Two weeks!" Beth's words came out in a squeak.

"That's right, my love, two weeks! I was due to fly home in three days but I've changed my booking and the tickets for Mr and Mrs Brady will be ready for collection tomorrow morning."

"You've got tickets for Mr and Mrs! Oh Kevin, slow down! You're going way too fast. This whole thing is getting out of control again. I haven't said that I will marry you and even if I had, two weeks just isn't enough time. I have to give notice at work, on my apartment. I have to notify my Aunt and Uncle and all my friends and relatives and make all the arrangements. Kevin, I'm just not going to have time to get it all organised."

"What is there to organise? I've already talked to Sean's priest and he has agreed to marry us on Friday, the day before we fly home. Naturally it will be a very quiet ceremony - just your close friends and any of your relatives who want to come. I talked to Sean after you left work today and he agreed to be my best man. If we have the ceremony in the morning, we can have a luncheon reception, say at Luigi's so that your friends from there can be present, too. Then you and I will have the rest of the day and evening together on our own. And then there will be the night," and he pursed his lips in a kiss.

Beth was sitting, stunned, her mouth open in disbelief. "*How could you?* How *could* you go ahead and speak to my friends and make these arrangements without speaking to me first? I hadn't said that I would marry you, let alone when, yet here you are, merrily taking charge of my life and all my affairs as if you have some sort of mandate to do so. You astound me. I don't know whether to get up right now and walk out of here or just laugh at your audacity. Are you really for real or is this some big joke?"

Kevin grasped Beth's hand in a vicelike grip, his eyes cold and hard, his voice harsh. "This is no joke! I am deadly serious and don't you ever think otherwise!" At the look of horror and pain on Beth's face he relaxed somewhat. "Oh God, I've done it again! I've frightened you yet again when I had already promised I would never hurt you. But you must see, Beth, that there is so little time. I must be home in two weeks and I will not leave without you. I've already told you that.

"I had a long talk with Sean this afternoon and he told me all he knows of your background. I'm very sorry to hear about your parents, but it really does make things easier for us. There will be very few emotional ties for you to break. I gather your Aunt and Uncle won't exactly be heartbroken at your leaving and you have no brothers or sisters to leave behind. I know you have a few close friends but you can always write and visit back and forth.

"I'll pay whatever your landlord wants to release you from your tenancy agreement. I have already tendered your resignation from the Gallery on your behalf and Sean has accepted. So all you need to do is pack your possessions and find yourself an outfit for the wedding. I'll pay for whatever you want for yourself and your bridesmaid. I imagine you will want to ask your best friend. Cathy, isn't it? Sean said she is a lovely girl and a very good friend to you. This may be a small wedding but you will be the most beautiful bride Boston has had all year." His voice and face had softened as he talked and he was now gazing at Beth with such tenderness.

"You appear to have taken no end of liberties," Beth responded. "I don't know who to be more angry with, you or Sean, for discussing my private life that way and yet I don't feel angry. I feel as though I've just come off a giant roller coaster. I feel breathless and scared and elated and all blown to pieces. I don't even know now if I have said that I will marry you."

"You may not have spoken the words with your voice, but you have with your heart and they are shining out from your eyes now, for all the world to see. Sweet Beth, sweet Beth, we will be so happy, you and I. So very, very happy."

A quiet, tactful cough from behind Kevin brought the two of them back to earth and an awareness of their surroundings. Their waiter was standing by patiently, ready to serve their champagne. When it was poured and the waiter had left, Kevin raised his glass. "To the future Mrs Kevin Brady," he toasted.

"Mr Brady," breathed Beth and she sipped her wine.

When they looked back on that evening, neither could recall what they had had for dinner, other than that it was exceptionally well cooked and presented. Their waiter was more than pleased with his very generous tip, as were the *maître d'hotel* and the cab driver who took them back to Beth's house.

On the doorstep, they shared their first kiss. It was exquisite and leftthem both breathless. Beth took her arms from around Kevin, placed her hands against his chest and gently pushed him away.

"Go home," she whispered. "*Now*! I daren't let you through the front door, let alone upstairs. Besides, I need to be alone now. Come for me at 7 o'clock tomorrow evening and no sooner. There are things I have to take care of before I see you again."

"You win," said Kevin. "Seven o'clock it shall be. Sleep well, sweet Beth. Dream of me." He bent his head to kiss her once more. "I love you. I love you. I love you." He turned and ran quietly down the steps.

Beth watched him as he hurried along to the corner of her street, looking for a passing cab. She leaned back against the door jamb, oblivious to the cold, biting wind that was swirling around the porch. She felt so warm inside, so full, so content, so loved. "I love you," she whispered into the darkness. "I *do* love you."

7

Beth arrived for work as usual at ten o'clock the next morning. Sean was waiting for her just inside the main doors. He seemed to be agitated, fidgety. "Let's go to my office," he said and bustled Beth away to his private domain in the far corner. He seated her in one of the chairs in front of his desk but did not sit down himself. He paced up and down, round and about, wringing his hands and then running them through his hair distractedly. Several times he started to say something but stopped himself before pacing on again. He stopped suddenly at the corner of his desk, put both hands on the desk top and leaned forward towards Beth. He looked long and hard into her bemused eyes.

"Are you sure you know what you are doing, Beth? Is this what you *really* want from life? Dear girl, you don't even *know* the man and here you are running away with him to the other side of the world."

Beth smiled up at Sean. "I take it you are referring to Kevin and Ireland is just across the ocean, not the other side of the world. Besides, I'm not running away with him. We are being married here in Boston, by your very own priest and you will be best man so you can see that there will be no foul play. He's hardly a Bluebeard, you know," and she laughed softly.

"This is not a laughing matter, child. This is a very serious thing you are doing. Have you really given it sufficient thought? Or have you just let that sweet-talker sweep you off your feet? You've led such a sheltered life. What do you know of love? How would you know the difference between a genuine man and some smooth-talking Lothario?"

"Sean, *please*! That's enough!" Beth interrupted. "You're right that I've led a sheltered life but I'm not a complete innocent and I am also not a fool. It's true I've had very little experience of love and, yes, he *has* swept me off my feet but, Sean, he really does love me. And I love him. It is a wonderful feeling and I have never been so happy. I thought you would be pleased for me that at last I've found someone who loves me, who wants to take care of me, someone who *cherishes* me. What does it matter how long we have known each other? The fact is that we both know this is right for us. I'm going to marry him, Sean, and I'm going to live in Belfast with him."

"My dear, I'm sorry. I didn't mean to upset you," Sean sighed. "It's just that this is all so very sudden. My concern for you is genuine. I've come to think of you as one of my own and I shall miss you very much." A blush of self-consciousness crept up his neck and into his face.

Beth reached up and gently touched his cheek. "Oh Sean, I'm sorry I snapped at you. I guess I'm feeling a little defensive. As you say, this is all very sudden, but that doesn't mean it is wrong. I've done a lot of thinking - most of the night, in fact. I've tried to put up every argument in the book for and against this whole thing and I still come out with the same result - I love Kevin and I want to marry him. This has taken me as much by surprise as it has you."

"You're absolutely certain?"

"Yes."

"You won't change your mind?"

"No."

"So there's no going back?"

"No, Sean."

"Very well." Sean stood up and walked to a davenport that stood in the corner of the room. He took a key from his waistcoat pocket and unlocked one of the drawers. From this he took a flat metal box the size of a large book, which he placed on his desk. He unlocked the writing flap of the davenport and removed one of the little drawers along the top. He pressed a little button and the back of the drawer space sprang open. Inside was another key. This he brought back to the desk and unlocked the metal box. He lifted out a large packet wrapped in dark blue velvet. This was unfolded to reveal a beautiful icon. It was a picture of the Madonna and Child, embossed in gold, surrounded by a brilliant background of the most dazzling lapis lazuli. The Madonna and Child appeared to be radiating in the bed of glorious blue. Beth caught her breath at the sight of it.

"Sean, it is *exquisite,*" she whispered. "I never knew you had this. It's never been on display."

"Oh, this is a very special piece, not for the general public to see. A few people know of its existence and I've had a few offers for it, but I would never sell it. I somehow knew I had to keep it for a very particular reason. And now I know what that reason is."

He came and leaned against his desk beside where Beth was sitting so that he was facing her. He reached down and took both her hands in his.

"Beth, I want you to listen very carefully to what I have to say." He brought his face down close to hers, his voice low, urgent, very serious. "Please don't take this the wrong way; this is said only from true and deep concern for you. For all intents and purposes, you are alone in this world. When you go to Ireland you will be even more alone. There will be no-one other than Kevin that you know, no-one familiar to whom you can turn if needs be. If, and I repeat, *if* you should ever find yourself in a position of great need, of whatever kind, I want you to have the wherewithal for survival. It will give me great peace of mind to know that you will have some form of security to fall back on. Therefore I am giving this icon to you; I reiterate, *to you*. Not to you and Kevin, but to you alone. Kevin has plenty of money of his own and is part of a family of considerable standing in Belfast. You are taking nothing with you to this marriage because you have nothing. So please, I beg you, don't be offended; just take this gift with my love and in the knowledge that you will be making me very happy. Believe me, Beth, I *need* peace of mind - for reasons I am not at liberty to divulge. You will be doing me a great kindness by accepting this. I will sleep more peacefully at night, knowing you will have the means of independence should that ever be necessary."

Beth studied Sean's face intently. She felt a strange sadness take hold of her as she listened to him.

"Dear Sean, my sense of propriety tells me that I should refuse such a magnificent gift. It is so valuable - beyond anything I could ever own - that I can't imagine how I could be worthy of such generosity. But something I do not understand tells me that I *must* accept it and that is the only reason that I will do so. I'm not sure I'm entirely happy about it. In fact, the whole thing makes me feel sort of creepy, but I think I understand a little of what you are trying to say. I just hope and pray that one day I will be showing it to my grandchildren and telling them stories of the very dear and ever-so-slightly eccentric man I used to work for back in the 'good old

Boston days'. I really hope that is the way it will be, Sean."

Sean leaned forward and kissed Beth gently on her forehead. "Bless you, child. I hope and pray for the same.

"And now to practicalities!" and he abruptly stood up and moved briskly to his own chair, once more the employer and master of his domain. "You will be wanting to leave work immediately, I imagine, so we need to settle up your final salary cheque, etc."

"If you don't mind, I would like to work until the end of this coming week. That will give me the following week to pack my things and get ready for the wedding on the Friday. Kevin has got pretty well everything organised and there's really nothing for me to do. I can't just sit around all day, I would go crazy and there's no way I could concentrate on painting right now. I have a feeling it will be some time before I pick up a paint brush again.

"I'm just sorry that this is such short notice for you. I hope you will be able to find a replacement soon."

"No-one could ever replace you, Beth. You are unique. In your quiet, gentle manner you have found a way into my tough old heart as no-one else has done. As you know, I have never had a daughter of my own, but if I could hand-pick one, I would choose you. I shall miss you more than I can say."

He stood up and came around to her chair. He took her hands and drew her up to himself. They shared a long, tender embrace during which no words were, or could be, spoken. When they drew apart, both had tears running down their cheeks. Beth reached up and kissed Sean's cheek.

"I shall miss you, too, so very, very much. I love you."

8

"So, how was the big date? Come on, 'fess! All the gory details, please!" Cathy was sitting opposite Beth, tucking into her ravioli with great enthusiasm. Her large green eyes danced with glee as she looked at Beth. "Tell all to Aunty Cathy!"

Beth was sitting back in her chair, half-heartedly pushing food around her plate. She really had no appetite at all, not even for the delicious ravioli, Luigi's special of the day, served by the man himself. To her amazement, he had come to greet the girls as they entered the restaurant, had shown them to a table and taken their order himself, fussing around Beth as though she was a cherished friend. Kevin's aura seemed to linger in the atmosphere.

"Cathy, I don't know where to begin," she said.

"Try the beginning, kiddo."

"Okay, brace yourself!" and she took a deep breath. "He is tall, dark, very handsome and very charming. I met him yesterday at the store. His name is Kevin Brady and he is a businessman from Belfast, Ireland. Two weeks today he is flying home and I'm going with him. We are getting married the day before. Will you please be my bridesmaid?" The words tumbled out of Beth's mouth in one long rush and then she collapsed back into her chair.

"Are you *crazy*? Have you lost your mind? Is this some sort of joke? Oh my God, you are serious! This is for *real*!" Cathy squealed.

"*Shh*!" Beth hissed. "People are looking at us!"

Cathy put down her fork and sat back in her chair, shaking her head in disbelief.

"Hey Kid, let's take this slowly, from the beginning. You met some guy yesterday, a stranger and a foreigner and today you are engaged to be married. In two weeks you *will* be married and on some plane flying away to his home, as his wife. I don't know if this is a nightmare come true or a fairy story. Are you really serious, Beth? Are you really sure you know what you are doing? I mean, this is totally out of character for you. 'Miss Straight Lace, No Nonsense'. That's what my Dad calls you - not unkindly, of course. It's just that you are so cautious about everything. You're the last person anyone would expect to do something like this.

"Oh my God!" She drew in a long, noisy breath. "What will your 'olds' say? Your aunt will have a *fit*! We'll be able to hear the screams of anguish all the way down here!"

"She already knows," Beth said quietly. "I phoned her before I went to work this morning. She listened politely, said she was not really surprised, considering who my parents were, said she and Uncle Douglas would not be coming and hung up. I think she is a little disappointed with me, to say the least.

"Oh Cathy, I know this is 'out of character' for me. But honestly, I feel now as though I've been walking around in an emotional straight-jacket ever since my parents died. No-one has ever shown me any love or affection, except you and your family - and Sean, in his own way. Now I've met Kevin and for the first time in fourteen years I feel *alive* - really alive. It's as if he's some sort of catalyst, as if he's somehow unlocked the padlock on that straight-jacket and now, at last, I'm free! I'm still me, I'm still Beth, I haven't changed. It's just that now I have this wonderful sense of freedom. I feel so alive, so happy. Oh Cathy, I feel wonderful!"

"But Kid, this is all so sudden. Oh, groan! That's what the girl usually says to the guy, not the best friend to the bride-to-be."

"I know it's sudden, believe me. No-one is more surprised by all this than I am. I don't think my feet have touched the ground since yesterday morning. Honestly, I put up every argument in the book against this. I told Kevin he was crazy and to go away, but he just wouldn't. He was so persistent and he made me listen, not only to him but to my heart. I've been up all night thinking and the only conclusion I can come to is that I do love him, I want to be his wife, I want to share my life with him.

"He is offering me something no-one else ever has - a future, a sense of belonging. He *needs* me. He could have his pick of women, but he wants *me*. He has chosen *me* and I don't ever have to be alone again. I can't begin to describe what it feels like to be wanted, to be needed, to be loved. There simply aren't any words appropriate enough. I feel complete."

Cathy had tears in her eyes and her voice broke as she said, "Beth, I had no idea! I thought I knew you better than anyone, but I just didn't know how alone you really were. I guess I've never known anything but love all around me and can't begin to comprehend what it is like not to be loved. I think maybe I can understand a little bit how you feel now. Oh Beth, I'm going to miss you so much!" and she started to cry. "I'm so sorry," she spluttered as she wiped her eyes on her napkin. "I'm making a fool of myself, I know I am, but I can't help it! What am I going to do without you?"

"Come and visit me - often!" Beth fished around in her handbag and handed her friend a packet of tissues. "Here, have a Kleenex and do the job properly. Please try to stop crying or I just might start myself. If we're not careful we'll be thrown out of here for making a public nuisance of ourselves. Come on now. Smile, please," Beth encouraged. "By the way, you haven't told me yet whether or not you agree to be my bridesmaid. Sean is to be Kevin's best man and I need some support, too. Please say you will."

"Dope, of course I will," Cathy replied, a little less tearfully. "I had hoped, in my daydreams, that one day I would be your bridesmaid and that I would walk up the aisle ahead of you and there would be Steve, grinning all over his face, waiting to claim his bride. Then you would be my sister-in-law as well as my best friend. But I guess that's not the way it's going to be, huh?"

"*Only* in your dreams! Steve is a heck of a nice guy, but can you really see us as a couple?"

The two young women giggled loudly at the thought.

"No, you're right," spluttered Cathy, as she wiped tears of mirth from her face. "I love my brother dearly but am the first to admit he's not the greatest in the intelligence department. Sports, yes. Intelligence, no. What he really needs is some cute little blonde who thinks he is 'really cute' and they'll live in a 'really cute' little house and raise themselves a bunch of 'really cute' kids.

"Oh boy, does that sound bitchy, or what! I didn't mean it that way but you know what I mean. In truth, you and Steve would be a disaster. I just didn't want to finally admit it.

"So now you're going away." Her eyes filled once more. "Please don't forget me in your lovely new world, Beth. Don't forget me, *please*!" she pleaded. Beth reached across the table and gave Cathy's hand a gentle squeeze.

"As if I could," she said gently. "You are the only true friend I have ever had and nobody could ever mean as much to me as you do. Besides, you'll be godmother to my first 'offsprung'! All my kids are going to *love* their American Aunty Cathy!"

Cathy blew her nose loudly and wiped her eyes. "I had better get my passport and visas up to date. I'm going to be doing a lot of travelling in the future." The two smiled a little shakily at each other.

Beth was toying with her fork, picking it up and putting it down, not quite knowing what to do with it.

"Do you think," she asked shyly, "if I asked your father in the right way, he would possibly be willing to give me away? Or would you ask him for me?" she added in a rush. "I've come to think of your family as if they were my own and I would love it if he would."

"Oh Kid, of course he will. You ask him yourself. He'd be thrilled. I know Dad would be really proud to walk you up the aisle. He and Mom really love you.

"Now, tell me. What are we going to wear for the big day?"

The next hour or so was spent in detailed discussion about the wedding, about Kevin and about the events of the previous day and evening, Beth quite forgetting that she was supposed to be at work.

From where he was standing at the front window of his gallery, Sean could see across the road into Luigi's. The sight of Beth's dark head, bent close across the table towards Cathy's flaming tresses, tugged at his heart. He would miss her terribly but more than that, he truly feared for her.

9

Beth woke with a sense of unfamiliarity. Sleepily she gazed around the bedroom in the half-light of early dawn that seeped in around the edges of the curtains. A jolt of non-recognition shot through her body and brought her up to a half-sitting position. She trembled as if with fear. By now she was fully awake and was aware of someone else breathing slowly and rhythmically. Her eyes grew accustomed to the dim light and as she looked about her more carefully she gave a little chuckle. What a clutz she was! She had stayed the night at Cathy's house and it was Cathy she could hear breathing as she slept deeply and contentedly in the other twin bed next to her own.

Then the full realisation dawned and a shudder of apprehension mixed with excitement tingled all through her. Today was Friday. Today she was to marry Kevin. How could this day have come so quickly? All last week she had worked as usual. Except there was not much that was usual about it. She was scarcely able to concentrate properly and yet more people appeared to be buying rather than just browsing at the Gallery. Beth was totally unaware that she was glowing with happiness. She positively radiated joy and this acted like a magnet to the customers. More than once Sean observed a 'casual shopper', as he thought of them - the type who wander in out of curiosity, browse around for a while, picking up this and that, perhaps showing a modicum of interest in one particular item, but then putting it down and wandering out into the street again; not the type to make him fat! - begin their ritual of superficial perusal, become aware of Beth and leave with a package under their arm and their money tucked safely in his till. He really was going to miss her! She was even better for business than ever before. He already knew that her replacement wasn't a patch on Beth - Beth as she had been before Kevin. This *new* Beth was positively dazzling! Still, he would enjoy the benefits while they lasted and take his personal delight in Beth for the short time that remained.

Beth had chosen to work a full day each day of her last week at the Gallery, rather than her usual part-time, as she would not be doing any painting before the move to Ireland. Kevin was not too pleased about this but Beth felt it was only fair to Sean as she wasn't able to give more notice. Also, it limited the time she spent with Kevin. Instinctively, she felt it was important to keep a little distance between them. Their relationship was so intense, so all-consuming, that she was a little frightened of losing sight of her own self, that somehow Kevin would devour her uniqueness and she would become a non-person. So by restricting their time together she was able to remain in control of her own individuality whilst coming to know Kevin better.

This week had flown past in a wave of hectic activity - shopping, cleaning, packing, crating up all her paintings and equipment that were to be air-freighted to Belfast, farewell parties. Shopping had been such fun, as Beth had never had much money before to spend on her clothes, for Kevin was so generous both with her and Cathy. As the ceremony in Boston was to be a simple affair, Beth did not want a traditional wedding dress - that would wait for the Nuptial Mass to be held in Kevin's church when they got home. Instead, she settled on a pale ivory dress in a very fine wool, the quality evident in its simplicity. They chose a similar style for Cathy, but in a rich shade of emerald green that highlighted her beautiful eyes and glorious red hair - perfect Irish colouring!

The two dresses were hanging side by side in Cathy's wardrobe, awaiting their one and only outing together. Thinking of this brought tears to Beth's eyes as she sat in bed, reflecting on the last two weeks - the weeks that had turned her life upside down and changed it irrevocably. Her emotions were so mixed; sadness to be leaving Cathy and her family, Sean and her job, her friends and the way of life in Boston she had come to love; apprehension about meeting Kevin's family and beginning a new life in a strange country; nervousness about this day and the night to come, for this was all to be a completely new experience for her in every sense; but overall, a joyousness, a deep and tender love for Kevin that had been developing over the past two weeks and was now, she was sure, strong enough to overcome all the other negative thoughts and feelings.

Beth got out of bed and crossed over to Cathy's bathroom, closing the door quietly behind her so as not to waken Cathy. She turned on the shower and stepped under the steaming water, revelling in the exhilarating spray. Her whole body tingled as the power of the water stung her skin, enlivening all her senses. As she emerged from the bathroom, swathed in towels, she saw that Cathy was sitting up in bed, sipping a cup of coffee.

"Salutations, Kid," Cathy called out. "I've made you a morning heart-starter, too, although from the raucous singing (if that racket can be classified as singing) emanating from behind my bathroom door, it doesn't sound as if your heart is in need of a jump-start today. What sort of time do you call this? Even the birds aren't awake yet. How can you be so cheerful in the middle of the night?"

"You angel. How lovely," said Beth as she picked up her cup from the dressing table and drank thirstily. "*Ouch*! *Ouch*!" she gasped. "That is really hot! I've burned my tongue!"

"Oh, too bad! We'll have to call off the wedding. You can't get married if you are injured and in pain and Kevin has to go home tomorrow, so I guess you'll have to stay here after all."

"You are such a clown, Cathy!" laughed Beth. "I doubt I shall meet anyone in Ireland who makes me laugh the way you do. I'm not so sure I even want to."

"You'd better not!" retorted Cathy. She climbed out of bed and walked over to the dressing table where Beth was sitting on the bench stool. She nudged Beth with her hip. "Shove up, Innocent," she said as she sat down beside her. The two friends sat looking at each other in the mirror as they drank their coffee.

"Oh Kid," Cathy said wistfully. "I feel like a big sister who should be giving her kid sister the 'morning-of-the-big-day' talk, but I don't really know where to begin."

"Don't even *think* it," retorted Beth. "I may be lacking in experience but not in knowledge. The last thing I need now is a facts of life heart-to-heart. Actually, what I do need is a hug."

They turned and held each other in silence for a long time, each thinking thoughts and feeling emotions that they couldn't or wouldn't dare express in words. Beth was the first to break the mood. She sat back, holding Cathy at arm's length. She looked at her fondly, then leaned forward and kissed her gently on the cheek.

"Dear Cathy," she said softly. "I am so blessed to have you for my friend. I love you so dearly and shall cherish your friendship always. And now, unless we both want to show up in church with red blotchy faces, this indulging in sentiment will have to stop, here and now! You go and have a nice hot shower and then we'll both go downstairs and have a good hearty breakfast before we make ourselves even more beautiful than we already are!"

When she looked back on the day, Beth found she could remember very few of the details. It was as if the time had passed in a kaleidoscope of images; the beaming smile on Mr Sinclair's handsome, ruddy face as he walked Beth down the aisle; the cool, sweet smell of the flowers in the church, so beautifully arranged by Mrs Sinclair; the tears glistening in Sean's eyes; the strange diffidence in Kevin's voice as he made his vows and his triumphant, proprietorial air once the service was over; the laughter and noisy exuberance of the wedding breakfast at Luigi's that lasted until late in the afternoon; the quiet dinner for two at their hotel in the evening; the unaccustomed sensation of lying awake in the early morning listening to Kevin's soft snores and feeling the warmth of his body beside her and the weight of his arm flung carelessly across her. She would have liked to prolong that moment, savouring the newness of the experience, for there would never again be a moment just like that, the first, unguarded awareness of Kevin as her husband, but then the bedside phone rang with their wake-up call and it was all one big rush to get ready and out to the airport where Cathy and the rest of the Sinclairs were gathered to wish them God speed on their way home, to Ireland, to a new, uncharted future.

Maelstrom

It is not in the storm nor in the strife
We feel benumbed, and wish to be no more,
But in the after-silence on the shore,
When all is lost, except a little life.
Lord Byron 1788 - 1824
'On hearing that Lady Byron was ill' (written 1816)

1

Beth's welcome to her new home and family was hardly what she expected and very far from what Kevin had promised. As they came through the arrivals area at the airport, Kevin started waving enthusiastically.

"Look, over there," he said excitedly to Beth. "There's Michael. My brother. He's come to meet us. Oh boy, is he in for a surprise!"

From Beth's vantage point of almost a foot shorter than Kevin, she was having great difficulty seeing beyond the passengers in front of and beside them. Those directly in front veered off to greet their own relatives and through the gap left by their disappearance she saw a man who was unmistakeably Kevin's older brother. The family resemblance was remarkable. If anything, Michael was even taller than Kevin and a lot stockier. He had obviously been just as handsome as Kevin but his good looks had coarsened with age and he now looked quite dissipated, as if his life style had done him no favours. Beth knew that he was thirty-four, seven years senior to Kevin, but he looked a lot older. As yet he had not noticed Beth and was smiling broadly at his younger brother.

"Welcome home, Kev. This has been quite some trip, hasn't it? Your most successful yet, I gather."

"You can say that again, big man, and in more ways than you know." Kevin put his arm around Beth's waist and drew her forward. "Michael, meet your new sister-in-law, Beth. Sweetheart, this is my brother, Michael - the Big Man!"

Michael took a step backwards in shock and stared down at

Beth with a look on his face that chilled her to the core and filled her with a dreadful fear. He turned his thunderous look to Kevin.

"You *bloody, stupid* fool," he spat the words out. "Just what the hell do you think you are playing at? Are you trying to kill off the old girl? My God, she will have heart failure when you get home. You know full well you were supposed to propose to Eileen Conlon when you got back from this trip. Ma has already told old Paddy that you will be going over there tomorrow to do the deal."

"Well, she can bloody un-tell him, can't she," Kevin countered petulantly. "There is no way I'm going to marry that po-faced, fat old cow. I don't care how much money her old man has. God, haven't we got enough money already?"

"It's not just the money, you stupid fool!" shouted Michael. "The Conlon clan are getting too big for their boots and for our good. This marriage was to put an end to the competition. Oh God, you are so *stupid*! I wonder you have lived as long as you have. God knows, you don't deserve to!"

"*You just shut your mouth*!" Kevin shouted back. "It's all right for you. Your wife may be stupid and docile but at least she isn't fat and you don't have to put a paper bag over her head!"

"My God, I could kill you myself if Paddy Conlon and his boys don't do it first!" Michael raised a huge clenched fist and would have hit Kevin then and there but was stopped short as he heard Beth's cry.

The two brothers started with surprise and looked about them. They had been so engrossed in their hateful shouting match that they were completely unaware of the gawping, curious onlookers and even less aware of Beth, who was staring at them with a look of devastation on her face and tears pouring down her cheeks. Her pain and humiliation were clear for anyone to see.

Kevin pulled her rigid body to him. He buried his face in her hair, kissing the top of her head.

"Oh sweet, sweet Beth. I'm so sorry. You mustn't pay any attention to us. The fireworks always start when we get together, especially when Michael starts throwing his weight around." This latter comment was directed bitterly towards his brother. "Come on, sweetheart, let's go home."

Home! If Beth had been at home she would have walked out of the airport, hailed a cab and gone straight to the sanctuary of Cathy's house. But here, the place she was *now* supposed to call home, she had nowhere to go. She couldn't even get another flight back to the States because she had no money and Kevin had her passport in his pocket. She felt more desolate and alone than she had ever felt in her life. What had she done? What had she let herself in for? Had she been foolish not to heed Sean's warnings? What did he know that she did not? And who was this Eileen Conlon? That question could wait until she was alone with Kevin. She would not give Michael the satisfaction of seeing her question Kevin in front of him but she *would* have an answer to that particular question, if nothing else. She would know exactly why Kevin had married her and when she did know, she would *then* decide what action she would need to take.

Not a word single was spoken in the car on the journey to the Brady home. The atmosphere was thick with menace and unspoken accusations. Beth sat tight up in the corner of the back seat, gazing miserably out of the window, seeing nothing of the passing scenery. She was dreading the meeting with her mother-in-law, the ruler of the roost, the head of the small but powerful family - just how powerful, Beth wondered? *Dangerously* powerful? It appeared, from what she had seen of and heard from Michael that that just might be the case.

Michael! Where was the adored older brother whom Kevin admired so, almost worshipped, whom he always referred to as 'the Big Man' as if his qualities were larger than life? From what Beth had seen so far, he was a bully and a tyrant, someone to be feared, not respected and admired. And what of Kevin? Where had her loving, domineering, authoritative, impetuous husband gone? The man who was sitting on the other side of the car from her was no more than a petulant little boy who had done wrong and been caught out and was now sulking peevishly - a thoroughly unpleasant little brat!

Beth was so shocked she felt numb and empty inside, all the euphoria and glow of the last two weeks now extinguished and cold. The emptiness was a dull, heavy ache within. Please God, let all this be simply an aberration, a momentary flash-in-the-pan brought about by Kevin's impetuosity (she didn't know until now that he hadn't told his family of their marriage) that would be dispelled when they recovered from their initial surprise. Please don't let this present state be her new reality. She didn't think she could bear it if it was.

2

Beth was aware of the car slowing down and turning into a driveway, the entrance to which was set in a tall, thick hedge. The drive was lined with trees and curved sharply to the right so that the house was fully secluded from the entrance. The grounds were extensive and well-stocked with shrubs and trees which all looked rather sad in their winter bareness, accentuated by the cold, drizzly rain and the backdrop of a grey, sullen sky. The drive curved once more, this time to the left and there stood the Brady house, large and imposing in its Victorian grandeur - so much larger than Beth expected.

As the car drew up in front of the wide stone steps, the front door opened and a tiny figure emerged, dressed all in black. Her steel grey eyes were softened by the warmth of welcome for her favourite son. Her equally steel grey hair framed her face with soft curls that did little to relieve the harsh, cruel lines in what had once been a famously beautiful face, a beauty reflected in the handsome looks of both her sons; for this tiny person, despite her lack of physical stature, was undeniably Clementine Augusta Brady, Beth's new mother-in-law.

As Beth got out of the car, the instinctive realization of who she was tightened Clementine's cruel mouth. Her eyes, as she watched Beth coming up the steps towards her at Kevin's side, were as hard as granite and they seemed to bore painfully into Beth's soul as an icy dread settled in the pit of her stomach. Those cold, implacable eyes never left Beth's own as Clementine spoke for the first time.

"Ever since you were a very little boy, Kevin, you always loved to bring home a little surprise from your ramblings for your dear Mama, didn't you, my pet?" The harshness of each clearly enunciated word cut into Beth like a whiplash. She was rooted to the spot by the violence of the hatred that poured from her mother-in-law.

"Darling Mama, this is the most precious surprise I have ever brought home for you. What could be lovelier than a beautiful new daughter-in-law when I know you have longed for me to be happily married and settled down? I just know that you will love each other dearly because I love you both more than anything in the world."

Kevin's voice was tight and high with nervousness as he blundered on carelessly.

"You dare to call me Darling?" Her words were heavy with sarcasm. "Oh do stop your gibbering, you stupid boy!" She turned and swept indoors, Kevin scurrying after her like a frightened rabbit.

Beth remained motionless, too stunned to move. Michael took her arm roughly, pulling her forward. "Come on, indoors," he said harshly. "You're letting all the cold air into the house." As if it was all *her* fault!

After the door had been closed, Beth felt the warmth from the central heating begin to seep into her body but nothing could alleviate the iciness that surrounded her heart. This was a thousand times worse than anything she had experienced at Aunt Mildred's. Kevin and his mother were still arguing in the middle of the hall, her voice brutal and pitiless, his, whining and petulant but the words they were speaking did not register with Beth.

A door at the far end of the hallway opened and out bustled a sprightly elderly woman with a shock of pure white hair and sparkling blue eyes.

"Welcome home, Master Kevin," her lovely lilting voice rang out, shattering the tension that hung like a thick pall in the air. Kevin turned gratefully toward her, bent down and enveloped her in a huge hug.

"Oh my lovely Bridie! 'Tis grand to see you again, sure it is! You're the light of me life and the joy of me heart, so you are. Sure, I'm only half a man when I'm away from you. Give me a kiss and make me whole again!"

"Away with your nonsense, you big daft boy," and she slapped his hand. "You need your head looking into, as always." She came over to Beth with a smile of such sweetness that Beth instantly felt tears sting her eyes. "And what you need, my child, is a cup of good, sweet tea and a warm cosy bed. You look all done in. Come away upstairs with old Bridie and I'll show you to your room. Then I'll bring you a nice cup of tea and a wee bit of cake for you look as though you've not eaten for a month. Then you can have a lovely wee nap before dinner. 'Tis a good sleep you'll be needing to refresh you after your long journey."

Beth found she had been led upstairs and into a large, airy bedroom. The sight of the big, comfortable-looking bed was almost too much and her legs buckled under her. Bridie's arm, which had been lightly about her waist, tightened with amazing strength for one so tiny. She led Beth straight to the bed-side and urged her to lie down, deftly lifting her feet from the ground and slipping off her shoes.

"Just you lie there, my pet, and don't you worry about a single thing. Old Bridie will look after you, never you fear." She slipped a light, warm coverlet over Beth, tucking it in around her shoulders. Impulsively, she bent down and dropped a little kiss on Beth's forehead. "There now", she said. "I'll be back with your tea so quick that you won't even know I've been gone."

As the door clicked shut behind Bridie, Beth felt a corresponding click within herself as if the tight rein she had been holding on her emotions had given way and she felt hot tears flowing down her cheeks. She was utterly, utterly exhausted, so much so that she only vaguely realised that not only had she not thanked Bridie for her kindness but she had not spoken a single word since that first, dreadful moment of meeting Michael.

She did not hear Bridie return to the bedroom with her tea tray. Nor did she see the look of deep compassion on Bridie's face or hear her as she whispered, "Oh you poor, sweet child. Whatever has brought you to such a dreadful place as this? God help you from becoming like poor Miss Mairead and if you will let me, I'll do all in my power to keep you from that dreadful fate, too. I'll always be here for you, child. You'll always have a friend in old Bridie." She bent and kissed Beth's sleeping cheek and then hurriedly left the room as she heard heavy footsteps approaching along the landing.

"Yes, old Bridie," she muttered to herself, "you've got your work cut out for you, protecting that little one. She needs all the help you can give her and then a lot more. God grant me the strength."

"Your little wife is sleeping now, so you leave her be," she said to Kevin as he drew alongside her on the landing. "Come away down to my sitting room and tell me all about your trip while we have a nice cup of tea. Joseph can bring your cases up after the little lady has woken. And if you're very good, I might just find something a little stronger than a cup of tea, if you promise not to tell your old Ma."

"Oh Bridie," laughed Kevin softly. "You're a wicked old

woman who'll be the ruination of me yet. What would I do without our little get-togethers in your room and your wondrous 'cups of tea'? God knows I need one now - and a kind and loving shoulder to cry on. You're a God-send, Bridie, you are that!"

3

The sound of doors and drawers being opened and closed none too quietly brought Beth out of a deep, dreamless sleep. Kevin was busy unpacking his suitcases, seemingly unaware of his sleeping wife. Beth lay for some time watching him, trying to find something familiar about him, something she recognised of the man she had married such an incredibly short time ago but who now seemed like a stranger to her. Even his physical appearance had changed. He seemed to be much shorter, less substantial. There was no denying his exceptional good looks but somehow they had lost that sparkle and brilliance that had so captivated her in Boston and now he looked years younger, immature and vulnerable and decidedly not in control and masterful as he had been. His whole personality seemed to have undergone a complete change from the moment of that first, violent outburst with Michael at the airport. Beth was bewildered and confused and also very frightened.

Kevin at last noticed that Beth was awake and he hurried over to the bedside, trying hard to recapture his air of self-confidence and authority.

"Beth, my sweet," he murmured to her as he lay down beside her and took her in his arms. "You must be so tired after such a long journey and all the excitement. Awfully sorry your welcome wasn't as warm as it might have been, but you know how things are with families! Actually, none of this would have happened if Michael had just kept his bloody big mouth shut. He's so damn jealous of me that he can be positively poisonous. You see, his was an arranged marriage, if you can believe that such a thing still exists in this day and age in a civilised society. Mairead's father was setting up in competition with us and it was decided that the two families would merge and the old man would get his daughter off the shelf at the same time. You'll meet her later on but don't expect any rational conversation from her. She always was a few sandwiches short of a picnic but now it appears there's absolutely no chance of her having a family of her own (she's years older than Michael) it's tipped her right over the edge. Michael had words with the old man about 'supplying him with damaged goods' and suggested a complete buy-out so now her family has nothing to do with our business, or with Mairead, anymore. I think they were just glad to get rid of her. We may have got their business but Michael sure has been lumbered with a halfwit for a wife, poor old sod. So I guess when he saw me with a luscious young thing, his jealousy got the better of him and he just flipped."

Beth lay rigidly in Kevin's arms, scarcely believing what she was hearing. It sounded like a horror story and Kevin was so casual, almost callous, about it all. Poor Mairead! What a dreadful life she must lead. An arranged marriage! Softly, she spoke two words - "Eileen Conlon." She felt Kevin stiffen slightly, then relax again as he laughed lightly.

"Don't you worry your pretty head about that! That was just Michael trying to stir things up. As I say, he's just jealous and can't bear to see me so happy. He's a miserable old bastard but if you get in his good books, he'll look after you to the end. He's not all bad, you know. He just has his moments, like we all do. You'll get used to him in no time and soon you'll have him eating out of your pretty little hand." He lifted one of her hands and kissed the palm seductively. Beth felt nothing at all at this. Perhaps she was too shell-shocked and jet-lagged just now for anything to register properly.

"You get yourself up now and have a nice hot shower. It's almost time for afternoon tea - one of Mother's little rituals - and it doesn't pay to be late! If it weren't for that, you wouldn't be getting up at all!"

As Beth stood under the steaming water, letting its heat seep into her emotionally battered body, she thought back over all Kevin had said. There had been a distinct ring of untruth about it all, Beth was sure. Then she felt a twinge of guilt. Here she was, a bride of two days and she was already being disloyal to her husband by doubting him! Surely he had some justification for feeling as he did. Surely not everything he had said was untrue. Besides, she must hurry so as not to be late for tea with her mother-in-law. The thought of this filled her with dread. After the reception she had received with Clementine, she would have been more than happy not to set eyes on her again. It was strange, she thought suddenly, that Kevin had gone to great pains to explain away Michael's behaviour but had never once made reference to his mother until the mention of afternoon tea and even that held a veiled threat.

When she came back into the bedroom she found that Bridie was unpacking her things. There was no sign of Kevin.

"Ah, there you are, Miss Beth. Are you feeling nice and refreshed after your wee sleep? You were away with the angels when I brought you your tea tray. But never mind that now because there will be a grand tea laid down in the drawing room soon. You come and get yourself dressed now and I'll away downstairs and finish organising the tea. It will be ready to serve in fifteen minutes and it won't do to be late, certainly not on your first day here. Mrs Brady is a stickler for traditions and very set in her ways, but if you don't let her see that she frightens you, you'll be all right. If you're worried about anything at all here in the house, you come and see old Bridie and I'll set you right.

"Now, how about this lovely outfit to wear? 'Tis a lovely shade of blue that will make you look even more beautiful than you already are. Your underthings are all in this chest of drawers over here," she added, pointing to a beautiful walnut chest near the window. She laid out on the bed a checked wool skirt and matching cashmere sweater. Giving Beth her lovely sweet smile once more, she slipped out of the door, closing it softly behind her.

Beth went to the bed and ran her fingers lightly over the skirt and jumper, a little shudder travelling up her arm and down through her body. At least when she went to live with Aunt Mildred and Uncle Douglas she had her own clothes and toys about her. Now she didn't even have the comfort of the familiarity of her favourite old jeans and cosy sweaters. Kevin had bought her a complete new wardrobe, all very expensive and very elegant, but so alien! All her lovely, comfortable favourites had been given away to a charity shop before she left Boston. All she had brought with her of her own was her paintings and they were all crated up, Heaven knew where, awaiting collection or delivery or whatever, she certainly didn't know. Kevin hadn't explained anything to her. Good grief, he hadn't even told his own family he was married! A wave of anger hit Beth and she felt an upsurging of inner resolve. Right, she said to herself, I'll show you, Kevin Brady, that you did not marry a doormat. I will not lie down and let you and your family walk all over me the way they seem to have done with poor Mairead!

Beth quickly towel-dried her hair and applied her make-up - a little blusher to warm her cheeks, a touch of mascara to accentuate her lovely long eyelashes and the pretty pinky-mauve lipstick that suited her so well. She slipped on her new skirt and jumper and put in the beautiful sapphire and diamond earrings Kevin had given her as part of an extensive jewellery collection - her wedding gift from him. She daren't even think about the vast amount of money he had spent on her!

Lastly she stepped into the new Bally shoes and walked about the room for a few moments to accustom herself to the high heels, so much higher than anything she had had before. Taking one last glance in the cheval-glass to check that she was looking her best, Beth quickly left the room, instinct drawing her along the corridor that led to the long, sweeping staircase down to the hall, which in turn led to the drawing room and afternoon tea with the family.

Beth paused at the top of the staircase and nearly turned and fled back to her room. But then she drew herself up as tall as she was able and began her descent. With each step she took she said to herself, 'I am my parents' daughter', and drew the comfort of their remembered love about her like a mantle, counteracting the sinking feeling in the pit of her stomach as the bottom step loomed ever closer. 'I am a Brady by marriage, but I am a Morgan by birth and by nature!'

When she reached the hall, Beth looked around in dismay. There were six doorways leading off the hall, two of which had double doors, and they were all closed! She glanced at her watch in panic and saw that it was now exactly 4.15, the designated time for tea. She didn't have the time to open all the doors to see which one led to the drawing room!

Just then a door at the far end of the hall opened and out stepped Kevin. Beth caught a glimpse of the end of a billiard table as he closed the door behind him.

"Perfect timing, my sweet! You look beautiful." He came up to her with his hand outstretched. Beth took it gratefully. Kevin led her up to the double doors on the left of the hall, opened them and together, hand in hand, they entered the drawing room.

4

As Beth came into the drawing room, she glanced quickly around, trying to get her bearings, her trained artist's eye taking in as many details as possible. It was a room of enormous proportions, dominated by a vast fireplace with an elaborately carved surround. A large ormolu clock stood foursquare in the centre of the mantelshelf, itself cluttered to overflowing with old family photographs in ornate silver frames, figurines and ornaments of every size and shape, all with a very definite Victorian appearance. This was reflected in the furnishings of the room, the heavy, over-stuffed sofas and armchairs, the large mahogany cabinets and occasional tables, the dark-maroon velvet drapes and pelmets shrouding the windows overlooking the side and rear gardens, barely visible in the fading light behind the fussy lace curtains. The general effect was overwhelming. Despite the considerable size of the room, it felt overcrowded, cluttered, claustrophobic.

This is like stepping back in time, thought Beth, giving an inward, wry smile as she noticed what could only be an old-fashioned bell-pull hanging within easy reach of a high-backed wing chair drawn close to the blazing fire. The large chair dwarfed its tiny occupant and yet, at the same time, Clementine's aura emanated with an almost malevolent power from where she was sitting amongst all the cushions. She looks like a sinister version of Queen Victoria holding court, Beth chuckled to herself. Oh, I shall have to be careful. I can feel myself becoming positively vindictive and I don't like it!

Beth felt a sudden, uncomfortable shudder run through her and she turned slightly to find Michael was standing at the other side of the fireplace, coldly looking her up and down. All her senses seemed to be heightened as a whole mishmash of impressions appeared to bombard her from all directions, the overriding ones being antagonism from Michael and his mother and a distinct fear seeping from Kevin, standing rigidly at her side.

He cleared his throat once or twice and then said, "Good afternoon, Mama. What a splendid fire on such a miserable day." His voice was brittle with anxiety. "I trust Bridie won't be long with tea. I'm ravishing!" and he laughed nervously.

"Oh yes, my pet," Clementine's voice was icy cold. "You always were 'ravishing', as you call it. Ravenous for excitement, ravenous for adventure, ravenous for danger and ravenous for beautiful women." Her frosty glance flicked cruelly over Beth. "I doubt you will ever change."

Beth felt Kevin recoil with embarrassment. She wanted to say something, anything, in his defence but words failed to come. She had never encountered such maliciousness before and she was stunned into silence. While she was still desperately trying to rack her brains for some words of comfort and support, a door in the far corner of the room opened and Bridie emerged, pushing a large, three-tiered trolley, laden with delicious-looking food. Following behind her came a short wiry man, carrying a large tray on which was arranged a beautiful silver tea service - obviously Georgian, thought Beth, her quick eye, well tutored by Sean, taking in all the fine detail and elegant shape of the various pieces. This family certainly believed in quality of possessions.

There was a perceptible easing of the tension in the air, as if everybody had been holding their breath and had suddenly exhaled at the same time. Their spent breath made no sound but the air about them moved slightly, stirring each of them to the awareness of their surroundings and the remembrance that they were supposed to be members of a well-to-do family of considerable standing. Beth observed this as if at a distance, as though she were an unseen observer of some obscure play written by Ibsen or Chekhov. A case of 'not in front of the servants', mused Beth.

As the elderly couple drew near to where the family stood in front of the fireplace, Kevin placed his hand under Beth's elbow, drawing her forward.

"Beth, my dear, this is Joseph, Bridie's husband and our gardener and handyman and there is no-one handier with a tea tray than our Joseph." His attempt at levity had a hollow ring and certainly no-one in the room responded to it in any way.

After he had settled the heavy tray on a side table beside Clementine's chair, Joseph turned to Beth. "I'm delighted to meet you, Miss Beth. Welcome to Ireland. God willing, may you find great happiness here."

Beth wondered whether anyone else had seen the look that

Bridie shot at her husband. She sincerely hoped not, for although it was the briefest of looks, the words it spoke were almost audible and to Beth's ears, seemed to reverberate around the huge room. 'You stupid old fool!' Bridie's eyes seemed to snap at him. 'How can you expect a poor wee thing like the little lady to find happiness in this God-forsaken house?'

In an instant Bridie's face had resumed its normal bright, cheery expression. Beth half wondered whether she had imagined that strange interchange but she knew it had transpired when Bridie smiled at her with that extraordinary sweetness and said, "Oh yes. God willing, Miss Beth, you will be very happy with *us*." The emphasis on 'us' was so subtle that Beth, with all her senses so heightened, was scarcely able to detect it. But detect it she did and it was like an open invitation of friendship and of refuge whenever she might have need. The knowledge that there was at least one person in this strange, unwelcoming household to whom she could turn for comfort was like an injection of courage for Beth. She felt her shoulders straighten fractionally as she drew in the strength and reassurance that the old lady's words imparted to her. It was almost a tangible thing and Beth wrapped it around herself like a garment - a cloak of peace that would protect her from all the unpleasantness that seemed to permeate the whole house.

When she later reflected on that day from the safety of her exile, she found that she was not surprised when she recalled that she had not considered Kevin as someone to whom she could turn for friendship or refuge. It was as if she knew instinctively, after so very brief a time, that her life with Kevin would be unreliable, unstable, without any strong foundation or substance. But at the time, these future realisations were just unformed, elusive feelings; feelings she would have been incapable of putting into coherent thought.

Clementine's harsh voice brought Beth back into focus. "Bridie, for goodness sake, fetch that useless creature over here or tea will be totally ruined and that I will not countenance. There have been enough delays already." Beth shivered at the look of cold contempt on her mother-in-law's face, for that last, sarcastic comment had been directed at her. She rapidly averted her eyes and caught Bridie's quick look of reassurance before the old lady scurried off to the other end of the drawing room where there was a deep window seat under the huge casement that overlooked the rear gardens.

Beth was astonished to see Bridie reach in behind the long, heavy drapes and emerge holding the hand of a tall, elegant woman. She was strikingly beautiful, but thin to the point of emaciation and so very, very pale. She had been completely hidden by the curtains and so quiet and still that no-one could possibly have been aware of her presence. When they drew near, Kevin said shortly, "Beth, this is Mairead." Then he abruptly turned away, reaching for the cup of tea his mother held out to him and helping himself to sandwiches from the trolley.

Beth went to stand before Mairead and looked up into eyes of the most unusual violet that would have been breathtakingly beautiful except that they appeared to be absolutely lifeless. She felt a wave of infinite sadness wash over her.

"Hello, Mairead," she said gently. "I am Beth. Kevin's wife. Your new sister-in-law." Something in Mairead's eyes flickered fleetingly. Was it pain or was it pity? Whatever, Beth felt that now familiar iciness creep up her spine. She had never encountered such desolation in a human being before - and never wished to again.

Just then Michael appeared at her shoulder, thrust a cup and saucer into Mairead's hand and turned away. He never once looked at his wife or addressed a single word to her. Beth led Mairead to a chair, collected her own tea and sat in the chair next to Mairead's - and so began the most uncomfortable meal she had ever endured.

The brothers sat close by their mother, their previous disagreements seemingly forgotten, the three of them eating and drinking heartily and discussing their various business ventures in an intimate and animated fashion that excluded the two younger women. Bridie and Joseph had withdrawn to take their own tea in the kitchen. Mairead sat like a statue in her chair, occasionally raising her cup to her lips and taking minute sips of tea. She ate nothing at all.

Beth once again felt an odd sense of unreality, of dislocation, as though present in the room but not present at the same time. The voices of the brothers and their mother had a strange muffled quality as if they were reaching her down a long, distorted tunnel. She could hear their speaking but not their words. The brothers and their mother - strange how she thought of them thus. Was it jet lag and emotional exhaustion that gave rise to this sense of disconnection or an innate foreboding? Dear Lord, what am I doing here? She felt the words moving in her mind. Even her own thoughts appeared to be coming from far beyond her.

Finally, exhaustion took full control and Beth fell suddenly and deeply asleep, spilling her tea cup onto the carpet and bringing her husband to his feet with a shout of annoyance.

5

Beth awakened from her deep sleep to find herself lying on her bed, fully clothed and with the coverlet tucked around her. She felt as though she had been heavily drugged. She yawned deeply and stretched her body as if trying to force out every ounce of tiredness from her muscles.

Kevin, alerted by the movement from the bed, sprang out of the armchair where he had been agitatedly awaiting Beth's waking, and rushed over to the bedside. He slammed his hands down either side of Beth's shoulders, tightening the coverlet and pinning her firmly to the bed.

"*Thank you very much! Thank you very much, indeed!*" He spat the words angrily down into her startled face. "You really excelled yourself, didn't you? If you had wanted to antagonise my mother even more than you already had, you couldn't have chosen a better way! One of her finest china cups smashed and tea stains all over the drawing room carpet! My God, you know how to put on a performance, don't you?"

Tears of bewilderment filled her eyes. "Kevin," she pleaded. "Please stop this. I don't know what you are talking about."

"My God, are you *stupid* as well as deceitful?"

"Deceitful?"

"*Yes, deceitful*! What sort of a wife are you, anyway? All your protestations of undying love and loyalty! Have you shown one iota of loyalty since we got back home? *You have not*! Dear God, what a fool I've been to be taken in by those big beautiful eyes of yours! I actually believed you could be useful to me but you've been nothing but one big bloody disaster from the word go!"

"How *dare* you speak to me like that?" interrupted Beth.

"I dare because I have every right to. I'm your husband and don't you forget it!"

"You may be my husband but I am also your wife!"

"Hah!! And you think that makes you something special? You are only special if I say so and right now you are nothing but trouble! Have you any idea how long it will take me to get back in my mother's good books? Or how long it will take to get that bloody, supercilious look off Michael's face? You have made a complete fool of me in front of my family. You have disgraced me!"

"No, Kevin. You have disgraced yourself. My only crime is that I was so jet-lagged and exhausted that I fell asleep during afternoon tea. You are the one who has been deceitful by not telling your family about us to start with and by not telling me about Eileen Conlon - as if I would have married you then!"

Kevin swung out and caught Beth hard across her face with the back of his hand.

"Shut up! Do you hear me? *Shut up*!! Don't you ever answer me back again. Just remember your place in this family. You are the lowest of the low! You are on the bottom rung and if you ever want to progress up the ladder, you just watch your step. Be very careful, Beth, or your life could end up being very miserable indeed."

"Do you think it is anything other than miserable now?" sobbed Beth.

"I warned you! Be very careful! And never, *never* answer me back! Learn your place, watch your tongue and things will be fine. Step out of line and you will regret it, I promise you." His voice was low and threatening, menacing.

Beth experienced genuine terror for the first time in her life. She stared at the face above her with eyes wide with this new-found terror. The face glaring down at her was one she had never seen before - a face dark with violence and brutality. Oh dear Lord, help me, she prayed silently. I've married a madman! He is insane, I know he is! How am I going to cope? How can I stand this? Oh dear God, I can't bear this! The panic welling up within her threatened to explode forth in a scream. It felt like it was hammering inside her head and would burst her skull open.

Kevin suddenly released his savage grasp on the bedclothes and hurtled across the room to the door, upon which someone was hammering hard. He unlocked the door and flung it open but was brought up very short as Michael grabbed him around the throat and thrust him back into the room, kicking the door shut behind him.

"Sweet Jesus, you bloody maniac!" he hissed at Kevin. "Your screaming and yelling can be heard all over the house. Haven't you upset the old girl enough already? Do you want to finish her off for good?"

"It wasn't my fault," whined Kevin. "It was Beth. She let me down. She disgraced me in front of Mama."

"Shut your snivelling little mouth! Trust you to hide behind some little petticoat. You'll never be a man, will you? You never could own up to a single mistake you made. You always had to try to shift the blame on to someone else. But to blame some helpless little woman is really beyond the pale. You really are disgusting!

"Now for God's sake, pull yourself together. Dinner is in half an hour and you had both better be on time and on your best behaviour. I will not tolerate any more upsets today. Do I make myself clear?" He shook Kevin to emphasise his words, threw a cursory glance at Beth and left the room, leaving the two occupants in shocked silence.

Beth was the first to move. She flew off the bed and into the bathroom, locking the door behind her. She leaned against the door, her heart pounding. Then she started to shake quite violently. When her legs could no longer support her, she sank to the floor, tears pouring down her cheeks, her body convulsed with soundless sobs. What she wouldn't give to be safe at home in Boston, or even back in Canada with Aunt Mildred! Better still, back in her childhood, enwrapped in the security of her parents' love. No-one had ever loved her as they did! The remembrance of their love calmed Beth. As she had done so many times in her life, she drew the warmth of that special love about her and her shaking subsided.

She rose from the floor and turned on the shower. As the hot water gradually warmed her body, so her inner resolve strengthened. Nothing in her past had ever defeated her and she was not about to let that change now. She would bide her time, do what was expected of her and try to determine what would be the best route to take. Now, however, was not the time to make decisions of any sort. Now was the time to prepare herself for the next confrontation with these strange people who were now her family but were alien to her in every way.

6

The passing days had a dreamlike quality for Beth - sometimes nightmarish but mostly of an unreal nature. Always, hovering in the background, was the sense that she was an observer of some macabre play, as if all the others were acting out strange, unnatural roles whilst she, the only non-participant, was the spectator, detached and remote from their unfamiliar reality.

She realised by now that there was something wrong with each member of the family. She could understand and sympathise with Mairead's damage, for if she was not very careful, her sister-in-law's dreadful, mindless condition could become her own fate. The oppressive dominance of the Brady men was soul-destroying but she, Beth, was resolute in her determination not to be bowed down by their attitudes.

Her mother-in-law was an enigma to Beth and would, she thought, remain so. There was a strange dichotomy in Clementine. On the one hand, she was a lover of beauty in all things, a woman of strong principles and high standards. And yet she was tyrannical and brutal and was, Beth feared, downright evil. She demanded absolute loyalty and obedience from her sons and their devotion to her was not just based on love and respect but also on fear, predominantly so in Kevin's case.

Beth had plenty of time to observe the characters and the goings-on in the house from her position of non-participant, for she rarely left the house except with Kevin. She was unable to drive and Kevin would not let her go out on her own. He said that it was far too dangerous for her to do so because of the political situation. Beth was fully accustomed to seeing armed policemen for that was standard in North America, but she still got a shock each time she saw fully-armed soldiers on patrol and armoured cars driving around the streets.

Kevin had never disclosed his political affiliations to Beth (indeed, he never discussed anything of importance with her) but each time she was with him and they saw the soldiers, he quietly muttered something in Gaelic. Despite her requests, he flatly refused to translate for her and she gave up asking.

Her painting equipment still hadn't been delivered to the house and Beth found that time weighed heavily upon her. She spent a good part of each day in the library which was surprisingly well stocked with contemporary novels as well as historical and non-fiction books. There were several volumes on the history of Ireland and Beth found these fascinating. Perhaps there might be clues within them that would give her some inkling as to what had made her new family the people they now were. Wishful, fanciful thinking! she told herself sharply. These are self-made people, not the product of some airy-fairy ancient myths and legends!

Beth wrote long, chatty letters to Cathy, describing the huge, beautiful house and gardens, the positive attributes of the various household members (few though some of them were), the goings-on of darling Bridie and Joseph, of whom she was becoming ever fonder, their delightful accents, the delicious food so different from anything she had ever had at home. She told Cathy of Mairead's exceptional beauty, her elegance, her gentleness and softness of nature, but not that the life and soul had been crushed out of her by living with these people.

As much as she loved Cathy and treasured their friendship, she could not possibly confide in her of the darkness within the family. She did not understand it herself and until she did, she felt she could share it with no-one.

Beth spent long, often lonely, hours pondering her situation and what she should do about it. The only legacy her parents had left her was her Catholic faith and she clung to this now. But even this she could not share with Kevin or the others. She had been to Mass on Sunday with the family and the familiarity of the ritual was greatly comforting. The priest had appeared kindly and benevolent during the service but when she was introduced to him afterwards, she was saddened by his behaviour. She didn't mind his dismissive acknowledgement of her - heaven knew she was well used to that! - but she was distressed to witness his fawning obsequiousness towards Clementine. And Clementine accepted it with barely concealed contempt which only made him grovel even more.

He was most decidedly not someone to whom she could come for spiritual guidance or *any* guidance, for that matter. She doubted that, if she dared to confide in him, anything she said would remain sacred. She had a nasty feeling that his allegiance was more to

Clementine (and her considerable wealth and power) than to God. How very different from Father Kelly, her priest when she was at University, with whom she spent many long, companionable hours in spirited conversation and with whom she shared many a game of tennis! He had been a true friend and confidant.

So, what to do and where to turn? There was certainly no-one within the family to whom she could speak. Any attempts at even the most mundane conversation with Mairead were futile. A simple greeting was met with her perpetual blank stare. When she looked at you, her eyes didn't see you. That brief flicker in her eyes the first time Beth had met her had been the one and only reaction Beth had ever witnessed in her.

Michael and Clementine she avoided at all costs, enduring the family meals with outward pleasantness but inward dread, speaking only when spoken to and 'being on her best behaviour' as ordered by Michael!

As fond as she had become of Bridie and Joseph, they were, nonetheless, the old family retainers and surely their loyalties belonged to Clementine and the others, in spite of the kindness they extended to Beth. They were, by nature, kindly people but not, she reckoned, to be confided in. She must 'keep her place', in Kevin's words.

As for Kevin himself, she scarcely knew what to think. She knew that she had no personal love for him, if she had ever had. All the euphoria of those early days in Boston, his bedazzling charm, the way he swept her off her feet, had been just that - euphoria. Wishful thinking, a fanciful fairy tale as insubstantial as a snowflake. She felt a deep, burning inner shame that she had so foolishly lost not only her head, but her standards of correctness, of decency; for what she had done, she now realised, was not decent. It was shameful, wilful and totally selfish. How many lives had she blighted by her thoughtless actions? Eileen Conlon's, for one! (or had hers been a lucky escape?). Kevin's, most assuredly. Her own, but that, surely, was natural justice and to be borne as such until she could do something to right her wrongs.

In Boston, in church, before a priest, in the sight of God, she had made vows of commitment and obedience. Those vows were made for life. She prayed God's forgiveness that she was unable to love Kevin as a wife should and for His strength to enable her to do all within her power to make the best marriage possible and to find acceptance in Kevin's eyes and those of his family. It was the only way forward. Anything less would lead to an existence like Mairead's and that would destroy her completely.

7

Kevin's behaviour continued to cause Beth grave concern. He was so volatile. She never knew from one minute to the next in what frame of mind she would find him. He was either frenetically cheerful, as if he were on overdrive, or darkly morose; rarely anything in-between. Beth quickly learned to tread with great caution in his presence, careful never to give him cause to raise his hand to her again - the bruise on her face from that first dreadful blow had taken several days to fade but the inner bruising still caused her great pain.

Try as she may, she could not in any way communicate with her husband at any meaningful level. He simply wouldn't allow it. She knew better than to ever ask him again about Eileen Conlon, even though she longed to know the full story. She knew that it was in some way wrapped up in their business life from which she was totally excluded. She was aware that Kevin and Michael left home at 8.30 every morning and were always home at 3.45 to partake of afternoon tea at 4.15, according to Clementine's dictate. Clementine spent her days shut away in her study, rarely venturing out with her sons. After tea, the three of them would return to Clementine's study - that inner sanctum to which Beth and Mairead were never admitted - and spend the hours until dinner deep in discussion, occasionally their raised voices drifting out into the hallway.

Many times, in an attempt to draw closer to Kevin and take a fuller, more active, interest in his life, Beth asked him about the family business. All she could get from him was that they were involved in financial matters and real estate, and a terse, 'Just be thankful that we make enough money to keep you in the lap of luxury!'

Sometimes she felt she was merely an ornament to be taken out of wraps when required, dusted off and put on public display. *Then* she was expected to shine! *Then* she was a valuable asset! When they returned home or visitors had left their house, she was simply put back on the shelf and forgotten until the next social occasion.

One Friday Kevin came home from work in especially high spirits. He was most attentive to Beth during afternoon tea. Later, at dinner, he seemed to be positively effervescent. He was full of banter and amusing anecdotes. Beth hadn't seen him so animated in a long time. This was more like the Kevin she had first met in Boston. She was so enjoying what she hoped was the return of her true husband, that she was totally unaware of the wary looks that passed between Michael and Clementine or the underlying air of tension that was slowly building. However, the two visibly relaxed when, at the end of the meal, Kevin stood up from the table and held out his hand to Beth.

"Come, my sweet," he said. "I think it is time for you and me to spend a little more time together. Good night, Mama. Good night, Michael." He bowed his head slightly to each in turn and led a bemused but delighted Beth from the room.

When they got upstairs, Kevin took Beth straight through to their own private sitting room, a room in which they had never before sat together. Now at last, thought Beth, they would spend some quality time as a married couple. Indeed, in the time they had been together in this house, they had spent *no* time as a married couple.

Kevin led her to the sofa, fussing around her while she settled herself. To her disappointment, he then went to sit in one of the chairs by the fireplace, in which Joseph must have lit a fire while they were still at dinner. The room was suffused in a warm glow from the flames and from a single lamp, placed at the far side of the room so as not to be intrusive. There was such a soothing, almost romantic, atmosphere in the room, reminiscent of the candle-lit dinners they had shared in Boston, Beth felt herself relax for the first time since her arrival in Ireland.

When Kevin spoke, he took Beth completely by surprise.

"Tell me about your childhood, before your parents were killed. I want to hear all about when you were happy and loved. You look so beautiful in the firelight that I could gaze at you forever. I just want to drink in all your beauty while you talk. Come on now, tell me, from back as early as you can remember."

It was a strange request as he had never before shown any interest in her life. Perhaps this was to be a fresh beginning for them. Perhaps he had resolved whatever difficulties had kept him on edge for so long and now felt free to be his true self with her at last. Having longed for this sort of gentle intimacy, Beth slipped her legs up onto the sofa, settled herself comfortably and let her mind drift back as far as she could, back to the days of warmth and laughter and love.

She talked and talked as she never had with Kevin. Until now, she had always been the listener. Kevin sat all the while with his legs stretched out in front of him, his elbows perched on the arms of the chair, fingertips together, lightly tapping his pursed lips from time to time, his slightly narrowed eyes never once leaving her face.

Suddenly he sat forward, breaking into her reminiscences.

"Enough, my sweet. Enough for now. You're looking very tired. Come away and get ready for bed now while I pop down to the kitchen and get you a nice hot drink."

Beth was touched by his solicitousness but reluctant for him to leave the room, thereby breaking the tenuous rapport that had been building up between them. Wanting to hold on to it and maintain the warmth of their closeness she asked, "Can't you ring for Bridie, just this once? I'm sure she wouldn't mind."

Kevin drew her towards him, slipping his arms around her tiny waist. He dropped his head and gave her a long, lingering kiss that sent lovely shivers running up and down her spine. He raised his head, his eyes dancing in the firelight.

"But I would mind," he whispered. "I want to do this for you myself - my special treat. Now you hurry into bed and I will be back as quickly as possible." He kissed her once more and slipped noiselessly out of the room.

Beth was amazed at how a man of his size could move so absolutely silently. He reminded her of a panther - so sleek and dark, handsome to the point of beauty, so gentle to look at, but so dangerous to encounter. She shuddered at the turn her thoughts had taken so unexpectedly. Enough, she reprimanded herself. No dark thoughts tonight. Be thankful he has returned to you and enjoy him all the while he is here with you.

Beth took extra care with her bedtime preparations, choosing a beautiful silk nightdress she hadn't worn before and spraying on a little *'L'air du temps'* which she enjoyed so much because of its delicate scent, even though Kevin thought it wasn't expensive enough for her!

She climbed between the lovely fresh linen sheets and lay, propped against the plump pillows, expectantly awaiting Kevin's return. He crept into the room like a little boy, with a huge mischievous grin on his face, bearing before him one of the best silver salvers, in the middle of which rested a large, battered kitchen mug. Beth laughed delightedly at the spectacle before her.

Kevin came and put the tray down on her bedside table and

sat on the bed beside her.

"Ah, sweet Beth, it does my jaded old heart good to hear you laugh like that. I don't hear it often enough. We shall have to see what we can do to remedy that.

"Now while I get myself ready for bed, you drink up your Kevin Special, prepared by my own fair hands against the wrath of old battle-axe Bridie who thinks I have defiled her kitchen and insulted her in the process by not letting her heat the milk for you herself."

"You've made me hot milk!" exclaimed Beth. "Yuck!!"

"Ah, but this is made to my own secret recipe, handed on to me by the Little People and it's like nothing you've ever tasted before. Sure, 'tis the nectar of the gods. Now, drink it all up while I have a nice shower and then we'll see what we can find to talk about, maybe... perhaps!" After planting a quick kiss on Beth's laughing mouth, he disappeared into their bathroom.

Beth sipped her hot milk reluctantly. All right, Kevin Brady, she laughed to herself. You win. I hate hot milk but this doesn't taste too bad. For you, I'll drink it. For anyone else, I would rather die of thirst!

She could still hear the shower running by the time she had finished the last drop of her drink. The sound of Kevin's raucous singing brought further laughter from her. He truly was tone-deaf! His voice was appallingly bad. At least this was something at which he didn't excel, she chuckled, something at which she could best him, for she, herself, possessed a beautiful clear soprano voice not unlike that of a young boy whose voice had yet to break.

Beth snuggled deeper into her pillows, revelling in the delicious feel of the smooth linen sheets - another new experience for her! - and the warmth from the milk that spread so nicely through her. She felt happier and more contented than she had done since ..... oh, she couldn't remember when. She felt so toasty-cosy she couldn't even bother to remember!

She was scarcely aware of Kevin slipping in between the sheets beside her and certainly didn't hear as he whispered her name several times. Nor was she aware of his slipping out of bed again some hours later and silently, stealthily, leaving the room, closing the door soundlessly behind him.

8

"He is up to no good! I *know* he is up to no good!" Bridie kicked shut the connecting door between the kitchen and her little sitting room. "God help the poor little lady, but I know he is up to no good!"

"Oh hush, woman," snapped Joseph. "Will you stop your wittering? I'm trying to watch television."

"Hush yourself, you stupid old man! Sure, who could be interested in some stupid television programme when that sweet little lady could be suffering God knows what at the hands of that man. And don't I know it, if nobody else does, for haven't I raised the little he-devil myself? Didn't I give him every bottle of milk he ever had, morning, noon and night and God knows when else in between, since the day he was born in that great room above because herself was too grand and too idle to put her own teat into his greedy, bleating, little mouth!

"God help me, I tried all I could to bring him up decent, seeing the fine example he had to follow in his nasty big brother and that weak, poor excuse of a man that called himself his father, having somehow managed to sire two demons from his milksop loins. But the evil was bred into the wee lad from his mother's milk, that she couldn't even be bothered to drip into his mouth! And look at the creature he has become, God help us. He is wicked through and through.

"I don't know what his game is tonight but I know it is a dark and dirty game. 'Just come down to make my sweet Beth a night-time drink. Want to make it with my own loving hands!' My old Aunt Fanny! The only person he has ever loved is his own wicked self and the only thing he has ever done for the little lady is to black her eye and make her the saddest creature that I have ever seen in all my days - sadder even than poor wretched Mairead for she, poor soul, had very little spirit to break. But if he breaks the little lady, so help me God, if I rot in hell, I'll break him myself! God knows, I'll swing for the evil bugger!"

The last word brought Joseph sitting to attention. He was well used to hearing Bridie rant and rave, sure he scarcely paid any heed to a word she said. But to hear her swear like this! Now he knew she was seriously upset. Things were looking exceedingly bad if his Bridie swore.

"Whist, woman. Keep your voice down. Do you want us to be thrown out on our ears? For if we leave here, we go without a reference, you know that as well as I do and jobs are few and far between for anybody these days but for the likes of you and me there would only be the workhouse. Now hush and don't fret yourself any longer. The little lady is no fool. She can look after herself. Come away and have a nice drop of whiskey with me."

"I'll take the whiskey but I'll not hush. The little lady is no match for that amount of evil, you mark my words. If somebody doesn't put a stop to that demon soon he'll take her with him all the way to hell."

"Woman, woman! Be quiet for the love of God in heaven! You will get us thrown out of here and out of the church, too, with talk like that! You know the power that evil old woman wields, even in her church."

"In *her* church, yes, but not in ours, for you know as well as I do that Father Patrick will have nothing to do with her or her kind. He would sooner rot in hell than climb into bed with her and that wet smack who kisses the ground every time she sets foot in his church."

"Oh, be quiet. Do be quiet!" pleaded Joseph, as he helped himself to another large whiskey. "Think of my poor heart!"

"Bugger your poor old heart! There's nothing wrong with your heart that a good kick up the arse wouldn't fix! Dear God, I can't talk to you, you're as useless as tits on a bull!!" Bridie slammed out of the room and into their bedroom. "I shall visit Susan tomorrow and have a proper talk with her. She'll know what to do," she called out.

Joseph took another gulp of his drink and reached again for the bottle by his side. He was deeply shocked at Bridie's outburst and equally deeply frightened. Never in all his life had he seen her like that. And Susan - dear God, what was to happen to them?

Susan was Bridie's younger sister and was herself a housekeeper, the difference being that she was not married and was housekeeper to Father Patrick, whose church was at the far end of town. It was also the church which Bridie and Joseph attended, despite the long haul to get there, whatever the weather for, as Bridie had said many a time, nothing would induce her to enter the local church, presided over by that bought-and-paid-for, pathetic excuse for a priest who danced attendance on Clementine at every opportunity, waiting breathlessly for the 'crumbs' from her purse! She would sooner dance with the Devil himself!

Joseph sweated profusely in his increasingly drunken fear. Tomorrow old Bridie was going to talk to Susan and tell her God knew what! Who knew what Father Patrick would do then! Dear God, what was to become of them?

At heart, Joseph was a good man, but he was weak and fearful. Bridie was the strong one in their relationship and for all their life together, for the most part, he had been happy to let her be so. But when she was like this!! He was truly afraid.

9

Beth awoke slowly the next morning. She felt pleasantly languid and heavy with sleep. She turned her head and found that Kevin was still beside her, sleeping deeply. This was unusual, for normally he was already in the shower when she awoke. She felt all nice and snuggly-warm inside and she reached out her hand and ran her fingers lightly along his bare shoulder but he didn't stir. That really must have been some night, she chuckled to herself and she nestled back into her pillows, eager to mentally relive that lovely evening. But to her puzzlement, she could remember nothing after finishing her hot milk. Try as she might, there were no recollections to be dredged up from anywhere.

Just then Kevin came to with a start. He took a quick deep breath, looking around him as if he did not know where he was. Then he noticed Beth and reached out hungrily to her.

"Come here, you gorgeous thing. Give your poor old husband a big kiss, you luscious creature, you!" and he buried his face in her neck.

Beth traced the muscles in his upper arm with her fingers, feeling him shudder slightly under her touch. Very tentatively she said, "Kevin, about last night..."

"Oh God," he moaned. "You were spectacular! I've never known a night like it! What a lady you are!"

"But darling, I hardly know how to say this but I'm ashamed to admit that I can hardly remember a thing about it."

"Ah, but you see, that is the true power of love. It has taken all that glorious ecstasy away from your mind and straight to your heart where it belongs! And doesn't your heart feel grand and full this morning? And isn't it a beautiful fine day today? A day for adventure and fun!"

"I've never met anyone with as much of the Blarney as you," Beth laughed. "How can you possibly know it's a fine day when the drapes are fully shut and it's been raining for over a week?"

"Ah to be sure, I feel it in me bones! 'Tis another of the wee gifts given to me by the Little People!"

"You are such a card when you want to be. You and your Little

People! I sometimes think you actually believe in them."

"Careful, Bethy! Do not mock the Little People. You do not know with what you would be tangling. Treat them with respect and they'll fall all over themselves to help you. Scorn them at your peril, for all manner of ills could befall you." Despite his exaggerated Irish brogue that he always adopted when he spoke of his 'Little People' or when he was teasing her, Beth felt that Kevin was deadly serious. What a strange, complex man he was!

He continued to stare intently into her eyes for what felt like an eternity. Then he suddenly sprang up from the bed and halfway across the room where he gave a leap into the air, half-turning so he landed facing her as he clapped his hands together.

"Come on, my girl! Up and at it!" he called. "You and I are going exploring today - out to the countryside, away from all 'cilivization' and maybe, just maybe, we might find where the Little People live!" He gave her an impish grin and disappeared into the bathroom, singing a haunting, lilting song in Gaelic.

'Cilivization', indeed! Beth lay back, speechless, breathless at his mercurial behaviour. Her mind was reeling under the onslaught of his rapidly changing moods. And she thought her mother-in-law was an enigma! She wasn't a patch on this strange, capricious man who was, at one and the same time, her husband, her occasional lover, her even more infrequent friend and her emotional jailer. Would she ever know the full extent of this man whom she had married but didn't know if she loved, wasn't sure if she particularly liked, of whom she was most definitely afraid, but who intrigued her, fascinated her, made her laugh and who aroused such feelings of pity and tenderness in her? Someone, somewhere, had said that life was an adventure but whoever it was had failed to add that it was also the most complicated, intricate, emotional maze!

10

They left the city and drove out into the countryside. Kevin most certainly had been right about the weather. The very air seemed to be alive and sparkling in the dazzling sunlight. The cloudless sky was a rich, clear blue and the fields were like huge, deep-pile carpets as if a giant Bridie had just finished vacuuming them in her meticulous way, every blade of grass in its place, soaking up the glorious sunshine.

Beth had never seen countryside like this in all her life, for this was the first time she had left the city since her arrival and certainly the first really sunny day she had experienced in Ireland. She was breathless with delight, her head turning from side to side as she strained to catch each passing scene from every angle, instinctively storing minute details in her artist's mind for further development. Her fingertips tingled and itched with the desire to paint.

"Oh," she whispered. "I must paint this! I've never seen such colours! And everything is so green!! It's winter-time and everything is still so green! I guess that's why this place is called the Emerald Isle?"

She turned to Kevin for confirmation but found that he hadn't heard her at all. He was deeply absorbed in his own thoughts, a look of tightly suppressed excitement on his face. Perhaps he hadn't heard her over the noise of the engine. But as she listened, Beth realised that the engine noise was virtually inaudible, almost as though it wasn't even turned on despite the fact that the big, powerful Mercedes Benz was hurtling down the lane at considerable speed.

As Beth focused on the car and the road ahead, it suddenly dawned on her how desperately narrow the lane was. She gripped her seat in panic, calling out to Kevin as another car appeared from around the bend, flying straight at them. High banks and hedgerows afforded no chance of escape from what must surely be a head-on collision and Kevin made little effort to slow down. She tried to scream but her voice froze in her throat.

Kevin let out a roar of laughter as the two cars whizzed past each other.

"You Americans are all alike! You're so used to your big, wide highways that our little lanes terrify you. Soon you'll be driving them yourself as if you've never known anything different."

"I don't know how to drive," snapped Beth. "And I'm not American, I'm Canadian and there's a very great difference between the two and don't you forget it!"

"Hey, hey! Don't be so silly. There's no need to get snappy just because I called you American. It's no big deal!"

"I'm not being silly! You could have warned me about the roads. I was really scared."

Kevin glanced across at Beth and immediately slowed the car down and pulled into an opening by a farm gate. She was as white as a sheet and shaking from head to foot. He gathered her into his arms and rocked her gently to and fro, resting his cheek lightly on the top of her head. She was so tiny and frightened, like a little bird quivering with fear. His heart surged with tenderness for her.

"Oh baby, baby," he murmured into her hair. "I'm so sorry, really I am. I just never thought that it would bother you this much. I didn't realise you would be quite so frightened. I honestly didn't mean to upset you. Forgive me? Please?"

Beth drew back a little from Kevin's embrace and looked up into his face. She was quite shocked to realise that he had deliberately set out to frighten her. She had a sudden vision of him as a young boy, one of those horrible little boys who pull the wings off flies for the sheer pleasure of inflicting pain and torment. Somehow she could see him quite clearly, a look of concentrated enjoyment on his little face. Then she gave herself a brisk mental shake, dispelling the considerably disquieting vision.

"I wasn't just frightened, Kevin," she said. "I was genuinely terrified. I really believed that we were going to crash. I *will* forgive you this time, but please don't do anything like that to me again. It really was unfair. I know I have a lot of adjustments to make now that I live in Ireland, but I really need your help and support if I'm going to adapt quickly and easily. It certainly hasn't been easy so far."

"Beth, I'm genuinely sorry. I promise I will try much harder in future. And now, what say we find somewhere to park the car and go for a walk? We don't want to waste all this wonderful sunshine, do we? Then I'll take you to a lovely little hotel I know where they serve the most delicious seafood."

A little further down the lane they found a lay-by where they could safely leave the car. Changing into sturdy walking boots, they set off across the fields towards the nearby hills that looked so inviting. They walked for over two hours, mostly in a companionable silence, neither feeling the need for much conversation; Kevin occasionally pointing out scenes of particular interest; Beth asking the odd question about unfamiliar plants and such like; both drinking in the sweet, cool air and the soft, warm sunshine, feeling them invigorate, renew, refresh bodies and souls grown stuffy and stale by the cold, depressing, wet weather of the past weeks.

Beth was enchanted with all she saw. The gently rolling hills, scattered with farms and clusters of little cottages, were so different from anything she was used to. Even the winter trees appeared to be more beautiful, their graceful branches like fine filigree against the blue sky. Perhaps it was because there were so few evergreen trees which seemed so overpowering back home, especially in the winter time. Here, these deciduous trees, which seemed to be more sparsely, more naturally planted, gave a feeling of openness, of freedom.

Beth let her thoughts, fanciful and otherwise, wander where they liked as she revelled in the quiet peacefulness of the morning. This is the first time I have ever felt at peace since I've been in this country, she thought to herself. She was standing on a hilltop overlooking a valley with a delightful, tree-lined river flowing along the bottom, the fields, outlined by dry-stone walls and hedgerows, scattered up each side, cattle contentedly grazing in some, sheep in others. She absorbed the beauty, the stillness, the peace into herself, storing it up as if to fortify herself for whatever lay ahead for her back at 'the House' in Belfast. I really must learn to drive soon so that I can get out here more often, thought Beth. I could learn to cope with the dragon Clementine if I knew I could come here to recuperate!

Intrusive thoughts of her life in Belfast threatened to invade Beth's feeling of tranquillity and she fought hard to maintain it but to no avail for at that same moment Kevin called to her. He was some distance away overlooking the roadway and appeared agitated.

"Come on," he called. "We must go. Now!" He was jigging from foot to foot, slapping his hands against his thighs. "*Come on*! *Come on*!"

Fearing something was wrong, Beth hurried over to him, looking anxiously up into his face. She saw that his eyes were dancing and the suppressed excitement she had sensed earlier was emblazoned across his face.

"Whatever is the matter?" she asked anxiously.

"It's Guinness time! I'll race you to the car!" He set off down the path at a jog, turning to call to Beth. "Come on, slow coach, or the Little People will catch you and then I'll have to drink your Guinness as well as me own!"

"You can have mine with pleasure," Beth called after him as she ran to catch him up. "I wouldn't drink that stuff if you paid me to. It's disgusting!"

"Hush your mouth, woman, or you'll be had up for treason! Just remember where you are! A person can be deported for making comments like that!"

"You can deport me or put me in a dungeon or do what you like. I will still not drink that filthy black stuff! It is awful! It's not fit for human consumption!"

Kevin stopped abruptly and spun around in time to catch Beth as she careered into him. "You wicked woman, you. I don't know why I put up with you!"

"At least you get my share of Guinness. You can't complain about that, can you?"

"True, but I've noticed you've taken quite a liking to our finest Irish whiskey. Now that needs some considerable thinking about. Should I permit you to continue to deprive me of that very special luxury? Perhaps I should get in a supply of American bourbon just for you."

"Don't you dare! That's even more disgusting than Guinness!" Beth laughed. "Do you know something? I think you are quite, quite mad!"

"Ah, little Beth, you could well be right." Kevin held her gaze for a long time, suddenly dropped a quick kiss on her lips, spun around and leapt off down the path. "Last one to the car buys the first round!"

They were approaching the car from a different direction and Beth noticed a blue flashing light down below them to the right. Through the trees she glimpsed the roof of a small building in a clearing - an old barn or a deserted cottage. As they drew nearer she was aware that Kevin had tensed considerably. He seemed to be walking on the balls of his feet, almost springing with each step, his hands tightly closed at his sides. He kept glancing quickly to the right and back to the pathway, all the time half-whistling tunelessly.

They came around a bend in the pathway and were able to see into the clearing more easily. The flashing blue light came from atop a police car. There was also an armoured personnel carrier parked in front of the cottage and several heavily armed soldiers were milling around. Beth shivered as if she had been hit by a blast of icy air. Kevin was now whistling cheerfully and he reached for Beth's hand, drawing her to his side. As they passed the pathway that led to the cottage, guarded by a young soldier, Kevin gave him his most dazzling smile and called out. "Good morning. Beautiful day, isn't it? Under his breath he muttered, "A fine day's work! A fine day's work!"

When Beth asked what he meant, he said that the soldiers were probably on manoeuvres, protecting the country against 'undesirables', so that the likes of her could sleep safe in their beds at night. Beth wasn't at all sure that she liked his tone of voice and found little comfort in what he said. She also felt that it would be unwise to say anymore. Besides, they were now back at the car and Kevin was anxious to get to the hotel and his first Guinness of the day. She, herself, felt more than ready for a glass of Jameson's!

11

As Kevin had predicted, the food at the hotel was excellent. The monkfish and scallops in filo pastry was particularly delicious and was followed by a delectable fresh fruit brulee. Having finished their meal, Beth and Kevin were now relaxing in large, comfortable armchairs in front of a big picture window in the lounge. This is like being in someone's home rather than an hotel, Beth thought as she gazed around the lovely room. A huge fire blazed brightly in the inglenook, its flames reflected in the copper coal scuttle and log basket. The rest of the furniture in the room looked just as comfortable as the chair in which she now sat. All the pictures on the walls were watercolours of the local countryside, adding a more personal touch to the décor. It was all so much more cosy and restful than the dark, heavily Victorian drawing room back at the House and Beth sat back deeper into her chair, thoroughly enjoying the peaceful, relaxing ambience, slowly sipping a delicious Irish coffee.

Directly opposite her chair hung a delightful watercolour, beautifully and skilfully executed. Turning her head slightly to look outside, Beth realised with a little start that the view in the painting was the exact one at which she was now looking through the window. Even the sheep seem to be grazing in the same places, she chuckled to herself. This is really blissful, she thought as she sighed contentedly. I could sit here and look at this scene all day.

She didn't feel any great desire to paint what she could see but was content, rather, to just sit and let the peacefulness and beauty of the scene soak into her being, dispelling any disquieting thoughts or feelings she had experienced earlier, forgetting completely about the disturbing sight of the soldiers at the deserted cottage.

She jumped slightly, startled from her reverie by Kevin leaning over the back of her chair.

"No need for you to disturb yourself. You just stay put and relax. I have to make one or two business calls. I may be gone some time but don't worry, I won't forget you! I'll be back at least in time for tea before we go home, if not sooner." He dropped a kiss on the top of Beth's head and was gone before she could say anything.

She felt a momentary flash of anger at being abandoned so

peremptorily but shrugged off the feeling as the young barman smilingly brought her over another Irish coffee, obviously ordered by Kevin on his way out.

Oh, what the heck, she thought. Do as the man says and just sit back and enjoy the peace and quiet. This was the first time, she realised, that she was able to be alone and away from the House and its oppressive atmosphere. This was her first taste of freedom since leaving Boston and she was now rather pleased that Kevin had absented himself as he had.

Beth sat back with her drink and let her mind wander, not thinking of anything in particular, just drifting dreamily. She was vaguely aware of two ladies coming to sit near her, their voices chattering away in that still strange-to-the-ear Northern Irish brogue. She closed her eyes and unashamedly eavesdropped on their conversation just to see how much of it she could understand. They spoke so fast in their unfamiliar accent that it was almost as if they were speaking a foreign language. Beth lazily listened as she tried to familiarise herself with the sound of their voices. Kevin and his family had much more anglicised accents and she had had little exposure to people other than their very select friends.

Listening more now to the conversation rather than just their voices, Beth was astonished to hear that the two women were discussing their plans for Christmas. *Christmas!* Could it really be that time of year already? So many new and strange things had happened to her in the last few weeks that she had lost all track of time. And now, it seemed, in just over three weeks it would be Christmas. She shuddered at the thought of Christmas in that big, dreary, stifling house. What on earth would it be like? She couldn't imagine any sort of festivities going on there. How very different it would be from last year when she had stayed with Cathy's family over the Christmas period. That had been the best Christmas she had ever experienced - so very different from those she spent with Aunt Mildred and Uncle Douglas.

Aunt Mildred's God was stern, exacting, authoritarian; someone to be treated with pious, reverential respect. Therefore His Son, being created in His Father's image, was to be treated in the same way. She knew no joy in her faith, only doom and gloom, for hadn't Jesus died a cruel and horrible death (she gave no apparent acknowledgement to the Resurrection and the glorious promise of eternal life)? And He had suffered such 'humiliating agony and a shameful death' because of 'man's vileness'. He was 'born to die for man's wickedness' and wickedness was most certainly not something to celebrate. Therefore Christmas was a time to contemplate man's dreadful state and not a time to rejoice at the birth of a baby who was 'born to die'. So when the invitation came to share in the Sinclair family Christmas, Beth accepted with both alacrity and some reservation, for she really didn't know what to expect.

In the end, she had spent five gloriously happy days as part of a large and loving family. Two of Cathy's older brothers were married and between them they had five children, Daniel at five years being the eldest and Bethany at five months, the youngest. The house, large though it was, was bursting at the seams as the two brothers and their families all came to stay, as did Mrs Sinclair's parents. With twelve adults and five children in the house, there was always lots of noise and laughter. Everyone pitched in and helped, the ladies doing the cooking and the men doing the dishes and clearing up (Mrs Sinclair had her sons well trained!).

For Beth, the highlight of those five days was Christmas Eve and she knew that she would carry the memory of it all through her life. After the children had eaten their supper and were bathed and in their pyjamas ready for bed, Grandpa Sinclair called everyone into the reception hall. It was a large hall, as large as Aunt Mildred's whole living room, and set in the wall that adjoined the dining room was a huge carved-oak fireplace. The mantelpiece was decorated with evergreens and straw, with a group of three fat white candles of different heights at either end. In the centre of the mantel stood a beautiful porcelain angel with a golden halo and enormous, fine, gossamer-like wings edged in gold. Beth had never seen an angel so beautiful and later learned that it had belonged to Cathy's great-grandmother and was handed down from eldest daughter to eldest daughter and so one day would be Cathy's.

In the hearth was the most wonderful Nativity scene, all lovingly carved by Cathy's great-grandfather. It appeared to be perfect in every detail, including a beautifully painted backdrop depicting the night sky and the hillside behind the stable.

All the family gathered around the fireplace, the children in the very front and Beth, being so much tinier than any of the other adults, to their right so that she could see everything that happened. As Grandpa Sinclair lit the candles on the mantle, Great-Grandpa Wilson (Mrs Sinclair's father) slipped out of the hall and into the living room, turning off all the lights as he went so the only illumination there was came from the candles on the mantleshelf and the blazing fire, in the living room, that cast its warm glow out though the open double doors into the hallway.

The children gazed at the Nativity scene in silent wonder, their eyes huge and glowing in the candle-light. Even baby Bethany, held in her father's arms, seemed to have caught their mood, as she pointed at the stable, her mouth open in a silent 'Ooh', her eyes sparkling.

Someone, somewhere, flicked an unseen switch that lit a bulb concealed behind the backdrop. The whole scene suddenly came to life, the night sky bright with stars as the light shone out through pin-holes in the backdrop and the big, central, cut-out star, unnoticed until now, shining brilliantly, its light radiating out and falling directly onto the stable. Everyone gasped with delight and clapped their hands, even those who had witnessed the same event year after year and yet were moved afresh by the beauty of the experience.

Then Grandpa Sinclair came to young Daniel and wordlessly placed something in his outstretched hand. Silently, his eyes shining with the awareness of the honour of his task as the eldest grandchild, Daniel turned and placed the carved model of the Infant Jesus in the cradle. At the same moment, on some unseen signal, Great-Grandpa Wilson began to play 'Away in a Manger' on the piano in the living room. Daniel and three year old Thomas sang the words with innocent beauty as only a child can sing, two year old Chloe and her eighteen month old cousin, Nathaniel, 'aahed' and 'laahed' and baby Bethany added her coos of delight, the adults joining in softly.

After the singing was over, the children were led, unprotesting, up to bed, all seemingly spellbound with awe and childlike wonder. Beth found that tears were flowing down her cheeks but did not feel in the least embarrassed or ashamed as not a single adult had dry eyes.

"It's the same every year," Mrs Sinclair whispered to her. "No matter how many times we go through this family ritual, it always is the same. We are completely overcome. I don't know if it's just because of the children's reactions or whether it is our own personal awareness of the miracle of that first Christmas. Perhaps it's a little of both."

The rest of the evening was spent in the big living room, sipping hot punch in front of the fire, some placing last minute gifts under the huge tree, parents filling stockings for the children, ready to hang from the fireplace once the fire was out, others quietly singing as Great-Grandpa Wilson continued to play Christmas carols, all enjoying the gentle loveliness of family unity on a very special occasion. At half-past eleven they all left the house to walk through the falling snow to the local church for midnight mass, Cathy's youngest brother, Rick, and his girlfriend having volunteered to babysit.

Sitting by another fire, thousands of miles away in a place where she knew virtually no-one and where she had not one friend, Beth knew she would never again experience a Christmas like that one. It was as if it had been given to her as a special gift, made all the more beautiful and precious by its rarity. Although she now knew an almost overwhelming sadness, she nevertheless felt the privilege of that experience and knew that the memory would remain with her and would sustain her no matter what might lie ahead.

12

Beth looked around her and noticed with considerable surprise that it was now dark outside. She had been so absorbed with her remembrances that she had lost all track of time. Her second Irish coffee stood unfinished on the table beside her. The two ladies who had been sitting near her had left and an elderly couple had taken their places and were now enjoying a most delicious-looking afternoon tea.

Just then Kevin entered the lounge and it seemed that every head turned and followed his progress across the room towards Beth, appreciation of his good looks and fine build on all their faces. Beth felt a surge of affection for him as she sat quietly watching his approach. She raised her face to receive his kiss as he dropped down into the chair beside her.

"Hello, beautiful. Did you miss me while I was gone? Hey!" He leaned forward and peered closely at her face. "Have you been crying? Your eyes look wet and a bit puffy. Are you all right?"

"Don't worry. I'm fine. I've just been sitting here quietly reminiscing and I guess I got a little emotional, but I definitely have not been crying."

"If you've been reminiscing, it has to have been about Boston or Canada. I've told you before that all that is over and done with. It's all in the past and must stay there. Your life is here and now, with me, in Ireland. All that has gone before is done and finished with. You are to forget all about it, do you hear me? I won't stand for any of this sentimental nonsense. Understood?"

Beth recoiled at the harshness in his voice.

"Kevin, that is outrageous! How can you possibly expect me or anyone to forget about their past? For one thing, it is simply impossible and for another, what you are asking - no, demanding - is grossly unfair. Anyway, I was not wallowing, as you would have it, but merely remembering a particularly happy occasion that is very important to me. I don't regret my life in Canada or Boston but if you carry on like this, I shall most certainly come to regret my life here in Ireland."

"Okay, point taken." Kevin slumped back in his chair and let his long legs slide out in front of him. "So, share."

"I beg you pardon?"

"Come on, share. Tell me all about this 'particularly memorable occasion'. I want to hear what's got you all dewy-eyed and soppy."

"I think not," Beth replied in as restrained and impersonal a voice as possible. "Now is not the time and place."

"But I want to hear about it!"

"And I choose not to tell you. Now, you tell me. How did your business calls go? Everything to your satisfaction, I trust."

"Oh baby, if only you knew! But then, I choose not to tell you!" he added, sounding just like a spoiled brat, 'naah, naahing' in the playground.

"That's fine by me. I'm sure you will, if and when you wish to." Beth had to fight hard to keep her irritation under control. When he was like this, Kevin could be very dangerous as well as being extremely childish. She felt an overpowering and all-too-frequent desire to reach out and slap him. His infantile behaviour was so exasperating and thoroughly embarrassing.

Fortunately for all concerned, at that moment a waitress arrived with their afternoon tea, ordered by Kevin upon his return. Beth was relieved to be able to busy herself with pouring the tea, keeping in check the decidedly childish urge to dump Kevin's in his lap!

The silence in the car on the homeward journey was strained and uncomfortable. Beth still felt angry with Kevin and was so very disappointed that he had allowed what had been such a happy day out to degenerate into pettiness and unpleasantness. What was it with this man, she wondered to herself? In the space of just a very few minutes, he had been charming, concerned, appallingly cruel, childish and spiteful. It seemed that the longer she knew him, the less she knew him.

She was beginning to feel decidedly cheated in their relationship - a relationship into which she had entered with full commitment, dedicating her life to a man who now appeared to be little more than a figment of her imagination. She felt she was now living a lie, at times feeling almost as if she was a bigamist, the Kevin she had married being so totally different from the Kevin sitting beside her now, preoccupied with heaven-only-knew what thoughts.

If only there was someone she could talk with about all these conflicting thoughts and emotions. Maybe by talking them through she might be able to make more sense of things, might find some fresh purpose and direction in her life. But who was there for her? Perhaps in the new year she would see about getting the help she needed. What she *really* needed was a friend like Cathy in whom she could confide - not that anyone could take Cathy's place. But it takes time to develop that sort of trusting friendship. In the meantime, she would do as she had so often done in her life: draw on her inner strength that had been built up through all those long, lonely years of living with Aunt Mildred. She would continue to survive until she was able to truly start living again.

Later that evening, the family all sat watching the television news. Usually Beth mentally shut herself off from the catalogue of tragedies and disasters that occurred with sickening regularity, not because she didn't care but because she cared too much. How was it possible that in the midst of such a beautiful country, full of delightful, happy, loving people there could be so much hatred and destruction? She knew she would never be able to come to terms with such wanton violence, especially that which was supposedly in the name of God, whether here in Ireland or in the Middle East or the Far East or wherever. It was all so meaningless and unnecessary.

The headlines included the discovery of yet another murder victim and a camera shot of the site of the murder brought Beth upright in her chair with shock. It was the deserted cottage she and Kevin had passed earlier in the day! She turned to look at Kevin who appeared transfixed, his body taut, his eyes unblinking as he watched the story unfold on the screen. With a feeling of sick horror rising like bile within her, Beth turned her eyes back to the television and listened as the gruesome details were relayed.

It transpired that an army patrol had noticed recent activity around the cottage and upon investigation, found the body of a young man inside. He had been horribly tortured, both knees and both elbows had been shot away and finally he had been shot at point blank range through the middle of his forehead. His mouth was taped but there was no indication that he had been blindfolded and so presumably had been able to see the gun placed against his forehead and very likely the face of his murderer.

According to the report, this was the ninth such murder, the other eight having occurred earlier in the year. As in the previous cases, no-one had claimed responsibility, all terrorist and para-military groups, in fact, speaking out against such barbarism. The police were convinced that the same person or persons were responsible for all nine killings, even though this latest one came four months after the eighth and all those before had been just weeks apart. Also, most puzzling to them was the fact that the first eight victims had all been Protestant whilst last night's victim was a young Catholic man, Declan Conlon.

"My God!" said Michael, the words seeming to explode from his mouth. "That's Paddy Conlon's boy! Eileen's young brother!"

"Stupid bastard!" muttered Kevin. "Who's for a drink?" He sprang to his feet and headed for the drinks cabinet. "Your usual G and T, Mama? How about you, old man?" This to Michael who was still staring at the television in stunned silence.

The enormity of that dreadful crime filled Beth with a revulsion she had never before experienced and prayed she never would again experience. How could one human being do such indescribably heinous things to another human being? How could it be possible? What sort of monsters must they be? Nausea welled up within her and she waved away the whiskey that Kevin was holding out to her. Surely if she opened her mouth to take even a tiny sip, that revulsion and abhorrence would come spewing out from her and wouldn't stop. How *could* it stop?

She turned to look at her in-laws and saw that shock and repugnance had drained all the colour from their faces and their eyes, filled with an alien fear, were turned on Kevin. Mairead was rocking back and forth in her chair, moaning softly, her eyes vacant and unseeing.

Kevin's face was flushed, almost feverish.

"Oh for God's sake!" he snapped. "What is the matter with you people? It's only another murder and God knows, they're common enough in these parts. All right, this time it's somebody we know, but after all, it's only stupid Declan, the original waste of space. You lot look as though the world is about to end.

"For God's sake, drink your drinks and get some colour back in your cheeks. You all look like a load of corpses yourselves. And for the love of God, Mairead, shut up your wailing! You sound like a bloody banshee!"

A cry escaped from Beth's mouth as she rose from her chair and fled the room.

"Oh God!" shouted Kevin. "Bloody, *bloody* women!!" He stamped across the room to pour himself another very large whiskey.

Beth raced up to her room and threw herself across her bed, weeping uncontrollably. Shortly afterwards, the door opened and Bridie crept in. She sat upon the bed beside Beth, gently stroking the young woman's hair, crooning softly as she listened to the heart-wrenching sobs.

"You let them come, little lady. Let them wash away all that dreadful pain. Sure, you've had a terrible shock this evening, so you have. You'll not be used to hearing about such wicked goings on. God keep us all from ever getting used to such wickedness."

Beth raised herself up and slipped her arms around the old woman, resting her head against the bony shoulder.

"Oh Bridie," she whispered. "He's a monster! *He is*! He's a dreadful, *dreadful* monster!"

"I know, my pet. I know. They're all monsters, the lot of them. Wicked, evil monsters." And she stayed, holding Beth, rocking her gently until her tears ceased and she fell into an exhausted sleep. Beth didn't stir as Bridie laid her on the bed. The old woman stretched out the cramp in her back as she gazed down at Beth's face, peaceful at last in sleep. But the pain in her old aching muscles was nothing compared with the pain in her heart.

13

The following day, after the family had returned from Mass and had eaten a large roast dinner, beautifully prepared by Bridie and fully enjoyed only by Kevin, Clementine declared that they would all go around to the Conlon house to pay their respects.

Kevin, who had been in remarkably good spirits all day, brightened even further.

"An excellent idea, Mama. We must all go now to present our condolences." He rose from the table and swept grandly across the dining room. "Come, my dear," he called to Beth from the doorway. "We must make ourselves presentable." He turned and made a sweeping, theatrical exit from the room and up the wide staircase, leaving the doors open and the remaining occupants of the room in dumbfounded silence.

Michael was the first to speak. "I just don't believe that man! My God, he gets madder by the day! We'll have to lock him up soon."

"Hush, Michael," Clementine answered in a surprisingly subdued and shaky voice. "It's just the shock. It has to be the shock. You know he and Declan were close."

"Close, my ...!"

"Michael!" Clementine's voice of authority cut through Michael's retort.

"Well, I ask you. How can you say they were close? They hated the sight of each other, especially after Kevin came home with his surprise bride and left Eileen virtually at the altar in all her wedding finery and with no groom."

"Michael, enough!" This time it was a command. Clementine had actually noticed the distraught expression on Beth's face. The pain and bewilderment that radiated from her was almost tangible. She took her serviette from her lap and laid it carefully beside her plate, all her movements exact and deliberate as if for fear that one slight, uncontrolled action would shatter her composure completely. In a barely audible voice, she excused herself from the table and left the room without looking at anyone.

"Dear God, Michael," her mother-in-law's words followed her up the stairs. "I know you don't like the girl and I can't honestly say

I do either, but sometimes your insensitivity astounds me."

Beth entered her bedroom, closing the door quietly and precisely and stood leaning her forehead against the cool wood, listening in disbelief to the sound of the shower and Kevin's voice penetrating above the noise of the rushing water. He had left the bathroom door open and both the steam and his raucous singing poured into the room.

Fear, incredulity and a feeling perilously akin to hatred churned inside Beth. She felt isolated, dislocated from any sense of reality, as if she was caught up in the middle of some horrific nightmare and try as she may, she could not wake up. Waves of despair and nausea washed through and through her and only the awareness of Kevin's presence in the bathroom prevented her from rushing in there to be sick.

Oh dear Lord, she cried out silently. What is going on in this madhouse? But then the enormity of it all overwhelmed her and a great inertia swept over her and seemed to infill her, taking away all thought and feeling. Her last conscious thought was that she had become an automaton. Is this how life is for Mairead, she wondered lethargically.

Kevin's exuberance appeared to have been heightened by his hot shower, as he swept into the bedroom, enwrapped in a bath towel, an aura of vitality and sharp, tangy aftershave.

His vivacious cheerfulness seemed offensive to Beth as she numbly watched him bustle about the room getting dressed, brushing his hair, putting on a heavy gold neck-chain she hadn't seen before and tucking it beneath his shirt before tying his sombre black tie, all the while whistling and humming with great gusto. Whereas on anyone else the black suit and tie and crisp white shirt would have had a subduing effect, on Kevin they seemed to accentuate his virility and astonishing good looks. He appeared almost indecently vital and alive, his vibrancy crackling like electricity.

"Come on, old girl!" his bright, cheery voice shattered through to Beth's benumbed senses. "Chop, chop! Time to make yourself beautiful. Must impress the opposition. Come on, get glammed up, there's a good girl. I shall await you downstairs!" He swept out of the bedroom just as dramatically as he had from the dining room a short while ago.

Or was it another life time ago? Beth wondered impassively. Reality was suspended and if asked the time, the day, the month, the year, she would hardly have known what to answer. She wandered aimlessly over to her dressing table, picked up her hairbrush and drew it once or twice listlessly through her hair. She stood for a while, holding the brush against her breast, gazing into the mirror, not knowing at what or whom she was looking. Then she carefully replaced the brush on the table top and turned and left the room.

All the family were waiting for her in the hall and she silently, numbly, joined them and filed out to Michael's large Mercedes waiting at the front door. Beth was totally unaware of the journey to the Conlon house as she sat on the back seat between Kevin and Mairead. Her mind had gone on a journey of its own, somewhere she had never been before. She was vacantly, distantly conscious that her body was still alive but wondered vaguely if her mind had died all by itself and was now dwelling in some sort of hell.

The loud peal of a doorbell brought her suddenly back into focus and to her amazement, Beth found herself standing in front of a house not dissimilar to their own. She had no recollection of the car stopping or of getting out and walking up to the front door. The door was opened by a maid with swollen, red, tear-filled eyes and they were ushered unceremoniously and unannounced into the drawing room.

Beth was aware of a large number of people and an overpowering feeling of grief and anger that permeated the whole room. On a large, overstuffed sofa (remarkably like one in their own drawing room) sat a middle-aged woman of vast proportions, weeping inconsolably, two younger women either side of her trying unsuccessfully to offer some comfort and sympathy.

Several young men stood near the fireplace (again, very like their own - in fact the whole room could have been a replica of theirs at the House) and it was from them that the waves of rage flowed. They turned with questioning looks as the Brady family entered the room, looks that rapidly turned to anger and hatred. A short man with a huge barrel chest stepped forward. This was Paddy Conlon and he was very far from pleased to see who his visitors were.

Surprisingly, and despite the antagonistic expressions on the faces of the Conlon men, Kevin took control of the situation, extending his right hand to Paddy and drawing Beth forward beside him with his left.

"My dear Paddy," he intoned smoothly. "I can't begin to tell you what this news mean to us. My wife and I felt we must come over straight away to offer our heartfelt sympathy."

Paddy's sharp intake of breath hissed around the room, his black eyes brittle with loathing. He knocked Kevin's outstretched hand viciously to one side as he glared menacingly up at him.

"You take your oily charm and your American whore and you get out of my house! If you come anywhere near me or mine ever again, so help me God, I'll kill you with my own bare hands." Then he turned and very deliberately spat in Beth's face.

The last thing Beth was aware of was Michael grabbing Kevin and pinning his arms behind his back as she sank to the floor in a dead faint.

14

The doctor removed his stethoscope from around his neck and placed it in his old-fashioned Gladstone bag, the bag that had been his father's when he was family doctor to Clementine's parents. Beth listened to Dr O'Keefe's stuffy voice droning on about the trauma of being a poor wee thing miles and miles away from home, being accosted by that boorish brute of a man, Conlon, who wasn't fit to be in the same room as a Brady. But not to worry, for there was nothing wrong with her that a couple of days rest in bed wouldn't cure, for wasn't it the truth that here she was in the bosom of her loving family and all she needed now was lots of their special TLC?

Beth almost laughed aloud. *Hah*! *Loving family*? *TLC*? What did *he* know? Instead she felt hot, sharp tears sting her eyes and she turned her head away so that she could no longer see the sanctimonious face of Dr O'Keefe and the cold, disdainful one of her mother-in-law. Who was there in that miserable household to offer her any love, affection or understanding?

Seeing Beth's distress, Bridie, who had been anxiously hovering whilst Dr O'Keefe completed his examination, suddenly shooed the doctor and Clementine from the room, admonishing them to go quietly so that Beth could sleep and assuring them that she, herself, would attend to all Beth's needs. They were not to worry themselves at all. As if you would give her a second thought, you miserable old bat, she said silently to a relieved Clementine's retreating back.

Bridie firmly closed the bedroom door, shutting out the dreadful sound of raised voices coming from the study downstairs where Michael and Kevin were shouting at each other like madmen.

"They're all mad," muttered Bridie. "They're all mad. Every last one of them is absolutely bloody mad, even that poor wee soul, Mairead, God help her. But never you fear, little lady," she said to Beth as she drew near to the bedside. "I promise you, by Jesus, Mary, Joseph and all the saints, that I'll not let you end up like them. I will look after you, so I shall, God give me strength. With His help I'll keep you safe, never you fear."

"Oh Bridie, what would I do without you?" Beth whispered as the tears flowed down her cheeks. "It seems I've done little else but cry ever since I came to Ireland. And I'm so tired of it all. I never want to have to cry ever again but I can't see how I can do anything else!"

"Well, we'll have to see what we can do to stop all those tears. You'll soon become a public hazard. We've enough rain as it is in Ireland. With all these tears we'll soon be flooded out of the house."

"Oh Bridie, I do love you," Beth laughed through her tears. "You are so good to me - and for me. I can't think why."

"Away with you and your 'I can't think why!' It's a very long time since anyone told me that they loved me and probably even longer since I said the same to another body, but I can say to you now that I love you as if you were my own grandchild, if God had seen fit to allow me to be a mother in the first place. So there, now you know. I'm just a cranky old woman who never had a baby of her own and would dearly love to have had a daughter as lovely as you. So while you have need, I'll fuss you as I would my own."

"Thank you, Bridie. That was a lovely thing to say. Believe me, I'm more than happy for you to make a fuss of me any time. It just might keep me sane."

"That's what I pray for, every day! Now, I want you to have a good sleep and then I'll bring you up a tea tray a little later. You'll not be coming downstairs again today, my girl." She tucked the blankets in around Beth and bent to place a kiss on her forehead. "Rest now, my pet. Rest now."

It was dark when Beth awoke. She lay with her eyes closed listening to the sounds in the room, scurrying, almost furtive sounds. Kevin was up to something but she really didn't want to find out what, didn't have the energy or the heart. After a while she opened one eye and peered around the edge of the bed covers. Kevin had propped a small flashlight on his chest of drawers, its narrow, concentrated beam of light pointing into his open wardrobe.

With mounting unease, Beth watched as Kevin took a small key from his key ring and unlocked one of the top drawers of his bureau - she hadn't even known that he kept it locked! From the drawer he took another key and walked over to his wardrobe. Inside it was a set of four drawers and he used this second key to unlock the top one of the four. This is just like Sean, thought Beth, when he was getting out the icon to show me. Except from this drawer Kevin did not take out a flat box containing a priceless artefact but a set of clothing that Beth had never seen before - black trousers, black polo neck sweater, black socks and black soft-soled shoes, even black gloves and a black balaclava.

He slipped off the bathrobe he had been wearing and donned the black outfit. Beth lay rigid with horror as she watched the transformation of her husband into something more sinister than she could ever have imagined. Her heart was pounding so hard she was sure he must hear it. As if he could read her mind, he suddenly turned towards the bed and moved swiftly and silently to where Beth lay. She closed her eyes the moment he turned towards her and lay absolutely still, praying desperately that he wouldn't find her out. He stood over her for what seemed like an eternity before moving over to his bureau again. She waited another few moments before risking opening her eyes again.

Kevin was reading from a small black book she hadn't seen before, the look of sadistic delight on his face filling her with revulsion and dread. Then he picked up the same heavy gold neck-chain she had seen him wearing earlier in the day, held it up in the dim light, turning it from side to side as he chuckled silently to himself before once more fastening it around his neck and tucking it inside his sweater. He placed the book and the key inside the drawer before locking it and very carefully put his keys down on the bureau top, so as not to make a sound. Finally he pulled on the balaclava and gloves, extinguished the torch light and slipped silently from the room.

Beth remained perfectly still, not daring even to breathe until it became absolutely necessary. The sound of her breath as she finally exhaled made her start with fright. Surely he had heard and would come rushing back into the room to do who-knew-what to her! Her mind seemed to be shooting off in a dozen different directions all at once, each one painting a scenario worse than the last. What was Kevin up to? Where was he going? Why was he dressed in those strange clothes that had to be so mysteriously locked away? Where had that unfamiliar neck-chain come from? What was in the notebook that brought such an evil, sinister look to his face?

The panic rose within her, threatening to choke her. She nearly cried out with fright but stopped herself just in time, strangling the sound in her throat so that it became a pathetic whimper.

She turned her head to look at the clock on the bedside table and was alarmed to see that it was only twenty minutes past three. How could she get through the hours until daylight? When would Kevin return? How could she keep from him the fact that she had witnessed his middle-of-the-night clandestine behaviour? If he found out, would her life be in danger? She had a very real and very dreadful fear that it would be.

Beth began to pray in earnest for help and gradually a tenuous peace started to ease out the panic. She allowed herself to sink into the nascent calm, feeling it gradually, almost imperceptibly grow stronger and more definite. Little by little her pounding heart slowed to a more normal rate and she began to breathe more easily. As the peace seeped further into her mind and her thoughts became more rational, she determined that tomorrow, somehow, she would get some time alone with Bridie and would ask her for help. She had promised to look after Beth and Beth was now going to take her up on that promise, even if it was in a way that Bridie had not envisaged. For now Beth knew of a certainty that she must leave this house, possibly for ever, but at least until Kevin's unbalanced, irrational behaviour had been resolved. Then she would see whether or not there could or would be any future for them together.

What she really needed was her passport but Kevin had that locked away, she knew not where. Perhaps Bridie could help her locate it. Also, she was going to need some money of which she had none except the little spending money Kevin had given her from time to time and there was precious little of that. However, she did have a lot of valuable jewellery, some of which, hopefully with Bridie's help, she could sell so that she could afford to keep herself whilst all these dreadful problems were being rectified. Perhaps she could get a job. She wondered what the rules and regulations were concerning foreigners working in Ireland. Perhaps she could go home for a while. Perhaps... She slept.

15

Her bedroom door smashed against the wall as Michael crashed into the room.

"Where is he? Where is he?" He was shouting like someone crazed. Beth had scarcely opened her eyes when Michael grabbed her by the shoulders, shaking her unmercifully, slamming her back and forth onto the pillows.

"Where is he? *Where is he? Oh God, it can't be him!! It can't be!!*" He let go of Beth and sank down on to the bed, deep, dreadful sobs tearing from his body.

Beth struggled to free herself from the weight of Michael's body, collapsed across her midriff. Painfully she pulled herself up to a sitting position, staring down at her brother-in-law, open-mouthed with incredulity. A ghastly, keening moan joined forces with Michael's hideous weeping, a moan that grew and grew until it became an unearthly shriek of agony. Beth looked up to find Clementine standing in the open doorway, abject horror written all over her face, the appalling shriek pouring unchecked from her mouth.

Then a high-pitched, monotone cackle of laughter split the air. Beth dragged her eyes away from the terrifying spectacle of her mother-in-law and saw Mairead being propelled along the landing to her own bedroom by Bridie. At the door she turned to look across to Beth's and Kevin's room and Beth saw that although she was still laughing, her face was totally blank and expressionless. Bridie pushed Mairead into her room and slammed the door, muffling the terrible sound.

Bridie scurried back around the landing to Beth's room, collecting an ashen-faced Joseph along the way and dragging him with her. She stopped in front of Clementine.

"Stop it!" she shouted at Clementine. "Stop it at once, do you hear me?" Clementine made no acknowledgement of Bridie. She just continued to stare at the empty space in the bed beside Beth, her dreadful wail rising and falling unabated.

"The good Lord knows, God forgive me, that I've wanted to do this for many a long year!" Bridie's small bony hand flew out and cracked across Clementine's face with such force that her head was thrown back and her wailing was instantly silenced. She stared at Bridie, unblinking, unseeing and then she suddenly collapsed in a heap, Joseph managing to catch her just before she hit the floor.

"That's it, Joseph," said Bridie. "You take her along to her room and then get downstairs and call for Dr O'Keefe first and then the police. I suppose you had better phone that wastrel of a priest of hers, too. I'll go and deal with the big man in here."

"Bridie, Bridie! Can't you make the phone calls? Please! I don't think I can face it."

"For the love of God, man, will you pull yourself together? I know you've had a dreadful shock, horrible so it was. I have all this lot to handle meself and I just can't be coping with you now as well. I need your help for once. So just for now, be brave and you can weep into your whiskey later. God knows, we'll all be needing some before much longer. Now, away and do as I say."

Bridie came into the bedroom and grasped Michael by one shoulder, pulling at him roughly.

"Michael! Michael! You big lummox. Will you shut up your caterwauling right now or will I have to lay you out the way I did your mother, big as you are? For God knows, I'm that angry right now I could lay out Goliath himself with me bare hands, so I could. Come on, now. The police will be here any minute and you'll need to deal with them. Joseph is useless with shock and fear and your mother has more need of O'Keefe and her priest than you do so you'll have to pull yourself together and act like a man for a change."

Her voice was harsh, almost cruel, but it penetrated sufficiently into Michael's consciousness for him to drag himself up from Beth's bed and stagger from the room. The two women could hear his repeated "Oh my God! Oh my God! Oh my God!" keeping time with his footsteps as he lurched and stumbled down the stairs.

While all this had been going on, Beth had been sitting, wide-eyed and open-mouthed, feeling as if she was watching a very badly acted, macabre play, somewhere between a melodrama and a horror story. She turned bewildered eyes to Bridie and whispered, "Bridie, what is happening?"

Bridie quietly closed the door and climbed up on to Beth's bed, settling herself facing Beth in the place where, normally, Kevin would be lying. She reached out to take Beth's hand in her own, stroking the soft, young skin with her old, gnarled fingers.

"This is the most difficult thing I have ever had to do in all my life and I wish and pray with all my heart that I didn't have to do it at all but it is best coming from me. The other lot are insensitive at the best of times but just now there's not an ounce of sensitivity in a ton of them." She drew in a long, shuddering breath. "Oh God, I don't want to do this, truly I don't!"

Every cell of Beth's body thrummed with a horrible dread.

"Tell me, Bridie. Please! Whatever it is, please just tell me."

"All right. I think it best if I just tell it to you straight - no frills or fancies. Okay?"

"Bridie, *please*! I shall go mad if you don't tell me *now*!"

"Well, Joseph decided, as it was a fine day today, that he would get out and about early. So he went down the drive first thing to rake the gravel before the men went off to work. Just inside the gates, tossed into the shrubbery, he found a body. All he could tell at first was that it was a man and that he was very dead. He was dressed all in black but Joseph couldn't recognise him because his face had been so badly beaten. He had been shot through the elbows and knees and through the forehead, just like the Conlon boy on Saturday and the other eight lads earlier in the year.

"This is the only time, though, that one of the bodies had been found in the city. All the others were in isolated places, like Declan. And as far as I know, this is the only time there has been a note left on the body. Joseph brought the note into the house when he came to fetch Michael. I saw the note. It said, 'Enough is enough. This time you have gone too far. P.S. We've taken the neck-chain back.' I don't know and I don't want to know what that note means but I fear that I just may know if I think about it, so I burnt it in the kitchen fire. Michael hasn't seen it and knows nothing about it. Joseph is too terrified to tell anyone about it and I know that I never shall."

"It's Kevin, isn't it, Bridie?" Beth's words were scarcely audible.

"Yes, my pet, it is. Michael recognised his ring and his watch. There are few enough watches as fancy as Kevin's, at least here in Belfast. It was nearly impossible to recognise him from anything else, least of all his clothing. None of us has ever seen him in any of those clothes. That's why Michael came crashing in here to see if Kevin was with you. He just couldn't accept it was Kevin. None of us could."

"You've seen him?"

"Aye, my pet, I have. But bad as he was, and I think you were beginning to see just how bad he really was, I would never wish what happened to him on anyone, except the Devil himself and then probably not even him. Whoever has done these things is truly a devil and must be stopped. But somehow I feel there won't be any more killings like these again."

"Bridie, I saw Kevin. In the middle of the night. He didn't know, but I saw him changing into those clothes. He keeps them locked away in his wardrobe and I saw him put on a neck-chain I had never seen before yesterday. The note mentioned a neck-chain. Oh Bridie, what does all this mean?" Her voice was steadily rising with panic.

Bridie let go of Beth's hand and grasped her by the shoulders.

"Listen to me!" she said sharply. "*Listen to me*! You must forget all about this, do you hear me? *All* about it!"

"Bridie! How can I? My husband has been killed - horribly murdered! How can I possibly forget about it?"

"Of course you'll not forget that. But all the other - the clothes, the neck-chain, the note - that you must forget about. You tell no-one, do you hear me? *NO-ONE*!"

"But Bridie! ..."

"No buts! There's more to this than you or I know about and believe you me, it is not safe for us to know."

Both women jumped with fright at the sound of a sharp rap on the door. Then it opened and Michael stood in the doorway, a Michael grown old and haggard, his face drawn and grey, his voice stiff and impassive.

"Beth. Bridie," he said. "Would you please come down? The police are here and they would like to speak with you both." He immediately closed the door and went back downstairs.

"Not a word, do you hear?" hissed Bridie as Beth flew out of bed and grabbed her dressing gown. "*Not a word*!"

16

The police were very solicitous, asking just a few basic questions. Had Beth noticed any sudden change of character in Kevin lately? How could she tell them that she didn't even know what her husband's character was like? That she never knew from hour to hour who it was she was living with - he could have been any one of a hundred strangers, so alien had he become. It was easier simply to say no.

Had she noticed anything unusual about him the previous evening? Had she been aware of his going out? Bridie's eyes bore into her from where she was sitting just behind the detective inspector, out of his range of vision but clearly visible to Beth. Keeping her own eyes averted from Bridie's intense gaze and sending up a quick but earnest prayer for forgiveness for lying, Beth's answers were again negative and noncommittal.

Bridie's responses to the questions put to her were equally circumspect. She was giving nothing away. They would hear no tittle-tattle from her. And there most certainly would be no cosy little chats over a cup of tea 'below stairs'. She was keeping well out of sight.

As soon as their few questions were answered, Bridie asked permission to take Beth upstairs so that she could 'look to the needs of her mistress'. Let them think she was just a simple, servile old crone! She didn't care. At least that way they couldn't be pestering her with more probing questions.

And in truth, Beth did need looking after. She was deeply shocked but no-one had thought to send the priest or the doctor to her - not that she would want either of those pompous old frauds in her room, fawning unctuously over her. She, Bridie, would do all she could to help Beth over the initial shock herself.

Once upstairs, Bridie tried to persuade Beth to go back to bed, but Beth refused.

"Bridie, *please!*" she snapped. "I'm not ill! I don't want to go to bed. That is the very last thing I want to do. In fact, I never want to sleep in that bed again. Now please stop fussing!"

She saw Bridie's mouth tighten and hurt fill her eyes and was immediately contrite.

"Oh Bridie, Bridie! I'm so very sorry. I shouldn't have snapped at you like that. That was really mean of me, especially after you have been so kind to me."

"Oh now, don't you fret yourself. It's just me being a silly old woman. We've both been through enough this morning already. We're bound to be touchy. So we'll say no more about it. Now I do think you should rest. So why don't you go and settle yourself on the sofa in your sitting room and I'll pop down and make us both a cup of tea. I know I'm ready for one!"

"Fair enough. I agree to that. And I would love a cup of tea." Instinctively, Beth reached out to put her arms around Bridie and the old woman's bony arms locked about her, holding her close in a fierce, protective embrace.

"I will look after you, so help me God, I will!" Bridie's voice was harsh with passion. "I will not let you be destroyed as well!" She abruptly let go of Beth and turned quickly to leave the room, but not before Beth had seen tears glistening in the old, faded-blue eyes.

As soon as the bedroom door was closed, Beth flew over to Kevin's bureau where his bunch of keys still lay beside his hairbrush. She slipped the little key for the top drawer of the bureau from the ring and quickly unlocked the drawer. Now her nerve failed her and she felt she couldn't bring herself to open the drawer, but the sound of a door slamming out on the landing spurred her into action. She yanked the drawer open, grabbed the little black book from within, slammed the drawer again and raced into the bathroom, locking the door behind her. At least she wouldn't be bothered in here. In fact, it was the only place in the house where she could be truly alone and safe.

She sat on the closed lid of the toilet seat and stared at the black book in her hand, trying to keep it steady as she began to shake, great juddering shakes that pulsated uncontrollably through her body from top to toe, over and over again. She was sick with apprehension. The book seemed to be on fire, burning painfully into the tender flesh of her hands. Fear held her transfixed in its vicelike grasp. The longer she looked at the book, the deeper and more terrifying became her fear.

"Oh God, help me, please!" she pleaded softly. "I don't want to know what is in this book but I *have* to know! I just know it's something terrible, but if I am to make any sense out of this mess my life is in, I have to know what is in here. Please give me the strength to do this!"

Drawing in a long, shaky breath, as if to imbibe strength deep into every cell of her body, Beth opened the book to the first page and plunged into a nightmare beyond her wildest imaginings.

There were nine entries, eight dated some months previously, the ninth being made at 5.32 a.m. on Saturday, just two short days - and two lifetimes - ago. Each entry detailed the name, address and age of Kevin's victims. Then followed, in gruesome and explicit detail, the exact manner in which they had been tortured and kneecapped. Their elbows had been shot away first so that they could offer no resistance to their solitary tormentor. Kevin had even included their conversations, if such pitiful, desperate pleadings for mercy could be described as conversation.

Beth was so numbed by the mindless, abhorrent violence that when she turned to the last entry she was not surprised to read the name, Declan Conlon, aged nineteen. His manner of torture and death were the same as the other eight but this time Kevin taunted the young man about his 'ghastly sister' and how he had deliberately set out to find himself a 'proper wife' whilst on his fund-raising trip to America so that he wouldn't have to marry 'the fat old cow, Eileen' and how the Conlon family would all 'go to hell' now as he, Kevin, had laid plans to ruin them completely.

The IRA had been delighted with the results of his American trip, so much so that they hadn't a clue just how much money he had secreted away for himself. Old Paddy Conlon might be good at his sums, but not so good as Kevin. And now Kevin had the means by which he could secretly expose 'upright, goody-two-shoes, pillar of the community Conlon' and destroy him and his nauseating little clan while still being able to protect his own family. No-one would be able in any way to connect the Bradys to the demise of the Conlons or their mutual, illegal activities. It would just take a few phone calls on Monday to set the mysterious, inter-connecting wheels in motion and by Friday at the latest, the Conlons would be no more.

And as a reminder of this last, oh-so-pleasant time together,

Kevin would help himself to Declan's heavy gold neck-chain and would wear it with such fond memories. And then he pulled the final trigger.

Even worse than the catalogue of atrocities was the manner in which it was written. Beth could feel the sadistic fervour pouring from every pen stroke as if it were acid eating into her soul, burning, searing its vileness into her so that she felt she would never be clean and free again. Nausea seeped from every pore, drenching her in a vile, putrid sweat, her nightdress clinging to her damp, icy body.

A jarring noise thundered in her head and she shook it violently to dislodge the sound but then realised it was Bridie banging on the locked door, calling frantically for her. In panic, Beth crammed the book into her cosmetics drawer of the vanitory unit before unlocking the door and opening it a fraction.

In answer to Bridie's beseeching enquiry, she said, "I'm all right, Bridie, really I am. I just feel a little sick. I'm just going to run a bath and if there is a cup of tea handy, I'll drink it while I soak."

"If you're sure you're all right, then I'll just have to believe you. I'll just pour the tea now. If you leave the door ajar, I'll pop it in to you when it's ready. Then I'll lay you out some nice warm, fresh, clean clothes to wear. You take your time with your bath. The soak will do you the world of good. I'll be waiting for you in your sitting room. Mind you have a good soak now. Take as long as you like."

All eternity won't be long enough, thought Beth bitterly. Once she had her cup of tea and the bath was ready, she closed the door and quietly locked it again. She stepped into the hot water, feeling it sting against her icy skin, wishing it was hot enough to burn her up to nothing, to annihilate her so that she didn't have to think or feel ever again. She lay back in the bath and let the scalding tears pour in rivulets down her cheeks and neck, longing to be the tears themselves, drowning in the bath water, flowing into oblivion, unnoticed, undetectable with no sense of identity any longer.

17

Beth spent the rest of the morning lying on the sofa in her sitting room under the watchful eye of Bridie, the old woman sitting in a chair opposite her, ostensibly reading magazines but in reality totally attuned to Beth's every move, even the flutter of her eyelids which she was determinedly keeping firmly shut so as to ensure her privacy. In fact, she was in complete turmoil, reliving the events of the early morning time and again, mentally going over each ghastly page of that appalling black book repeatedly, as if each word was tattooed on her inner eyes and she could not blank them out to save her life - or her sanity, which she was convinced she was rapidly losing.

As much as she loved Bridie, she just wished the old woman would go away and leave her in *peace*! She almost laughed aloud at the thought but didn't dare as she knew that hysteria was only a hair's breadth away and if she gave in to it they would only send for that obnoxious, pompous doctor or, worse still, that slimy, obsequious priest. So she stayed as still as possible, praying that Bridie would soon leave her alone.

Eventually Bridie did stir herself and, saying that she must go and prepare lunch, not that anyone would be particularly interested in eating it, she was sure, she left the room. Beth was suddenly and blessedly alone. She picked up one of the scatter cushions from the sofa and stuffed as much of it in her mouth as she could and screamed and screamed and screamed, confident that no-one would be able to hear her muffled, strangulated howling. Although the effort gave her a headache, at least it released some of the dreadful tension that had stretched her to breaking point within.

Dropping the soggy cushion back on the sofa, Beth leapt up and rushed into the bathroom, grabbed Kevin's vile book from her drawer and hurried into the bedroom. She yanked open the bottom drawer of the bureau, scattering her sweaters to left and right in her anxiety to get at the flat box buried at the bottom of the drawer. Throwing the box onto her bed, she stood up and grabbed her jewellery box, spilling pieces everywhere, frantically searching for the little key she kept amongst her brooches.

Finally, with the precious key in her grasp, she ran over to the bed and tried to unlock the box, her fingers grotesque and flabby in their clumsiness, tears of panic blinding her vision. At last the key slipped home and turned easily in the lock. The lid sprang open and Beth threw the book in on top of her priceless icon, slammed the lid, relocked it and raced back to the bureau. She dropped the box into the open drawer and then tossed the key back into the jewellery box, scooping up the various pieces scattered across the bureau top and throwing them back in any old how. Then she dropped to her knees and frantically gathered up her sweaters and dumped them back on top of the box and pushed the drawer shut.

On her hands and knees, Beth crawled backwards away from the bureau, bumped into her bed and sat back against it, knees drawn up under her chin, her arms wrapped tightly around her legs, her eyes wide and wild with horror, staring at the drawer in which now lay the sickening evidence of her husband's depravity. She was shaking violently and waves of nausea washed through and through her but she stayed where she was, transfixed, unable to move, shocked almost senseless.

All rational thought was suspended - indeed, *all* thought was suspended. Fear and abhorrence were Beth's only reality. They had seeped deep into the very core of her being, paralysing all other senses. She was unable to stop the violent shaking that racked her body, just as she was incapable of tearing her eyes away from the bureau drawer, wherein lay the evidence of such vileness.

She didn't hear the tap on the door, nor the sound of the door opening or Bridie's cry of alarm when she saw Beth huddled against the side of the bed. Bridie only just managed to put the luncheon tray she was carrying safely on the bed before she dropped to her knees beside Beth.

"Oh, Miss Beth! Miss Beth!" she cried as she grasped Beth by the shoulders. "Oh Miss Beth, whatever is the matter? Whatever possessed you to sit on the floor like this? Talk to me, Miss Beth! *Say something,* for the love of God!" She tried to hold Beth to stop her shaking but ended up shaking her by the shoulders even harder, trying desperately to get some response from her.

Beth turned to look at Bridie, dragging her eyes painfully away from the bureau drawer. Bridie cried aloud at the tortured expression on Beth's face and opened up her arms as the younger woman leaned over and placed her head mutely against her shoulder, too numb even to cry. The two sat on the floor silently for an hour or more as

Bridie's tears washed over Beth, the old woman's heart aching as it had never ached in all her life.

Eventually the pain of Bridie's old arthritic joints penetrated through her grief.

"Come along now, little lady," she said gently to Beth. "This is not doing either of us any good, sitting here on the hard floor. You come away now to the other room and put your feet up again. I'll tuck that nice warm afghan around you and see if we can't chase away the chill from your bones.

"Our lunch will be ruined now and I don't suppose either of us is up to eating cottage pie anyhow, so I'll take it away downstairs now and heat up some soup that I made yesterday for us. It's all nice and tasty and we both need some warmth and nourishment inside us. Come along now. Let's get you across the way and comfortable."

She coaxed Beth to her feet and into the sitting room, tucking the afghan snugly around her and turning on the gas fire before she left to collect the abandoned lunch tray and trudge wearily downstairs to the kitchen once more.

Where will this all end? she wondered dismally. What is going to happen to the little lady? I can't see her staying in this morgue of a place now and if she goes, I don't know that I want to stay either. But just what would Joseph and I do at our time of life if we did go? And if we did go who would look after poor, sad Mairead? What would become of them all?

A stab of fear shot through her, quickening her steps and she hurried through into the kitchen, kicking the door to behind her with some considerable vehemence. Enough of these thoughts, she told herself sternly. There are troubles galore here and now, without imagining any more!

18

Beth stayed in her room all afternoon, refusing to see anyone - the doctor, the priest, her in-laws - only Bridie would she allow to be with her, for with Bridie she knew she didn't have to talk. The old woman was content just to sit silently, keeping a watchful eye on Beth, anticipating her any and every need, protecting her in the only way she could for the time being.

With great reluctance Bridie left Beth alone later in the afternoon so that she could prepare dinner for the family. No-one appeared to notice the lack of afternoon tea, strict family ritual for once overlooked. Bridie had no idea what the rest of the family had been up to all day and cared even less. She was just grateful that they had left her alone with Beth as much as they had, for she was genuinely fearful for Beth, for her sanity and in some inexplicable way, for her safety.

Dinner was to be early this evening as they all had to be at church by seven o'clock when there was to be Mass said for Kevin. Bridie had yet to inform Beth of this, her reluctance stemming from her desire for Beth to have as much peace and quiet as possible and not to have even more to think or worry about than she already had.

Beth had spent the afternoon in complete silence, lying on her sofa, scarcely moving a muscle, totally devoid of thought or feeling, as if her mind had left her completely, her eyes open but empty and unseeing. Hence, Bridie's fear for her sanity.

However, when Bridie returned with their dinner trays and told Beth of the evening service, Beth's voice was strong and sure as she replied with a very emphatic "No!" Bridie made no response - just carried on eating her dinner, trying not to think of the reactions of Michael or Clementine to Beth's refusal.

When Bridie had managed to finish her meal, Beth waved her hand dismissively at her own tray.

"I'm sorry I couldn't eat anything, Bridie. It does look good and I'm sure it tastes delicious but I just can't face food today. Perhaps tomorrow?"

Again, her voice sounded perfectly normal, perfectly in control. Bridie felt her spirits rally a little at the sound. She had always known that there was something very special about Beth but hadn't realised just how much inner strength she had. It gave her considerable hope that Beth would be able to come through this ordeal reasonably intact.

As Bridie was leaving to take the trays down to the kitchen, Beth called after her.

"Please tell the others that I will not be going to church. I do not wish to see any of them tonight. I want to be completely alone."

"I'll tell them for you, Miss Beth, but they're not going to like it one bit."

"I really couldn't care whether they like it or not. I am not going and that's all there is to it. They can hardly drag me screaming and kicking into church, can they? That really wouldn't be seemly now, would it?"

Bridie was a little surprised at Beth's sarcasm but secretly relieved that she hadn't lost her 'spunk'.

As she feared, Michael exploded when Bridie told him of Beth's decision and tore out of the dining room and upstairs to Beth's room. Bridie went to follow him but Clementine called her back.

Michael burst into Beth's bedroom and finding it empty, went through to the sitting room where Beth was still reclined on the sofa. His eyes were blazing and his lips white-rimmed with anger.

"All right, young lady," he shouted at her as he ripped the afghan off her and grabbed her by the arm, yanking her to her feet. "You've had all day to sulk in your room, playing the grieving widow. Now you are going to get yourself dressed in your widow's weeds and act the part properly in public, for the sake of Mama and your dead husband. How can you even think of not coming tonight? You're his *widow*, for God's sake! What do you think people will say? Have you no *decency*?"

Beth looked up at her brother-in-law, trying hard not to flinch with pain as his fingers bit cruelly into her arm. With a controlled, impersonal voice she said, "Please remove your hand, Michael. You are hurting me.

"Quite frankly, I couldn't care less what people would say. It is precisely because I *do* have a sense of decency that I am not going tonight. Nothing on earth would get me inside that church and certainly not any false sense of duty to you or your mother. That man who was my husband, may God forgive me, was a sadistic, brutal murderer and I am glad he is dead. I, for one, will not be mourning his passing and will not under any circumstances pretend otherwise. If nothing else, I am not a hypocrite."

"*A murderer*! What do you mean, a murderer?"

"Precisely what I say, Michael. A murderer. I know it to be true and I'm sure you know it equally as well as I do."

"*You lying bitch*!" Michael spat at her.

"I am not lying, Michael. I have proof - absolute, incontrovertible proof."

"*You lying bitch*!!" Michael screamed at her and hit her so hard that the impact of his hand against her face lifted Beth off the floor and flung her back on to the sofa.

"*You lying bitch!! You lying bitch!!*" He kept repeating the same three words as his fists rained down upon Beth. She tried her best to curl out of his way to protect her face from the powerful blows but he had put one knee hard onto her stomach, pinning her down onto the sofa, immobilising her whilst his fists drove relentlessly into her face, heedless of the blood and her agonized screams.

Hearing the commotion coming from upstairs, Bridie ran out of the dining room where Clementine had kept her in mindless, useless conversation and into the drawing room where she grabbed a large poker from beside the fireplace. She raced upstairs, her heart and legs seemingly unaware that she was seventy and not seventeen, and into Beth's room, flailing the poker above her head.

Blind with rage, she set about Michael, her anger giving almost superhuman strength to her puny arms. One of her blows glanced off Michael's shoulder and cut painfully into his ear. He sprang away from Beth, clutching his bleeding ear and howling with pain. He was stunned to see that it was Bridie who had caught him such a blow and he was instantly subdued, the raging madman vanished in a flash, the imperious, autocratic Michael firmly back in place as if the other had never been.

Scarcely glancing at Beth, he sneered sardonically, "I shall give your apologies this evening - the poor young widow, prostrated with grief and all that." Then menacingly he added, "I'll deal with you properly in the morning. Looking like that, you'll be going nowhere tonight!"

He left the room without a second look at Bridie, his 'I'm the lord of the manor' demeanour in no way diminished by the blood still trickling from his damaged ear.

Bridie dashed into the bathroom, filled the basin with water and plunged in two hand towels. Wringing them out and grabbing a dry bath towel on her way out, she hurried back to where Beth lay moaning in agony. As gently as she possibly could, Bridie bathed the terrible wounds on Beth's face. Both eyes were rapidly closing, the eyeballs themselves red as though blood vessels had burst. Her nose was so swollen and bloodied that Bridie feared it may be broken. Her lips were badly split, the swelling painfully forcing the cuts open wider. Cuts, bruises and abrasions so covered her face that there was hardly any undamaged skin to be seen. All through her ministration, Bridie crooned softly to Beth, trying to calm and soothe her.

As soon as she heard the front door close and the car drive away, Bridie grabbed the telephone from the desk and punched a number. At the other end of the line the phone was answered by Susan, Bridie's sister, to whom she said, "Get me Father. 'Tis terrible urgent. I need him right away."

When the priest came on the line, Bridie felt weak with relief at the sound of his voice.

"Oh Father Patrick, there is terrible trouble up here at the house and I don't know who else to turn to. I knew you would not be away up at the big church for the Mass for himself. His brother has beaten the young lady something terrible and has threatened to 'deal with her' tomorrow. I honestly fear for her life. I have just got to get her out of this house!"

"You've done the right thing by phoning me, Bridie. I'll be along with you in about fifteen minutes. She'll be safe with Susan and me." The warmth of his voice steadied and strengthened the frightened old woman.

"Bless you, Father. We'll be packed and waiting for you when you get here," she replied and cut the connection. She flew out onto the landing, shouting for Joseph who came rushing out into the hallway, looking up at his wife, his mouth open in amazement at this uncharacteristic behaviour.

"Don't stand there gawping, you silly old fool. Fetch me up some suitcases from the store room. *Now*!!"

She hurried back into the bedroom and began flinging open

cupboards and drawers, tossing clothes and shoes onto the bed. When Joseph staggered in with several cases, Bridie grabbed them from him and tossed them onto the bed along with the clothes.

"I'll deal with all this," she said as she pushed her astonished husband out of the room. "You go now and get Miss Beth's painting things out of the store room and put them ready by the front door. Then get back up here and carry these down when I've got them filled. Father Patrick is on his way to collect the little lady and she'll not be coming back here again - and you will tell no-one where she has gone, not if you want to live another day for, so help me God, if you do I'll kill you myself and you know I will and all!"

Joseph turned tail and fled downstairs to do as his wife instructed. He did indeed know that she would be true to her word. His life would not be worth living if he went against what she said. Indeed, it would be over! There was no way on the face of this earth that he would breathe a word of the goings-on in this house tonight to another living soul.

His fear of Bridie was considerably greater than both his love for her and his unquestioning devotion to her. And he had never loved another person from the first time he met her when he was seventeen and she only twelve. In the fifty-three years they had been married, he had given her his heart and his absolute loyalty. He had never once felt un-manned by the knowledge that she was the stronger and the wiser of the two. He was just so grateful that she loved him. That was enough for him. He didn't even mind the fact that they had no children - in fact, was pleased about it for it meant that he didn't have to share Bridie's love with anyone else. It was all for him and he would gladly die for her - but not by her hand! So his silence was assured.

As Bridie was emptying Beth's bottom drawer of its sweaters, she came across the flat box which held the icon. She had never seen it before but instinctively felt it was of great importance. She put it to one side to go in the overnight bag, along with Beth's jewellery case and other more personal things. As she picked up the jewellery box, she was surprised to hear Beth speaking from the doorway, her voice weak and cracked with pain. She had dragged herself up from the sofa and as far as the door where she had managed to prop herself against the jamb.

"Not the jewellery, Bridie. I don't want the jewellery. I don't want anything he gave me. Only the key. I must have the key."

Bridie dropped the case onto the bed and hurried over to Beth, leading her gently to an armchair that stood near the wardrobes.

"Don't you fret about anything, do you hear? You're taking that jewellery, all of it. There's so much there and it must be worth a small fortune. You don't have any money, I know that, and you'll be needing some soon. So that lot can be sold so that you'll have money to get yourself set up in a new life as soon as you are fit. So you're taking it all with you and no arguments.

"Now you sit here while I finish this packing and then we'll get you safely away from here."

Just as she was finishing with the last case, Joseph returned and quickly took all the luggage downstairs, returning without being asked to help Bridie with Beth. Between them, they gently guided Beth down the long staircase and up to the front door where all her worldly possessions stood, including her precious painting equipment that she hadn't even known was in the house!

She was beyond tears and almost beyond speech so she reached out her hand and gently stroked first Bridie's cheek and then Joseph's, wiping away their tears.

"Thank you," she whispered. "With all my heart, thank you." She could say no more. Painfully, she drew the elderly couple to her and the three stood silently in an embrace, filled to overflowing with emotion - unspoken love and unvoiced farewells.

The lights of Father Patrick's car shone through the window in the front door as he pulled up in front of the house. They stepped apart from each other, not able to speak but their eyes saying all that needed to be said.

19

Father Patrick had witnessed many distressing things over the last thirty years or so in his role as parish priest and confidant but the sight of Beth's severely battered face caused him to catch his breath in disbelief. Dear Lord above, he said to himself, who could do such a vicious thing to anyone, let alone to such a little scrap of a thing as this wee lady. Trying his best to keep his surging anger to himself and not betray his feelings of revulsion, not of Beth but of the crime, he worked silently alongside Joseph as they loaded his big old estate car with all Beth's possessions.

When the job was completed, he turned to the two women waiting in the hall, reaching out to them both with his hands and with his heart, drawing first Bridie to his side and then Beth. Turning to where Joseph hovered diffidently in the background, he motioned with his head for the old man to join them. He looked from Bridie to Joseph and back again, his admiration for them being surpassed only by the look of love on his face.

"I know we haven't time to talk now, but I do want you both to know that I am more than aware of the great risk you have taken tonight. I am fully aware that you have placed yourselves in some considerable danger, but I know equally well that the Good Lord will watch over you and protect you, for goodness will always triumph over evil and what has gone on here is nothing short of evil. I will pray for you and for your safety tonight and every night."

"Please don't concern yourself about old Joseph and me, Father," Bridie answered him. "Just you concentrate on getting the little lady well and keeping her safe from harm."

"That goes without saying, but nevertheless, I shall continue to pray for you both with gratefulness for your love and concern for her. Never fear, she will be well looked after and only those who *need* to know will know where she is and they will be kept to an absolute minimum. Susan will keep you posted as to her progress and I will see you as often as possible at mass. And now I must be away and get this little lady medical assistance. God be with you both. Only His love can be greater than my respect and admiration for you. God bless you mightily."

Then, taking Beth gently by the arm, he led her down the steps and into his waiting car, settling her as carefully as possible in the front passenger seat. He drove as quickly as he dared, to put as much distance as possible between them and the influence of the Brady household. The sooner she was cleansed from all that had gone on there, the better, he thought. With time he would learn more fully of the events of the last few months, but from the little he already knew from Susan and judging by the present state of Beth, he knew she had been through a living hell. He was determined that, with the Lord's help, he would do all he could to ease her pain and wipe away the horror that she had so obviously endured.

When Michael, Clementine and Mairead returned from church, Bridie was waiting for them in the hall. Michael went to walk past her to get to the study and a more than needed very stiff whiskey, but Bridie laid a restraining hand on his arm.

"Just a minute, my fine young man," she said, her voice heavy with sarcasm. "Before you go any further, I just want to tell you that she is no longer here. Now I'll tell you this only once and then we'll talk about it never again, do you hear? She has gone and gone for good. I'll never, and I mean *never*, tell you where she has gone, and you'll never find her. She'll come to no more harm at the hands of anyone in this household. Don't ever ask me where she is or anything about her, for I'll tell you nothing and neither will Joseph. And if you think that you can frighten us in any way you are very much mistaken. And if anything should suddenly happen to either or both of us, then there are those who know what to do with certain documents and who to speak to, if you get my meaning. So don't even think of doing anything unfriendly or having any of your nasty little cronies do your dirty work for you. Understand?

"I had thought that staying here was the only thing for Joseph and me to do for our security because where else would we get a job at our ages, but now I realise that the only way to keep the little lady safe from you and your kind is to stay here and keep an eye on you. So just remember, I know more about you and your family than anyone else alive and unless you want the world to know just what sort of people the high-and-mighty Bradys really are, then you forget about Miss Beth altogether or there will literally be hell to pay. Do I make myself clear?"

"You are an evil old witch!"

"I may be old and a witch, but the good Lord knows only too well that it is not Joseph and I who are the evil ones in this household. You lot were born and bred evil and you reek of it. God knows I've witnessed enough of it over these last fifty years and have always kept my mouth shut, may God forgive me, but I'll not be answerable for what I might do and say if you harm Miss Beth in any way ever again. You've done your worst for her already. I just pray that it isn't too late for her to be made right again. So we say no more about this and you will do nothing more about her or I'll know about it and the world will know Michael Brady for what he really is."

Clementine had been quietly listening to this intercourse and as soon as Bridie had left, slamming the kitchen door behind her in anger, she walked to her study door, turning to Michael and saying, "In here. *Now*!"

"Well," she sneered at her son. "You have everything under control, do you? The interloper is fully taken care of! You can handle her and keep her mouth shut, can you! Just you pray that she does keep her mouth shut or if what Bridie says is true, we are ruined, you and I and this I will not tolerate. I have not spent over forty years of my life building up our business empire to have it destroyed overnight. I managed to salvage it after your father's mismanagement almost brought it to complete devastation but even that incompetent couldn't best me. I will not be thwarted now by you, by Bridie or by anyone else."

"If Kevin hadn't been so stupid, none of this would have happened. Trust him to go and bring an outsider into the family and then get caught at his 'little antics'. You should have dealt with him properly years ago when he was still controllable but no, you had to pander to your little pet and spoil him to the point where he was completely ruined! You just couldn't ever say no to him, could you. Anything darling little Kevin wanted, he had. Every time he got into any trouble, whatever it was, even getting that stupid Colleen girl pregnant when he was only sixteen, you always bailed him out. He always had to have his little adventures and when they weren't exciting or dangerous enough, then he made them all the more so and now it looks like he just might have become a murderer. Knowing him, there was probably nothing political in what he did, more likely just pure devilment. And you forgive him anything and everything, don't you? It's no wonder he turned out as rotten as he did. You always blamed the old man because in your eyes he was a weakling but I can assure you that you are the one to blame for Kevin's deviancy. He truly is the product of your making. I hope you are proud of him now!"

"And you've always been jealous of him, haven't you? You never could accept that your baby brother was more handsome than you or that he had more success with girls. Even that he was more intelligent than you. It has always rankled with you that though you were the elder, you were at the same time the lesser."

"Well, now I'm all you've got, aren't I? So you're stuck with me just as I'm stuck with you and that pathetic excuse for a wife you lumbered me with, all in the name of business and family empires! What a lot I have to thank you for, haven't I? Well, old thing, I guess we just have to stick together whether we like it or not, all in the name of family unity!

"But I promise you one thing, that little bitch will not get the better of us. When I track her down, and I will whatever Bridie may threaten, she'll not see the light of day again. My God, I'll not let some jumped up little American upstart bring this family down!"

Redemption

But now, thus says the Lord, *who created you, O Jacob,*
And He who formed you, O Israel:
"Fear not, for I have redeemed you;
And I have called you *by your name;*
You are *mine."*

Isaiah 43 vs 1

1

As soon as the old estate car pulled into the garage at the priest's house, Susan was waiting at the pedestrian door that led into the hallway. She opened the passenger door and reached in to help Beth out and into the house while Father Patrick secured the locks on the inside of the garage door. Despite the warning phone call from her sister, Bridie, Susan was not prepared for the sight of Beth's face. She was deeply shocked by what she saw. The poor young thing looked as though she had gone a full fifteen rounds with a heavyweight boxer and come off decidedly the worse for the experience. Susan had never seen such a battered face in all her life and it seemed to worsen by the minute as the bruises deepened and the swelling increased.

She and Father Patrick helped Beth into the priest's study and laid her on the large sofa. Susan had pillows and warm blankets ready and these she tucked snugly about Beth. Father Patrick went straight to the telephone on his desk and dialled a well-remembered and frequently used number. As soon as he heard the familiar voice on the other end he said, "Dermot, I have urgent need of you, now."

"I'm on my way."

Dr Dermot Kearney went back into the dining room where his wife was attempting to entertain her sister and husband who were visiting for their annual two weeks prior to Christmas. He leaned down, kissed his wife on the cheek and said softly, "I must be away. Paddy is in great need. I don't know how long I will be so don't wait up for me."

"Take care, darling, and do give my love to Paddy."

As Dermot was leaving the house, collecting his doctor's bag from his study on the way out, he could hear his sister-in-law's strident voice. "Why on earth should Dermot have to go out on night calls? Surely his junior partner should be doing that sort of thing. After all, what's the use of having a junior in the business if you don't take advantage of them? That's what they are there for, surely. It really isn't good enough that a man of Dermot's standing should have to do such menial tasks."

"But Dermot is not that sort of doctor, Kathleen. You know that as well as I do. Besides, Paddy is a very special case. He only calls Dermot when there is great need and Dermot wouldn't dream of not attending to his needs personally." Mary's gentle voice was the last thing Dermot heard as he closed the front door and made his way quickly to his car. He pondered yet again on the astonishing differences between his wife and her younger sister. Kathleen was a born misery-guts and her doom-and-gloom husband, Arthur, was no better. They came up every year from their home near Bantry in County Cork to spend the fortnight before Christmas with Dermot and Mary but fortunately always left promptly after lunch on the 20th, which gave Dermot and Mary a few days to recover before their children arrived with their respective families for a noisy but *happy* family Christmas.

It is strange, thought Dermot as he sat, impatiently waiting for the traffic light to turn green and allow him on his way, that those two could be so totally different and yet be full blood sisters. You would never think that they had grown up in the same house. Kathleen never stopped moaning or putting on airs and graces whereas Mary was sweetness itself. She had been the most delightful, vivacious young girl when he had met and fallen in love with her almost forty years ago and now, after thirty-seven years of marriage they were even more in love with each other than they had ever been. Perhaps that was something to do with Kathleen's peculiar behaviour. It could well be that there was just a touch of jealousy on her part because her sister's marriage was such a happy and fulfilling one whereas her own was empty, almost loveless. Arthur was the most uninspiring of men with a total lack of a sense of humour, whilst there was always so much laughter and gaiety in the Kearney house.

Dermot let these mundane thoughts have free rein as he negotiated the streets to Patrick's. When the priest, one of his oldest and dearest friends, called him in the way he had tonight, it was because there was something serious afoot. Dermot never knew what to expect when he got there but without exception it would be something serious. People only took their sick and wounded to Patrick when it wasn't safe to take them to the hospital where they would have to face awkward questioning by the authorities.

The two men had implicit faith and trust in each other and were fiercely loyal, one to the other. They had grown up together, being the closest of friends from early childhood. Dermot never questioned Patrick about the various people who came and went at night to the priest's house, all too often in need of Dermot's expertise. Patrick was a ministering angel to all in need, most particularly those who could not fend for themselves or those with no-one else to whom they could turn.

Out of long-established habit, Dermot parked his car down a quiet side street occupied only by factories and warehouses. He walked back up the street a way, keeping a careful eye out for any passers-by. When it was obvious that there was no-one else about, he slipped down a little alleyway that led onto a lane running down behind the church. He tapped lightly on the fence at the back of Patrick's garden, an unobtrusive gate opened and he slipped in.

"Good evening, Susan," he whispered as he ran lightly up the path to the back door.

Even though it was pitch dark, he knew it was none other than Susan who had opened the gate and was now latching it securely behind him. He let himself into the kitchen and made his way quickly along the hall to Patrick's study. The priest was sitting on a chair pulled up to the sofa, holding the hand of someone whose face was turned away so that Dermot could not see who it was. He stepped over to Patrick's side, placed his hand on his friend's shoulder and looked down at his new patient. Revulsion lurched through his body as he gazed at Beth's battered face.

He turned to where he knew Susan would be waiting by the door for her instructions. "Water and towels, please, Susan."

The old woman scurried down the hall to the kitchen where

the kettle had already boiled and fresh towels were laid out ready. How many years had they been doing this, she wondered. All the time the troubles had been raging they had been taking in victims of beatings and worse, patching them up and sending them on their way, sometimes straight away, sometimes after a few days if they weren't fit to leave that night. But never had they had such as this young lady in the other room. This was something different again and she would not be on her way for many a day yet.

When she returned to the study, Dermot was already laying out his things, both from his bag and from the little cupboard over in the corner of the room in which was kept an emergency supply of medicines, antiseptics and such like. It was always well stocked, for they never knew when they would have need of its contents, although things had been much quieter of late and they all prayed that the day would not be far off when there would be no further need for them.

All Patrick said was, "Her name is Beth", as he stood up to make room for Dermot to attend to her. Dermot sat down in the chair vacated by Patrick and took Beth's limp hand in his.

"Beth", he said gently. "My name is Dermot and I am a doctor. I'm going to clean you up a bit now and see what damage has been done. I will try my best not to hurt you any more than I have to. Try to bear with me and we'll get you as comfortable as possible as soon as possible. First of all, I want to give you an injection for the pain. Are you allergic to any drugs that you know of?"

"No," whispered Beth.

"There now. That's all the talking you will have to do for now. You just lie there and I'll do all that's necessary now." Dermot worked quickly and efficiently and with infinite care and gentleness, his inner rage at her condition not affecting the delicacy of his touch in any way.

By the time he had finished Beth was fighting to keep awake, the analgesic having taken away the worst of her physical discomfort. She longed to be left alone so the others would not see the tears that threatened to flow at any moment. The solicitousness of the doctor was almost more than she could bear. After so much brutality, all this kindness was overwhelming - Bridie, Joseph, Father Patrick, Susan and now Dermot. They were all being so good to her and all she wanted to do now was cry herself into oblivion.

Dermot tied off the last of the stitches that he had put in Beth's torn cheeks and dabbed the area once more with antiseptic. He gathered up his paraphernalia and handed it all to Susan. Then taking Beth's wrist in his hand, he checked her pulse again.

"We'll leave you in peace now to have some sleep, child. If you should need anything, we'll be in the kitchen just down the hall, but you needn't disturb yourself because one or the other of us will be in to check on you regularly. You try to get as much sleep as you can. That will be the best for you just now. Any talking necessary can be done much later, when you are ready and strong enough."

Beth was asleep before the others had left the room, pulling the door to behind them. In the kitchen, Patrick reached for a bottle of Jameson's from one of the cupboards. Without a word, he took three glasses from the cupboard and poured a hefty measure into each one. He handed a glass to Susan and to Dermot and then raised his own in mock salute.

"That was a night's work I'm sure none of us ever wish to repeat. That any man could raise his hand to a lady is beyond me, but that was viciousness such as I haven't seen before. Although the physical wounds are bad, they're not life-threatening at all, but it's the inner damage done that causes me disquiet. She has been seriously traumatised. I'm certain that with your excellent care, Dermot, the physical will be healed rapidly, leaving few if any scars. I dread to think how deep go the emotional scars, though. I shall have to call our old friend, Paul, to come and stay for some time once she is well enough to take the next step to her recovery. That will not be easy for her, judging from the outer symptoms. This could take quite some time to resolve, but with the Lord's love and guidance and all the prayers we can put up between us, I'm sure we will succeed.

"God bless you both for your invaluable help and your unquestioning loyalty. They mean more to me than I could ever express." He raised his glass once again towards his friends and downed the contents in one long swallow. He picked up the bottle, offering it to the others. "Tonight, a refill is most definitely the order of the day, as it were!"

2

Father Patrick awoke from a deep, heavy sleep, an after-taste of sadness clinging to him like early morning mist. It was unusual for him to be other than bright and eager for the new day ahead and it took some minutes for him to push his way mentally up through the unfamiliar grogginess. Then the memory of last night's events registered upon his consciousness and the reason for the sense of sadness became apparent to him.

At least I'm not becoming senile and maudlin, he thought to himself. There is cause enough for this feeling, asleep, pray God, on the couch downstairs right this minute.

He turned his thoughts to Beth, and please Lord, she really was sleeping for she would need all the sleep she could get if she was to be strong enough to face the next few days in which she would be embarking upon the path to her inner healing. And he was more than sure that there was a very great need indeed within her for inner healing. He had lost track of the number of people who had come to him for help over the past years and their problems had been as numerous and diverse as the individuals themselves. But somehow he had never experienced the sadness or disquiet that he felt when he looked at Beth. He did not yet know the details of what had brought her to his door, only the little he had gleaned from Susan and Bridie and yet he knew that this would be, without doubt, the most complex and deep-seated 'case' he had had to deal with in all his years of work.

This work that he so dearly loved - bringing people to the Lord so that He could minister to their individual needs on a one-to-one, personal level - went far beyond his responsibilities as a parish priest and was not looked upon favourably by his bishop. Patrick often wished he could share with his fellow churchmen the joy of this mission but with very few exceptions, especially within the Catholic church establishment, his work was frowned upon and so he had to operate in an almost clandestine manner. For no matter how much censure he might receive from his superiors, there was no way that he would not continue with this calling. And the poor, damaged souls who found their way to him would, under no circumstances, be turned away without his having done all of which he was capable to aid their recovery, whatever their predicament.

Few, if any, had been in the predicament of that wee battered thing downstairs in his study. He would need all the help he could get, both from his friend, Paul, who shared in this ministry work and, above all, from the Lord, Himself. To that end, Patrick sprang from his bed, surprisingly agile for a man of his not inconsiderable girth, and knelt at his prie-dieu for his morning prayers - always a pleasure for him, but this morning with an added poignancy and urgency, for there was much work to be done.

Prayers over, he went to his bathroom for his morning ablutions and then downstairs for one of Susan's delicious breakfasts that could fortify the neediest of men. As he passed his study door, he peeked in and saw to his relief that Beth was still sleeping and, praise the Lord, it would appear, peacefully. He pulled the door to gently after him and hurried down the hall towards the kitchen, the smell of frying bacon giving impetus to his steps.

Unlike many others in a similar position, Father Patrick chose to take most of his meals in the kitchen. He was not a man of pretension and did not enjoy eating alone, especially in his large, draughty dining room at the table that could easily seat twelve people. He was a gregarious man and much preferred the cosy warmth of the kitchen and Susan's friendly chatter. Besides, her gossip often proved most beneficial to his work. He often learned more about the people who availed themselves of his services at his own kitchen table than he did in the first few sessions in his study.

"Good morning to you, Susan," he said as he entered the kitchen. "Did you manage to get much sleep last night? I'm sorry that the bulk of the vigil fell to you. May the good Lord restore you if you have been unduly taxed."

"Good morning, Father," replied Susan as she started to fry his eggs. "And thank you, I did sleep very well. After two or three looks at the young lady I could tell that she was deeply asleep so I allowed myself to doze off, too. That big old chair of yours is surprisingly comfortable and whatever Dr Kearney had given her certainly seems to have done as it ought. I looked in a few minutes ago and she was still away with the angels."

"Aye, I've just peeked in myself and was most heartened to see her sleeping so peacefully. The best thing for her just now. No end of healing can take place during sleep and if nothing else it will strengthen her for the work ahead. And I feel there will be a lot of that to come. After we've done justice to your delectable breakfast I shall away and telephone Paul. I sincerely hope he can come down to us as soon as possible for I shall be in great need of his help during the next few days, if not longer."

"And when we've finished I'll prepare a little something for Miss Beth for she'll be in need of nourishment by now. Heaven knows when she last ate anything. Bridie said she had hardly touched her food since that husband of hers died and there's nothing of the poor wee thing to start off with. She'll need building up and I'll do all I can to make sure she is."

"That you will, Susan. That you will and an excellent job you will make of it, too. Sure, aren't I living proof of your building up? It will do me good for you to have someone else to build up for a change. I might just stop expanding, myself. I can hardly do my belts up anymore as it is."

"Away with your nonsense and eat up your breakfast before it goes cold!" admonished Susan, her brusqueness not entirely hiding her delight at the compliment. Her mother had been an exceptional cook and had passed her talents on to both her daughters, to the delight of Joseph and Father Patrick.

After Patrick had blessed the food, the two tucked into their food with gusto, Susan eating almost as much as Patrick. Tiny she may be but she could eat as well as any man!

When he had finished his meal, Patrick went upstairs to his bedroom to phone Paul. For one thing, he didn't want to disturb Beth and for another, he didn't want her to overhear anything he might say to Paul. Until he had all the facts of her case, he could only surmise the full extent of her damage and he wouldn't like her to hear if he had any points incorrect. That could make her feel worse than she obviously already did.

"Good morning to you, Paul," he said cheerfully when his friend answered the phone. "And how are you this fine morning?"

"Either you haven't looked out of your window yet today or you are on the cadge again, my fine friend," came the jovial reply.

"What else would you be calling for at this time of the day? Certainly not to enquire as to the state of my bunions, I'll be bound. Come on, you rogue, out with it. Creeping never did suit you. You're far too big a man to creep anywhere."

"Now which of us is the pot and which is the kettle today, I wonder? Seriously though, Paul, I do have a genuine need of your help and I was wondering if you could come down to stay for a while. I have a wee slip of a girl downstairs in my study who was widowed two days ago. Her brother-in-law gave her a monumental beating last night and after he went out we were able to secret her out of the house and she is now 'in hiding', as it were, with me. She is in a dreadful state of shock as well as being in a pitiable physical condition. Dermot is seeing to her physical needs but it is her inner, spiritual needs that concern me. And I genuinely fear for her life."

"I'll be more than happy to help, Pat, but shouldn't she be in hospital if she is that ill?"

"That's not what I meant. Unfortunately her brother-in-law is an evil brute of a man if ever there was one and a very powerful one at that and it is my belief that he has the word out for her. I have a line into his household, as it were, so I'll be able to get some idea of his movements with regard to the little lady, but I don't trust him one little bit - he's a nasty piece of work. I don't know the full details about her history but it is not pretty and she is in great need of our help. I know it is dreadfully short notice and so close to Christmas but I don't think we can put this off."

"Patrick, my dear friend, you are a God-send. Of course I shall be delighted to come, you know I will. Your timing could not be more perfect. That sister of mine is driving me to distraction with all her plans for Christmas. She is constantly trying to involve me in all sorts of trivia. This is the perfect get-out, I can assure you."

"That is good of you, Paul, but are you sure that Isobel can spare you? I wouldn't want to be in her bad books, you know."

"Perish the thought. She'd do anything on earth for you, Pat, and well you know it. She has adored you from the time we were all kids. It's only the fact that you wear your collar back-to-front that keeps you safe from her machinations."

"Don't forget that you wear your collar back-to-front, too,

Paul."

"Ah yes, but mine is a different colour, so as to speak, and doesn't have quite the same protective effect as yours. If it were otherwise, then she would have had a ring on her finger and one through your nose many a long year since."

"You cynical old goat! Get your things packed and get down here as soon as possible. Susan will have your room ready for you and a veritable feast for this evening. You know how she loves to feed you."

"And I love to do justice to her cooking, too. One of the great pleasures in life! I shall be with you before lunch, all being well."

"Bless you, my friend. This is *greatly* appreciated, I assure you. Drive carefully and the Lord go with you."

Patrick was still chuckling as he went back downstairs to the kitchen where he found Dermot sitting at the table with a steaming cup of coffee in his hand.

"Dermot, old man, it's good to see you," Patrick held out his hand to the doctor. "Did you manage to get back here without any undue problems?"

"Things looked pretty quiet as I came up the street. So I parked outside and came up to the house, minus my bag, as if I was just making a social call. So if anyone is watching this place, they shouldn't be too suspicious about my visit."

"Good man," said Patrick as he took the coffee cup that Susan was holding out to him. "I just wish we didn't have to go about in this clandestine manner. It's all so unnecessary but for the sake of that poor girl in the other room, we really have no choice. We can't take any chances with her safety, from what Bridie has already told me and from the little I've seen of her myself."

"I agree with you, Paddy. So until it is safe to do otherwise, we shall have to carry on as if this were a 'safe house', which, of course, it is in so many ways."

Patrick handed his empty cup to Susan. "Thank you, dear. That was lovely. If we could have a refill each and a cup for Beth, Dermot and I will go and see if she is awake now. By the way, Paul will be here by lunch-time. I trust that will not inconvenience you too much and if you could find the time to get his room ready, I would be most grateful."

"Sure, 'tis no trouble at all. Mr Hopkins is a delight to look after, he is that." She bustled about preparing a tray for their coffee and slicing some freshly-baked Madeira cake that she hoped Beth might be tempted to eat.

Handing the tray to Patrick, she said, "Make sure she drinks her coffee and find out what she wants for her breakfast. And don't take 'No' for an answer for that young lady needs her food, whether she thinks she does or not. Now, away out from under my feet and let me get on with my work!" And she shooed the two men out of the door.

3

When Patrick and Dermot entered the study, they found that Beth was sitting up on the couch with the blankets wrapped tightly about her. She turned to look at the men as they came through the door and both felt an icy shiver go down their spines at the sight of her face. There was such a depth of emptiness in her eyes that one felt one could vanish without a trace in the dark abyss.

No-one of such a young age should know sadness and pain such as this, thought Patrick angrily. He placed the tray he was carrying on a small table drawn up to the couch and handed Beth the cup of coffee. She reached for it with hands that seemed to have lost all their flesh, her skin was so transparent and sunken around the fine bones. They shook slightly as she took the cup in both hands.

"Thank you," she whispered faintly and she lowered her gaze away from Patrick while she sipped at the coffee.

Patrick was at a complete loss to know what to say in the face of her grief - a most unusual experience for him. It was like looking at a small bird whose feathers had all been plucked out by some nasty little boy. She had that same naked, pathetic air of helpless vulnerability about her. His heart ached for her.

Dermot pulled out the chair from Patrick's desk and placed it facing Beth, slightly to one side so that she would not feel hemmed in or threatened. He chose not to sit beside her on the couch for the same reason. She was looking so desperately fragile that he knew he would have to be especially gentle with her.

"Good morning, child," he said, his voice soft and kindly. "Do you remember who I am?"

Beth raised her eyes and looked blankly at him for a moment or two. Then recognition slowly dawned.

"You're the doctor who tended to me last night, aren't you?" Her voice was weak and shaky. She quickly sipped some more coffee as if to gain strength from the hot, strong drink.

"That's right. I'm Dermot Kearney. And this is Father Patrick, if you remember him, also. This is his house you are in and I'm here this morning to see how your bumps and bruises have fared overnight. Would you have any objections to my giving you a quick check over? You had a bit of a rough do last night and I'd like to make sure that all is in order - at least as much as it can be."

Beth sighed wearily and placed her cup back on its saucer. "Go ahead and do what you have to," she said.

"I'll try my very best not to hurt you." Dermot first took her wrist in his hand to feel her pulse. Then he took a thermometer from his inside jacket pocket and popped it under her tongue. Beth sat back against the plump cushions and closed her eyes. Dermot looked at Patrick and jerked his head towards the corner cupboard in which he kept his emergency medical supplies.

Glad of something to do, Patrick went and unlocked the cupboard and brought the large box from inside it over to Dermot.

"Ask Susan for some freshly boiled water, please, will you, Paddy? I'll be needing to change some of these dressings. And another cup of coffee all round wouldn't go amiss, either. If Susan asks, tell her we'll sort out the young lady's breakfast as soon as I've finished here."

Patrick hurried out of the room to do as he was bid, thankful for a few minutes in which to gather his emotions together. He felt all knocked to pieces again, having seen Beth and felt the desolation coming from her in waves. For some inexplicable reason, he was moved by her plight as he had never been moved before. She was affecting him in ways he had never before experienced. His anger at cruelty and injustice was something he had had to struggle against all his life. When he was a young man, studying for the priesthood, it was the one thing that got him into more trouble than anything else. He had been known to come to blows with a man who was ill-treating his dog. The dog had been badly beaten but his owner ended up in a far worse state when Patrick had finished with him. And it was almost the end of Patrick as a priest, as well. However, his overpowering desire to serve the Lord and his obvious love for his fellow men had won the day for him, though he had had to tread very carefully for some considerable time after that. And now he was struggling again with an anger that burned with a passion, the intensity of which he hadn't felt for many years.

When he returned to the study, Dermot was busy examining Beth's face, gently prodding around her nose.

"At least it isn't broken," the doctor said with obvious relief.

He didn't add that he was more than glad that Beth would not have to go to hospital to have her injuries attended to. That would be an incredibly dangerous risk to take.

He tenderly bathed Beth's face with the water that Susan had brought in, before re-dressing where necessary and leaving other areas open to the fresh air.

"Although things may look pretty bad as far as bruising and swelling goes," he said, "I'm confident that all will heal quickly and with little or no scarring. Now, for my part, I want you to get as much rest as you possibly can. Patrick and Susan will take better care of you than anyone else possibly could, except perhaps old Bridie herself. You just allow them to do what they must and enjoy being waited on hand and foot. I'll be back to see you this evening and as often as possible and necessary. Are there any questions you would like to ask of me?"

"No, thank you," replied Beth. "I can't think of anything at all."

"I doubt you can. You're not really in any state at the moment to do much thinking at all. So, doctor's orders! Rest all you can and enjoy Susan's wonderful cooking. She'll have you fattened up in no time. I'll be away now."

"Thank you, doctor. You've been so kind to me." Beth's eyes filled with tears but she blinked them away rapidly.

Dermot reached out to take her hand and gave it a little squeeze. "You've no call to thank me, child. It is a pleasure to help you. Just you get yourself well for me. That's all I ask of you."

He stood up and shook hands with Patrick. "Until this evening then, old friend."

"Aye," Patrick replied. "Until this evening. Paul will be with us by then."

"Ah good! I shall look forward to seeing him again. He's a grand man, is our Paul. None finer, with the exception of yourself, of course!"

"Get away out of my house and let the rest of us get on with our work. Not all of us have lackeys to do our bidding."

Their laughter, though a little strained, helped to dispel the heavy air of sadness that pervaded the room. It was like opening the curtains and unexpectedly finding the sun shining.

Susan busied herself clearing up the coffee things while she waited for Patrick to return from showing Dermot out. She didn't want Beth left alone for a minute now that she was awake. Upon Patrick's return she said, "I'll away to the kitchen now to make Miss Beth some breakfast and then prepare some soup for lunch. Mr Hopkins will be wanting something warm and nourishing when he arrives after travelling all this way in such dreadful weather."

Without asking Beth, she had already determined that she would prepare the young woman some scrambled eggs, for just by looking at the poor battered face it was obvious she wouldn't be able to chew much of anything. But she needed good nourishment, that she did. And between old Seamus's beautiful free-range eggs and her good healthy home-made soups, she would make sure that Beth had all the sustenance she needed. Perhaps a nice junket or a milk jelly for pudding, she mused as she bustled back to her kitchen, her mind flicking through her stored memory of invalid foods. She was going to enjoy having this young lady in the house. It would be a joy looking after her and nursing her back to health. No wonder Bridie was so fond of her. Even after such a short acquaintance, Susan was captivated by Beth, as were Patrick and Dermot. There was no denying that she was a very special person.

Actually, it wasn't strictly true what Patrick said to Dermot about lackeys, for didn't he himself have the services of his young assistant, Father William, a keen, eager young man not long out of the seminary? Mind you, neither Father William nor young Jenkins would be any too pleased to know that they had been referred to as lackeys, even in jest. The young priest had been pushing for some time now to have more responsibility. Well, now he would have his chance. Patrick was going to be fully occupied with Beth and Paul for some time to come so William would now have the chance to prove himself.

Patrick pondered these thoughts as he sat back in his easy chair. He reached over to his music centre (last year's Christmas present from his very indulgent nieces and nephews), switched on the CD player and the strains of Kiri Te Kanawa filled the room. Ah, he thought as he revelled in the sound of her exquisite voice, no-one sings 'Sanctus' quite the way she does. He stretched out his long, somewhat chubby legs and lay back in his chair, his fingertips together, teepee-style, his eyes closed in delight.

The sound of Susan clearing her throat none too gently brought Patrick up with a start. How could it be possible that he had forgotten all about young Beth? I must be getting older than I realised, he thought to himself with horror. What must the poor wee thing be thinking of me, silly old fool that I am? He glanced quickly and furtively in her direction only to find that she also had her eyes closed and was obviously enjoying the music herself. That comforting knowledge in no way negated the look of reproach that Susan shot at him.

Susan settled a tray on the table near Beth and sat down in the chair vacated by Dermot, gently touching Beth's arm to get her attention. She shook a large linen serviette open across her lap and tucked another under Beth's chin, like a small child. Silently, Beth looked at the old woman with astonishment, not fully realising what was going on.

"I've brought you some breakfast, child, and I want you to eat it all up."

"Oh Susan, I couldn't possibly eat anything," replied Beth. "I'm far too sore to chew and I really don't think I can be bothered with the effort. Thank you anyway, but no thank you. It was very kind of you and I'm sorry to waste your cooking but it really is too much for me to handle."

"Aye, it's just as I thought. That's why I've just prepared you some nice creamy scrambled eggs and that is also why I'm going to feed it to you myself."

"Feed me? Like a baby?" Beth sounded shocked. "I haven't been fed like a baby since ... since I was a baby, I should imagine!"

"Well, you're not a baby now, but you're in no fit state to do much of anything for yourself so I shall be doing what is necessary for you myself, as the good doctor so ordered. So now, you close your speaking mouth and open your eating mouth and I will fill it up for you. Come on now, open up, there's a good girl."

Beth was so astounded, she found herself doing as she was told. She had to admit that the eggs were delicious. It seemed like years since she had last eaten and she now found she was ravenous.

Patrick rose from his chair, stifling his desire to roar with laughter at the sight of Susan playing mother hen. "If you don't mind, ladies, I'll leave you alone for a few minutes. I must go and have words with Father William. I'll be back at least in time for

Paul's arrival."

With relief he left his study, closing the door behind him. He found that he really didn't know what to say to Beth just now. It was impossible to simply pass the time of day with her because of the very nature of her presence in his home and he didn't want to get into any detailed discussion of her circumstances until Paul was there and they had had a chance to pray together about the whole situation. Susan and her mothering were a positive God-send and genuinely gave him the opportunity to speak to William about his new duties. He left the house by the side door that gave directly onto the church, hurrying through to the opposite side where William had his own little office. Patrick himself would not be seeing much of the inside of the church for some time to come but at least he had his own little sanctuary within his study where he could make his devotions and they could all pray together, as and when necessary.

Susan finished feeding Beth, surprised but delighted that the bowl was scraped clean. She handed Beth a large mug of chocolate, still hot and steamy.

"There you are, now. I'm sure you can manage that yourself. And doesn't it feel better now that you've something inside you other than yesterday's stale breath."

"Oh Susan," Beth laughed weakly. "You are so like Bridie! I felt sure that the mould must have been thrown away when Bridie was born but obviously they saved it for you, too. And I'm very glad they did. You are a tonic, you really are."

Susan blushed and bent quickly to retrieve her needlework from a basket she had placed by her chair, hoping that her heightened colour would be attributed to her bending forward. She was used to Patrick's appreciation and his banter, but compliments such as these were new to her - and very pleasing, too.

"Ah well, Bridie, now. She's a true character is that one. Why, when we were girls there was no end to the mischief she could get up to in a single day - more than our brothers could in a whole month. Why, the sisters up at the school were fair set to know what to do with her. No punishment could ever daunt her and our poor mother got greyer by the day. Sure, she didn't have a dark hair on her head by the time Bridie was thirteen. But you couldn't not love Bridie. A freer, more loving spirit never lived."

Susan's needle flew in and out of her embroidery as if it had a life of its own while the old lady regaled Beth with tales of their childhood, at the same time keeping a close eye on Beth. To her delight, she saw many a smile flicker almost painfully across Beth's face and the sound of her gentle laughter at Bridie's antics was music to her ears. There is hope yet, she thought. There is hope.

4

Patrick was strangely on edge and the unfamiliar feeling irritated him. He paced up and down the hallway as quietly as he could so as not to disturb the two women in his study.The sound of Susan's soothing voice, chatting away pleasantly and the intermittent, soft laughter coming from Beth did his heart good but did little to alleviate his nervousness. His meeting with Father William had taken far less time than he had hoped it would. The younger man, being delighted with his new responsibilities and eager to put them into practise, had ushered Father Patrick out of his little office with almost unseemly haste and had rushed off on his morning's pastoral visits with enthusiasm. And so Patrick found himself back in his own house with too much time on his hands until Paul's anticipated arrival.

At long last, the front doorbell rang and Patrick rushed to answer it before Susan had time to put down her needlework.

"Paul, my dear fellow," Patrick beamed with delight. "What a joy it is to see you. Come in. Come in. Did you have a good journey? Was the weather too awful? Whatever, you're here safe and sound now. Come away into the kitchen and get yourself warm. There's fresh coffee in the pot or could you do with something a bit stronger to revive you after all that driving?" He fairly dragged Paul into the hall, suitcases and all, as he slammed the door shut against the driving rain and wind outside.

"Good gracious me," exclaimed Paul. "I don't think I have ever had such an enthusiastic welcome in all my days. I think I'll just go out and come in again, just to see if I'm as welcome the second time around."

"Don't you dare, you old goat. Down the hall is where you are going, to the kitchen and a wee libation. Coffee can wait. I can't tell you how good it is to see you, my friend."

"I must confess," said Paul when he was seated at the kitchen table with a glass of Jameson's in one hand and a cup of coffee on the table in front of him, "that I don't think I have ever seen you so agitated before. This is most intriguing. This young lady has had quite an effect on you, so she has. If I didn't know you better, old man..." he laughed.

Patrick took a long drink from his glass, gazing out of the window at the storm-lashed garden, feeling strangely in harmony with the wind-tossed bushes.

"You're right, in a way, Paul," he replied. "She has had a major impact on me and I'm not altogether sure why or in what way. It's most confusing. I *do* know that she pulls at my heart strings as no-one ever has before. I credit myself with being a man of compassion - I wouldn't be in this job if I was otherwise - but this little one moves me in ways I've not experienced previously. I just want to pick her up and cuddle her and soothe away all her hurts and fears as you would with a little toddler who has fallen over and scraped its knee. And yet, it's so much more than that. For some reason, I feel deeply, personally involved."

"Are you sure you can manage the counselling sessions? Will not this sense of involvement be an intrusion or a distraction to you?"

Patrick sighed and took another drink of his whiskey. "No, no. I shall be fine. I know that the Lord will protect me from myself and enable me to do that which is necessary. And with your help and prayers, everything will work out as it should, I know. After all, it's the Lord who is in charge of this whole operation, anyway. All *we* need do is co-operate with Him."

"And then some," replied Paul. "And then some!"

"Aye, it isn't always easy to be objective and uninvolved but we always manage somehow. And I know we will be strengthened and guided in our dealings with young Beth.

"And speaking of whom, let's you and I go along to the study so that you can make her acquaintance while Susan comes on out here to finish getting our lunch. I'm sure you must be hungry after your journey and the smell of that soup is making my tummy rumble!"

"I wondered where Susan was," said Paul. "She's in with Beth, is she?"

"Yes. She's taken a very big shine to her and won't have her left on her own for a minute. I've never known her to be so protective. It's rather sweet really. A bit like a mother hen with a wounded chick."

Patrick pushed open the door to his study slightly and peeked in, his spirits lifting at the sight of Beth's expression. Her eyes had lost that empty, haunted look and her face was relaxed and peaceful as she lay, snuggled in amongst the fat cushions, wrapped in blankets while she listened to Susan's tales of her childhood. He opened the door wider to usher in Paul and Beth looked up at their approach. Paul caught his breath as Beth smiled her sweet smile at Patrick, his heart constricting with pity at the contrast between her beautiful smile and the appalling damage to her face. Patrick threw a brief, knowing look at his friend, sensing his emotions and reactions, so similar to his own. Then he drew him forward to the couch.

"Beth, my child," he said gently. "This is my very dear friend, Paul Hopkins, who has come to stay with us for a few days."

Paul reached down to take Beth's proffered hand in his own, amazed that so tiny a thing could belong to an adult. It was difficult to determine her size as she was lying swathed in blankets but if her hand was anything to go by, she must be just a tiny slip of a thing, he thought.

"It is a great pleasure to meet you, Beth. May I call you Beth?"

"You may," replied Beth. "And I'm pleased to meet you as well, Mr Hopkins."

"Please, if we are to be friends, and it is my sincere wish that we are, you must call me Paul. I won't feel quite so much the old granddad figure if you do." He smiled warmly at her and settled himself comfortably in his chair with a familiarity born of long association.

"I wonder if our dear Susan - and it is grand to see you again, my dear - would be so kind as to fetch us all a cup of her exceptionally fine coffee?" He turned his charming smile to the older woman who was gathering her needlework together, preparatory to leaving the room.

"And you, Mr Hopkins, are a shameless flatterer who gets worse with age and acquaintance. Sure, I don't know how we put up with your flannel, so I don't. You'll have one more cup of coffee and no more or you'll have no room for your lunch." Her waspish tone of voice was tempered by the smile she flashed at him (so like Bridie's, thought Beth) and the pat she gave his shoulder as she passed him on her way to the door.

"And don't go tiring Miss Beth with your nonsense talk, either. She's in no fit state to be tormented by your teasing today."

"One thing I love almost more than any other, coming here," Paul laughed, "is that I get such a tongue-lashing from Susan every time."

"Don't I know just what you mean, Paul, for don't I suffer the same treatment from her every day of my life. It's like being back at the Christian Brothers, only she uses a feather duster, as it were, rather than the whip-cord of a tongue that Brother Brendan used on me all too frequently. That man could strip the skin from your back with his voice, I swear."

"Ah yes," Paul said, smiling fondly. "Your Susan gives as good as she gets and more. She's a delight, that she is."

"Mind you, you ask for your tongue-lashing, Paul, for you wind her up as no one else can possibly do," chuckled Patrick. "And she loves every minute of it. You're her pet and you know it. Each of you is as bad as the other."

Beth listened to the easy banter between the men with quiet amusement. She really didn't know why they were here or, for that matter, why she was here herself. She was fully aware of and deeply grateful for her precipitous departure from the Brady house and the part that Father Patrick, Susan and the doctor had played. And now Mr Hopkins had arrived and she felt somehow that his presence was far from coincidental and that, in some way she didn't understand, it was very much to do with her.

As if reading her thoughts, Patrick broke into her puzzled musings. "My dear," he said. "I'm sure you must be wondering why there is such a gathering of bodies about you, as it were. Let me do a little explaining as to the function of this decidedly unorthodox household.

"As you are only too aware, we secreted you out of your former home last evening at the behest of Bridie for she feared, and with all too obvious reason, for your safety. It is not an uncommon occurrence for people such as yourself to be brought here by their friends or relatives or for me to effect a rescue such as I did last night. It is well known amongst the community that anyone in need can come to me for help. For one thing, it is part of my responsibility as the parish priest and I would be failing in my duties if I turned away such as had need of my assistance. It is a sad reality that all too often in these troubled times, it is not possible for these poor souls to seek their help through the normal channels, and so they come or are brought to me. It is not my place to judge and so I do whatever I can to bind their wounds and heal their hurts.

"Occasionally, I come across some who are in greater need from inner hurts than any outward injury and it is to these that I feel a special drawing. If I remember my scripture correctly, our Lord instructed His disciples to go forth in His Name to preach the Kingdom of God, to heal the sick and to cast out demons. As far as I can see, the church is usually pretty good at preaching, although I'm not all that sure that the Kingdom of God enters into much of the preaching with any great regularity. I am sure, however, that most of the clergy would run a mile if they ever encountered a demon. They certainly wouldn't know how to go about casting it out with any great effect. Furthermore, precious little is done about healing the sick and this causes me much grief, for I see such great need for healing in this world. I'm not just talking about physical healing, although I do know of cases and have witnessed such where, through the power of prayer, there has been miraculous, instantaneous healing of physical ills. And others where the healing has come with time and further prayer.

"What concerns me more is the inner hurts of people who have been traumatised by life or by their fellow men. It is in this area that I have come to realise my true calling. Herein lies my great desire - to bring to people the knowledge that through prayer, by the Love of our Gracious Lord, they can be redeemed from their pit of hell and pain, that they can be healed, they can be saved, if you like; that the Lord loves them with a love that is beyond our comprehension and He wants them - us all - to be whole. This is not airy-fairy, pie-in-the-sky, wishful thinking. This is reality. This is His desire for us and it should be our desire for ourselves.

"Paul and I have grown to this awareness over the years and we have sought out places, mainly in England, where we have received instruction in Christian counselling. We are now fully qualified and authorised to counsel those in need, but I can assure you that our true authority lies in our great desire to serve our Lord and do His work. And it is a privilege beyond measure to help to bring someone through the nightmare of their damage out into the glorious light of their freedom. For in healing lies freedom; freedom from pain, freedom from guilt, freedom from fear, freedom to live as the Lord intended us to live, freedom to love - ourselves, our fellows, our Lord.

"As anyone can see, you have been appallingly treated at the hands of your family and from what I have heard from Bridie, your suffering has not been confined to the beating you received from Michael. I gather that there has been some considerable emotional abuse from all sides. That is the sort of thing with which we can help you, if you would like us to. The decision is yours. In no way whatever would we try to force upon you something that you would not want. But should you wish to talk about the goings-on that have brought you to us here, then we would be more than happy to listen and do whatever we feel the Lord wishes us to do to ease your distress. I repeat, the decision is yours and yours alone.

"Would you like some time to think about what I have said? I have been rabbitting on for some considerable time now and I know it must be quite a lot to take in at one go and certainly is not your average morning's conversation over a cup of coffee! There must be quite a lot of what I have said that is completely new, if not foreign, to you and if you have any questions at all, Paul and I would be happy to answer them."

Beth had been listening intently to all that Patrick had been saying, trying to take it all in, her thoughts and emotions hurtling about like a whirligig. The pain deep within her seemed to be growing and growing, threatening to burst from her, tearing her asunder in its passage. At the same time, she felt she could hardly breathe, that she was suffocating, drowning, frantically flailing about for a safety line - and now it appeared that one had been thrown to her and all she had to do was to reach out and take hold. Tears stung her eyes as she tried to speak, her voice breaking with emotion.

"*Please* help me. I so *need* you to help me. I don't think I can go on any longer. I can't cope any more." Hot, burning tears overflowed and flooded down her ravaged cheeks. "I just don't know where to begin!"

Patrick leaned forward in his chair and took her hands in his while Paul dug through his pockets, searching for a hankie, praying that he hadn't already used it. Mercifully, it was still pristine and he gently wiped at Beth's face with it until Patrick released one of her hands so that she could do the job properly.

"Dear child," Patrick's voice was filled with compassion. "Don't upset yourself just now. We'll not be jumping head first into this right away. In fact, I'm not so sure we will be doing much of anything today. First of all, it is almost time for lunch and I think our best bet would be to have a little time now for some quiet prayer to bring you some peace and quieten that awful panic that I know is threatening to choke you."

He smiled in answer to her unspoken question. "Ah, I know full well what emotions are chasing themselves about inside you. They're running full pelt across your face! So for starters, we calm them down and then, when we have all fortified ourselves with Susan's lunch, we'll take things one step at a time. There's no time schedule to follow, no races to be run or won. We've all the time in the world that's needed. So now, let's all quieten our minds and ask the Lord to bless us with His peace and love."

Beth lay back against the cushions and let the gentle Irish voice of the priest wash over her, the words of his prayer not registering on her consciousness but the effect seeping softly and steadily into her being, soothing her frayed nerves, stilling the tumultuous thoughts that had been racing hither and thither through her mind. Peacefulness gradually settled upon her and she found herself cocooned in its tranquility.

Susan's light tapping on the door brought the three occupants of the room back from their respective contemplations. Patrick had finished speaking some while since and they were all enwrapped in a beautiful aura of serenity. In unison, they each released a sigh of contentment, laughing at their spontaneous and synchronised exhalation. Each felt restored. Each felt hopeful and positive. Each felt hungry, for Susan's lunch and for the task that lay ahead.

5

After they had taken their fill of a substantial lunch of home-made onion soup, fresh crusty bread and a delicious mature Irish cheddar followed by warm apple tart with lashings of thick cream, Patrick, Paul and Beth gathered around the fireplace where a roaring blaze dispelled the gloom of the winter afternoon. Outside, the wind howled and the rain fell in torrents but inside, all was warm and cosy. Paul lit his pipe and the rich aroma of the tobacco drifted about the room. The sky outside darkened even further as huge black clouds, swept along by the wind, turned the afternoon to night. Patrick got up and closed the curtains against the gloom.

"It's as black as the inside of a goat out there and we want none of that in here." He turned on several table lamps as he made his way back to his chair. "There now, that's much cosier, isn't it? We can't talk properly if we are not comfortable and all that gloom outside is hardly conducive to comfort now, is it?"

He settled back into his chair and placed his elbows on the arms with his fingertips together. He tapped his index fingers against his pursed lips while he gazed contemplatively at Beth, who was tucked up on the sofa. She looked back at him somewhat apprehensively, nervousness beginning to build within her. Patrick raised his head slightly and then dropped his chin back down onto his fingertips, nodding his head slightly as he continued to study Beth's face, the shadow of uncertainty in her eyes, the tightening of anxiety around her nose and mouth, the pallor in her cheeks. His heart surged with compassion at the signs of such obvious need on her face.

"Before lunch, you said that you would like us to help you but you didn't know where to begin." Patrick kept his voice soft and gentle in an attempt to soothe Beth's mounting fears. "Have you any clearer idea where we should start, now that we've had some prayers and you've had a little time to think?"

Beth shook her head as she struggled to find words to express the turmoil of feelings within her. "I really have no idea," she whispered, her voice tremulous with emotion.

"In that case, may I make a little suggestion? There is

something we have found over the years that proves to be most helpful in so many ways and that is for a person in need to write a letter to Jesus."

"A letter to *Jesus*?" Beth said in amazement. "But surely He already knows everything there is to know about me. Why should I need to write to tell Him what He already knows?"

"Exactly so. He most certainly does know all about you. But the purpose of this exercise, if we may call it that, is for you to bring into focus all that is troubling you. As you have already said, you don't know where to start. Well, this might just provide the start.

"The Letter to Jesus exercise can be useful for various occasions, such as helping a new Christian to know how to make a fuller commitment to God, to learn how to give himself - or herself - *to* Him and how to receive *from* Him - a most important lesson, that one is, I assure you! However, I find it also invaluable in cases such as yours where you are in considerable need and equally considerable confusion. It can help you to see things a little more clearly and also help Paul and me to know where your most immediate need lies.

"That doesn't mean to say that we will be reading your letter. That is for you to decide once it is finished. You may wish to show it to Paul and me or you may decide just to mention the broad outline or simply give us a single thought that will be the starting point that we need. As I say, that is up to you. There is no pressure upon you to do anything at all. Just that with which you feel comfortable or that which you might feel the Lord is guiding you to do.

"As to the format of this letter, well, there is no specific pattern to follow. But as a guideline, may I suggest the following? First, we will all pray together some more and then Paul and I will leave you alone. After we have gone, you may wish to pray again by yourself, or not, just as you feel. I do believe it important that you be completely honest in this letter, both with yourself and with the Lord. Don't be surprised if you find that a lot of anger or other strong emotions come out during the writing. There is a place, after all, for righteous indignation. The Lord Himself was not above such as He demonstrated when he threw the moneychangers out of the temple or when He berated the Pharisees. The important thing is to allow those feelings deep within you to come to the surface and from there we will deal with them together, with the Lord's gracious help and guidance.

"And don't think you will shock me. I assure you I am completely unshockable. Paul and I are not here to condemn you or to judge you. We have no such authority. Only the Lord can judge you and even He does not condemn you. You are His child and He loves you. Remember that above all else - He loves *you*. He wants *you* to be whole.

"So if you are comfortable with all this, then I suggest that we sit quietly and turn our thoughts to the Lord and pray that He will guide us all in this venture."

As she had done earlier that day, Beth sat back and let Patrick's words wash over her, feeling the power of his prayers strengthen her and confirm in her the desire to be free from her inner anguish. His love for the Lord was a palpable thing, as was Paul's. She had never encountered such love and devotion before and its effect upon her was to create such a longing within her that it was like a pain in her heart. But a pain like she had never known before. *This* pain she didn't want to stop. This pain would have driven her to her knees if she hadn't been so firmly tucked in by her blankets, so she knelt in her mind and in her heart and in her kneeling, she felt a desire begin to burn within, a desire to know and to love the Lord as these good and kindly men knew and loved Him.

When he had finished his prayers, Patrick rose from his chair and went to his desk. He took a writing pad from a drawer and placed it in the middle of the desk, along with several pens and pencils. He also put a large box of tissues close to hand - "The essentials, when one is writing to Jesus, I can assure you from personal experience! Help yourself, do."

He came over to where Beth was getting up from the sofa and he drew her into his arms in an embrace. He smiled over the top of her head at Paul who nodded in return. Then Patrick drew back and smiled down at Beth.

"Bless you, child," he said. "The Lord be with you and please, do not be afraid. I promise you, there is nothing whatever to fear. You are in the safest hands in all the world for you are in the hands of the Lord of all the world and you are His precious child. And now we will leave you in peace." He kissed her gently on the forehead and he and Paul quietly left the room.

Even before Patrick had closed the door Beth had picked up a pen from the desk. She looked at the blank paper in front of her for a few seconds and then wrote, quite deliberately, "I hate him." And again, "I hate him! I HATE HIM! *I HATE HIM*!!" Each time, the rage within her increased until it flowed over in great, burning tears that poured down her face, searing into the bruises and grazes, catching painfully on the stitches, the weight of each drop seeming capable of ripping open the neat sutures, leaving gaping wounds on her face that mirrored the gaping wounds in her heart.

Beth's whole being was suffused with agony. Her face burned with it, her head threatened to burst asunder with the pressure of it. Her heart was being crushed, compressed to nothingness by the weight of it. Every cell of her body screamed with the intensity of her agony. She rubbed wildly at the cascade of scalding tears, the pen in her hand catching at the stitches on her cheek and she cried out in pain.

The sound of her anguished cry sliced through the thick band of grief that had her encircled, entrapped, and a modicum of peace flowed through the breach and into her tortured mind, halting the madness that threatened to engulf her and drive her over the edge into insanity.

Very carefully, Beth placed the pen back on the desk. She took a couple of tissues from the box Patrick had placed strategically near by, gently wiped her face dry and then blew her nose, long and hard.

She picked up the pen once more and studied the twelve words scored deeply into the writing pad. This time yesterday she would have torn the page off and destroyed it in her shame - and all the pages below that bore the imprint of the pen that had been wielded with such force, a force that, until now, she would have believed was entirely alien to her nature. But now she recognised the anger for what it was and the fact that she had every right to be angry. Perhaps this was the righteous indignation of which Father Patrick had spoken.

And yet the intensity of her anger surprised her considerably. She hadn't known that she was capable of such depth of feeling.

Even the initial love she had felt for Kevin was lukewarm in comparison with the violence of emotion she had just experienced. Although somewhat disturbed by this new awareness, Beth nevertheless felt a sense of release from the fierce inner tension and turmoil and thought that now she could begin her letter properly.

'Dear Jesus,' she began. *'There is so much I need to say. I know that You know everything about me there is to know but I need to say these things myself so that I can bring them into focus and learn how to deal with them.*

'There is so much hurt and pain inside me and so much anger that I am shocked by the intensity of it all. It makes me ashamed and even more guilty to realise that I am capable of hatred. It goes completely against the grain but I have to admit it is there. I just pray that with the help of Patrick and Paul, I will learn how to cope with it.

'As this letter is supposed to be honest and truthful, then I guess that's what I have to be - gloves-off, bare-knuckle honest with myself and You about how I really feel and no more hiding behind politeness and false decorum. If I am honest, the thing I am most aware of now is anger. And painful as it is to admit, I feel such anger towards my parents, for by dying they left me with that awful, dreary Aunt Mildred and her boring, morose husband. They cut me off from all happiness and love. They abandoned me to a life of loneliness and emptiness. They still had each other and their incredible love but I was totally alone and loveless.

'Aunt Mildred and Uncle Douglas were useless. I was an encumbrance to them, a "duty" they had to fulfil, a penance of some sort. Oh, they fulfilled their duty all right, but boy, didn't I know it! I don't think they ever liked me but if they did, no-one would ever have guessed. They perpetually wore that pinched look of martyrdom. "Look at us. Aren't we good, sacrificial Christian people, bringing up that heathen's child, allowing an infidel into our home, raising it as if it were our own?" Oh, I heard them talking many times. I know just what she thought of my parents and of me. She despised them and she had no right to and all her hatred for them was dumped on to me. God forgive me, I could hate her myself if she wasn't so pathetic.

'And it's because of her that I married Kevin. If I wasn't so empty, so bereft of love, I would never have fallen for his clever words and his silky charm. I would never have allowed myself to be taken in by his poisonous lies, to be brought back here to be abused by his evil mother and brother. I would never have made love to a vile, sadistic murderer.

I hate them all but I hate myself more because I have been duped and I have been tainted. I have lain with a monster. I have been defiled by a devil and I will never be clean again. I am despicable beyond words.

'Oh God, *I fear there is no saving for me. I feel so lost, so dirty, so vile, so beyond help!'* Beth pushed the note pad to one side, put her head on her arms and wept.

From outside the study door, Patrick could hear Beth's weeping; his heart filled to overflowing with compassion at the evidence of her distress and pain and joy that at last her defences were crumbling. Hope loomed large on his horizon and he sent up a grateful prayer of thanks that his work was showing such signs of useful progress .

6

Patrick and Paul waited for about another twenty minutes and then tapped quietly on the study door and went inside. Beth was still seated at the desk, elbows on the desk top, her head resting dejectedly in her hands. Her tears had stopped but her shoulders shook convulsively as she drew in deep, shuddering breaths.

Paul went over to tend the fire while Patrick cautiously approached the desk. He gently placed one hand on Beth's shoulder, drawing her around to face him. Tenderness welled up in him as he gazed down into her grief-stricken face.

"Come away over to the fire now," he said. "A wee drop of sherry will not go amiss for any of us, I think. Then, if you feel you want to, you can share with us any of your thoughts or feelings." He led her to the sofa, not entirely sure whether her shaking was due to cold or shock, but either way she would benefit from sitting comfortably with the blanket tucked around her again and a warming drink inside her.

When she was settled on the sofa, Beth accepted her drink gratefully and leaned back against the cushions, weak with exhaustion. Patrick and Paul stared at the leaping flames in the fireplace, sipping their drinks contemplatively, neither wanting to be the first to breach the uneasy silence.

A long, sad sigh escaped from Beth and both men raised their eyes to look, first at each other, and then at Beth. The time had come to take the next step and they both knew that it would not be easy for Beth or, in many ways, for them, but there was no good to be served by postponing matters any further.

"Well, my dear. Have you anything you would like to tell us just now?" Patrick was the first to speak and Beth turned her head slightly to look at him, her eyes heavy with sorrow, her beaten, bruised face accentuating her pitiable state of mind, so plainly evident for anyone to see.

"To be honest," Beth replied wearily, "I feel too exhausted to do much talking. If you don't mind, I think I would prefer it if you each read my letter. It is awful and horrible and I am appallingly ashamed of what I have written but it is the truth and maybe when you know all about me you will know if it is possible to help me or not."

"My dear child," Patrick answered firmly. "There is one thing I can promise you with all possible surety, that there is not a single person on the face of this earth who is beyond the help of the Lord. Even the vilest murderer is not beyond His forgiveness."

Beth let out a strangled sob, gesticulated towards the desk and turned her face away from the men to hide the tears that had started flowing again. Paul, sitting the closest to the desk, got up and retrieved Beth's writing and handed it to Patrick. He then drew his chair closer to the sofa and took Beth's tiny hand in his huge fist. Softly and gently he stroked the back of her hand.

"Don't be ashamed of your tears, little Beth," he said, his voice low and soothing. "Let them come. There is great healing in their release." He continued to talk to her gently, his deep, soft voice calming, soothing her more than the words themselves.

Patrick read the words of anguish, written with such force and with such heart-wrenching poignancy. Almost in disbelief, he read the pages again, shock registering more fully with the second reading. When he had finished, he wordlessly handed them to Paul, holding on to the pages after Paul had taken them, tugging them slightly to get the other's full attention before releasing his grasp. His eyes bored into Paul's with a silent message that warned the other man not to show his reactions too obviously.

Paul released Beth's hand, sat back in his chair and read through the papers. In stunned silence, he, too, read them a second time, as had Patrick. He raised his eyes to find Patrick staring at him intently. Again, an unspoken message passed between them. This was far more serious and far more involved than they had realised. They were only too aware that Kevin had been murdered but to find that he, himself was a murderer was almost beyond belief. Dear Lord, just where do we go from here? Paul asked silently. How to proceed? Delicately and with infinite care, without a doubt!

Patrick moved to sit beside Beth on the sofa, taking her hand in one of his and smoothing her hair away from her forehead with the other.

"Beth, my dear," he said gently. "I think what is best for you, just now, is to go upstairs and have a good sleep. You have been through quite enough for one day and what you need now is a good rest. Susan has prepared your room for you and you should be comfortable there, I'm sure. I'll take you up there now if you are ready and then send Susan up with a tea tray.

"While you are resting, Paul and I will go through your letter together and spend some time praying for guidance. One thing I do not want you to do is to worry about anything. The Lord is in control of everything and for that we can be truly thankful. We don't have to strive for the answers ourselves, just allow Him to guide us in the right direction."

Upstairs, he led her into a warm, cosy room dominated by a big, four-poster bed covered in a very pretty patchwork quilt.

"Susan is a talented needle-woman, as well as an excellent cook," Patrick remarked. "There's not a lot that she can't turn her hand to with great accomplishment. She makes me feel quite inadequate at times," he chuckled.

Beth smiled briefly at his comments but did not speak. All she wanted to do was fall into the comfortable-looking bed and sleep for a hundred years. Maybe then, when she awoke, all the horrors of the present would have disappeared.

Moving away from Patrick's protective hand on her elbow, she looked about the room and noticed that all her things were stacked neatly to one side, her overnight case placed on a chair beside the dressing table. Catching her breath sharply, she ran over to the case, yanked open the zipper and frantically scrabbled about inside it until she found the one thing she was looking for. She placed the flat box on the dressing table, reached back into the overnight bag for her jewellery box and took from that the key she needed. After unlocking the box, she lifted the lid and stood looking into it, breathing rapidly and deeply. Then she stretched out her hand and took up the black book that had been lying there, so sinister and menacing.

Slowly she walked back towards Patrick, holding the book before her at arm's length, anguish etched deeply into her face.

"You will be needing this, as well," she whispered and then turned abruptly away so that he could no longer see her shame.

Patrick took a step forward and reached out his hand to touch Beth but withdrew it, sadly shaking his head. Without another word, he left the room, closing the door behind him and went back downstairs, his footsteps as heavy as his heart.

When Patrick returned to his study, he found that Paul had poured two large whiskies, one of which he handed to his friend. "I think we are both in need of a stiffener to fortify us," he said grimly. "That was quite a letter, was it not?"

"Thank you, my friend," Patrick said as he took his drink. "You may well be right. And I think there is a lot more to this than we know." He held up the black book Beth had given him. "I have a very nasty feeling that what is contained within these pages will not make pleasant reading."

"What have you there?"

"I don't know the contents, but Beth was most anxious that I have it, saying that we would be needing this, for what, I'm not too eager to find out. But find out we must if we are to help that poor wee mite upstairs. I don't think I have ever seen such tragedy written on a face before. It almost breaks my heart."

"I know, I know. I just feel I want to gather the poor little lass up in my arms and cradle all that hurt away. How can anyone be so cruel to such a lovely, gentle creature? Sure, I wonder at the mentality of some people. I despair, sometimes, for the future of this world when man can be so abominably wicked towards his fellow men. This is not what we were created for, to hate and mutilate.

"Oh God, if there was no God I would do myself in for I couldn't live in this world another minute without the hope that only He gives us! There's precious little hope or joy to be found without Him, and that's a fact!"

"I couldn't agree more, but at least we have the sure knowledge that He is there, not just for us, but for everyone. So there is hope and we can take comfort from that certainty. And now that we have vented our spleens, as it were, we must set our minds to doing what we can to help that wee lady who has found her way to our doorstep and, if I may add, into our hearts, for I'm certain she has affected you as deeply as she has me."

"There's no doubt about it, old friend. She's a very special soul and, unfortunately, a very damaged one, as well."

"Aye, she is that and I'm afraid that we're only just beginning to see how damaged she really is. Now, do you want to have first go with this book?"

"Oh no, thank you. This is your house so you can have the privilege!"

"Some privilege, I'm sure!"

Patrick settled down in his chair by the fire and held his empty glass out to Paul. "You can do the honours then."

"Fair's fair," answered Paul. "Then I want to re-read that letter. I'm not really sure I took it all in at the first two readings." He replenished their drinks and then took his place beside the fire, opposite Patrick who had started to read the black book, the shadow of disbelief and abhorrence darkening his face. His hand shook as he turned the pages and every now and then he kept muttering, "Oh dear God. *Dear God!*"

Paul watched his friend with growing alarm and apprehension. What on earth is in that book? he wondered. It must be pretty bad for Pat to react like that. He tried to concentrate on Beth's letter but his concern for Patrick kept distracting him and so he gave up and sat, watching the emotions chasing themselves over his friend's face.

Eventually, Patrick put the book down in his lap and leaned back, exhaling deeply, over and over as if he was fighting nausea. He sat, shaking his head with incredulity, scarcely believing what he had read. The words on the page seemed to have a life of their own, as if they were repulsive, alien monsters oozing their poison into his mind so that he saw in full and horrific detail the heinous atrocities they described.

Mutely, he passed the book to Paul and then covered his face with his hands, as if trying to blot out the diabolical mental pictures that seemed to be burnt into his brain. Blindly, he reached out for his whiskey glass, slopping the liquid over his trousers in his haste to get the glass to his mouth. His mind reeled to and fro, shell-shocked by the gruesome revelations. The man was an aberration, he thought. He wasn't human, surely. Dear God, no wonder that child is so traumatised!

Paul's hands were shaking by the time he had come to the end of the last page. He swallowed hard several times and then took a few deep breaths, exhaling noisily. He looked over at his friend speechlessly and then reached for his drink and gulped it down, shaking his head as the liquor burned its way down to his stomach.

"What can I say?" whispered Paul. "What can anyone say, reading something like that? What sort of devil was he? What sort of motive could he possibly have had for such barbarism? Surely no-one deserves to die that way, except he, himself."

"And that is precisely the way he did die," Patrick answered shakily. "Bridie and Joseph told me but we all assumed that he was just another of the victims. I had no idea until now that he was the perpetrator who, it would appear, received his just come-uppance. I can't help but think that he did get exactly what he deserved. But when I think of that poor wee lass finding this book and reading it, I could weep."

"I know, I know. It's like reading some revolting horror story only to find that it has come to life. I'm sickened to the very depths of my soul. We've seen some pretty dreadful things and heard some horrendous confessions over the last years, you and I, what with the troubles and all, but never have I heard of anything so wicked and debased as this. It's almost beyond comprehension. If we didn't have the proof of the dead bodies - oh dear Lord, I almost said the *living* proof! - then there would be no way I could believe what I have just read. I would swear that it was the ramblings of a very sick mind."

"Unfortunately, it's not just the ramblings but the *actions* of a very sick mind," replied Patrick. "I've known that family ever since I came here to Belfast and that's more years than I care to remember. I've seen those two Brady chaps grow from what appeared to be quite normal boys into powerful business men. I've always had my suspicions that not all their dealings were above board or moral but I would never have suspected either would be capable of anything of this magnitude. Kevin was by far the more wayward and headstrong of the two, if not a little wild, even, always dancing along the very outer edges of the law, charming his way out of one scrape after another. Michael assumed the role of the man of the house after their father died and became a bit of a sober-sides then, although Clementine was always head of the household, even when her husband was alive. It was a case of he wore the trousers but she told him which pair to put on, if you know what I mean!

"There is something about that woman that makes my blood

run cold; something, dare I say, verging on the sinister, and so I keep my distance. I have very little to do with the family, on principle as much as for any other reason, because I simply do not like their method of operation. They seem to have very few scruples and a greatly exaggerated idea of their true standing. They seem to think that because they are very wealthy and powerful in the business community and because they are overtly generous to their own church (their priest is 'bought-and-paid-for', as Susan's sister says, much to my amusement), that they are in some way above the law of the land and even above the laws of God; as if their financial investment in the church has bought them some kind of spiritual superiority. Yet you couldn't meet a more ungodly tribe than the Bradys, I can assure you."

"They sound a charming lot, I don't think," Paul responded with irony. "I must confess to being a little puzzled, though. Your description of the family is not a pretty one by any stretch of the imagination and yet Beth is a Brady, even if only by marriage. Didn't she realise what sort of people they were, what sort of family she was marrying into? I don't somehow envisage her as being a mental or emotional lightweight or one to be taken in by the trappings of wealth. Somehow I can't reconcile the two."

"Well, all I know is that she met Kevin in Boston when he was there on a business trip and he swept her off her feet and into matrimony in no time at all and, from what he has written in the last entry in that ghastly book, he did it quite deliberately so that he didn't have to marry poor Eileen Conlon. Obviously, Beth had no knowledge of that or we all wouldn't be here right now trying to save her battered sanity!"

The two friends sat companionably beside the fire, each cogitating silently, until Susan called them for dinner. Just as they were finishing, Dermot arrived to check on Beth's progress. Susan showed him up to Beth's room and then prepared coffee for them all which she took through to the study. Dermot joined them shortly afterwards and gave them his report on Beth.

"Well, I must say that I'm delighted with the way her physical wounds are healing. Although she looks a dreadful mess with all the bruising and swelling just now, she is making very good progress. I should be able to take out most, if not all, of the stitches in the next few days and that will certainly improve her appearance greatly. However, I must admit that I'm most certainly glad that I will not have to tend to her mental condition. That I gladly leave in your most capable hands. For there is no doubt whatever but that she is seriously traumatised. You two really have your work cut out for you and no mistake. Still, she's definitely in the right place to receive the help she needs. She won't go wrong with you chaps."

"Thank you for your vote of confidence," said Patrick. "What we would be even more grateful for, however, is your prayers. We shall be needing all that we can get, I assure you."

"You have them, my friend, unquestioningly. Now, I know that I don't really need to ask you to tread very carefully with Beth, but I'm going to anyway. She is in a very fragile state of mind and is in need of serious kid-glove treatment. Not that I'm trying to teach granny egg-sucking techniques, you understand."

"Have no fear, that little lady will be handled with the most delicate of care. After all, the Lord Himself is in charge of all we do and He knows just exactly what it is that she needs. We just have to be open and receptive to Him."

"*Just!*" Dermot exclaimed. "You make it sound so simple! I'm sure, I really don't know how you do the work that you do. All I do know for certain is that I admire you unreservedly. And on that note of sentimentality, I shall take myself home to my bed and if I'm lucky, a night of undisturbed sleep. I prescribe the same for you both, too. I doubt that Beth will awaken again tonight. She is thoroughly exhausted and was asleep before I left her room. I shall be thinking of you all tomorrow and will try to pop in sometime during the day. If you're engrossed when I call round then I'll leave you to it and come back in the evening."

"Bless you, Dermot. You're a good man and my life would be the poorer for not knowing you. On your way now and drive carefully. There's another gale howling outside, I see."

Patrick showed Dermot to the door, closing it quickly after him to keep out as much of the bitter night air as possible. Then he and Paul went up to their rooms, leaving Susan to her nightly ritual of putting the house to bed.

7

The following morning, having breakfasted well in bed, Beth wandered downstairs, hovering uncertainly in the hallway, not knowing whether she should wait in the empty study, finally the soft rumbling of deep voices joined in amiable conversation drawing her towards the kitchen. She tapped timidly on the door which was standing slightly ajar, tentatively pushing it further open. The men, absorbed in their dialogue, were not aware of Beth's diffident entrance but Susan turned to her immediately, welcoming her into the warm, cosy kitchen.

"Come in, Miss Beth, come in. Will you have a fresh cup of coffee with us now?"

"Ah, my dear," exclaimed Patrick. "How are you this morning? It's good to see you up and dressed. Are you feeling refreshed after your long sleep? I do believe you look a little brighter today. Come and sit here and have your coffee." He hoped that he didn't sound as nervous as he felt. He knew that he was talking too much and too fast, self-conscious in his anxiety over Beth. He raised his coffee cup to his mouth and drank quickly to cover his embarrassment but only succeeded in burning his mouth.

Paul, sensing his friend's discomfort, offered Beth the sugar bowl and passed an innocuous comment about the perpetually dismal weather. Beth shook her head in response to the offer of sugar and sat silently sipping her coffee, not knowing what to say to whom. There was a distinct feeling of unease in the room, even Susan seemed affected by it as she clumsily dropped a juice glass she had been drying. The sound of the shattering glass broke the tension and Patrick, pulling himself together, said cheerfully, "Come along, you two. Let's head off to the study and leave poor Susan in peace. We can take the coffee with us and sit more comfortably in there."

"That sounds like a very good idea to me," Susan responded tartly. "You're not doing my housekeeping account any good sitting in here. At this rate I'll be needing a whole new set of dishes if you don't get out from under my feet. And there'll be no food to put on the table if I have to spend the whole morning clearing up after you. Now, scoot! Out of my kitchen, the lot of you!"

Beth couldn't help but laugh. "Oh Susan," she said. "You are a *tonic*! You're *so* like Bridie."

"And speaking of Bridie," answered Susan. "She'll be coming down tomorrow afternoon for her tea, as usual, it being her regular day off. We thought it best to stick to the normal routine of things, so as not to appear suspicious. She'll be able to fill us in on what is going on up at the big house. She can't tell me anything over the phone in case anyone is listening in."

Beth shuddered at the mention of the big house, the earlier momentary lightness overshadowed by the evil aura of the Bradys that reached out for her even in this place of refuge. Patrick took her arm and steered her purposefully from the kitchen and down the hall.

"We'll be ready for more coffee in a couple of hours, Susan," he called out.

"You'll be lucky!" came the sharp reply. "You'll be lucky."

"What a woman!" Paul laughed. "You don't know how lucky you are to have Susan to run your house for you, Pat."

"Oh, I do, believe me! She is heaven-sent. And furthermore, it's not just my house she runs, but it seems at times, my whole life! She is a great character and a great joy to me. I would be thoroughly lost without her, I can tell you."

While this cheery banter was going on, they had all settled themselves in the study, the two men in their chairs by the fireplace, where blazed another glorious fire to ward off the inclement elements, and Beth once more ensconced on the sofa, taking comfort from the blanket tucked snugly about her. I feel like Linus must feel, she thought to herself. He was never without his 'security' blanket. All she needed was a Snoopy dog and the mental picture would be complete. To everyone's amazement, she began to laugh aloud. Patrick and Paul looked at her in astonishment as she flapped her hands at them, unable to speak as tears of merriment rolled down her cheeks.

"I'm sorry," she wheezed. "It's just Peanuts!" She laughed even louder. "I can't possibly explain!"

The two men looked from Beth to each other and back again, shaking their heads uncomprehendingly. They hadn't a clue what was going on but at least they could tell that Beth's laughter was genuine amusement and not hysteria. The atmosphere lightened appreciably and they all felt themselves relax as Beth's laughter subsided into little chuckles.

"Oh!" she gasped. "I couldn't begin to explain what brought that about but whatever, I feel a whole lot better for having a good laugh. In fact, I feel more relaxed than I have done for a very long time."

"Hallelujah!" cried Paul.

"Amen!" echoed Patrick. "What you will find, child," he continued to Beth, "is that laughter is a wonderful gift from our Heavenly Father. As there is great healing and release in tears, so there is in laughter and in many ways, even more so because it can be shared and is such a delightful pastime, as well."

Beth took a deep breath and looked at Patrick for some moments.

"May I ask you a question?"

"My dear, you may ask me anything you like."

"Except how much he spends a month on his favourite whiskey!" Paul interposed with a bellow of a laugh.

"That's enough out of you, my friend!" retorted Patrick with a smile. "You're more than happy to partake of your fair share whenever offered."

"This is a true fact," replied Paul. "A true fact, indeed."

Beth laughed with the two men, feeling a great fondness for them both growing within her. They were such good, kind people and she was so fortunate to be here with them, but there were some puzzling aspects of which she was starting to become aware, now that her headache was easing a bit and her thoughts were becoming clearer. Just what was she doing here, other than the fact that she had been rescued from Michael's violence and was in need of a good doctor and a friendly shoulder on which to cry? What else was in store for her?

"And now, my dear," said Patrick, turning his attention once more to Beth. "Ask away. Just what would you like to know?"

"Well, I must admit that I'm a little confused about things and don't fully understand what I'm doing here. Please, don't think for one minute that I am in any way ungrateful. Nothing could be further from the truth, for if you hadn't been so kind as to take me in, I dread to think just where I would be now - and in what state

I would be, as well. However, I am somewhat puzzled.

"If I remember rightly, you mentioned something yesterday about helping me through the awful time I've been having lately and that the letter to Jesus that I wrote would help us all in figuring out what to do with me. I was wondering if you could please explain to me just what this all entails."

"First of all, before we go any further, I have a word of warning for you that I should really have mentioned earlier. Now that you are up and about I must ask you not to go anywhere near the front of the house, except after dark and when the curtains are closed. If the front doorbell rings, I want you to keep out of sight. You're absolutely fine back here in the study or in the kitchen or in your bedroom or bathroom upstairs because the back of the house cannot be overlooked by anyone."

He reached over to give Beth's hand a reassuring squeeze at the look of consternation on her face.

"Don't worry, child. You really are safe here but we just don't want anyone else to know that this is where you are. If you are seen or if you leave this place unprotected, then I'm very much afraid that you will be in considerable danger. I do know that Michael Brady has put the word out and there are a good few men looking all over the city for you. I don't really know why, myself, but I imagine it must have something to do with what you wrote in your letter."

"Yes," whispered Beth. "I don't know if he knows about Kevin's book, but I told him that I had incontrovertible proof that Kevin was a murderer and that is when he hit me."

"Well, that absolutely settles it. You're not setting foot outside this place until it is completely safe. For one thing, at the moment, you could hardly walk down the street unnoticed with your face the way it is. All eyes would be on you and no end of questions would be asked. Besides, where would you go? It would be out of the question to try to fly back to America just now, for the airport, train and bus stations will be well watched by his look-outs."

"But I can't stay here indefinitely. That would be unfair on you, especially now that Mr Hopkins has come to visit and it is almost Christmas. I couldn't possibly impose on you any longer than necessary. I know that I can't leave the country because I don't have my passport and I have very little money, but perhaps

I could find a small town somewhere and get a job of some sort. There must be something I can do that doesn't require identity papers. Anyway, I can't keep you from your work like this. This must be a terribly busy time for you with all your church activities and all your other parishioners needing you."

"No, my dear. You are not going anywhere, not until you are fully recovered and we have found a completely safe place for you to go. Paul has come specifically to help you and my young priest, Father William, is revelling in his new-found authority and independence. I have let it be known that I'm a little under the weather - I honestly had a very bad cold-cum-flu virus thing until recently and those who can be bothered to question my absence from my duties will assume that I still have the wretched bug - and William has been champing at the bit to do more on his own in the parish, so now seems as good a time as any to give him his head.

"Susan will put in regular appearances at church and I will attend occasionally, bundled up to the nines as though I really wasn't very well so that things will look as normal to outsiders as possible, but you will never be left here alone. Paul will always be with you when Susan and I are not here and I will always make a point of seeing William in the church office. He very rarely comes in here anyway, so that will not seem unusual to him. He's a nice enough young chap but we do not have a particularly close relationship and tend to keep our distance from each other. Needless to say, he is unaware of your presence here and I want it to remain that way. He is more than a little sceptical about my extra-curricular activities, as he sees them. He is a most earnest and devout young man but I find him decidedly blinkered and narrow in his judgements. So no questions will be asked about my being less in the public eye.

"And as to Christmas. Well, I assure you that your presence here will be nothing short of an added joy to us. If you like, you will be able to observe as much of the church activities as you wish, for we have a hidden peep-hole in our old church! It is accessible only from the house here and is always under lock and key, the one and only key being in my personal possession at all times. So you will be perfectly safe, if not a little cold, for it is a little room 'up in the gods' that has no electricity and therefore no heating or light but if you wrap up warm, you should be all right. You can see quite a lot from up there but cannot be seen from anywhere in the church. I've checked! So that, I think, is all your arguments shot down in the proverbial flames.

"And now, I think it best to fill you in on a little background as to what brought Paul and me to this work that is so important to us. The best place I always find to start is at the beginning and the beginning for us was a long time ago when we were just wee lads in a small village further north from here. Paul can take over here while I rest my voice for a while. It will do you good to hear someone else talking for a change, too!"

Beth turned to Paul expectantly, her fears allayed somewhat now that she knew she was welcome to stay where she was. And in truth, she really didn't want to leave these wonderful people, at least not yet awhile, especially now she knew that Michael was actively looking for her. She gave herself a mental shake to dispel her disquieting thoughts and listened attentively to Paul, who now began to speak.

"Indeed, as Pat says, we two old fogeys go back a long way, back to infancy, in fact, for our mothers became friends when they were both carrying us. Theirs was an unusual friendship in itself because although there wasn't the tension and troubles that we know today, there was still a very definite divide between the religious denominations then, especially in a small village such as ours. But then, both our mothers were social outcasts and so it was almost natural that they became friends, for they had precious few others.

"My father was a solicitor and a Protestant from Coleraine, which is where he met my mother. She was a nurse and a Catholic, working in the local hospital, although her family home was out in the country. They fell in love and my mother became a Protestant so that she could marry my father in his church. Both families were very upset, to say the least, and my parents were completely ostracised by them and most of their friends for what was seen as a betrayal of their faith. If it had been the other way around, if it had been my father who was the Catholic and my mother had changed from the Church of Ireland to the Church of Rome, then I doubt there would have been such an uproar. So in the end, to get away from all the ballyhaloo, my parents moved out to a village far enough away so that they weren't known there, but close enough that he could still commute each day to his work in Coleraine.

"But bad gossip travels just as fast as bad news, if not even faster, and my mother was soon to become a social pariah in the village as well. Father was busy rushing back and forth to his office, working hard at building up his practise, wining and dining his way up the social ladder in town. It seemed that now my mother was out of sight, she somehow became out of mind and father regained his acceptability in the sight of the business community, at the expense of his relationship with my mother, much to his shame and my disgust as I grew older.

"By this time, my mother was expecting me and was having a pretty lonely time of things at home. Until, that is, the day she met Pat's mother in the village shop. My Auntie Mary, as she was to become, was expecting her second child (Pat is just seventeen days older than I am!) and was as much an outcast as Mother, her 'crime' being that she was an abandoned woman! Pat's father had gone over to England to try to find work (this was the hungry thirties, don't forget) and had never bothered to contact Auntie Mary again. It wouldn't have been so bad if Joe Filey, the village black sheep, hadn't gone at the same time and hadn't been so eager to write home to tell everyone that Big Jim (as Pat's father was known) had not only found himself work, but had also found himself a new woman of decidedly dubious repute and had set up home with her in the back room of the local pub. Poor Auntie Mary was devastated beyond belief, but I have never in all my life known a woman with more dignity. She quietly got on with her life, bringing up Ann, who was only four months old when Big Jim left, and then Pat, who arrived three weeks before Ann's first birthday. My mother - her name was Elizabeth, like yours - and Auntie Mary became the closest of friends, especially as Father was away more than he was at home, and so it was natural that Pat and I should become friends, too. My sister, Isobel, is fifteen months younger than I am and although Ann was that much older, the two girls became inseparable. I suppose in some respects it was simply a case of there not being anyone else any of us were allowed to play with, but I think we all would still have been great friends, even if our family circumstances had been much different.

"I suppose, in retrospect, Pat and I both suffered quite a lot at school (presumably, our sisters did also), not just because of our home life, but because we had such close friends on the opposite side of the religious divide. We both very quickly learnt how to use our fists and they got plenty of use, I can assure you!"

"They certainly did!" interrupted Patrick. "I'm surprised we haven't got permanent scars across our knuckles! I know that Paul's schoolmasters were pretty scathing about our friendship but the Brothers were downright cruel to me about it. I had many a sound beating, 'for the good of my wayward soul', and endless exhortations to repent of my 'ungodly behaviour' or fear for my immortal soul. Although Paul and I both stood up to it all pretty well, it nevertheless did have a very damaging effect upon us, very nearly irreparable."

"Eventually, we all grew up and went our separate ways," continued Paul. "My younger sister, Helen, who is eight years Isobel's junior, married a Catholic farmer and crossed 'the great divide' into his church and was welcomed with open arms - strange how it works so successfully one way but not the other! They have a dairy farm not too far from where we grew up and have happily raised themselves seven 'offsprung'. Isobel never married. The only man she ever loved was our fair Patrick, here, and if she couldn't have him, then she would go without. Second-best never figured anywhere in Isobel's life. I honestly believe that our parents' non-marriage had affected her very deeply and there was no way she would submit herself to anything short of a true love match. So to this day, she lives with me, drives me half-mad from time to time and dotes on our nieces and nephews and their burgeoning families.

"Pat's sister, Ann, married a very fine chap, one Joseph Dennehy, a doctor from Dublin. So she moved south with him and they had themselves six wonderful children. Brendan, the eldest, is a priest, now living in Australia. The four daughters have all made good marriages and are happily raising their various broods. And that brings us to the second son, John. A finer man you couldn't want to meet. He is now, what, thirty-two, thirty-three, unmarried as yet, a successful art dealer with his own galleries in Dublin and Donegal. Not only is he a great success commercially but, of far more importance he is also a great success as a human being. He is a man of great humility, gentleness, compassion and such fun. He is the delight of his old uncle's heart, for I honestly believe that if Pat could have had a son of his own, he would have chosen John.

There is a bond between the two of them that is wonderful to behold."

"Aye," Patrick said softly. "He is a rare and beautiful man, one of God's special treasures."

"Well, as for Pat and me," continued Paul. "We both went away to study for our respective priesthoods, Pat to the Seminary, I to theological college. There, the pressure on our friendship was pushed almost to breaking point. For one thing, we were both so ardent in our desires to do well, to serve the Lord, that we allowed the religious divide to finally intrude into our relationship and so, eventually came the parting of the ways, and none too amicably, either."

"We didn't have any contact with each other for several years," Patrick said, "until my mother passed away and I returned to the village for her funeral. To my surprise, Paul was there, also. It appeared that the rift between us did not extend to our families and nothing would have kept him away from Mother's funeral."

"This is true," added Paul. "Auntie Mary was much, much more than a surrogate auntie to me. I loved her almost as much as I loved my own mother. She was more special than anyone else I have ever known. All jesting aside - and we do kid each other mercilessly, I know - it is from her that Pat gets all his good traits. His gentleness, his compassion, his absolute love for the Lord and his burning desire to serve Him are all a mirror-image of Auntie Mary. She wasn't able to go out into the world, so to speak, and so found her service through bringing up her children in such a wonderful, unprejudiced and loving way. Her children, Pat and Ann, proved to be people of exceptional qualities, all due to her exceptional, selfless love. Auntie Mary was a rare and beautiful soul, a true jewel in the Lord's crown."

"Saved by the coffee!" cried Patrick, who was by now blushing furiously, as Susan entered the room, bearing a heavy tray. He sprang to her assistance, hiding his discomfort in busyness, as he pulled a table to the fireside, clearing magazines away and wiping down the surface of the table with his jacket sleeve.

"Away with your fussing, man!" said Susan. "What's got into you this morning? Have you been at the bottle already today or are you getting senile in your old age?" She put the tray down on the table and flapped her hands at him, gesturing him back to his chair. "Away and sit down. I'll see to this. Sure, you're not fit to pour coffee, except all over the carpet and that is not what I slaved all morning for your to do."

Beth and Paul roared with laughter at the spectacle of big burly Father Patrick being ordered about by his tiny little housekeeper. Patrick sat down and sheepishly joined in their laughter, then, as it took hold of him, wholeheartedly.

"Didn't I tell you that she runs my life as well as my house?" he wheezed at Beth. "No one alive talks to me the way that old besom does."

"Enough of your besom or you'll be getting no dinner from me, young man. You'll be having to fend for yourself but not in my kitchen, so think on." Susan bustled about the room, straightening this and that, plumping up cushions that didn't need plumping, finally catching Beth's eye and giving her a wink before she scurried out to the kitchen, muttering, for Patrick's benefit and the others' delight, "Men! They'll be the death of me yet, so they will!"

8

As they sat drinking coffee and eating Susan's delectable, freshly-baked rock cakes, Paul resumed his story.

"We discovered that we were still friends but that a major cloud hung over our relationship, dampening and subduing it. There was between us an air of politeness that had never before existed - that politeness reserved for very new acquaintances, those of whom one is most unsure of the suitability of any progression of the acquaintanceship. We were strained and estranged. However, we did agree to keep in touch when we parted at the railway station in Coleraine, I to go to my new home in Londonderry and Pat to his, here in Belfast. And true to our word, we did make an effort - the odd, cursory note at Christmas time, an occasional birthday remembrance - but it was all very superficial.

"Then came the Troubles during which time we were both tested to the full. The worse the troubles got, the greater became the theological divide but the closer we drew to each other. It seemed that the more suffering we experienced, the more we needed our nearest and dearest; as kids, we had been totally reliant upon each other for friendship (with the exception of Dermot, who was also a friend of Pat's up at the Christian Brothers, although I didn't know him all that well at the time) and so it was to each other that we now turned. However, things were still not as they had once been.

"Then a few years ago, when we were both at the point of physical, emotional and spiritual exhaustion, a friend sent me a brochure about a place he had recently discovered. It was a beautiful mansion house, set in the most glorious countryside near the sea on the south coast of England. It was a place of Christian teaching, counselling, healing and retreat. Ostensibly Church of England, there were in reality no denominational barriers. Pink, purple, green or yellow - it didn't matter what you were; the only prerequisite was that you loved the Lord Jesus, but even that wasn't strictly necessary, for many apparently went there not knowing Him and left transformed, having met Him and accepted Him into the lives.

"Well," Paul continued, as he waved his hands in the air in

the most casual of manners, "we were 'quids in', for we both knew and loved the Lord - *or so we thought*. This place was exactly what Pat and I needed at that time. So we booked ourselves in for a two-week retreat - we certainly didn't need counselling or healing, although the odd prayer or two wouldn't go amiss. What we needed was peace and quiet and long, lovely, contemplative country walks. And this was how we passed the first three days, strolling through springtime woods, carpeted with bluebells and primroses, along the private beaches as the waves gently washed the sands and the peace washed through our battered souls.

"On the third evening, after dinner, we sat in the lounge debating doctrinal issues. The more we tossed about our thoughts and ideas, the more barbed and caustic became our comments until we were very close to verbal fisticuffs. Another chap was sitting nearby, observing us closely. Eventually, and fortunately, he moved nearer and intervened before things degenerated into a school-yard brawl. He introduced himself - we shall call him Hugh - as a vicar from the Midlands. After the usual pleasantries, he commented on our 'spirited discussion' and asked if we had a problem we would like to share. Naturally, I said that of course *I* had no problem, but that Pat was the one with the problem. And of course, Pat immediately replied that he was *perfectly* unperturbed and that *I* was the one with the problems. Then, with awful clarity, we both actually realised what each had said and shame engulfed us. We hardly knew where to look and then, almost in desperation, looked to Hugh. He gently asked if we would like him to pray with us and if we would like some help with our very apparent difficulties. The excruciating detail of our altercation is long forgotten and rightly so; it was the dialectic itself and the reasons behind it that needed dealing with. Hugh suggested that we meet in the morning in the chapel and a friend of his - we shall call him David - would join us and together we would talk things through. This sounded eminently sensible - so often the intervention of a third party can smooth over little difficulties with consummate ease. And so all was agreed and we departed to our separate rooms, confident of a pleasant chat the following morning.

"What a shock we had in store! Neither of us could have imagined what was to come out during the next five days. It was searingly painful, deeply humbling, intensely soul-searching. We discovered hidden hurts we never dreamt existed and even if we had been vaguely aware of some of them, they had been brushed off as a mere by-product of our youth, the normal emotional bumps and bruises anyone can expect to pick up along the way through life. And yet how deeply they were buried and how monumentally they had affected our lives.

"I had to face and acknowledge my deep-seated resentment of my father for his high-handed indifference towards me, my mother and my sisters; my disappointment, verging on disgust, in my mother for being so submissive and acquiescent to him; my resentment at being ostracised because of my parents' flouting of their faith to marry. I found that I felt that if it had been a successful marriage, then it would have all been worthwhile but it had rapidly become a mockery and that made me all the more bitter and angry, especially as I had had to suffer so much ridicule at school. I felt that their sham of a union was a major reason why I never had the courage to marry and for this I was very angry.

"As for Pat, he discovered that he had been harbouring a profound bitterness, hatred almost, for his father for deserting them and causing his mother such appalling humiliation. There was also great anger towards the Brothers for their brutality and mental cruelty. These hurts were lovingly prayed into and we were able to forgive those who had wronged us, each other and ourselves and we found that this forgiving brought a spontaneous and wonderful healing and release. We came to see that all parties concerned were, in one way or another, damaged souls - we were all the walking wounded, as it were - and that we are all, every one of us, God's children, created by Him, loved by Him, each worthy and in need of His love and forgiveness.

"But *worst* of all, and *best* of all, we discovered that the Lord we both thought we loved and served was a charade - a man-made charade, a Lord we had both, separately and respectively, been taught about; my 'gentle Jesus, meek and mild', Lord of platitudes and niceties; Pat's Jesus hanging lifeless on the cross, Jesus the son of Mary and God. All very well and good in their place but there was no real substance to our respective Lords, about whom we had been taught all our lives. I say 'Lords' deliberately, for these were not two aspects of the one Lord but two very different creations, seemingly unrelated to each other and, least of all, to the *real* Lord Jesus.

"One afternoon, we sat in prayer after a particularly difficult soul-searching time. Our eyes were closed as we listened to Hugh and David. As they asked the Lord to send His Holy Spirit to cleanse us through, Pat and I were, at the very same time, overwhelmed by the most exquisite experience. We both experienced the living reality of the Lord Jesus. He showed Himself to us in a way that virtually defies description, for there truly are no words adequate, in any earthly language, to describe the love, the peace, the gentleness, the power, the *reality* of the Lord Jesus. And having *experienced* that reality, there is not a soul in heaven or on this earth who can take away from us that reality. That is because it *is* reality - *absolute* reality, given to us by the Lord Himself."

Paul paused for a moment in reflective contemplation, hardly wanting to drag himself from the memories of that very special awakening in his soul.

"I have said that it is barely possible to describe what it is like when one experiences the living Jesus, but I will, nonetheless, try, just so that you will have some indication of what is in store for you when your turn comes, for come it will - if you earnestly desire it. Of that I am absolutely certain, for the Lord delights in drawing close to His 'little ones'. Those who love Him and are ready to welcome Him into their lives are in for treats such as they could never have imagined possible. For when the Lord draws close and makes Himself known, every atom of your being experiences His 'livingness'. You are filled to the very top and overflowing with His love, which floods you with a radiating, pulsating, super-charged energy that can literally knock you off your feet. There is an ecstasy beyond all earthly comprehension, a heightening of all the senses so that you feel and see things in ways that you never before imagined. You experience a totally new dimension of awareness within, the likes of which no experience this world can offer comes anywhere near. *This* is spiritual reality. This is *JOY* - Jesus Overwhelming You, the most beautiful definition I know of that lovely little word. And if this seems far-fetched and fanciful, then all I can say is, *try it*. For it is there for you. Yes, *you*, Beth, if you truly desire it. So all you have to do is to lovingly, openly, willingly invite Jesus to enter into your life, to take up His rightful place at the very centre of your being. And you will know joy and happiness such as you have never glimpsed before - and *such fun!!* For the Lord Jesus has a wonderful sense of humour. So, if you truly desire this, then simply invite the Lord in. Give your life to Him anew.

"Pat and I did just that and for us, this was life-transforming. We wanted to rush out and tell the whole world. Why shouldn't everyone have what we had been given? We were ready to rip off our dog collars and start a new crusade, because who needs dogma and denominations when they can have the *real, living* Lord? But, of course, we couldn't and we didn't. Sanity prevailed once the initial ecstatic euphoria settled down.

"It was interesting that we both felt the initial urge to 'down dog collars', as it were. At first it seemed to us that this new - at any rate, new for us - Jesus was so different from the one we had previously 'known' in our churches that we thought we no longer belonged within the organised church structure. I do believe it was something akin to the experience of that young chap, Cliff Richard, who questioned whether or not he should remain a pop-singer after he became a Christian but then decided that the Lord could use the public exposure and popularity to get His message across to young people. After all, the Lord cannot permit a single opportunity to go to waste.

"And so it was with us. We were both trained priests and if we were open and willing - and who could not be, after all we had experienced? - then He would use us to gradually and gently bring a new awareness of Himself to our parishioners. Unfortunately, there are all too many of our fellow clergymen and seniors who are not of like minds with us and we have had to tread very carefully. However, we are now starting to see signs of an ever-increasing renewal within and without the church, which is enormously encouraging for us. The Holy Spirit is moving mightily in this renewal, bringing greater and greater strength and drawing people in larger and larger numbers to the *real* Jesus. So we have great hope.

"Pat and I both tried to introduce a healing ministry into our respective churches but met with seemingly immovable resistance. So that is why, when the need arises, we offer Christian counselling and prayer ministry, either here or up at my home, on a private basis. We would dearly love to set up a centre where people in need could come to stay and where we could hold regular services open to the public, but of course, something like that would take vast amounts of money, far more than two old codgers in their early sixties could ever scrape together.

"Still," he added with a shrug, "the Lord knows all about it and we give Him a little nudge every now and then, just to remind Him, so as to speak! For having been on the receiving end of such wonderful healing of *our* inner hurts and having studied and qualified as Christian counsellors, the desire to help others find healing for *their* inner hurts - and their physical ones, too - through the love and graciousness of the Lord, has become a deep, burning desire. To bring others to the Lord so that they can truly know Him, can experience His living reality in their hearts, so that they can develop that very precious, personal, one-to-one relationship with Him that He so longs to have with each and every one of us, is now our true life's work and we could want for nothing more fulfilling. This is our joy, our hearts' delight.

"And this, my dear Beth, is why we want so very much to help you. Because of your deep suffering, the Lord, by His grace and His very great love for you, has brought you to this place of safety for not just your physical healing, but, I earnestly believe, for your inner healing, too."

Beth was spellbound, enrapt, tears of wonder, joy, pain and fear glistening in her eyes as she drank in Paul's words.

"Help me," she whispered, as the tears spilled over and down her cheeks. "Help me, please!"

"That is precisely what we are here for, my dear," said Patrick, as he handed her the ever-present box of tissues. "But first we are all in need of more physical nourishment. Any minute now, if past form is anything to go by, Susan will be calling us in for our lunch."

A sharp tap on the door, an 'I told you so' and Patrick helped Beth to her feet, offering her his arm as Paul led the way out of the room, delicious, tantalising aromas, promising yet another wonderful feast, drawing them rapidly and eagerly towards the kitchen.

9

After lunch, at the suggestion of Patrick, Beth went up to her room to rest for a while. The two men wanted time alone to pray about Beth's situation and she needed time also to pray and to prepare herself for the coming session. Paul had counselled her to take some time to sit quietly and ask God, through His Holy Spirit, to guide her in sharing her problems with them. She was to make notes of any thoughts or feelings or mental pictures that came to her and to bring them with her when she joined the men later.

However, Beth found that she was so nervous that at first all she could do was to pace around the bedroom and then to sit by the window, looking out at the relentless rain. The sight of the grey, wind-tossed trees and the driving rain made her feel even more depressed and she quickly closed the curtains against the miserable weather.

She turned away and noticed, for the first time, hanging on the wall, a lovely painting of coastal scenery. The sunlight danced across the deep blue of the sea, tingeing the tops of the white caps with a soft golden hue. The hillside that swept dramatically down to the seashore was dotted with tiny white sheep, contrasting vividly with the almost luminescent green of the grass and the dusky tones of heather. A few white cottages were nestled near the foot of the hill, a small inlet providing a narrow, sandy beach and mooring for two or three boats tied up to landing stages. The overall effect was one of peace and tranquillity and Beth felt the ambience gradually seep into her, calming her fears and steadying her shaky nerves. What a perfect place to which to escape, she thought. I could run away to a place like that with no trouble at all! It looked exactly her sort of haven - a virtual paradise with no outward indication of anything nasty or violent.

Feeling more composed, her equilibrium restored by the beauty of the painting, Beth went to sit in the armchair by the window, picking up from the little table to the side of the chair the Bible Patrick had lent her. She leaned her head back against the cushions and closed her eyes, the Bible lying heavily in her lap. She felt unable to pray, so she just sat quietly for some time, trying to hold on to the feeling of tranquillity but feeling it slipping away as the reasons for being in this place came back into focus. Fear raised its ugly head once more, bubbling up in her throat, fluttering nervously in the pit of her stomach.

As much to distract herself from these uneasy feelings as anything else, Beth picked up the Bible from her lap and opened it at random. It fell open at Psalm 103, with which she was unfamiliar. She started to read, uncomprehendingly at first but then forced herself to go over what she had already read. The words were beautiful but somehow she could find little comfort in them. However, the words of verse four, 'who redeems your life from the pit and crowns you with love and compassion' seemed to repeat themselves over and over. Tears welled up and trickled over and down her cheeks. Surely she was beyond redemption? Surely the pit of her sin was too deep, the sides too steep, for anyone to rescue her? How could anyone feel love and compassion for *her*? Who could love *her*? Nobody in their right mind, thought Beth, could possibly love someone as unclean, as defiled and worthless as she was.

She didn't know how long she sat in the chair, silent tears falling from her closed eyes, before the door opened and Susan entered the room.

"Here you are, my dear. I've brought you a nice cup of tea," she said as she placed the cup and saucer on the table beside Beth. "The men have theirs below. When you've finished this you're to go away down to the study and they'll be ready for you."

Susan appeared to be unaware of Beth's distress, but perhaps it was just her kindness in not wishing to embarrass Beth by drawing attention to the tears. However, as she turned to go, she reached over and squeezed Beth's hand.

"Bless you, child," she said gently. "God bless you and give you His strength." She slipped quietly out of the room, pulling the door to behind her.

It's strange, thought Beth as she sipped her tea, that having been independent for so many years, I have come to think of myself as very much the adult. And yet all these people call me 'Child' - Bridie and Joseph, Patrick, Paul, Susan and even the doctor. But I don't find it insulting; in fact, in some ways it's rather comforting, as if they see me as a child in need of ..... of what? Comfort? Help?

A cuddle? Oh, I need *all* these things and more! I just don't know which I need most. Maybe it just might be the cuddle! Whatever, I am really blessed that all these wonderful people are so loving and so giving, that they all seem so eager to help me.

Fortified by the tea and the reassuring thoughts, Beth took herself down to the study, tapping timidly on the door and entering in at Patrick's bidding. She found that the sofa had been pushed back away from the fire and three chairs were gathered in a semi-circle in front of the hearth.

"I think it best," Patrick said to Beth, "that for this next session you sit in a chair, here between Paul and me, rather than lying on the sofa. You can still have the blanket around you, if you need it."

"Thank you, but I will be fine without it," answered Beth.

"Well, it's there if you change your mind. We must make sure that your physical is as comfortable as possible.

"I will explain a little of what will be happening this afternoon. Only a little, though, for Paul and I don't even know all that will be happening. One thing of which you may always be certain is that you never can tell what the Lord will do next. He is the Master of surprises, as well! However, in a moment we will start with a prayer and then I think it best if we just sit quietly and see what the Lord reveals to any of us. And then we will take it from there, one step at a time, as He guides and directs. But most importantly, don't be afraid. You are in the very best hands in all creation, for the Lord has you held firmly and securely right in the palm of His hand and He will not let you go under any circumstances.

"And now we will just have a quiet prayer and ask the Lord to send His Holy Spirit to quieten our minds, to take away all thoughts of anything that has gone before today, to take away all anxieties so that we can be free to receive that which He wishes to reveal to us, to enfold us in His protection as we open our hearts and minds to receive His guiding."

Despite Patrick's exhortations to the contrary, Beth did indeed feel nervous and anxious. This was all so very new to her and she felt very self-conscious because all this was for her benefit - she was the centre of attention, something she had always loathed. All the old feelings of guilt arose suddenly in her and she wanted to run away and hide. Forcing herself to take slow, regular breaths, she found that a tentative peace was creeping over her and the panic was subsiding a little.

Beth glanced quickly at the two men, sitting either side of her, and noticed that they both had their eyes closed and their hands open, palms facing upwards, resting on their laps. She decided to do the same and immediately felt calmer. She could hear Patrick and Paul praying very softly, but wasn't able to catch more than the occasional word and Paul actually sounded as though he was speaking a foreign language - was it Hebrew? She had certainly never heard any language like it before. She must remember to ask him.

Then Patrick spoke. "I feel it is very important that, although the events of the last days and, possibly, weeks are by far the most immediate of your problems, there are things much further back in your past that need dealing with first. For some reason, I feel that these past experiences have a great bearing on the present situation and that the resolving of them will help us greatly in dealing with these later difficulties.

"So I think we should ask the Lord to bind up all the recent troubles, the wounds both physical and mental, and keep them safe in His care until it is the right time to deal with them. And now, let us sit quietly and ask the Lord to bring to the surface, that which He wants us to know."

Again, the three sat in silence, the men praying silently and Beth panicking at what might be revealed. Fear gripped her around the throat and she felt that she was about to suffocate. Help me! she shrieked silently and her eyes flew open, for she was sure that Patrick and Paul must have heard her desperate plea; however both their faces were serene and peaceful as their quiet prayers continued.

"Don't fight whatever you may be feeling," Paul spoke softly, his eyes still closed. "Just breathe gently and rhythmically and draw in the peace. There really is no need to panic or to fear for anything. There is nothing for you to feel guilt or shame about. Just be still and receive."

His gentle voice flowed over and through Beth, soothing her raw nerve-endings and she found herself relaxing once more.

"If I remember rightly from reading your letter to Jesus," Patrick said, "you mentioned something about your parents going away and leaving you so that you were brought up by an aunt and uncle. I take it you meant that your parents had died. Would you like to tell us about this? If you can, I feel it would be very important and could have a major bearing on things."

Beth found it very difficult to start speaking. She had to take several deep breaths and virtually force herself to open her mouth. Still the words seemed stuck in her throat. She felt as though her throat was paralysed and that she would never be able to speak again. As the panic started again, she began to breathe quite hard, exhaling deeply through pursed lips as if she was desperately trying to keep from fainting. Patrick reached over and gently stroked her arm.

"Take a deep breath, very slowly and then, gently as possible, let it out with your mouth slightly open. And again," as Beth did as she was told. "Keep breathing slowly and gently and feel the peace flowing in. There really is no need to feel panicked at all. Remember, no-one is here to judge you or to condemn you in any way. We are here because of genuine concern and desire for your healing. So, just take your time and begin as and when you can."

All the while Patrick was talking, Paul seemed to be muttering in his strange, foreign language. Beth was slightly distracted by it, telling herself once again that she must remember to ask him about it. The realisation that she was thinking of something other than herself made her feel a little better. She told herself very sternly to pull herself together. After all, at twenty-four she was hardly a child anymore, despite the others referring to her as 'Child'. Theirs was a term of endearment, not a criticism of her behaviour. Now she must not give them cause to think that she really was a cry-baby.

Tentatively, she tried her voice again and found to her considerable relief that it hadn't packed up for good. So she wouldn't disgrace herself by not being able to talk. But who knows what shame she would bring upon herself by the things she might say? Either way, she was going to let them down, after all their kindnesses, but she felt that she would rather do it by opening her mouth than by sitting there endlessly like some half-witted mute.

"My parents were killed in a plane crash when I was ten years old. They had left me with my aunt and uncle while they went on vacation by themselves. We had never been apart for vacations before. If they had taken me with them, then I would have died, too, and then I wouldn't have had to live all these years without them. I wouldn't have had to be so horribly lonely, so completely unloved."

With a suddenness almost of violence, the long-buried, excruciating pain of remembrance swept through Beth, forcing its way into every cell of her body so that she almost screamed with the intensity of her agony. Burning, scalding tears poured from her eyes as she fought to breathe, each breath bursting forth from her lungs in great, convulsive sobs. Unable to sit upright a moment longer, she collapsed forward across her knees, howling in anguish.

10

Patrick and Paul continued their prayers as Beth's heart-rending cries continued for some time. After a few minutes had passed, Paul quietly said, "Dear Lord, please send Your Holy Spirit to wash through Beth, cleansing away all her pain."

As Beth went to take in the next deep, shuddering breath, she felt, to her utter astonishment, an exquisite peace such as she had never experienced in all her life flood into the top of her head and down through her whole being in a flash. Her tears ceased in an instant and with them went the tight, crippling headache caused by her crying. Slowly, she sat up again and looked at the two men in amazement. They both were smiling radiantly at her and she felt a reciprocal smile spread itself across her face as she shook her head almost in disbelief.

"If I hadn't just experienced what I have, and for the life of me I don't know what it was, I would never have believed such a thing possible," she said in a voice filled with awe.

"As I have already remarked," answered Patrick, "the Lord is the Master of surprises! I said earlier that Paul and I never really know what the Lord will do at one of these sessions and now, once again He has shown Himself at His unpredictable best. I know that sometimes He will act with amazing speed, quite miraculously so, but more often things take much longer to be resolved. However, in His wisdom and by His grace, He has seen fit to work through this first phase with remarkable speed."

"But what actually has happened?" gasped Beth.

"You tell us what you experienced and we will try to explain as best we can," replied Paul.

"Where to start?" was Beth's bemused response. "All too obviously I was deeply distressed and as I tried to take a deep breath for yet another sob, I felt the most intense peace - if that doesn't sound silly - pouring into me. It seemed to come in from the very top of my head and not really with the breath itself. Then it just flowed and flowed in the most gentle waves, through and through and through me. Oh, I can't describe it! It was the most beautiful thing I have ever experienced in all my life. This may sound crazy to you, but I feel as though I've been cleansed through in some way. I don't know how else to express it, whatever 'it' was!"

"That, my dear," replied Patrick, "was the Holy Spirit washing you through as we had prayed He would."

"But *how....*?"

"That we don't know, but what we do know is that He does and that it is usually in response to heartfelt prayer! And as His Spirit flows through you, it washes away the pain and the hurts and the fears that have held you chained and captive and separated from the loving grace of the Father.

"Now, I don't think for one minute that this is the end of all your problems but I do believe that the Lord has graciously released you from a particular entrapment of fear and pain and shown us - that is, Paul and me - basically where to begin. I now firmly believe that the root of your inner hurts lies in your parents' death and the catastrophic effect that had on your life. Do you agree, Paul?"

"Absolutely," Paul answered. "I can't think of a much more traumatic event in anyone's life and if it wasn't handled with love and proper care, then that sort of thing could have untold repercussions in later life. Do you feel able to talk a little about the circumstances of your parents' death and what it meant to you?" he asked Beth.

"Well," she began uncertainly. "I've never talked to anyone about my past, not even to Cathy and she was my best friend."

"To no-one at all? Not even your husband?" queried Paul.

"*Least* of all, him! Oh, he knew the bare bones, as it were, as did most people, that I was an orphan who was brought up by my aunt and uncle. Nothing remarkable in that, so hardly worth dwelling on it. As far as he was concerned, it just meant that there were no close relatives of mine who could in anyway be an encumbrance upon him or get in the way of his plans. One thing I learned very quickly about that man was that he did not appreciate being thwarted in any way whatsoever. So, he was just grateful that I was free from any 'excess baggage', as he put it."

"Charming!" Paul responded tartly. "However, enough of him for now. Today is not the time to deal with that stage of your life. Today is for yesterday, if I may put it that way. So what can you tell us of that time?"

"I really don't know what to say or even where to begin. I'm sorry, but it's all so difficult."

The sound of the front doorbell startled them all.

"Good heavens," exclaimed Patrick, looking at his watch. "I had no idea it was as late as that. I would suspect that old Bridie has arrived for her tea. Normally I would leave her and Susan to their own devices but I do feel it important that we all join in on this visit so that we know how lies the land. Besides, I do think, Beth, that you have been through enough for today and if you have now drawn a blank, then that is where we shall leave it. I think that, this being the case, then tomorrow, if you are willing, we might go through your letter to Jesus together and see where the Lord directs us, with that as our guide. Yes?"

"Thank you," Beth sighed. "It might be difficult as I am so ashamed of the things I wrote in that letter, but perhaps it would be easier than trying to find my own way blind. And I would dearly love to see Bridie!"

"That's settled then. Enough for today! Tea and gossip await us without! So for now, I think we shall close with a prayer. Paul, will you do the honours, please?"

"With pleasure," Paul replied. The three closed their eyes as he continued quietly. "Beloved Father, we thank You for Your perfect, unconditional love, given to us so freely, so willingly. And we thank You for Your guiding hand that leads us so surely, so steadfastly along the path that you have mapped out for us. Your constancy and Your faithfulness are our rod and staff. Your Light is a lamp before our feet. Your peace is a balm to our souls. We thank you for the work that you have begun in Beth today and we go from this place, confident that that which you have started, you will complete.

"And so, dear Father, we ask that You would bind up all that has been said in this room and keep it safe until we are ready to deal with it further tomorrow. I ask that You would now stand between me and Beth, between Beth and Patrick and between Patrick and me and that You will go before us from this place. These things I ask, in the Name of Your Beloved Son, our Lord Jesus Christ of Nazareth. Amen."

"Amen," echoed Patrick and Beth.

When Patrick, Paul and Beth entered the kitchen, they found that

Bridie and Susan were seated at the kitchen table, heads together in quiet conversation, looking like two old crones, uncannily alike. Patrick coughed, none too discreetly, and Bridie's head whipped around to face them. She let out a loud cry and sprang from her chair, rushing towards Beth. She flung her arms around the younger woman in a crushing embrace, Beth turning quite pink from lack of air. Just as suddenly, Bridie released her vice-like grip and stood back, holding Beth at arms length, studying her face intently, taking in every bruise, cut and stitch.

"Oh, dear God, little lady," she cried, tears glistening in her normally bright blue eyes, now dimmed with sorrow. "What has that evil man done to you? Dear God, I could kill him myself for what he has done and be proud of it and all. He's not fit to live, the evil old bastard, forgive me, Father."

"Bridie, Bridie," Beth smiled at the old woman. "It is so good to see you again. I have missed you and Joseph more than I can possibly say. Don't you worry yourself over the state of my face. It looks a lot worse than it really is. It's just the bruising that makes it look so bad. A lot of the pain has gone already and the cuts are all healing well. Dr Kearney says that there will probably be very few, if any, scars when it's all healed. But enough about me; how are you and Joseph? Tell me all your news. I'm so hungry to hear about you both."

"All of you, stop blocking the way and come and sit at the table and have your tea," snapped Susan, trying unsuccessfully to hide a big smile. "A lady can't move in her own kitchen without falling over huddled masses of folks. How am I supposed to see to you all if you'll not get out of me way!"

They all took their places at the table, laughing along with Susan who was happily fussing over them, laying out sandwiches, cakes, scones, jam and cream.

"You're a cantankerous old hag, you are, Susan," chuckled Patrick. "Sure, I don't know anyone else who would give you house room, so I don't, with your snappy old ways and your mean table."

"Mean table, is it? *Mean table?* You don't know the meaning of the word 'mean'. Sure aren't you fatter now than you've ever been in your whole life, even when you were a pudgy little fella at your mother's breast. And I'll tell you something else for nothing, I don't know anyone else who would put up with you and your lazy, complaining ways. Susan this, and Susan that! Just you be thankful that I'm as obliging as I am for I could go from here this very day and get meself a position such as you couldn't imagine, so I could!"

"You're right, I couldn't imagine. For there's not a better one anywhere that you could find and you know it, you old goat. You'd be as lost without me as I would without you and there you have it. An admission! We both have need of each other and right now my need is a big cup of strong, sweet tea, so hop to and get about your work!"

"Hop to! *Hop to!* I'll give you 'hop to'!" But as she leaned forward to place Patrick's tea before him, Susan rested her hand on his shoulder and stayed for a moment, the others noting with glee that she gave him a gentle squeeze before removing her hand, but not before Patrick had covered it with his own large hand, returning her squeeze with full measure.

Paul pulled his handkerchief from his pocket, wiped his eyes and blew his nose.

"I think it's a case of tissues all round," he laughed. "I don't know about anything else."

Indeed, they all had eyes brimming with tears of mirth. Beth was clutching her sides and gasping with laughter.

"I don't believe you people," she wheezed. "I've never come across anyone like you in all my life! Nobody would ever believe that you two were a priest and his housekeeper. I can hardly believe you are for real!"

"Ah, we're real enough," Patrick replied. "You'll get used to us and our ways in time, I assure you. Sure, I may be a priest but first and foremost, I'm the man God made me to be and it's not in my nature to be the sort to put myself above others. There are too many people in all walks of life who use their position to unfair advantage and to me that is abuse of power and privilege. If I wanted, I could be all smug and superior, extending my ring to be kissed all over the place, with people bowing reverentially to my collar and all it symbolises but if I did that, then I couldn't live with myself. I certainly wouldn't like myself and could hardly expect others to like me, either. I see respect as being a mutual thing that grows between two people, out of love and caring, with neither putting himself first before the other.

"And this dear lady couldn't put herself first if she tried. I have a deep and abiding love for Susan that is uniquely hers alone. She is far more to me than a simple housekeeper, although she does that particular job with consummate skill and devotion. She is also my very dear friend and confidante, my sounding board when I have a knotty problem to work through and the only one who allows me to call her names and gives as good as she gets!"

"Away with your silly nonsense," said Susan, blushing becomingly, her blue eyes sparkling with just a hint of moisture. "Now be quiet and eat the sandwiches before the bread curls up with old age. And I didn't spend all morning baking those cakes to throw them out stale in the garden for the birds." She took her own place at the large round table, giving Beth a big wink as she sat down. "And drink your tea before it goes cold," she added, with a grin that wouldn't stay hidden.

For some minutes, they all ate in companionable silence, the sandwiches disappearing in no time at all. As Susan rose to refill the kettle for more tea and Patrick reached for the knife to cut into a delicate, most delicious looking Victoria sponge, he said, "Bridie, tell us. How are things at the house? Are you and Joseph keeping well?"

"Ah, I tell you," she replied. "That place is worse than a morgue any day of the week. Sure, it's like living in one of them dreadful soap operetta things that they have all over the telly these days only this one is worse than the lot of them. The old witch, Clementine, spends half her days wandering about the place looking like death warmed up, weeping and wailing for all the world to see and the rest of her time locked away in that study of hers, scheming God knows what wicked plans, for you can be sure she is up to no good.

"And the Big Man - *hah*! 'Big Man', my arse, begging your pardon, Father - is up to his evil tricks, you can be sure. What with plotting some poor sucker's downfall and bleeding some other poor old sod - begging your pardon, Father - dry of all his money and spitting out the husk for the wind to blow away, he's like some monster, bent on total destruction and I can't wait for the day when it's his own destruction we'll be reading about in the newspapers. And I'll be raiding his own wine cellar for the best champagne to toast him on his wicked way."

"You're a hard woman, Bridie," Patrick interrupted. "I think it wouldn't hurt for you and I to have a talk one day about all this."

"Aye, well may I be hard, but it's living above in that hellhole that's made me hard, sure it has. God knows, it would make any poor, soft soul hard, having to live with that evil lot. Either hard or raving mad, and I know which I would prefer to be. Just look at that poor wee Mairead and what her marriage to the 'Big Man' has done for her. Why, she wanders around the place these days, cackling like a mad thing, which of course is just what she is, only now she's even worse. Himself treats her worse than ever and that's saying something, I can tell you. But I'll say this for him, and it's the only good thing I can say about him, and that is that he has never, to my knowledge, ever raised his fist to her and we all know what he can do with his fists, don't we?"

Bridie paused to drink her tea and eat a slice of sponge, looking over at Beth and sadly shaking her head. She replaced her cup in its saucer and sat back in her chair, folding her arms across her stomach, all the while studying Beth's face. Suddenly she leaned forward and placed her folded arms on the table, pushing her tea plate out of the way. She raised her right hand, tapping her pursed lips repeatedly with the side of the finger, looking intently at Father Patrick. Then she dropped her hand again and exhaled loudly, blowing her breath out between her partially opened lips.

"All right," she said abruptly. "I have to tell you, although God knows, the words stick in my throat when I even think them but tell you I must. He's got the word out on Miss Beth, so he has, and he's got his cronies looking high and low for her. He's that desperate that he's even had some of them up at the house of an evening and they're not the types that would be dropping by for a cup of tea in the afternoon, either, I can tell you. I know their sort and the part of town where they breed and carry on their evil deeds and it's not up around the big House, if you know what I mean.

"Just because my telly is blaring away in the evening doesn't mean to say that I'm sitting in front of it watching the drivel they put on for us eejits that lap it up night after night. I'm awful light on my feet and can flit around that house with no-one able to see or hear me but God knows the things that I see and hear. Himself would have me gutted and put out for fish meal if he knew the things that I know about him and his business."

"What sort of things, Bridie?" encouraged Patrick. "What have you heard him say about Beth? Can you be more specific?"

"Specific? God knows, I could tell you things that would turn your hair grey, if it wasn't already - begging your pardon, Father." She stopped suddenly at the look of fright on Beth's face and reached across the table to take her hand. "Now, don't you be fretting yourself about all this, little lady, for aren't you in the safest place in all the world for you to be right now? Sure, the good Father is looking after you. Both of them are - the One upstairs and himself here at the table. They'll not let that evil so-and-so or his no-good cohorts find you and do you any more harm, never you fear."

Patrick rose suddenly from the table. "I feel a sudden chill coming on," he said. "If we have all finished with tea, may I suggest that we withdraw to the study, with its nice blazing fire, and a wee drop of whatever you fancy to ward off whatever ails you? You, too, Susan - and Bridie. We'll all go through to the other room. I have a feeling that we'll be needing comfort around us as we listen further to what Bridie has to say."

11

When they entered the study they found that the fire was in danger of going out. Patrick hurried to tend to the dying blaze whist Paul busied himself rearranging the furniture, pulling his and Patrick's chairs back to their normal positions either side of the fireplace, dragging the chair in which Beth had been sitting over to its place by the window and hauling the sofa closer to the hearth. Happy now that the flames were leaping brightly in the grate, Patrick went to the sideboard upon which stood various bottles and assorted glasses.

"Beth," he called out. "What is your fancy this afternoon? A sherry perhaps - sweet, medium or dry? A gin and tonic? A drop of the Jamey's, perhaps? Whatever I have, my dear, is yours"

"I would rather like a glass of Jameson's, if I may, with ice and soda water, if you have it."

"Ice? Ice? Susan, do we have any ice in the house?" he bellowed.

"Hush yourself, man," Susan retorted. "I'll be away to get some if you stop yelling at me, otherwise you'll all go without!" She grinned at Beth on her way out to the kitchen.

"You won't be needing ice this weather," interjected Bridie. "All you need do is open the window and put the glass on the windowsill for a few minutes. It's cold enough out there to freeze the b....." She caught her breath at the look on Patrick's face. "The hands off a baby. Sorry, Father."

"You're a shocking woman, Bridie," Patrick said. "A shocking woman. But the Lord loves you - and I love you, too, you old besom. Well," he said, turning to Beth. "If I can call Susan names, I can do the same to her sister. Sure, she'd feel left out if I didn't, wouldn't you, you old goat?"

"Sure, Father, if you didn't call me names at least once a week, I'd begin to think I'd done something to upset you, so I would."

"Will you be having your usual Guinness, Bridie, while we wait on your sister? Or will you take a wee sherry instead, for a change?"

"It will be my usual, please, Father. Sherry, indeed! Sure, it's not much more than a swallow, so it is, and what good did that ever do anybody? It's not enough to wet your tonsils let alone anything else."

"Well, I'm pleased that you're sticking to your usual for I enjoy seeing you having to practise patience while it's being poured. It does you good in more ways than one, does this." He took the ice bucket from Susan as she returned to the study and dropped two large cubes into the prepared whiskey before handing it to Beth with a grin and a big wink.

"I have a feeling," said Beth as she took the glass from Patrick, "that I am going to get better more quickly here than I could in any hospital in all the world. In two days here, I don't think I have laughed so much as I have in all my life. I've heard that laughter is good for the soul, but I think it's good for the body as well!"

"Oh, it is that, Beth," said Paul. "As we've already said, more healing comes through laughter than through tears any day of the week. And we know only too well how much healing and restoration comes through the release of tears. But so much more through laughter. It's so freeing, so liberating and it feels so nice!"

"Well said, my friend," added Patrick, as he poured Susan's regular sweet sherry and two more whiskeys and soda (without the ice, this time) for himself and Paul. "Well said, indeed.

"And now, if I may," he said, raising his glass. "A toast. First to my very dear friends, here in this room - and a man could not wish for finer friends." He acknowledged each one of them with a nod of his head. "And then, to a successful resolution to dear Beth's predicament. May the good Lord guide us and strengthen us for the task ahead. And I'm sure He wouldn't be averse to our raising our glasses to Him, also, for wasn't His very first miracle that of turning water into wine. Anyway, He knows our hearts and how much we all love Him and how grateful we are for His constant love and help in our lives. And so, my friends, I give you, in all humility and love, the Lord Jesus Christ, our very dearest friend of all."

"Our Lord Jesus Christ!" Five glasses were raised and five hearts, filled to overflowing, were raised along with them.

Once the toasts had been drunk, the group all sat in their appointed places, the men in their chairs and the women on the sofa with Beth between the two elderly sisters. Instinctively, both Susan and Bridie slipped one of their arms through Beth's and snuggled against her in a warm, loving, cosy, manner as if to reassure her that they were there for her protection and that no harm would come to her all the while the McGann sisters had anything to do with anything.

"And now that our bodies are comfortable and our spirits are full," said Patrick, raising his glass again in a mock salute, "will you tell us, Bridie, all that has been going on up at the big house that affects our Miss Beth?"

"Well now," Bridie replied after drinking deeply of her rich, black drink. "I've already said that himself has the word out on the little lady, he that has a heart as black as this," She raised her glass. "But without a drop of its goodness, so he has. He's got his wicked fellas out looking everywhere he can think of - the bus-station, train station, airport, hospitals and God alone knows where else. The types and the number of them that that man knows is nobody's business. It's as if he's got his own personal army of cut-throats.

"Anyhow, he wants Miss Beth found and brought to him so he can find out just what she knows and doesn't know and then - and it breaks my heart to even think such things, let alone say them, but - he wants her silenced for good. And we all know what that means. The old witch has put up a large amount of money for the one who finds her, so the greedy bastards - begging your pardon, Father - are out on the streets, looking everywhere they can think of, and then some, to find her."

Beth sat absolutely still whilst Bridie was talking, scarcely able to believe her ears, as if she were made from stone and could not move a muscle, neither could she feel any emotion. Her ears listened of their own volition, as though they did not belong to her body and yet it was *her* brain that registered their signals, *her* mind that was imprinted with the awful message of doom. Once again, that strange sensation of being a non-participating spectator in the midst of some macabre play engulfed Beth and yet, at the same time, she felt the unreal reality of being centre stage. From a long way off, she saw herself, as it were, a prisoner in a dock, bound, shackled, gagged, forced to stand and listen whilst her own death sentence was passed.

Bridie paused to take another deep draught from her glass and in so doing, became aware of the tension emanating from Beth, sitting beside her on the sofa. She quickly put her glass down on the coffee table at her side and turned to take Beth's hand in her own.

"Aw, there. Now, don't you fret yourself so, Miss Beth. I didn't want to upset you at all, so I didn't. But the Father wanted to know what was going on and I had to tell him, for your own sake as much as anything else. You do believe me, don't you? I wouldn't hurt you for all the world, so I wouldn't. Come now, Miss Beth. Say you forgive me, please, for I couldn't bear to have you cross with me now, I couldn't, really." She squeezed Beth's hand hard in her anxiety to penetrate the younger woman's granitic rigidity.

The pain caused by Bridie's vice-like grip finally registered in Beth's consciousness and she came to with a start, shaking her head to clear it of the awful images, looking about her in bewilderment as though she didn't quite know where she was. Then the old woman's words echoed in her mind, as if she were hearing them on the rebound and instantly she was contrite.

"Oh Bridie, dear Bridie. Of course I forgive you, not that there is any need for me to do so. You have done nothing in any way to upset me. It was just the shock of hearing the words themselves. I should have known that Michael wouldn't let things rest the way they are. He will want his pound of flesh and at the very least, another ton, to boot. I guess he figures that I owe him for what he no doubt sees as my disloyalty, not only to my husband, but to the whole clan.

"Strangely enough, I don't feel any great anxiety for myself or my own personal safety, but I am getting very concerned about you, Father, and you, too, Susan. If he finds out that I'm here now or have ever been, then I feel sick at the thought of what he might do to you. I really think that I should be moving on from here as soon as possible, for all your sakes as much as my own. I can't have any of you being endangered on my account. That would be too much for me to bear, when you've all been nothing but kindness to me."

"*Tosh!* I think is the appropriate word," interjected Patrick. "I, for one, will not hear of your leaving this house until it is absolutely safe for you so to do and until we have been able to arrange for a secure future for you. And as the physical head of this household, I speak with no small degree of authority. And I am equally convinced that the spiritual head of this place is also more than content to have you here, safe under His care and *His* authority is beyond dispute. Not even him up at the big house would dare to challenge that authority, I can assure you. So we'll hear no more about your leaving but I would urge everyone here to be vigilant to the absolute extreme in keeping things under hats, so as to speak. We can take no chances whatever for that one and his mother are wily characters, to say the very least, and their associates are very far from virtuous or trustworthy. So we must take consummate care."

With a grunt, Patrick hauled himself out of his chair and made his way over to the drinks tray.

"Come along, Beth, my dear," he said. "You look as white as a sheet. Drink up your whiskey and get a little colour back in your cheeks. There's scarcely any room in your glass for a top up yet. Anyone else ready for a refill while I'm on my feet?"

Three empty glasses were lifted aloft. "Drunken sots, the lot of you," he retorted as he filled his own empty glass first, before collecting the others. "Still, we could do with the warming comfort today and not just because of the gale blowing outside, either."

Having done the honours all round, he flopped back down into his chair, the poor old springs groaning and creaking under his weight.

"Now, Bridie. Tell all. What's the gossip in the town this week? I've yet to have my weekly dose of scandal. Last week you were saying that prim Mrs Parkinson's new baby was a distinctly darker shade of pale than any of her other seven offspring and that he is deceptively large for a so-called premature baby, considering Mr P only came out of prison seven months ago."

"*Father Patrick*! You're a shocking old gossip-monger, so you are. If your parishioners only knew, they'd be too shocked to look you in the eye, let alone have you hear their confessions," Paul broke in, his laughing eyes belying the look of mock reproof on his face.

"And how else do you think I manage to keep calm during all those confessions if it wasn't for the fact that I had been prewarned by Bridie. Many's the time I'd like to reach through the grill and strangle the fawning wretches on the other side, for their sort come snivelling in, week after week, begging for absolution for the same thing time and time again, thinking that the absolution somehow gives them *carte blanche* to go out and do whatever all over again. All too often I end up needing absolution myself for the thoughts and feelings they engender in me.

"So come on, Bridie, my scandal levels are running mightily low this week and are in need of a serious top-up."

Beth allowed herself to be swept along with the casual chatter and laughter that Bridie's tales brought from the others, feeling strangely released from her fears for the time being. It was a relief just to sit back in front of the blazing fire, sipping her excellent whiskey and listening to the banter and chit-chat flowing around her, knowing that she was safe with these good, kind people in whom, despite the levity of their conversation, there wasn't an ounce of malice or ill-will.

12

The following morning, after breakfast, Beth found herself once again in the study with Patrick and Paul, the seating arranged as it had been the previous afternoon with three chairs in a semi-circle before the fireplace. After Paul had led them in prayer for a few minutes, Patrick picked up the letter that Beth had written to Jesus.

"Now, my dear," he said to Beth. "We can do this two ways. Either you can read the whole letter aloud to us, although I must admit that this we usually find is more beneficial after lengthy discussion and counselling has already taken place, or if you prefer, we can work through this together phrase by phrase, so as to speak. Whichever you are more comfortable with is fine by us."

"I'm so ashamed of the things that I wrote that in all honesty I would prefer to go away and hibernate for the next fifty years or so. Maybe then I could face it all!"

"And what do you suppose that might accomplish?" Paul asked gently.

"Oh, I know it won't do me any good at all but I just hate the thought of anyone knowing what a dreadful person I really am! It's so painful to admit that one is such a wretched creature. And I've always been such a private person that it is agony to allow others so close to my inner thoughts and feelings. I feel as though I'm betraying someone in some way but I don't know who."

"How do you mean, betraying?"

"I don't really know how to describe the feeling. I sometimes feel as though there are dozens of little 'me's' hidden away inside. It's as if all the different people I have had to become so that I would be acceptable to those around me are all separate entities within me rather than being part of me as a whole. I feel all full of fragments of me rather than being a single, whole me. I know it sounds crazy and I probably am but that's the closest I can get to explaining how it feels. Then if anyone gets close to any one of the hidden 'me's', I feel threatened and somehow as if I am betraying the privacy, almost the right to existence, of that particular 'me'."

"Can you tell me anything of the first 'me' you can remember? Was that the 'me' who was with your parents when they were still alive?"

"That was the happy, carefree me. We were so complete, my parents and I. All we needed was each other. There was always so much love and laughter then. When I think of those days, all I see is sunshine - warm, brilliant, dancing sunshine. My mother was so tiny, so vibrant, so beautiful and my father was so very handsome, tall, strong, and beautiful. They were both so beautiful inside and that came out in a kind of radiance. They exuded their love. It poured from them and all those around them couldn't help but be touched by it. I lived with it and in it for ten gloriously happy years. It was almost as tangible as the food we ate and just as important. I think I was as near to being perfectly happy as it's possible for any human to be. And then they were gone. No warning, nothing. They just were no more. The happy me died with them. My life was over. *That* life was over."

"And that is when you went to live with your aunt and uncle?" enquired Paul.

"Aunt Mildred and Uncle Douglas!" Beth spoke their names with surprising venom, enunciating each syllable, spitting them out with considerable force.

"You seem to have very strong feelings for them, although very different ones from those you have for your parents," commented Paul.

"I *wanted* to love them, but they wouldn't allow it. They didn't like me, they didn't want me, they scarcely tolerated my presence in their house. And that's all it was - *their* house! It was never a home, certainly not to me and I'm not sure it even was to them. They just seemed to be in it and not a part of it in any way. There was no comfort there. Oh, it was nicely furnished and all that, don't get me wrong. But there was no emotional comfort. There was no sense of ease or of belonging."

"And which 'me' lived there with them?"

"There were several of us by the time I eventually left but at first there was just the shameful me."

"Shameful? In what way?"

"Well, for a start, I looked far too much like my mother for Aunt Mildred's comfort. She herself was tall and heavy, plain and dowdy and she bitterly resented my mother's petiteness and beauty, seeing it as an insult to her famous - or should it be infamous - god who couldn't and wouldn't tolerate frivolity in any guise. And to Aunt Mildred, good looks were the height of frivolity. I was a constant reminder of the sister she outwardly pretended to accept but secretly hated with a deep bitterness and resentment.

"Coupled with that was the fact that I was a Catholic - my father had always been one and my mother converted when they married. My aunt never forgave my mother for what she thought of as her betrayal of her religion. To Aunt Mildred, Catholics were nothing short of heathens and she was outraged at my mother's so-called desertion of their Unitarian faith."

"Did she try to get you to change denominations?"

"No, to give her her due, she allowed me to attend the Catholic church and even arranged for me to go to the convent in our town. But I was never allowed to discuss school or church at home and was always made to feel as though my being Catholic was a source of great shame, to her as much as to me. She seemed greatly affronted by it and by me. I often heard her and Uncle Douglas talking at night when they thought I was asleep and she always referred to me then as 'the heathen', never by name."

Beth sat back in her chair and closed her eyes, as if trying to block out the vision of those painful, lonely years. Tears oozed from the corners of her closed eyelids and trickled down her cheeks. Paul reached forward and tucked a large, white handkerchief into her clenched fists. The look he threw to Patrick as he straightened up was one of deep compassion and he saw that it was reflected in his friend's face. He found that it was necessary to swallow quite hard a couple of times and quietly clear his throat before he was able to continue speaking.

"How did she refer to you face to face?" he asked when he was confident that his voice wouldn't betray his deep emotion too obviously.

"If she used my name at all, it was in full. She would sometimes call me Elizabeth, but never Beth. That was far too frivolous! But as there was an Elizabeth mentioned in the Bible and she was a good and godly woman, then Aunt Mildred could bring herself to utter the name occasionally. But usually she avoided calling me anything if she could do so."

"And what of her attitude towards you? How did she treat you on a day to day basis?"

Beth opened her eyes and looked for some minutes into the fire, trying to focus on the memories, so long stored away and so reluctantly, so painfully being brought to the surface again.

"Mostly, I think she was polite. Yes, that's it. Dutifully polite, as she would be to some stranger who had come under her roof. She did whatever was necessary to be done to provide for my daily care - food, clean clothes etc. - but that was about as far as it went. She never touched me at all, I don't think, from the day I started living with them. I don't ever remember seeing a smile on her face and there were most decidedly no words of encouragement or comfort or anything like that. Plenty of reprimands whether they were justified or not! And endless assurances of my everlasting fate of hellfire and damnation!"

"And your uncle? You've hardly mentioned him at all. How did he figure in your life? Did he never defend you or was his attitude the same as hers?"

"Uncle Douglas?"

Again Beth looked reflectively into the flames, thinking deeply, trying to capture the essence of that strange man, her uncle by the fact of his marriage to her aunt, but alien by nature.

"It's strange but when I say 'Aunt Mildred and Uncle Douglas', it's as if I'm just giving Aunt Mildred her full name. I don't see him at all. Now I think of it, he was always such a peripheral character, drifting somewhere in the background. He didn't seem to have any substance at all. Aunt Mildred was the dominant one in that relationship, as she was in every one she formed, whatever its nature. I don't recall that he and I ever had a conversation in all the years I lived there. I guess at the time it seemed natural, somehow, but looking back now I realise how abnormal it really was."

Beth fell silent, absorbed in these new thoughts. She had never thought of her aunt and uncle as individuals before but now saw them as desperately sad people, living an empty sham of a life. No, not even a life - barely an existence. She closed her eyes once more and let her mind drift, not holding on to any thought as it entered her mind but just letting it flow through and out the other side. In the background, she could hear Patrick and Paul praying softly and she let the sound of their voices wash over her. She didn't have the energy or the inclination at this point to focus on anything.

It was as though the act of wilfully concentrating on her past experiences had sapped all her mental and emotional strength. She didn't even want to know - indeed, didn't dare think - what her two kindly counsellors might think of her now.

After some moments, Paul spoke, tentatively at first and then more positively as he progressed.

"The Lord is showing me a picture," he said. "I see a very large church-like structure. It's bigger than any cathedral I have ever seen and yet it isn't like our general conception of a church building. However, perhaps it will come to me what it actually is.

"At the very back of the building, tucked down behind the very last pew, I see a little girl. She has long dark hair done up in pigtails. She is crouching down with her head and face buried and she is wearing a thick, dark cloak, I think it is. Yes, a very heavy dark cloak which is covering her almost completely, only her pigtails can be seen dangling down from the sides of her head.

"Now I am seeing the front of the church and there are very wide, deep steps. There is no altar and there are no other outward trappings of a normal church, except a huge, absolutely plain cross made from a beautifully grained wood. It's almost as if the wood itself is alive. There is an inner radiance to it that makes it positively glow with light."

He paused for a while, his eyes firmly closed, a little smile creasing the corners of his mouth.

"It really is alive! The Lord Jesus has just stepped out from the cross, as though He were the cross itself. Now He is walking down the aisle towards you, for the child is you, Beth. She is the 'shameful' you of which you have been speaking. The Lord is holding out His hands to you and the look of love on His face is almost more than I can bear to see. He *is* Love.

"He wants you to raise your head and look at Him. Can you see him?"

"Yes," whispered Beth, tears now pouring down her face, her hands outstretched.

"That's it," Paul said softly. "Reach out your hands to Him. He wants to take that cloak of your shame from you. It has no place on you. It is all falsity. You are His child and He loves you with a love that no-one else can give. Can you feel His love? I can feel it pouring from Him like a giant, cascading waterfall and yet its gentleness is beyond description."

Beth sat, unable to speak, as the waves of love washed over and over her, soaking into her being as new rain pours into a parched desert, awakening it from its scorched slumbers and releasing all the dormant seeds to spring into new life. So her heart responded to the inpouring love, leaping within her with a joy she had never experienced before.

"Can you see anything, my dear?" Patrick asked gently.

"Yes", whispered Beth. "But I scarcely know how to say it. I see a huge chair, more like a throne really, and Jesus is sitting on it. And He's .... He's ...." She stopped and shook her head, too moved to continue.

"Say it, dear. What is He doing?"

"He's holding me, the little me, on His knee. He has His arms around me, gently rocking me and stroking my hair." Her voice broke with emotion and she could no longer say anything.

Patrick and Paul opened their eyes and gazed at Beth. Her tears had stopped and her face was radiant and glowing. Then she opened her eyes and looked at them both in wonderment.

"It was *real*. It *was*, wasn't it!"

"It was and it is and it always will be," replied Patrick. "That was the Lord's special gift to you and it can never be taken away from you. What He has done is to remove that false shame from the little girl in you. The things that were said and done to you, as a child, that caused you to feel shame - uncalled for, unjustified, unnecessary shame - cannot be erased. They happened. The words were spoken. But your reaction to them has been altered. Your memory of them has been healed. When you think back on those times now, you should feel no shame, for the Lord has taken that from you and it is no more. This is the meaning of inner, or soul, healing - Jesus coming into the middle of your hurts and taking the pain upon Himself so that you can go forward, free from those shackles, free to become the person God created you to be.

"And how does it feel?"

"Wonderful!" Beth cried. "Absolutely wonderful!! Oh, I can't thank you enough for what you have done for me!"

"It's the Lord who has done all the work, my dear," said Paul. "We just held your hands, acted as 'jump-leads' for the Lord, so as to speak. And we were - and are - delighted to do so."

"May I suggest," interjected Patrick, "that we now take ourselves off to the kitchen for a cup of coffee? I'm sure we could all do with one right now. But before we do there are a few details to tidy up. You realise, of course, I'm sure, Beth, that this is still very much the beginning. I gather there are some other 'me's' that need to be discussed but I think the biggest hurdle has been overcome. I'm certain it will be easier now for you to open up and let the others emerge into not only the *day*light, but the Lord's light. The next stage after that will be forgiveness. But that will not be today for I feel you have had enough today to be going on with. Any more might be too much for you. A step at a time is always the wisest way to proceed.

"So, my dear friend," he said to Paul. "If you would like to close with a prayer, we will withdraw to the kitchen and physical sustenance!"

When Paul had finished his prayer, they all stood up and stretched hugely. Then Paul turned to face Beth and opened his arms wide. With a big beaming smile on her face, she stepped forward to be enveloped in a massive, tender hug such as she hadn't experienced in the last fourteen years. After a few minutes, she felt a light tap on her shoulder and a heard a timid, "My turn next," from Patrick. Laughingly she drew away from Paul and threw herself into Patrick's outstretched arms. They shared a loving hug whilst the two men exchanged looks of joyous delight over the top of her head.

13

"Beth, my dear, I'm afraid I shall have to leave you to your own devices this afternoon. Paul and I have rather a lot to discuss and I have some correspondence that really needs my attention," Patrick said, rather apologetically.

They were all gathered around the kitchen table enjoying a late-morning coffee whilst Susan busied around them preparing lunch. The delicious aromas of home-made soup and a boiling-bacon simmering away in two large saucepans on top of the Aga made Beth's stomach rumble. Breakfast suddenly seemed a very long time ago. Perhaps it was a reaction to the deeply emotional experiences of the morning or perhaps it was simply the cosy warmth of the kitchen, but she felt decidedly soporific.

"I'd love to be able to suggest that you take the time to go out and do some sightseeing but quite obviously that just isn't possible, especially considering the things Bridie was telling us yesterday. It is far too dangerous for anyone to know where you are just now, for you never know who-knows-who and word can spread with quite terrifying speed when you don't want it to. So all I can suggest is that you have a quiet time in your room - there are plenty of books of all descriptions in this house to choose from, should you feel like reading - or I'm certain Susan wouldn't have any objections to your stopping here in the kitchen with her. Paul and I shall be needing the study or you could have spent your time in there.

"I'm sorry that your movements, even in the house, must be so restricted during daylight hours," Patrick continued. "But your safety is of paramount importance. I sincerely hope that this house, meant to be a place of sanctuary for you, doesn't in fact begin to feel like a prison. It can't be easy for you, I am only too aware, but a little patience will help to make the time until your 'release' go more quickly, I trust."

"Please, don't concern yourself so about me," implored Beth. "I can't begin to put into words what your kindness means to me. Just being here, amongst such delightful company, is a tonic in itself. But to be receiving your wonderful help and counselling as well ... Well, I really can't express my thanks.

"Yes, it's true that I would love to get outside in the fresh air - even in the gale that is raging out there right now! - but I appreciate the feeling of safety too much to be remotely tempted to take any risks. So I am more than content to be snug indoors and will, in all probability, take you up on both suggestions. I don't want to get in your way at all, Susan," she said, turning to the older woman, who was busy checking the soup for seasoning. "But I would love to have the chance for another chat with you. You and Bridie are so alike and both such delightful storytellers. I could never tire of hearing the various tales of your childhood. And if I get in your way, then I would simply go up to my room to read or rest. I must admit that I am still in need of a lot more sleep than I would normally have. I guess it's all part of the healing process."

"Sure, you'd never be in my way," said Susan, adding liberal amounts of freshly ground pepper to the soup and giving it another stir. "And if you were, why I'd just tell you to be off, so I would."

"You wouldn't and you know it, you old fibber," laughed Patrick. "There's nothing you like more than a good old gossip except maybe a glass of sweet sherry or three."

"Away with your cheek," Susan remonstrated. "Or, priest or no, I'll set about you with me broom, so I shall. I'll not be maligned in me own kitchen. And if you've any fondness for your food, and we can all see just how much you do have, then you'll watch your manners or there'll be soup and bacon for the others and bread and water for you, so there will be, you cheeky man!"

The sound of the front door bell ringing was only just audible above their laughter.

"Come on, woman," Patrick called. "You're on your feet and closer to the door. Go and answer it. Quick."

"And how would you like to be called 'Quick' if 'twasn't your name?" retorted Susan as she left the room in an exaggerated huff.

"You're a wicked old so-and-so, Pat," said Paul as he wiped his eyes with his handkerchief. "I don't know why that woman stays with you, I really don't. But I tell you, you're right, Beth, when you said that it is a tonic just being here in this house. I laugh more here than anywhere else. It's a good thing I'm only staying a few days because I don't think my sides would hold up to much more of this. They're ready to cave in now from over-exertion."

The kitchen door burst open and Susan's voice rang out, "Will you look who I've got here?" and she scurried into the room, holding the hand of a young man, fairly dragging him through the door behind her.

Patrick leapt from his seat and threw his arms around the young man.

"John," he cried. "Aw, man, you're a sight for sore eyes! Tell me, what are you doing here? We weren't expecting you, lad. But what a joy that you are here, though." He gave him another monumental bear hug.

Beth watched this scene with amusement and amazement. She knew by now that Father Patrick was a man of considerable emotion but she had not witnessed a display of such intensity before. She looked in some wonderment at the source of his effusiveness and saw a youngish man, probably in his early thirties, with hair the colour of ripe wheat and eyelashes like spun gold, framing eyes of the most beautiful, soft cornflower blue - eyes that danced with delight and laughter. His fair skin had flushed a rosy red with the warmth of his emotion, his very white teeth enhancing a quite dazzling smile. He was of a slender build, some inches shorter than Father Patrick so that his head was thrown back as he looked up at the older man, and was so obviously a relative of some description for, despite the difference in their height and build, their facial features were a mirror image of each other and the love that poured from each to the other could only be that of close kinship.

"My manners, my manners!" cried Patrick. "John, you must meet my guest. Beth, this is my dearest, most favourite nephew, the finest young man in all the world!" He released his captive and turned him slightly to face Beth.

John's eyes were still dancing and his smile still flashing as his gaze sought Beth's, then they froze and a look of shock and horror registered on his face - just for a fleeting moment but long enough for Beth to see and recoil from his look. She was totally unaware that her own broad smile had added a grotesqueness to the swellings, bruises and stitches that adorned her face so that she looked like some awful caricature. Already, in three short days, Susan, Patrick and Paul had become so accustomed to her appearance that it scarcely registered on their consciousness any longer.

Immediately sensing the change in atmosphere, Patrick stepped forward to Beth and, taking her hand, drew her up beside him, slipping his arm around her waist and holding her tight against him.

"My dear, forgive me, please. I am a silly old fool sometimes and I do tend to get carried away. John, forgive me. I would have forewarned you had I known you were coming but the unexpected sight of you drove all sense and sensibility from my old mind.

"As you can see, poor wee Beth is not at her best, although she is making very good progress and is well on the way to recovery and I am rabbitting on because I am so angry that I have caused you both embarrassment and in particular you, dear Beth. Just now I feel a very silly old fool and hope that you really will forgive me, Beth. I wouldn't intentionally hurt you or embarrass you for the world, you must know that."

Beth slipped her arms around his ample middle and buried her face in his chest. Then she looked up at him, her heart tender at the look of consternation and mortification on his face. She smiled gently and reached up to stroke his cheek.

"Dear Father Patrick, I know you wouldn't and of course I forgive you. And, John?" she released her right arm from around Patrick's waist and extended her hand towards a most uncomfortable looking John. "I am very sorry to be the cause of your discomfort. I guess I must have come as quite a shock to you - hardly what you were expecting, I'm sure. However, I am very pleased to meet you."

"And I am sorry and more than a little embarrassed at my reaction to first seeing you," John took Beth's extended hand and shook it warmly, his smile genuine and sincere. "I assure you that I am not usually so insensitive and, knowing my uncle as I do, I should not have been so surprised, as one never knows just who he is sheltering at any one moment. I trust you will forgive me, also?"

"Of course," answered Beth, unaware that her hand still lay firmly within John's. Neither was conscious of the look that passed between Patrick and Paul, over their heads, a look that said, 'Well, who knows, eh? Who knows?'

Susan interrupted the proceedings by exhorting them all to

take their places at the table so that she could serve up the lunch, assuming correctly that John would be more than happy to join them for their midday repast.

"So tell me, young man, what brings you here so unexpectedly?" Patrick said as he put his soup spoon down and reached for the salt cellar, only to receive a sharp rap across his knuckles from Susan.

"There's more than enough salt in the soup and you know all too well what Dr Kearney said about salt and your blood pressure. So just you leave that where it is, do you hear me now?"

"You're a hard woman, Susan."

"But at least I care about your health, don't I? And I'm a good enough cook, if I say it meself, that you don't need all that salt in your food to make it tasty."

"Ah, you are good to me, Susan. So you are. And now, John, before we were so violently interrupted," he winked at Susan, "you were going to tell me the reason for your visit. Not that you would ever need a reason, for you're as welcome here as if it were your own home, you know that."

"I do indeed, Uncle Pat. But you know me, I just can't keep away for long. And as usual, I'm only here for the cabaret! Your double act, you and Susan, is the only thing that keeps me going. It's a hard world out there, you know, and if I didn't come here for my regular dose of comic relief, sure I don't know how I would cope."

"I just don't believe this." Beth put down her spoon and sat back in her chair. She looked around the table at the other four, shaking her head and chuckling with incredulity. "You guys are crazy! The lot of you! You're all as mad as each other. I've never come across people like you before and I don't think I have ever laughed so much in all my life."

"You will get used to us," laughed Paul. "And for your own good I think it would be wise that you do, as soon as possible."

"You may well be right," answered Beth. "You may well be right."

"Seriously, though, Uncle Pat," John continued. "I'm on my way to Dublin to visit the family before Christmas. I actually live in Donegal, Beth," he nodded his head in her direction, "where I have an art gallery. I also have one in Dublin - which is my family home, by the way - but I have a very fine young manager who runs that one for me as I find that I now much prefer the quieter life in Donegal to the bustle of Dublin.

"A woman who lives here in Belfast had asked me to try to obtain a painting of a particular local scene. She had seen some others that I had in the gallery, done by a local artist, when she was on holiday in the summer. Apparently she had spent her honeymoon in Donegal and she wanted the painting for her husband as a silver wedding anniversary present. I was able to get it done for her and it had to be delivered today at the latest as a surprise for their celebrations tonight. So I used the occasion as an excuse to drop in on you before heading off down to Dublin."

"Surely you'll not be making the journey today in this filthy weather?" Patrick asked. "You must stay over at least tonight. I'm sure that Susan can get a bed ready for you in no time at all."

"I don't want to put you to any trouble, Susan, but I was rather hoping I could stay, just for tonight."

"As if it would be any trouble," replied Susan. "Sure, your room is ready already for Christmas. I just have to make up your bed and that won't take but a few minutes."

"Christmas!" cried Patrick. "Oh, goodness. I'd quite forgotten that you are coming to us this year."

"Is there any problem with that?" enquired John. "If there is, I'm sure Aoife could squeeze me in somewhere. All my family are going to my sister's in Waterford, this year," he said by way of explanation to Beth, "but for myself, I chose to come to Uncle Pat's."

"No problems whatever, I assure you," answered Patrick. "Actually, this works out just grand for I've been a little concerned about poor wee Beth here, being lumbered with two old fogeys for her first Christmas in Ireland and now we will have some young blood to keep her company. That will be grand, now, just grand, don't you think?"

John looked at Beth, his colour heightening just slightly. "I didn't know that you were a house guest as well. I hope you have no objections to my being here, too."

"Far fewer than *you* are entitled to," Beth replied shyly. "After all, you are family. I'm just an interloper."

"Nonsense!" retorted Patrick with considerable sharpness.

"You are most certainly not an interloper. You are my guest! They'll be no more talk such as that from you or anyone. Understood?"

Beth was too stunned by his tone of voice to answer. She hung her head, not daring to took at him or anyone else in her embarrassment.

Patrick reached over and pulled her hands from where they were clenched in her lap. He squeezed them between his own great 'hams'.

"Oh, now, I've done it again! I've upset you when that was the last thing I wanted to do. I just couldn't bear to hear you speak of yourself in such a deprecating manner. You may only have been here a few days and you may never have heard of any of us before you came here, but I feel as though you've been part of our lives forever. It feels so natural and right, having you about the house that it came as quite a shock to hear you say otherwise. Now don't be upset, because we all love you dearly and want nothing more than for you to be happy. So take pity on an old man and give him one of those beautiful smiles of yours to take away his shame."

Beth leaned her head against his shoulder for a moment or two and then shyly looked up at him, a tremulous little smile on her lips. As he squeezed her hands more firmly, a quizzical look on his face, so her smile broadened until her lovely eyes were dancing and the discomforting atmosphere that had built so suddenly in the room was dissipated in an instant. Everyone relaxed and the easy camaraderie was restored.

14

After lunch, Patrick and Paul took their coffee through to Patrick's study, leaving John and Beth still at the kitchen table and Susan clearing away the lunch things and loading the dishwasher. When she was finished, she excused herself to go and make up John's bed and finish off her cleaning upstairs, refusing all help from Beth, as usual.

"You're here to get well, not clean house, young lady," she admonished as she went out the door, closing it after her. A little privacy won't do those two any harm, she thought to herself as she scurried upstairs.

Beth poured them both another coffee and then resumed her place at the table, surprising herself at how comfortable and at ease she felt in John's company. It was unusual for her to be so relaxed with someone who was little more than a stranger, especially considering the unfortunate beginning to their meeting. He seemed to be such a thoroughly nice person and so very non-threatening. It made a refreshing change from the people, and particularly the younger men, she had met in the last months, with the obvious exception of Patrick and his household.

After some minutes of companionable silence, during which Beth and John sipped their coffee whilst gazing out at the gale that continued to batter the trees and shrubs in the garden, John spoke, without looking directly at Beth.

"Do you mind my asking, and please tell me to mind my own business if you wish, what brings you here to Uncle Pat's?" He cast an unobtrusive, sidelong glance at Beth to try to judge her reaction, but could see nothing untoward in her face, which she turned slightly towards him as he started to speak.

"To be honest, it's a long story and a not particularly pretty one - in fact, it's downright ugly. I have been pathetically naïve and irresponsible and as a result, my life is now in danger and this is the only place I can be safe. Because of my stupidity and vanity, I am now little more than a fugitive with no place to go," Beth replied ruefully.

"You don't sound as though you are from around these parts

at all. Can you not go back home, wherever that may be?"

"I'm actually Canadian, although I've lived for the last two years or so in the States. But no, I can't go back because I don't have access to my passport. It's back at the house where I was living but I can never go back there again and there is nobody who can get it for me. I guess this must be a little like how it feels to be a refugee, although I doubt many refugees are as fortunate as I have been in finding sanctuary."

"Do you want to tell me about it?" John asked gently.

"Oh, I don't know. I find it so very hard to talk about myself and I seem to have been doing nothing else in the last couple of days." Beth put her cup back on its saucer and looked once more out of the window at the fierce wind and driving rain, feeling somewhat in sympathy with the bushes that were being ravaged by the elements. Then, very much to her surprise, she found herself talking, telling John everything. She talked for hours, about her childhood, about Boston, about Kevin and her sham of a marriage, about Michael and the very real threat to her life. Unconsciously, she accepted John's handkerchief when her tears started falling softly.

Not looking at his face, she did not see the torrent of emotions that chased each other across his countenance - anger, horror, anguish, compassion. Many times he had to force himself not to cry out in protest at the things she was saying, fearful that any sound he made might destroy her confidence. Finally, she was spent. Her story was told and she found that the shame she fully expected to feel, felt was rightfully hers, just wasn't there. She turned to look at John and at the sight of the expression in her eyes, his heart lurched in his chest and he felt an overwhelming desire to pull her to him, to enfold her in the safety of his arms and to never let her go. Instead, painfully but successfully exercising absolute self-control, he smiled gently.

"Thank God for Bridie," he said, when he felt calm enough to speak. "At least she was able to bring you to Uncle Pat. For all he is my uncle, I have to admit that he is an exceptional man and he does exceptional work. My admiration for him knows no bounds."

"I can quite understand why," replied Beth. "He is the loveliest man I have ever met and the most caring, closely seconded by Paul. I don't know what I would have done without them. They really have saved not just my life, but my sanity as well.

"It's strange, but before I came here, I had never heard of Christian healing, counselling or prayer ministry. When your uncle first mentioned it all to me I was terrified. For a start, it meant that I would have to talk about myself and own up to all manner of horrid things that I had pushed deep inside me for so many years. I just didn't see how I could possibly do such a thing - and so soon after coming here, too. It seemed far too much and far too soon.

"But looking back on, what - three days, no more, I can see already that it was not only the right thing to do but the right time, too. If I had not met your uncle, either until much later in my life or never at all, and had not had the chance of this help, I shudder to think of the damage that my association with the Brady family would have done to me. I'm realising already, from the little I have experienced so far, that the mind is capable of the most amazing feats of self-preservation. It will bury no end of hurts and damage deep within our subconscious in an attempt to alleviate the awful mental pain but it really is only papering over cracks. And now I can see that the only way forward is, as your uncle has explained and I have already glimpsed, to ask the Lord to heal the damage caused by past events and thereby remove the hurts bound up in our memories of them.

"I'm just amazed, now that I know of this, that everybody doesn't know and therefore benefit from it. It should be part of the standard education or something!"

"It should be preached from every pulpit in the world," added John. "I, too, have been on the receiving end of Uncle Pat's ministry. Nothing as serious as your situation but nevertheless, deeply painful at the time. Some years ago, I had a broken engagement that left me with suppressed, buried hurts, doubts and lack of self-worth. Outwardly, to all except Uncle Pat, as it transpired, I was still good old, cheerful John, relieved at the narrow escape, etc. But my dear old uncle knew me too well to be fooled. So he had me up here to stay for a few days and he showed me his bags of tricks, so to speak.

"Like you, I was terrified because I felt so vulnerable and so ashamed of my weakness and failure. I felt un-manned, emasculated. But soon I, too, was blessedly healed and my whole life was turned around. From being a good conscientious Catholic boy, off to Mass at the drop of a hat, I became a deeply committed Christian. I can tell you because you will understand, that when I received my inner healing I actually saw the Lord Jesus standing before me. He was holding out His hand to me, with such a loving, tender and understanding smile. It was an invitation for me to put my hand in His. He wanted me to give myself to Him. He was asking me to and I figured that if He wanted me to be His friend, who was I to say no!?

"Since that day, although things haven't been all plain sailing, by any means, my life has been transformed. Now I am able to ask the Lord into every aspect of my life; my home, my business, my leisure, everything. Too many people think that by being a committed Christian, by having the Lord at the head of your life then it's all dour piety, a bit like your aunt, from what you have said."

"A lot like my aunt," laughed Beth.

"But that couldn't be further from the truth!" exclaimed John. "As my faith grows and deepens and my confidence in the Lord grows with it, I find it becomes easier and easier to allow Him to do the things for me that He not only wants to do but has promised to do. He *delights* in doing things for us. And furthermore, He always does the *right* things for us, when we are actually willing to allow him, for He knows far better than we do just what we really do need. And just for good measure, He has the most wonderful sense of humour. I can promise you, Beth, that if you, too, ask Him to be Lord of your life, then things will never be dull!"

"I hope you're not expecting any commission!" Beth and John spun around to find Patrick leaning against the door frame, grinning all over his face. "Sure, that's a grand selling job you're doing there, my boy. And if I'm not careful, you'll be doing me out of a job."

"Not a chance, Unc!" John laughed. "I could no more do what you do than you could sell paintings! And how long have you been standing there eavesdropping?"

"Not long enough to hear any confessions, although that *is* supposed to be my line of work. I've just come along to ask if you'd like to join Paul and me in the study for a little drop of the O-be-joyful? I have a sneaky suspicion that Susan would like access to the kitchen and I'd be grateful if you could arrange it so that she can - or at least, my stomach would be grateful. She's been too polite by far in not disturbing you two but if we don't want to have to fend for ourselves or go out for fish and chips, then I think we had better let her back into her domain. Come along now. Paul's doing the honours."

Outside in the hallway, they found Susan waiting, sherry glass in hand. Both Beth and John started to apologise at the same time, only to be hushed with a smile and a 'bless you both' as Susan bustled into her kitchen, humming a sprightly tune, a lightness in her step that she herself hadn't experienced for quite some time.

15

Just after eight o'clock that evening, Dermot Kearney arrived, ostensibly to check on Beth's progress, but also to spend some time with his friends. He pronounced himself well pleased with the improvement in Beth's injuries but insisted that she have an early night, especially as she was undergoing counselling, as well. He felt that the emotional exertion was particularly draining for someone in her physical condition and so, having said her goodnights all round and collected a cup of hot chocolate from the kitchen on her way, she gratefully climbed the stairs to her bedroom. It seemed that as soon as Dermot mentioned the word 'sleep', she was suddenly aware of just how tired she really was.

After Beth's departure, the four men chatted together amiably for a while, until Patrick noticed that John was getting a little restless. He arose from his chair and stretched luxuriously.

"Come on, lad," he said to John. "Let's you and I take ourselves off to the kitchen where you can fill me in on the latest goings-on in your life. These two both look in danger of lighting up their filthy old pipes, so we'll leave them to stink the room out and pickle their brains a little further!"

"At last!" cried Paul. "I thought we'd never get rid of them. Now we can smoke in peace." He and Dermot eagerly dug in their jacket pockets for pipes, tobacco pouches etc. "Have you time for a game of cribbage while we puff?"

"Most certainly," replied Dermot, as he lit his pipe, drawing deeply on the stem and blowing great clouds of aromatic smoke in Patrick's direction.

"All right, all right. We're off," cried Patrick, his hands thrown up in mock horror and surrender. He and John quickly fled the room, a deep rumble of laughter following them down the hall to the kitchen. "Actually, I don't mind their smoking in the least. I just wanted the chance of a chin-wag alone with you. I don't see enough of you, lad, so I must make the most of the few times we do get together."

They found the kitchen deserted when they got there, Susan having retired to her room for the evening and her nightly dose of television. But, true to form, she had left plates of sandwiches and cakes in case anyone should feel peckish after the enormous dinner she had provided.

The curtains were closed against the dark and the fierce weather and the room was cosy with the warmth from the Aga. The smell of bread, freshly baked that afternoon, still hung in the air, blending enticingly with the aroma of one of Susan's famous stews, simmering in the low oven of the Aga, where it would cook very gently all night.

Patrick poured two glasses of Guinness and handed one to John as the two men settled themselves at the kitchen table.

"Tell me," said Patrick, leaning back comfortably in his chair, "how is the world treating you these days? Business good, is it?"

"Well, at this time, with the run up to Christmas, we've been pretty busy both in Donegal and Dublin. It's encouraging to see the business surviving the recession. Things looked a little dodgy there for some time, what with people not spending on luxuries, and one has to admit it that my line of business is very much in the luxury end of the market. People can always do without a painting or two but they can't do without food and the recession has hit the monied folk as hard as it has 'Joe public'. But things are definitely picking up again, certainly for me and mine. I do know of several others who have either gone down the tubes or are really struggling."

"It strikes me that your 'honest-to-goodness' approach to business is paying dividends. You are trustworthy and scrupulous, not out to do anyone down or take unfair advantage of your customers. People recognise this and that makes them want to come to you for their requirements. Even if they don't know what it is that makes you different from the rest - and we know, you and I, that having the Lord at the head of your Company is the difference - they recognise something, somehow intuitively sense, that at Dennehy's they will get quality goods and service at a fair and equitable price. It doesn't surprise me in the least that you are succeeding where others, especially those whose two great 'commandments' for life are 'do unto others before they do unto you' and 'thou shalt not be found out', are coming unstuck. They are getting their just reward, as you are yours. And so it should be."

John placed his glass on the table and leaned back in his chair, stretching his legs out comfortably in front of him.

"I must admit," he said, "that I have seen great changes in my Company's fortunes since I have asked the Lord to be C.E.O. By great, I don't mean that I'm making 'mega-bucks', but that business is coming my way much more frequently and usually when I least expect it, now that I'm not fretting about where the next sale is coming from or what I should be doing to drum up business. I am more than happy, now, to leave it all in the Lord's very capable hands.

"This would probably sound decidedly odd, if not downright bizarre, to anyone eavesdropping on this conversation, but it really is the truth. I get the distinct feeling that He is thoroughly enjoying running my little empire and takes the greatest delight in surprising me. If only others knew! Don't get me wrong, I still have to work and I do work - conscientiously - but there is so much more enjoyment in it for me and so much more satisfaction now that the awful pressures - and self-inflicted pressures, at that - are off me. No more of that nauseating sick panic as the month end draws nigh and I have wages to pay and creditors to settle. If things have been a little lean and money is tight, I now know that, when I least expect it, the Lord will come up trumps. He knows my needs and is more than capable of supplying them."

"It brings joy to my heart to hear of your experiences, John," Patrick said with a warm smile. "Jesus teaches us that God is more than able to provide for all our needs if only we are willing to let Him. This isn't religious nicety; it's cosmic law, incontrovertible reality, immutable truth, as are all the teachings of Jesus. All it takes is our desire, our willingness to let the Lord provide for us of His bounty, by simply co-operating with Him, by aspiring to live according to His teachings; and He will do the rest. And He will do it in ways we could never have imagined."

"I couldn't agree more, Uncle Pat. But so few people, it seems, are willing to surrender their self-will to that of the Lord, to allow His will to predominate in their lives. They seem to think that they will somehow lose all sense of personal identity, whereas in fact, they will find that they will become so much more fulfilled, if only they will give it a go. There's really nothing like it. I believe it was our old friend George Bernard Shaw who said, 'Christianity is such a good idea, I'm surprised no-one has ever tried it'. A touch cynical, perhaps, but I think I know what he was getting at.

"The more I practise this and the more used I become to allowing the Lord to run the show, the more comfortable and right it feels. I am really enjoying life now and the freedom it grants me - freedom to take time off now and again so that I can come and visit you, for instance, and not feel guilty about it and not panic that I might be missing a sale or such like. I have genuine *quality* of life now."

"Nothing missing, then, in your life?"

John was silent for a few moments, staring thoughtfully at his half empty glass before picking it up and taking a deep swallow.

"Just someone to share it all with", he added quietly. "But there again, I've asked the Lord to find the right girl for me. I'm certain that if He wants me to have a life partner - a 'companion of the Way' - then He is more than capable of bringing the two of us together. But, I confess, it's not quite so easy to be patient at times. I would dearly love to be married and have a family of my own. I'm the only one of our brood to still be unattached. The others think that I'm still over-cautious because of my past disaster, but I know that so far I just haven't met Miss Right. I do get lonely, though.

"Don't get me wrong," he added quickily at the look of concern on his uncle's face. "I've plenty of friends and don't go short of opportunities if I wanted to take them, but in all honesty, I really can't be bothered because I know they're not the right one. Maybe some day, though. Some day soon, I truly hope and pray."

Patrick placed his elbows on the arms of his chair and brought his fingertips together. He eyed his nephew over the apex of the triangle formed by his fingers. After a few moments, he spoke.

"Speaking of young ladies, what are your thoughts on our young Beth, then? You two had quite a talk this afternoon, didn't you?"

John's face instantly coloured up to a bright red blush. He flicked his eyes away from his uncle's steady gaze and cast them about the room, not settling on anything and finally dragging them back to meet Patrick's.

"That's not fair, Uncle Pat, and you know it," he said with a sigh. "You know me too well, don't you? It must be pretty obvious to you that I'm smitten already. But after all she has been through, I can't see her trusting any man again for a very long time to come, if ever. And I can't say that I would blame her, either."

"Never underestimate the Lord, John. He can literally work miracles. I know that He does not want Beth to remain damaged. Wholeness, in mind, body and spirit, is His desire for all His children and that little lady really does love the Lord. He won't leave her lonely and bereft any more than He will you."

"You're right, of course," answered John with a small sigh, akin to exasperation. "It's just that I'm all confused. A few hours ago I didn't even know that she existed and now here I am, positively captivated by a tiny scrap of a thing. Somehow all those dreadful wounds on her face make her look even more delicate and petite. She's like, oh, I don't know, gossamer, almost insubstantial, like a thistledown, that would blow away in the breeze. All I want to do is gather her up in my arms and hold her to me. If I did, I don't think I could bear to let her go again.

"Oh God, just listen to me! I sound like a lovesick school boy!"

"You're very far from being a school boy, but it definitely sounds to me as though you are in love," responded Patrick.

"How can I be? I've only just met the girl. And yet I feel I've known her for ever and a day. I thought I was in love with Abigail all those years ago, but this - this is all new to me. If this is love, why does it hurt so much? There is an aching here," he hit himself in the chest, over his heart. "And it *hurts*, Uncle Pat. It really hurts!" His eyes had filled with tears.

"It sounds distinctly like love to me."

"And I feel so angry," continued John, through clenched teeth. "Dear God, I could kill the bastard who did that to her with my own bare hands!" He squeezed his eyes shut tight and held his clenched fists against his forehead. He released a long, deep sigh and visibly relaxed his shoulders.

"No, I couldn't. Not really. But I don't think I have ever felt anger as intense as this, Uncle. It scares me, it really does."

"I shouldn't trouble yourself too much, John. What you are feeling is righteous indignation and you wouldn't be much of a man if you didn't feel as you do. The good Lord knows, I had a major battle with my own emotions when I first saw Beth and when I heard her story, not that I've heard it all yet, by any means.

So don't be hard on yourself. Give your anger to the Lord. In His hands, it will not be destructive, to you or to anyone else. And give Him your permission to do with that anger what He deems fit.

"For Beth's sake, we can take no direct action against her brother-in-law for that could lead him directly to her. Anyway, it is not our place to pass judgement. But be assured, John, that whatever happens, the Father's scales of justice will always be balanced. He knows the way and He alone knows the timing. We must commit all to Him and leave all to Him. But we can be absolutely confident in His justice."

"Bless you, Uncle Pat. Once again you have calmed me down and eased my mind. You're a pretty wise old stick, aren't you?"

"Enough of the wise, if you don't mind," said Patrick as he rose from the table, turning away quickly but not before John saw the blush of pleasure on his cheeks. "Will you have another drop of Guinness with me?"

"Is the Pope Catholic?" he said with a laugh, as he handed his empty glass to Patrick.

"Tell me, though, Unc, if you had the same feelings that I had about Beth, then surely what I feel isn't love? But at the same time, I can't believe that what you felt for her is the same as that which I feel."

"I'm absolutely certain it isn't, boy. I, too, experienced almost alarming anger - righteous indignation - and deep compassion. And I do most definitely feel a very real love for Beth, as if she could be my own child. The same sort of love that I feel for you and you know that if it had been the Lord's pleasure that my life would have been blessed with a child, then the only one I could ever have wanted would have been you. But as it is, I've probably had the best deal all round. For you and I have a truly special relationship that I think a father and son would be hard pressed to share, for we have had none of the parent-child angst that so often occurs. We have been free just to know and love each other.

"However, I do believe there is a very great difference between my feelings for Beth and yours. Speaking very much from the outside, as it were, never having been in love with a woman, it strikes me that you are very much in love and time has nothing to do with anything. But tread carefully, lad. She's still terribly damaged and dreadfully vulnerable. Whatever, she will need time to recover from the traumas of these last months in particular. Perhaps it's no bad thing that you live where you do just now. Knowing your depth of emotion and your tendency to be just a touch impetuous, a little distance will be a good thing. One gentle step at a time."

"Agreed, but that presupposes her interest in me. Somehow I don't think I would be the least bit attractive to her. I'd probably be the very last sort of person she would look at twice."

"You sell yourself short, my boy. Being as unbiased as I can possibly be, I can honestly say that you would be a very fine catch indeed. Who could want for a nicer, more decent, honest and loving person than you?"

"Can we please change the subject?" John broke in, as he squirmed uncomfortably in his chair. "Did Ma tell you that Aoife is expecting again?"

"Yes, she did. Three months ago!"

"Oh."

Just then the door opened and Dermot stuck his head into the room.

"Just to say that I'm on my way. That old crook in there has been cheating again."

"That means he's skunked Dermot yet again," Patrick said laughingly to John. "It happens every time Paul comes down but Dermot won't learn. He should stick to gin rummy. Paul rarely wins that. But he always thinks, 'maybe this time!' and loses yet again!

"Whatever, it was grand to see you, Dermot, and thank you for looking in on Beth. We're keeping her well fed and rested and she is making good progress mentally and spiritually, I sincerely hope, by the grace of God."

"Well, I'm certainly pleased with her and will possibly be taking out her stitches in a day or two. So I'll pop back, probably on Saturday. I'll pass the word that you're making slow progress but that it will still be some time before you are up and about. So just remember that you're supposedly on your deathbed and no gallivanting all over town, do you hear?

"It was good to see you again, John," he said to the younger man. "We'll see more of you at Christmas no doubt. You must come and take tea with Mary and me. It would be nice if you could bring Beth, but as things are, it wouldn't be wise now, would it?

"Don't get up, Paddy. I'll see myself out. It would hardly be the done thing for you to be seen at the door on a night such as this when you're supposed to be ill now, would it?"

With further cheery salutations, he was out of the room and away down the hall, calling out to Paul as he went. Patrick was still laughing as they heard the front door bang shut behind Dermot.

"He's a grand man, that Dermot, so he is. A fine doctor and an even finer friend. But I swear, he talks almost as much as Susan does, and that's saying something, that is."

"That's for sure, Uncle, and there's only one person I know who can talk more than Susan. So I'll be out of here and away to my bed before my ears drop off from all the listening!"

"Or before they get boxed off, you cheeky young thing!" Patrick laughed as John dodged past his chair on the way to the door, sidestepping his uncle's feigned punch.

Patrick stayed where he was for some time, thinking back on their conversation. John was the delight of his life. None of his nieces or his other nephew, lovely as they all were, were a patch on him. Nothing would give him greater pleasure than to see him happily settled with a good wife and a few fine children. Was Beth the wife for him? Lord knows, they have both suffered, he thought, although John's suffering was nothing compared with hers. Their backgrounds were so very different, John having come from a large, loving family, secure in every way. True, they had the shared love of art, but would that be enough? he wondered. Then again, the other thing they shared, probably - no, definitely - the most important thing of all, was their love for the Lord. If He has chosen Beth for John, and vice versa to be fair, then no-one would be happier than he, himself. For she was a dear and loving soul and would give herself unreservedly to the right man as John would to the right woman. All he, himself, had to do was to commit it all to the Lord - and not to interfere! The last thing they needed was an ageing priest playing matchmaker!

Again, the kitchen door opened and this time Paul came in, a beseeching look on his face.

"Will you please take pity on a chap and come and give me a decent game of cribbage. I feel like such a beast, having beaten poor old Dermot so easily. A challenge is what I need just now."

"Then a challenge is what you shall have," replied Patrick, hauling himself up from his chair. But not such a challenge as lies ahead of young John, he thought as he followed his friend down the hallway. That really will be some challenge, God bless him. God bless them both, in fact.

16

The following morning passed pleasantly for Beth, far more pleasantly, in fact, than she could have imagined. Patrick and Paul yet again absented themselves, to where she knew not, and she and John passed the time until lunch, before the blazing fire in Patrick's study. Their conversation was companionable and relaxed, flowing from topic to topic with an ease that surprised Beth. Her shyness seemed to have vanished almost completely and she found herself contributing to their discussions quite volubly. Usually she was so tongue-tied and nervous when she was with others of such a brief acquaintance and yet here she was, chatting freely and easily with someone she had met only the day before.

She took advantage of the casual nature of their chat to study John a little more closely. She liked the way his eyes crinkled at the corners when he smiled and their colour deepened from cornflower to a soft navy-blue. Yesterday, she had at first felt a little uncomfortable with the way he coloured so easily and so deeply, thinking that it was a sign of embarrassment or discomfort. But now she realised that it was just his natural colouring and was really quite endearing. In some way it seemed to accentuate the warmth of his personality, as if the goodness and congeniality of his nature radiated through his skin, transforming a pleasantly average face into one of exceptional appeal and attractiveness.

For his part, John had quite a struggle to keep his emotions in check. He was only too aware of his propensity to blush at the drop of a hat and hoped beyond hope that any excessive redness would be seen by Beth as natural, especially as there was quite a lot of accompanying laughter to their conversation. The last thing he wanted to do was to 'show his hand' and scare her off. She was so fragile and vulnerable just now and, besides, he himself was only just starting to accept the depth of his feelings. It was all so sudden and unexpected for him and she, at this stage, was in no state to be propositioned, however decently and sincerely, and most certainly not in any position, emotional or otherwise, to countenance involvement or commitment to another man. He had a lot of serious thinking and soul-searching to do before he could even dream of letting Beth know of his burgeoning feelings for her.

So John kept the conversation light and friendly, all the while drinking in Beth's beauty (in spite of her cuts and bruises, he instinctively felt he could gauge her true looks), studying her every move as surreptitiously as possible, storing every detail in his memory for future pondering and recollection. He was exhilarated at the thought of spending Christmas here with Beth. He must try to find a little gift for her, not too much to embarrass her, but just a small token that hopefully would remind her of him, with fondness, if he was lucky!

It was with great reluctance that John took his leave of Patrick and the others after lunch. He found that he had great difficulty releasing Beth's hand which she had proffered to him in farewell. The compelling urge to bend his head and kiss her lips, cut and swollen though they were, was almost overwhelming. He abruptly dropped her hand and turned with such fervour to envelop Susan in a huge bear hug that the poor woman could scarcely breathe, her ribs suffering the full impact of his unexpressable, pent-up emotion. She wildly flapped her arms, beating them feebly against his back. When he finally released her, her face was bright red with lack of air and her exertions in trying to get his attention.

"Good Lord, man," she gasped. "What ever has come over you? Anyone would think that your heart was breaking to be leaving me."

"Ah, it is, Susan. So it is. Sure, I don't see enough of you at all so I needed a big hug to keep me going 'til next time."

"Aye, well," she said, giving him a very sceptical look. "If I didn't know you better I'd think you were trying to flannel me. I still have my doubts, though. Now away with you. Get yourself off home before it gets dark. And if you've nothing better to do than to stand around, flirting with some old biddy, well, I have. Romancing is not going to wash the dirty dishes now, is it? Mind you drive carefully, so you can get back here safely for Christmas or there'll be none of my old grannie's special bread sauce for you."

"Susan, your logic defies me!" cried John, as they all roared with laughter. He was thankful that Susan had thoroughly distracted them all from his strange behaviour. He once more shook hands with his uncle and with Paul. Then, turning to Beth for a second time, he bent down and gently kissed her cheek, noting with some delight that she flushed most becomingly and her eyes brightened considerably.

"Goodbye, John," she said in a voice scarcely above a whisper. "I've so enjoyed meeting you and I really am looking forward to Christmas now." Then she turned rather abruptly and hurried into the study, leaving the others to go to the front door to see John on his way.

A few minutes later, Patrick and Paul joined Beth in the study.

"Well, my dear, do you feel you are you ready to carry on where we left off yesterday morning?" enquired Patrick.

Beth made a little grimace, wrinkling up her nose and hunching up her shoulders.

"I guess so," she replied.

"You don't sound too sure about it," remarked Paul.

"I guess I'm just a little nervous. The whole concept is still a little new and strange to me. I'm not used to 'baring my soul', although, come to think of it, that seems to be all I've been doing just lately. I talked with John like I've never talked with anyone in my life before. So maybe this next session won't be quite as bad as I feared."

"He's quite some guy, that nephew of Pat's," Paul said. "If it were in me to envy anyone anything, I think I would envy Pat his kinship with John. And yet, in reality, it's almost as though he were my nephew, too. He's called me Uncle since he was a wee lad and I feel closer to him than I do any of my own nieces or nephews. So I really have no cause to envy Pat at all, for my own relationship with John is a very special one, too."

"It strikes me that all three of you are really blessed. I'm sure that John couldn't want for better uncles, illegitimate or otherwise."

"Illegitimate?"

"Oops! Sorry! It's just a silly expression. My best friend's parents were like family to me and I always called them Aunt Sheila and Uncle Roy. Cathy's brothers thought that was really cute and called them my illegitimate aunt and uncle and I guess the expression has just stuck in my memory. I promise you, it is a term of endearment and nothing offensive is meant in any way."

"None intended, none taken!"

While they were talking, Patrick had rearranged the furniture into the now familiar semicircle and when ready, they each took their places. Again, Paul started the proceedings with a lengthy but heartfelt prayer and Beth felt that very special, new-found peace begin to flow into her. It felt so good to sit back, with eyes closed and hands open and just let the peace flow into and fill every part of her being. I could quite easily become addicted to this, she thought as the gentle waves washed over and over her.

After some minutes during which they all were silent, Patrick picked up Beth's letter to Jesus and quickly scanned the pages.

"Right, now," he said, gathering up the pages and his thoughts. "Yesterday we talked about your 'happy me' and your 'shameful me'. Are there any other 'me's' that you would like to tell us about? Any that you feel need releasing?"

Beth was still for a few moments. She forced her mind back to those desolate years in northern Ontario, feeling the all-too-familiar ache of loneliness encircle her heart, squeezing it painfully. Very quietly, she answered Pat.

"There are three that spring to mind; deceitful, secretive and lonely."

"In what way deceitful?"

"Oh, it was probably nothing too major, really. But when my aunt and uncle used to go to their church meetings in the evenings, I was left at home to do my homework or whatever chores Aunt Mildred could think of to keep me 'constructively occupied'. Sometimes, when I was feeling particularly rebellious or just plain angry with them, I would watch television, especially programmes that I knew she would disapprove of. They weren't bad programmes, but what she would call 'frivolous', her pet word for all things unacceptable to her. Laughter was the thing she disapproved of most, so I would watch comedy shows, most of them pretty awful and trite, not because I was that crazy about them but because I knew it would make her really mad if she ever found out. Needless to say, she never did. I was far too scared of her to ever let on but somehow it gave me a feeling of perverse satisfaction to be doing something that would really offend her, that would give her justification for calling me a heathen."

"Anything else?"

"No, that's it. My single act of rebellion. I know it may sound really silly and insignificant, but believe me, it was a big thing for me."

"How did it make you feel?" asked Paul.

"Strangely enough, it brought me very little satisfaction. I felt so guilty and yet I kept on doing it, not often, but just occasionally. I guess I was doing it for all the wrong reasons - not because I really wanted to see the programmes, but because I knew it would upset my aunt. I couldn't outwardly rebel in any way because I was so frightened of her, so I did that instead. I guess it's pretty childish when you think of it. I feel pretty stupid even telling you."

"What was it about her that frightened you so?" Patrick asked gently. "Did she beat you or such like?"

"Oh no! She never once hit me because that would have meant she had to physically touch me and that she would never do under any circumstances. She simply couldn't bear to touch me. I guess the thing I was most scared of was her disapproval. I had that all the time anyway but if I did something that upset her then she had a way of looking at me with such disdain, such icy contempt, that was a million times worse than any beating could ever be. At those times, she never said a word; she just looked. And that was so awful. It was so unbearably painful."

Patrick placed a couple of tissues in Beth's hands as tears were starting to ooze from her closed eyes. He looked up to find his own anger and deep sadness reflected on Paul's face. After a minute or two, Beth wiped her face and blew her nose. Taking this as a sign that she was ready to proceed, Patrick said, "Tell us about your 'secretive me'."

"Well, I guess I was secretive out of necessity, really. I couldn't have friends to the house and so what few friendships I ever had had to be kept secret. For years, all through school, I had to keep my love of art to myself because anything artistic or creative was 'frivolous' and therefore unacceptable. One of the nuns at school really encouraged me and gave me extra lessons during lunchtime, rather than after school which was the norm, so that I wouldn't have to explain any lateness at home time. I was only allowed to study art at University because I got a full scholarship and my aunt wouldn't have to fund me in any way and also it finally got me out of her hair, I guess. So in the end, she was happy to let me go - if she could ever be happy about anything, that is."

"And how did this make you feel?" asked Paul.

"It made me determined to do well at school so that I could get away from her. But really, deep down, it made me feel terribly sad. It reinforced the sense of being an outsider, of being unacceptable. I couldn't share anything at all with her because she simply didn't want to know. I couldn't even share my pain at my parents' death. I was never allowed to cry in front of her so all my grieving had to be entirely on my own, in secret. I guess that is what led to the 'lonely me'. The one created the other and the two really became intertwined, almost one."

"Is there anything else you can think of just now?" asked Patrick.

Beth thought for a few moments. "No," she replied. "I think that's all. Nothing else particularly springs to mind. Nothing of any significance at any rate."

"In that case," said Paul, "I think it best if we sit quietly and invite the Lord to come in to these areas that Beth has been describing. Let's prayerfully ask Him to infill us with His Holy Spirit so that we may see the way in which He wishes to release Beth from these hurts, so that these three aspects of her being - the deceitful, the secretive and the lonely - may be made whole."

The three of them once more closed their eyes. Beth found that this time she was more at ease. A little nervousness flickered around the edges of her consciousness but it was not as intrusive as it had been previously. She felt that she was becoming used to being prayed for, more comfortable and relaxed and therefore less aware of herself as being the centre of attention. Rather, she was aware that she was the focus of genuine love and desire for her well-being, for there was little doubt that these two dear and kindly men did indeed love her and genuinely desired her complete healing.

An overwhelming sense of gratitude flooded her senses. Tears welled in her eyes and flowed over and down her cheeks, as Patrick's words of loving entreaty on her behalf penetrated her awareness. As her tears turned to sobs, the intensity of Paul's praying increased and she could feel the great power of the sounds he was making even though she couldn't understand a word. The power seemed to wash over and through her in rhythm with her weeping, great waves pouring though her body, her mind, deep into the secret recesses of her soul.

At last her tears subsided and Beth felt a gentle peace begin to fill her, taking the place of the hurts that seemed to have been washed by her tears. Paul reached over and gently took her hand in his. She opened her eyes and turned towards him and saw that he was looking at her with eyes filled with love. His smile was so tender.

"The Lord wishes me to pass on to you these words," he said gently. "'Give Me the pieces of your life and I will give you back the wholeness.' He wants all the little pieces, all the fragments, all the broken bits and He will transform them into the whole you, stronger and better than you have ever been - your new creation. His great desire is for your wholeness and He longs to make you sound and complete in Him but He needs you to ask Him, to voluntarily give Him the broken bits with which He can work.

"I see Him looking at you with such exquisite love, beyond my capability to describe. He wants you to feel that love, His own deep personal love for you."

Beth closed her eyes as the impact of Paul's words hit her. Again she heard the same words - 'Give Me the pieces of your life and I will give you back the wholeness' - but this time it was not Paul's voice she heard for they came from within her, almost as if they were spoken inside her head. She hadn't said them, she hadn't thought them, she had *heard* them - distinctly, aloud but within! She shook her head in disbelief as though to clear her mind but again the words were repeated.

Then she saw Him. Although her eyes were firmly shut, she could see Him standing before her, His hands stretched out to her, love such as she had never imagined radiating from Him, filling her with warmth, deep into her very being.

"Beth," she heard Him, felt Him, sensed Him say. "My dearly beloved child. Come to Me."

She reached out her hands and placed them in His and then found that she was kneeling on the floor, tears pouring down her face. She cried as she had never cried in her life, tears of joy, tears of ecstasy. Deep sobs convulsed through her body but they were glorious, rapturous sobs, freeing her from the entrapment of her pain so that she laughed with delight and wonder.

Patrick and Paul sat silently watching Beth, their own faces awash with tears of relief and joy. They waited patiently, revelling in her release. Eventually she sat back on her heels, looking from one to the other.

"*He's real*!" she exclaimed. "He *really* is real! I have never in all my life experienced anything like that. I can't begin to say how wonderful He is. I wouldn't know where to begin. All I know is that I want more!"

"This is just the beginning, Beth," said Patrick.

"Oh, I know. I do realise that and I now feel a need, somehow, to actively give my life to Jesus, to make a commitment to Him. I'm not quite sure how to go about it, though."

"*Hallelujah!!*" cried Paul. "This is good news indeed! Nothing could be simpler, my dear. Just you stay where you are and we'll guide you. But first I must get some holy oil for I feel it is right to anoint you." He sprang to his feet, retrieved a small bottle from behind the cross on Patrick's prie-dieu and hurried back to the others.

Patrick stood before Beth and took both her hands in his, smiling down at her with exquisite tenderness.

"Now there's nothing to worry about, child. It's all very straight forward. The Lord is not a one for elaborate mumbo-jumbo or contortions and convolutions. Simplicity is the order of the day. The important thing is your desire, your *earnest* desire to ask Him into your life and to allow Him to have *complete* control. Is this what you truly want?"

"Yes. Oh, yes!" whispered Beth.

"Then all you need do is to tell Him so, here in front of us as your witnesses. In your own words, in your own time, invite Him to be Lord of your life. There's no need to be nervous or embarrassed. You are amongst friends who love you dearly."

Beth released her right hand from Patrick's and held it out to Paul, drawing comfort and courage from these two dear men who had come to mean so much to her over the past week. Hesitantly, a little falteringly, in a shy, quiet voice, she spoke from deep in her heart.

"Jesus, I want to give my life to You. I want You, I *need* You, to be in my life every day, in all things in my life. I know now that I can't cope alone and that You are the only one on whom I can completely rely in all things. So I commit myself, my life, my whole being to You and invite You to be the Lord of my life. I love You," she ended in a whisper.

She kept her eyes closed as she felt someone gently wiping the tears from her cheeks. Patrick's voice was deep with emotion as he blessed her and said, "Beth, my child, I anoint you in the Name of the Father who created you, the Son who loved you so much that He gave His life for you and the Holy Spirit who dwells within you", making the sign of the cross with the oil on her forehead. She felt the mark of the cross warm on her skin and its impression seemed to penetrate deep down, through her head and neck until it came to rest in her heart. She could feel it there, as if it were a real, tangible thing. The awesomeness of it left her speechless.

Patrick gently drew her to her feet and into his arms. He held her in a tender embrace before, almost reluctantly, releasing her into Paul's equally tender embrace.

"Welcome," Paul said. "Welcome to the Family of Christ. You truly are a sister of Christ, our little sister in Christ, now that you have voluntarily made this commitment. For, even though you have always been a child of God, because He it was who created you, now it is *your* reality, now it comes alive in you. And isn't it *glorious*?" he cried. "Isn't it the absolute best thing there is?"

"Oh, yes!" Beth replied, laughing with joy. "It is the absolute best! There is nothing like it in all the world!"

"Amen!" came Patrick's rejoinder. "Amen to that!

The three linked arms and danced a spontaneous jig, first this way, then that, driven by the joy, love and ecstasy that filled and uplifted their hearts. Gradually their exalted spirits came back down to earth and Patrick reluctantly said, "And now, my dear. I think that is enough for today. We mustn't overload you or wear you out. Let's off to the kitchen and see if we can rustle up a cup of tea. I think a quiet evening and an early bed is in order tonight. There's more work to do tomorrow!"

17

The next morning, Beth lay for a long time in bed after she had woken, analysing the events of the previous afternoon. She didn't think that she felt any major changes and yet there was a very definite sense of peace that hadn't been present before. She stretched luxuriously and snuggled deeper into the pillows, basking in the cosy warmth, both of the bed and her inner contentment. There was a tap at the door and Susan entered carrying a tray bearing two cups of tea. Beth struggled to sit up, drawing the blankets up under her chin, against the chill of the bedroom.

"Susan," she protested. "You shouldn't still be waiting on me like this. I'm perfectly able to get up and about properly now. I'm not an invalid. This is too much for you, surely."

"Nonsense!" Susan retorted, as she placed the tray on the bedside cabinet. "I'm as fit as a flea and you're still in need of your rest. Sure, you had a hard day of things yesterday, I'll be bound. Don't forget, I know that Father Patrick of old and he can be a hard task master when he puts his mind to it."

"It wasn't Father Patrick who was hard on me. I rather think it was me who was the toughest on myself." Beth shifted her legs to one side and patted the bedspread. Susan hiked herself up onto the bed and handed one teacup to Beth before taking the other for herself.

"Sure, isn't that usually the way of things. One of the many things I have learned from Father Patrick over the years - oh, I may just be the housekeeper but I'm not impervious to his ways and his teachings; I've shared endless hours in conversation with him, especially at the beginning of his new ministry when there was no-one else for him to share with - as I say, one of the things I have learned from him is that we are the harshest judges of ourselves, even more so than of others. And yet the Lord Himself doesn't judge us; He doesn't condemn us. We do that for ourselves, through ignorance, through fear. And I know all too well about all that, for sure, didn't I used to think that I was worthless myself."

Beth gaped at the older woman in astonishment.

"Susan, that's absolute nonsense! How could you possibly

think you are worthless? You're one of the kindest, most loving people I have ever known."

"Sure, I know now that I'm not worthless but there was a time when I really believed it. I guess I truly accepted what I had always been taught, that I was born in sin and would die in sin. There were always so many things we were taught that were wicked and evil and for which we would be punished in everlasting hell. God was always watching every move we made, ready to trip us up and condemn us. We children were always so fearful and lived in terror of the village priest. There was a time when Bridie and I thought that he could read our hearts and our minds and that he knew every little thing we thought and said and did. If we hadn't been so mortally afraid of hell we would have been too frightened to go to mass because of the old priest."

"I know what you're saying, although my own priest in Canada was a pretty benign sort of man. I guess, looking back, he was a bit insipid really, certainly nothing inspiring. But my priest at university, Father Kelly, was a really wonderful man. He was a great friend and confidant, as well. There was nothing frightening about him. Although he was very strict, he was always absolutely fair."

"Well, that's a lot more than can be said for the one who ruled our village with terror." Susan shifted her position and stretched her back, easing out muscles that had cramped with sitting awkwardly on the bed. Beth moved over in the bed and put the spare pillow beside her up against the headboard.

"Come and sit up here," she said, patting the space beside her. "We might as well both be comfortable. If you don't have to rush off, that is."

"That's much better," Susan said gratefully as she wriggled herself comfortably into the pillow. "Those two downstairs have enough food between them to feed an army and neither of them has lost an arm in the night so they're more than capable of making another pot of tea if they have need of it."

Beth laughed and leaned her head over on to Susan's shoulder in a gesture of affection.

"You are good for me, Susan, as well as to me. You make me laugh so and you make me feel as though I really belong here. My goodness, when I actually think about it, I've only been here for a week and yet it's as if I've known you all my life, you and Father Patrick and Paul. There is something about you three that I can't define but it is there - something unique, something very special, very precious. I feel really blessed just being here in this house with you all.

"Father Patrick and Paul are helping me in ways I would never have dreamed possible. But just as important to me is your caring, your nurturing and I don't just mean all the wonderful meals you've provided and this lovely cosy bedroom. You've been caring for me more like a mother than any housekeeper - 'just a housekeeper', indeed! You could *never* be that, Susan, any more than Bridie could. You both are so much more, so loving, so giving, so ... oh, I don't know how else to say it! So *caring*! It's such an ordinary word and yet the caring that you both give is so *extra*ordinary.

"I'm not very good at expressing myself but what I'm trying so badly to express is my deep appreciation for everything you have done and are still doing for me. I've become so fond of you both and you mean so very much to me. I hope I haven't embarrassed you with my soppiness but I really do want you to know how I feel."

Susan reached over and took Beth's hand, squeezing quite tightly. Beth peeked sideways to find that Susan was staring straight ahead, tears glistening in her eyes, her cheeks bright pink with emotion.

"Bless you, child," Susan's voice was far from its usual strong self. "You don't know what it means to me, either. I know that Bridie feels the same as I do. There's something about you, too, that is very special. You've brought something into our lives that we haven't had before. We've neither of us ever had any children and we've never had a young lady to look after before - you can't count that poor Mairead for she was almost as bad as she is now when she first came to that house and Bridie was never able to do anything for her other than the basics - so having you to look after - and we've both now had that privilege - has been a bonus to us in our old age. For it's been like looking after one of our own, so it has. We both feel that. I know it sounds odd, but there you are, that's the way of it."

Beth leaned over a placed a gentle kiss on Susan's damp

cheek.

"Thank you," she whispered. "You couldn't have said anything lovelier to me. I shall cherish this time together as one of my most precious memories."

"Bless you, Beth," Susan replied as she eased herself down off the bed. "But now I must away downstairs and get some work done. For here it is, almost ten o'clock and there's not a bed made or a baby bathed in the whole house."

She bustled from the room, taking the tray and Beth's delighted laughter with her.

After Beth came downstairs she breakfasted on a large bowl of delicious, creamy porridge, followed by freshly baked soda bread and lovely home-made rhubarb jam. Cradling a second cup of steaming coffee in her hands, she joined Patrick and Paul in the study where they, too, were enjoying their coffee.

"Did you sleep well, my dear?" enquired Paul.

"I had the best night's sleep in many months," replied Beth.

"And how are you feeling this morning?"

"Well, at first I wasn't really sure that I felt any different but now I realise that besides a sense of gentle peace, I feel in some way lighter, if that makes any sense to you."

"Most definitely," answered Patrick. "Don't forget that you've had a very real and very large burden lifted from you and although it was an emotional burden, it nevertheless had the effect of weighing you down so that your body would actually feel a physical heaviness. With the burden lifted, you will feel lighter and more full of energy. One of the many and great benefits of unburdening the soul!"

"Indeed," continued Paul. "The enemy is the past master at shackling people with the burdens of false guilt, false humility, false shame, unworthiness, self-condemnation, fear and any other means by which he can entrap them and keep them from the awareness of their rightful status as children of God. To give him his due - and I don't like to give him any credit of any description! - he is the master deceiver, so subtle - no, that's the wrong word, too good for the likes of him. Devious and insidious are much more appropriate descriptions. Yes, he is devious and insidious and never happier than when he has snared someone in his noose of fear.

"Fear is the greatest weapon of divisiveness that he has and it creates a seemingly insurmountable barrier between the entrapped person or people and the love of God but the key word here is 'seemingly', for the love of the Father is infinitely stronger than any bond or tie of the enemy. And by giving your life to Jesus, by asking Him to take control, those bonds are cut free and are no more! That is fact; that is reality. And what you are feeling now, today, is a little of that reality, for our work is still far from over. There's a lot more freeing yet to be done in you and *then* we'll have trouble keeping your feet on the ground!"

There was a tap on the door and Susan slipped into the room and began gathering up the coffee cups.

"I'll just be clearing up these things now and then I'll be out of your way."

She smiled sweetly at Beth as she took her mug from her.

"God bless you, child. You'll be in my prayers as I'm about my housework, as you always are."

"Thank you, Susan. I treasure your good wishes and prayers and I know they are of great help to me. Bless you."

After Susan had left the room and Paul had led the little group in prayer, Patrick once again referred to Beth's letter to Jesus.

"Before we go any further with this letter," he began, "I feel it is important to bring up the subject of forgiveness at this stage. There are two main aspects of forgiveness, as I'm sure you are aware, the first being the act of forgiving and the second, the receiving of forgiveness. They are equally important and, in truth, are often indivisible, for we cannot receive forgiveness if there is unforgiveness in our hearts. Our Heavenly Father longs to set us free, longs to forgive us our various and assorted transgressions, but we cannot be free, we cannot receive His forgiveness if we are harbouring resentment, grudges, ill-will in our hearts towards another."

Beth shifted uncomfortably in her chair, her mind shooting all over the place, pictures flashing into her mind of Aunt Mildred, Uncle Douglas, Kevin, Michael, Clementine and she felt her cheeks begin to burn with shame.

Sensing her unease, Patrick spoke gently.

"We all have areas in our lives, things in our past - distant and not-so-distant - of which we are ashamed. I like to think of that shame as the Holy Spirit nudging us, showing us that it is time to forgive; time to ask for forgiveness and time to receive forgiveness."

A little sigh of relief escaped from between Beth's partly opened lips and a slight tremor ran down her spine and tingled through her hands. She flexed her fingers and then rubbed them together as if in anticipation of what was to come.

"The Lord teaches us," Patrick continued, "in that greatest of all prayers, which I call the Kingdom Prayer and is commonly known as the Lord's Prayer, that as we forgive, so are we forgiven. As we actively forgive, actively let go of whatever feelings of ill-will we were holding, then we are free to receive the forgiveness from our Father. The reason we are unable to receive it without first forgiving is because we are already full up with unforgiveness! There simply isn't room in our hearts, our souls or anywhere else for the love and forgiveness from above until we have released the unforgiveness outwards. Then our own forgiveness - the forgiveness which our Father is waiting so lovingly to bestow upon us - can flow downwards into us from God. So, our own unforgiveness is actually the only thing preventing us from receiving forgiveness.

"You have come so far on your journey to inner well-being but I feel that your forward progress will now be aided if you are ready to forgive those in your past who have caused you pain. And you also need to think about areas in which perhaps you might need forgiveness yourself. Paul and I can't help you in this because only you know what is in your heart and in your memory.

"Do you feel the need to forgive your aunt and uncle and do you think you might be ready to do so? Do you feel it right to forgive your parents for abandoning you, however reluctantly, when you were so young?"

"How do you mean? And how can I forgive someone who is no longer alive? I don't think I understand you." Beth looked perplexed and troubled and she started to twist the cross she wore around her neck to and fro in her agitation.

"I think what Pat is really saying here," interjected Paul, "is that you might possibly have some degree of anger towards your parents even though you know that their death was an accident and that they would never have willingly or deliberately abandoned you. I recall your mentioning such feelings in your letter. By offering up forgiveness to them for this act that so dramatically and drastically changed your whole life, then you will be freed from that anger and be free to love them more fully and openly without any taint caused by anger or resentment.

"And don't worry about the fact that they are no longer in this life. We all know that they are with the Lord, so all you need do is to offer your forgiveness to Him on their behalf and He will take your prayers and use them and the power that is created by them in the way that He sees fit.

"We have to come to understand that such an act of forgiveness builds what we call a 'bridge of reconciliation' between the forgiver and the forgiven. Because that 'bridge' is of spiritual substance, it doesn't in any way alter its ability to function if one party is in this life and the other is in the next. So you can be assured that your forgiveness will be used in the very best possible way and bring about the very best possible results."

Beth released her grip on her cross and slumped back in her chair.

"Wow!" she exclaimed. "There is so much that I don't know and so much I didn't know that I don't know! How long it must have taken you both to come to these understandings. I don't know if I will ever be able to understand it all."

Both men chuckled.

"Don't worry, my dear," said Patrick. "I assure you that our lack of understanding is prodigious! But the Lord is gracious and infinitely patient. And by the gift of His Holy Spirit, He gives us that which it is necessary for us to know. And when He gives it, it is so much easier to remember because He gives not just the words but the reality of their meaning. With practise and with time, with daily devotions and study, you will more readily come to your own understandings according to your own needs and progress."

"I am impressed with your confidence in me!" Beth said with a wry smile. "I'm not so sure I have as much in myself, though." She ran her hands through her hair, ruffling the short hairs up the back of her head and giving her head a good shake. She puffed out her cheeks and then blew out a long breath. "I really do need this forgiveness thing, don't I?"

"You do, indeed," answered Paul. "We all do, regularly. Day to day, things occur that rile us, that rattle our equilibrium and we 'lose it', as they say - whoever 'they' might be! It can be something very minor or something huge but either way, if we hold on to it, it will come between us and the Lord and thereby cause an imbalance within. By releasing it in the act of forgiveness or by asking for forgiveness if we are the perpetrators of the incident, then balance is restored and peace follows in its wake.

"Lovely! So easy! So effective! But, and this is a very important 'but', we have to be prepared to *absolutely* let go of the incident, surrender it, whatever it may be. It will serve no purpose, other than to play into the hands of the enemy, to hold on to what we may have stated as a willingness to surrender but in reality - in our heart of hearts - we are actually not yet ready to do. That would be like building the bridge of reconciliation and then blocking it or even demolishing it again, which of course could cause us genuine harm in some circumstances. When God forgives us, He does so absolutely, unconditionally. With Him, it is forgotten! He doesn't remember it because He *chooses* not to remember it. That is to say, we have given our misdemeanour or our hurt to Him and He removes it from us totally. He never brings it back to beat us over the head with it. *It is finished*! And we must learn to do the same. When we forgive, we must be prepared to forgive unconditionally, absolutely, finally and permanently, or it is not, nor can it be, true forgiveness.

"And so, as Pat has already asked, do you feel the need and are you prepared, are you ready within your own heart, to take the next step?"

Beth looked from Paul to Patrick, back to Paul and again to Patrick, intently studying their faces, looking deep and long into their eyes. Then she closed her eyes and laid her head against the back of the chair. She was silent for a long time. Once again, she sighed deeply, opened her eyes and sat forward, her wrists balanced on her knees, tapping her fingertips together. She looked long and hard at a spot on the floor somewhere between her chair and the fireplace, breathing deeply and audibly. Her struggle was plain for the men to see but they remained silent, praying their own unvoiced prayers, watching and waiting for her to reach the decision that only she could make, the decision that they already knew she couldn't *not* make.

Eventually, Beth turned her head from side to side, looking

at each man in turn and then she straightened herself upright. She drew in a long, shuddering breath and then slowly exhaled.

"Okay," she said. "I'm ready."

"You're sure?" Paul enquired.

"Oh, yes. I'm very, very sure. You're right. I really don't feel I can go any further without this next step. It's silly, I know, but I'm really scared. But I know I have to do it. I *want* to do it. I *need* to do it. I just pray that I can do it properly."

"There's no 'properly' involved, child, " Patrick said gently. "All it requires is a willingness, a true *desire* to forgive and be forgiven. All you need do is simply say in your own words, from your heart, what you want to say. The Lord will do the rest. He already knows what is in your heart but He needs you to, if you like, give Him the ammunition with which to effect the forgiveness, to build the bridge. That is your part of the deal. He can't do it without your requesting, without your permission. Understand?"

"Yes. Yes, I see what you mean. So it's big breath time now and on with the job!"

Patrick reached over and patted Beth's hand and gave her a smile that brought a surge of joy and confidence into her heart.

"Take your time, my dear. When you're ready, you start. Paul and I will just sit here, praying quietly, lending our support. You have absolutely nothing to fear, I assure you. The Lord is eagerly awaiting your call for His help so that He can pour into you His blessings of love and forgiveness, of peace and healing balm. Remember, it is His great delight to give you of the good things of the Father and the greatest of these good things is His Love!"

"Thank you," whispered Beth and she turned her hand over under Patrick's so that she could give his a squeeze of acknowledgement of his kindness and gentleness towards her.

Beth released Patrick's hand and closed her eyes. She sat very tall in her chair, her hands resting in her lap, palms upturned. She took a few deep breaths to steady her nerves and, in a voice which quite surprised her with its steadiness and strength, she began her prayer.

"Dear Lord, I feel a great need within me to release to You the anger and bitterness I have held in me for so long and to ask Your forgiveness for these feelings. I can't do this face to face with any of the parties involved and so I ask that You will accept my request for forgiveness on their behalf, if this is the right way to do things."

She paused a moment to gather her thoughts and Patrick gave Paul a wink and a little grin of satisfaction, as if to say, 'she's on the right track here'.

"First of all," Beth continued, "I want you to let my parents know that I forgive them for dying the way they did and leaving me alone. I know they couldn't help it any more than I could help feeling abandoned by their deaths. And I ask for their forgiveness for being angry at them all these years.

"Then to Aunt Mildred and Uncle Douglas. There is a lot I need to forgive them for and if I went into detail, I would be here for a week at least! But I want to forgive them for not loving me, for being so horribly and unfairly strict with me, for not allowing me to have friends, for treating me as a stranger in what was, after all, my home, for calling me a heathen and treating me as such, for denigrating my parents and their memory, for simply not liking me or accepting me as the person I am. I offer my forgiveness willingly, sincerely, freely.

"I need their forgiveness, too, for thinking wicked thoughts about them, for calling them names behind their backs - but never to anyone else, only in secret - for being wilfully disobedient, for not being able to love them as much as I wanted and needed to, for resenting their discipline, for not being understanding of them and their ways.

"For all these things, Lord, and anything else I did that was not of You, I repent sincerely and humbly ask forgiveness."

Beth suddenly sat back in her chair, drained, tears flowing down her face. She was shaking with emotion and burning with embarrassment that Patrick and Paul should have been party to such a confession. Then Patrick's soft, gentle voice reached her through her distress.

"And now receive," he was saying. "Receive your forgiveness. Feel it. Experience it. Open your heart and your life and let it flow into you, soothing all the jagged ends of your emotions, washing away your shame and embarrassment, cleansing you, leaving you clean and pure. Freely you have offered forgiveness; freely receive your own.

"The Lord's word for you is 'Well done, my little one. I am

well pleased with that which has been accomplished this day. Receive of My love; receive of My life; receive of My blessing. Go forward in joy, delighting in your new awareness of Me as I so delight in you.' And He does delight in you, Beth, for I felt His delight. It was pulsing through me so strongly that I'm surprised you two couldn't see or hear it. It is a very real and very beautiful thing. Well done, indeed!"

Beth wiped her eyes with a tissue from the ever-present box beside her chair. She shook her head, almost in disbelief.

"I could almost say, 'was that it?' But I think there was a lot more going on than I could possibly imagine. For one thing, I was so horribly embarrassed and ashamed to have you two hear all that I said, and said so badly. And yet, now, I don't feel at all embarrassed. In fact, I feel relieved that I've shared this with you, that you were my witnesses.

"I didn't think anything had actually happened, mostly because of my feeling so uncomfortable. I've never done anything like this before. It's totally unlike going to confession although I somehow don't think it should be. Perhaps that's because confession always seemed a duty thing to do whereas this really was from the heart. Maybe that's the difference. But I do feel a lot better." She took a quick breath and then grinned. "Oh, I feel a lot more than a lot better! Actually, I feel great! It's almost as if my body has gone 'whoosh!' and a whole lot of garbage was gone hurtling out of me. I feel so much lighter and freer!"

"Have you any jesses handy, Pat? We'll have to tether this little lady soon or she'll be floating on the ceiling!"

"No more tethers for me!" cried Beth, laughing along with the two men. "At least, no more emotional ones, that's for sure."

Patrick pulled his handkerchief from his pocket to wipe his eyes and blow his nose.

"Oh, it's grand that the Father has given us this glorious gift of laughter. What a fellow He is, to be sure. But on a more serious note, Beth. We all know that there are still some major bonds that need breaking. We've dealt very successfully with the events of your past, but the present, or should I say the recent past, has yet to be addressed. Do you feel up to making a start on that this afternoon? I think that it's very much a case of 'the better, the sooner', if you follow me."

Beth's laughter ceased abruptly and she felt an icy shudder go through her.

"I've been trying so hard not to think of this at all, hoping that in some way it would simply disappear if I got all the other baggage out of the way, but I guess it won't go away of its own accord, will it?"

"No, my dear. That's not how things operate, as much as we might like them to. These things have to be faced before they can be overcome. So, shall we agree to the next session being after lunch?"

"I'd much rather never at all, but I agree with you, 'the better, the sooner'. This afternoon it is."

"Right then," said Patrick, "let's away to the kitchen before my stomach gives up on me and goes to live elsewhere in protest at all this neglect!"

"That man and his stomach!" Paul laughed. "Have you ever heard the like? Sure, he could live off his reserves for a month and not even see any difference."

"You old so-and-so," cried Patrick. "Some friend you are! Besmirching my good character before this lovely young lady. What will she be thinking of me now, I would like to know?"

"That you are the dearest man in all the world!" Beth thrust her arm into the crook of his elbow, squeezing it to her side. "And I love you dearly! And as for you," she said to Paul, slipping her other arm through his, "I think you are simply adorable and I love you just as much." She looked from one to the other, her eyes dancing with merriment and she burst out laughing at the looks on their faces. "And you both blush as beautifully as the other, too!"

"Enough of this frivolous nonsense!" blustered Patrick. "I'll have you know you're speaking to a priest!"

"And I'll have you know, you're enjoying every minute of it!" teased Beth.

"Away out of here! Cease and desist!"

"Balderdash and bunkum," Beth countered.

"And just where did you learn language like that?" Patrick came back at her.

"Sure, you don't think I was in a swoon all the time I was lying on the sofa with me eyes closed, do you? Sure I was after getting meself a fine Irish education, so I was!"

"Well, you ended up with a terrible Irish accent, so you did!"

"Stop! Stop!" called Paul from where he was leaning up against the edge of the open door, clutching his sides and wheezing with laughter. "You two will finish me off yet! You should be on the telly. What a double act!"

"And if you've finished with the comedy routine, your lunch is all but in ruin!" Susan's head poked around Paul's back. She cast a look of attempted serious reproach at Patrick and a big grin at Beth. "The next door neighbour's dog will be pleased with a drop of lamb stew even if you're not in the mood for it."

"Away with you, woman!" roared Patrick. "Next door's dog indeed. It'll be the job centre for you if you so much as open the back door right now, let alone put my dinner over the fence. Come along, Beth. The kitchen calls! Fortification time is upon us!"

They were a sight to behold, the four of them, as they made their uproarious way down the hall to the kitchen. Two tall, well set-up men with greying hair, faces creased with laughter lines; two tiny women, one with hair like spun silver and a face etched by the years with the warmth of the character within and the other with hair as black and sleek as a raven and a face unlined and radiant, the cuts and bruises scarcely noticeable, for the joy that glowed in her eyes diminished them almost to non-existence.

18

"Tell us, as objectively as possible, what you know about Kevin." The group had once again gathered in the study after lunch. Patrick was holding Beth's letter to Jesus in his hand and had Kevin's 'little black book' in his inside jacket pocket. His voice was soft with compassion for Beth who was sitting upright in her chair, staring unseeing into the fire, twisting the cross around her neck so hard that Patrick feared she would break it. He handed her some more tissues just so that she would release her grip on the cross. She looked at him as she took the tissues and he very nearly recoiled in shock at the look of utter desolation on her face - such a vivid contrast to the beautiful bright, cheery face of the morning!

"Can you tell us about Kevin?" Patrick repeated. "How he appeared to you when you first met him? It will help us have greater insight into the depth of your troubles, for all we have to go on right now is what you wrote in your letter."

"We appreciate that this will be very, very hard for you, Beth," added Paul. "But it is important or we wouldn't ask. Take your time and please don't be the least embarrassed. You know us too well by now to be uncomfortable with us."

Beth turned her head to give him a little, weak smile and he, too, was deeply saddened to see the expression in her eyes. Dear Lord, he thought to himself, if that creature wasn't already dead I could do him a serious mischief myself for all the pain and humiliation he has caused her. Forgive me, Father, but I can't help the way I feel. No one should ever be allowed to do the things he has done, to her and to others. I'm just thankful that he hasn't got away with these deeds indefinitely and that at last he will receive full justice, full recompense for his acts.

Beth sat back in her chair and closed her eyes. She willed herself, forced herself, to go back, in her memory, to those last weeks in Boston. They seemed a lifetime ago. Surely they had happened to someone else and she had just read about it all in some sordid, cheap dime novel! But no, she had to face the reality of her own experiences, no matter how painful, how shameful, how repugnant.

Beth clutched the wad of tissues hard, breathing very deeply, exhaling quite forcefully. Then she straightened her shoulders and began.

"I didn't like him when I first met him. I thought he was arrogant and conceited. But all too soon I found myself mesmerised by him. I found I was having lunch with him even though I had refused point blank. Then, that same evening, I allowed him to take me out for dinner, something I would never have done under normal circumstances.

"But somehow, there was very little normal about him. He just walked into my life and took over. I still don't know how it happened. I, the most level-headed of people, was swept completely off my feet and no matter how much I protested, to him and to myself, I found myself going along with all he suggested and arranged.

"Before I knew where I was, I had given notice at work - a job I really loved, working for a man who treated me like his own daughter and who taught me so much more about art than I could ever have learned at university. I had said goodbye to the best friend I could ever have had, had left my lovely little apartment where I was so happy and had married a stranger - a complete stranger! And I still don't know how it happened!"

Patrick and Paul sat silently listening, scarcely daring to breathe in case the sound of their breathing disturbed Beth and broke her flow. Now that she had started, they didn't want her to stop.

"He appeared to be so masterful, so authoritative, so commanding, so certain of himself. Then we came here and I saw him in his true colours. He was little more than a spoiled brat with no authority in his own home. He did nothing but whine and snivel or make a complete fool of himself. I was embarrassed and mortified by his behaviour and I was totally humiliated by his mother and brother. They treated me in the most appalling manner. Bridie and Joseph were the only ones in that house who kept me from going insane.

"In no time at all, I found myself a virtual prisoner in what was supposed to be my new home. I had no money - he never let me have any except for the necessities of daily life. I never went anywhere on my own. I don't drive and I wouldn't have known where to go even if I was allowed out on my own, which I never was. I still don't know where my passport is. I think it is in the family safe in her study but I can't be sure, so there is no way that I can go home or get a job or anything like that.

"Only once did I have a really nice day and that was the time he took me out for a walk in the hills and then on to lunch. Most of the time he behaved himself and treated me pretty well, but he was in a strange mood for a lot of that time. Then we found out, when we got home, that Declan Conlon had been murdered the night before and we had been right by the place where his body was found. In fact, we passed by when the police and the army were still there. It could be that Declan's body was still there, as well.

"I noticed that he started acting really strange when we saw the military. He was saying things in Gaelic half under his breath and wouldn't tell me what it meant. In fact I don't think he even knew I was there half the time. It was almost as if he was on some weird drug or something like that. He was really hyper and agitated. Then he suddenly seemed to be like the man I first met in Boston."

Beth suddenly stopped talking and caught her upper lip between her thumb and middle finger, tugging at her lip, oblivious of the stitches close by. She seemed lost in thought, concentration etching a deep furrow between her eyebrows. Patrick and Paul exchanged a look of some satisfaction, pleased that she had been speaking so freely and fully.

Then Beth let go of her lip and shook her hand, pointing her index finger as if accentuating some point or other.

"That's it!" she exclaimed softly. "Now I remember. I have been trying to recall something of the previous evening but just couldn't quite get hold of it. I knew it was something important and now it's coming back to me.

"He insisted that we spend the evening together in our rooms - something we had never done before - and then insisted that he would make me some hot milk. I can't abide hot milk but as he was really anxious to do something just for me - it was his own special recipe, he claimed - I agreed. From the way he was acting I thought that this was to be a prelude to a lovely romantic evening, but the last thing I remember is drinking the hot milk. I don't know what he had put in it, but even *I* enjoyed it! The next morning I could remember nothing. He was in such an exuberant mood, so happy and elated, that I was more than a little ashamed that I could remember nothing of the previous night. He laughed it off with some fatuous comment about the Little People and true love - *please* don't ask me to elaborate. It really is too embarrassing, especially as I fell for his smooth talking yet again.

"It was then that he suggested our day out together. When we got home and saw on the T.V. news about the murder of poor Declan, his behaviour became even more bizarre. Again, it was as if he was seriously stoned on some drug or other. I had never met Declan but I assumed that the two families were good friends and was really astounded at the way he was acting. I couldn't wait to escape up to my bedroom.

"Then on Sunday, after lunch, he insisted that we all go around to the Conlon's to pay our respects. I don't know if I have ever witnessed such outrageous behaviour and I know I had never been so ashamed of anyone in my life, but to think that I was actually *married* to that caricature, that *mockery* of a human being, was almost too much to bear. He insulted the Conlons in the worst way possible, feigning such phoney grief and acting as though he was the head of the household. Why Michael or Clementine didn't intervene I shall never know. Perhaps they were too stunned by his performance, as was everyone else.

"Paddy Conlon was the first to react and he threw us all out in no uncertain terms, but not before he had called me an American whore and had spat in my face. That was the clincher for me and I think that I just opted out of the whole situation because I simply fainted! It was all so horrible and so desperately embarrassing that I simply couldn't cope with it any longer so I just passed out."

Patrick and Paul exchanged knowing looks and raised eyebrows.

"When I came to at home, their nauseating doctor was fawning all over me because Clementine was there. He gushed on about my needing tender loving care and where else could I find better than right there in the bosom of my family. I almost threw up then and there! After he and Clementine left the room, Bridie took care of me. We could hear *him* and Michael shouting from downstairs. They both sounded like crazy, mad men, which was pretty true to character! Then I fell asleep. I was so exhausted I could have slept through an earthquake.

"However, when I did wake up it was the middle of the night and I saw him getting dressed in clothes I had never seen before, all black, everything. He had a small flashlight on so I could see all he was doing. That's how come I knew where he kept that black book hidden. I didn't look at it until the morning, after his own body had been found, because I was so scared that if I got out of bed he might come back and find me looking through his things and then I really would be in trouble. I feel sick just thinking about what would have happened to me if he had caught me. I really think he would have killed me, too."

Beth suddenly slumped back in her chair, exhausted, her dreadful monologue at an end. The two men sat quietly, allowing her a few minutes to recover from the ordeal of recalling so much horror. Paul was the first to speak.

"Can you tell us what you felt when you read the book?" he asked gently.

It was a little while before Beth was able to answer.

"I don't really know. It's quite hard to say because I haven't really analysed that part of things yet. I guess I've tried to block so much out, but I'll try now if it is really important."

"I do feel it is very important because your reactions have created the blocks which now are in need of being unblocked. These reactions, these emotions, need releasing if you are to go forward in wholeness."

"Okay, I'll try," Beth replied, her voice cracking a little in her uncertainty. "I think the first reaction was revulsion, followed rapidly by total disbelief. Then came the realisation that *my husband* had done these horrific, vile, wicked, evil things. *And he had enjoyed it*!" Her voice fractured with emotion as the tears once again poured from her eyes. "He really *enjoyed* what he did! He made notes of the most inhuman, barbaric things he had done. Everything was detailed. *Everything*! Oh God, he's crazy! Oh, I feel sick! I feel so filthy and vile! So *contaminated*!"

"Anger?" prompted Patrick.

"Of course, anger!!" Beth shouted at him. "I'm so angry I could scream!"

"Then scream. Howl out your anger. Tell him exactly what you are feeling. Tell him what he has done to you by his bestial behaviour, by his abuse of your trust and faith in him, by his abuse of your wedding vows, by his abuse of human dignity. Tell him. Scream at him. Let him have it in full force. You are fully justified in feeling this anger, more than justified. It is your absolute right to be angry and I want you to let all that anger come out. *Scream* it out. *Shout it out. Howl* it out. *Hammer* your fists. *Stamp* your feet. Let your soul cry out to the Father in its pain."

And Beth howled, like a wounded animal she howled. She screamed out her anger. She beat her fists and stamped her feet. She cried out in her pain until she was finally and totally spent. And Patrick and Paul wept with her.

19

"Oh! Wow!" Beth slumped back in her chair. She ran her hands through her short, dark hair, over and over, her fingers digging painfully into her scalp.

"I am absolutely shattered! I doubt if I have ever been so exhausted in all my life!"

"That's not surprising when you consider all you have been through in the last few days, let alone the last few months," replied Father Patrick. "All that you have experienced in such a short time is more than many will encounter in a lifetime. It's almost as if a whole incarnation of experiences has been encapsulated in such a brief time span. And if that is the case, then it is my understanding and belief that the Lord has a hand in all this. For He never gives to anyone more than they can handle at any one time. It is the Father's purpose to strengthen souls, not break them. So if someone is tried almost beyond human endurance, as you have been, then it is because He has some very special work for them to do for Him. You have obviously reached the stage - at least, obviously to me - where you are ready to embark upon His great plan for you.

"I firmly believe that we all come here for two reasons - to learn certain things and to do certain things. Only the Lord Himself knows what these are but it is our job - our destiny, if you like - to discover both these purposes. I believe that you have now reached the place of embarkation upon the great and wondrous adventure of your service in the Lord's Name. Hallelujah!"

"Amen!" echoed Paul. "My dear," he said, turning to Beth and reaching for her hands, "now the adventure really begins. If you have come this far and if you love the Lord as much as Pat and I believe you do, then you will desire, above all else, to discover what is purposed for you by Him in this life. Only you and the Lord can know that of a certainty, but whatever it is, do not fear, for you are already fully equipped for the job. We all have talents, some obvious, some not quite so. You have a great gift of an artistic nature. Perhaps you should look to that sphere for your means of service.

"On the other hand," he continued, "it might be in an area

as yet undetected or undeveloped that your real talent, your real gift from the Lord, lies. When you discover it, whatever it may be, you will recognise it and all will fall into place. Your heart and your soul will react in such a way that there can be no mistake, no misunderstanding. You will know with a certainty, a surety, that you had not known before. Your soul will recognise that which is its purpose to accomplish.

"And now," Paul said, as he slapped his hands smartly on the arms of his chair, "it is my suggestion - nay, my command, if you will - that you go upstairs to your room and rest for as long as you require. This has been a traumatic time for you. Your body and your mind will be exhausted. Rest. As long as you need, rest. We can talk further later. For now, though, all that matters is that you recover your equilibrium and regain your comfort levels. Away to your room - to bed, if you need. But rest, you must. Our love and the Lord's blessings go with you. Much - so much - has been accomplished today. Praise the Lord!"

Beth arose from her chair and walked first to where Paul was seated. She leant forward and placed her arms around his neck, placing her cheek against his, the roughness of his early five-o'clock shadow tingling against her skin.

"Paul, dear Paul," she whispered. "I can't find words to express my gratitude. Please know that my heart is full to overflowing. That's all I can say." She kissed his rough cheek, the short, stubbly hairs of his burgeoning beard rasping her lips and yet causing no discomfort to her rapidly healing cuts and bruises.

Paul's arms came up and around her slender body, holding her in a grip ripe with love and compassion.

"Bless you, child," he whispered, his voice thick with emotion. "Bless you!"

When Beth released herself from their embrace, she turned to Patrick to find that he had risen to his feet, his arms outstretched to her. She moved into his enormous bear-hug, feeling the power of his love as he enveloped her in his huge arms. Her own arms could scarcely encompass him, but her heart enwrapped him, enfolded him, with her love and gratitude. Raising her face to him, she said in a soft, gentle voice, "I love you."

"And I love you," he replied. "If you were my own child, I couldn't love you more."

Beth turned herself quickly out of Patrick's embrace and ran silently from the room. The old priest raised his hand to his cheek, not really sure that she had kissed him and yet the warmth of her lips was perceptible to his touch. He sighed gently and turned towards his friend, his eyes and his heart full, but no more so than those of Paul.

Beth lay for some time on her bed, all the recent events tumbling through her mind. So much had happened to her these last few days, more than she could possibly have imagined in her wildest dreams. And yet she knew with a certainty that what had transpired was more real than anything she had ever experienced before. Surprisingly, she felt no sense of dislocation as she had come to expect in her short time with Kevin. All that had taken place these past few days was more of a reality than anything in her life to date. She had been on the biggest emotional roller-coaster imaginable and yet she felt amazingly calm. Her emotions had run the gamut from A to Z and back again and yet she felt completely in control. Maybe, just maybe, she would survive. She *would* come through. She most definitely would triumph! With the Lord's help, she would most definitely triumph!

But there was something else, something of absolute importance that she must do. For her conscience's sake, for the sake of her self respect, she must make amends.

Rising from her bed, Beth walked slowly over to where her overnight case lay, unzipped, on the chair beside the bureau. She reached inside and withdrew the long flat box containing the icon, the gift to her and her alone, from Sean, the only other man who had loved her for who and what she was, the child he had never had.

Salvation

O come, let us sing to the LORD*!*
Let us shout joyfully to the Rock of our salvation.
Let us come before His presence with thanksgiving;
Let us shout joyfully to Him with psalms.
Psalm 95 vs 1-2

1

Patrick and Paul were enjoying a pre-dinner drink when the study door opened and Beth came softly into the room. She was carrying in her hand a long flat box that neither of them had seen before, a look of determination, of purpose, enlivening her eyes.

"I need to talk with you both," she said, as she took her usual place before the fire. "Please hear me out. I'm not quite sure how to put into words what I need to say but here goes anyway."

The two men exchanged glances of puzzlement but remained silent, allowing Beth time to gather her thoughts.

"You both know that the man I married turned out to be a multiple-murderer, a serial killer I think is what he would be called in today's parlance," she began. "I know - we *all* know - that I was in no way responsible for his depravity or his actions and yet, in some strange way, I do feel a certain sense of accountability."

"Just a minute," interrupted Patrick. "How can you possibly be held accountable for someone else's state of mind or their actions, especially those that took place months before you even knew the man existed? I don't understand your reasoning at all."

"I said that I didn't really know how to explain myself," replied Beth with a sigh. A deep furrow appeared between her eyebrows as she frowned, drawing her stitched brow up into an accent mark, making her appear both comical and quizzical at the same time. "I *know* I'm not accountable and yet I do feel a moral commitment to the victims' families. I feel that I need to do something, in some way, to recompense them for their loss at his hands. And I think that I just might have an answer of sorts but first I need to know something about the victims and their families, if that is possible. Do you know anything about them, Father?"

"Aye, a little," Patrick answered slowly, as he studied Beth's face, trying to fathom where this conversation was leading. "Of course, not as much as if they were Catholics for then I would probably know of them through the church. But I do know that they were all young, single Protestant men, all from the poorer parts of town - except, of course, for young Declan. It seems to me that so many of these young idealists who turn to violence as an answer to their problems come from the poorer elements of society. Not all, of course, but a large percentage. Whether it is due to poverty, unemployment, lack of material possessions, even jealousy of those better off than themselves, I know not, but it is a possible explanation. With time on their hands and anger and hatred simmering away inside them, things can rapidly blow out of all proportion and erupt into fanaticism and violence.

"So, yes, all the victims were young, disadvantaged men in one form or another. Their families must be having a bad time of it emotionally, if not economically as well, especially if the victims had been the breadwinners of the families. It must be devastating for those left behind not to have any idea whatever who killed their loved ones or why. With no-one claiming responsibility and the police completely flummoxed by all the deaths, they can not have even the comfort - if one can use such a word under the circumstances - of knowing who was responsible and why. It has been a deeply damaging thing for the community at large, with no end of suspicion and speculation causing even more division than there already was. No-one quite knows who to trust anymore.

"Things had settled down a few months ago after the eighth killing, when it seemed that it might have been the last. But young Declan's death has awakened all the old fears again. I hear quite a bit of what goes on that you wouldn't read about in the papers or see on the television for when something like this is happening, people close ranks and prefer to deal with it themselves. If it can in some way be resolved, behind the scenes as it were, then I think a lot of heat will be taken out of the tempers of far too many young men and things will settle down again, at least to what passes for normality these days."

"Well, I've been giving this all quite a lot of thought and I hope that what I have come up with just might be a means for that resolution," said Beth. "In here," she ran her fingers over the box, stroking its surface almost tenderly, "is something of considerable value. It was a gift to me, a wedding gift, a going away gift, a 'time of need' gift, that was for me - not *him*, not both of us, just me. My old boss, Sean, gave it to me before I left Boston and he said to me at the time that it was so that I would have something to fall back on if ever I was in great need. It was almost as if he had some inkling, some foreboding of what could possibly happen to me over here. I know that he already knew *him* but I don't think he really liked him or trusted him. That's why this was just for me - *he* never even knew about it - and now I know just what to do with it."

"Beth, my dear," interrupted Paul gently. "Not wishing to change the subject, but I can't help noticing that all your references to Kevin are simply 'him' or 'he'. You never use his name or refer to him as your husband or whatever. Is it still a great problem for you?"

"No, not a problem. I just prefer not to use his name or make any reference to a relationship with him if at all possible. Perhaps with time I shall be able to but for now I simply have no desire to acknowledge him in any personal way at all. Maybe it's all still too fresh and too painful. I'm not harbouring any hatred or unbearable anguish, if that is what is worrying you. I just am not able right now to focus on him personally. It's not a denial, it's just preference - self preservation, if you like. So please don't worry about me. I really am okay but I do need a little time yet."

"Yes, I see. That makes sense. I'm certain that with time you will feel more at peace within yourself and more detached from Kevin and all the circumstances surrounding your relationship with him. Obviously that will take time. I was just a little concerned in case there was something troubling you that we had not yet dealt with. But if you're certain that there is no major problem within, then that's fine with me. Now, tell us more about this mysterious box and its contents. It sounds most intriguing."

Beth unlocked the box and withdrew the velvet covered packet from within. She unfolded the material and gently lifted the icon, turning it first to show to Patrick. He drew his breath in sharply and reached out instinctively to touch it, but then drew back, raising his hands to his face in delight.

"Oh, my goodness!" he cried softly. "It is beautiful! Sure, I don't think I've ever seen anything so beautiful before." He crossed himself, almost without thinking, an action - a reaction - of awe and veneration.

Paul had risen from his chair and come to stand behind Patrick. He was rendered speechless by the sight before him. The firelight glinted on the gold, imbuing it with a warmth that was almost unearthly. The picture seemed to come to life, as if the Madonna was living, breathing, smiling her love down into the face of Her Child. He almost expected the Child to 'coo' with delight, His face radiant in the firelight and the light from His Mother's face. Whoever the unknown craftsman was who created this masterpiece, there could be no doubting his love for the Lord, for it was there in every line, every detail, for all to see. Paul raised his eyes to look at Beth, shaking his head from side to side in wonderment.

"I know," she whispered. "It had the same effect on me when I first saw it. It never ceases to amaze me that anyone can be so gifted as to create such a work of art."

Finally Patrick did reach forward and take the icon from Beth's hands. He drew it towards him, gazing at it in amazement, his face full of wonder and reverence. Slowly, he sat back in his chair, extending his arms so that the icon was held at arms length. Then he sat forward again, bringing the picture forward for a closer inspection. After a few minutes, he silently handed it to Paul, who looked as though he was almost too scared to handle it. Beth smiled with quiet satisfaction at their reaction. She knew its value, both as a work of the finest art and commercially and to see the veneration that it inspired in others made her even more resolute in her decision.

Paul gently handed the icon back to Beth and slowly resumed his place by the fire. Beth carefully refolded it in the velvet and then locked it safely in its box, which she placed on top of the box of tissues that lay on the table beside her chair. A touch of irony, she thought to herself. Pray God, I will no longer be needing the contents of that particular box because now the contents of this other box will free me from this last hurt. For the plight of the victims' families did indeed cause her great hurt, but now she could do something constructive about it.

She sat back in her chair, looking from one dear face to the other, her eyes dancing with delight. Then she sat forward in such a resolute, commanding way that both men started in surprise.

"Father Patrick," she said eagerly. "I need your help again. Or rather, that of your nephew. I have a plan that requires both his absolute confidentiality and his professional expertise. I wish to sell the icon."

"Sell it?" exclaimed Patrick. "How could you possibly part with such a thing as this?"

"Very easily indeed, I assure you. For I know now that it was given to me for just such a situation."

"Dear child, can you please explain?" Paul implored. "My poor old mind just can't fathom what you are up to and it really isn't up to mental contortions."

"All right," Beth said as she slumped back in her chair once more. "Here is what I have in mind. I want to sell the icon and share out the proceeds between the eight victims' families."

"Eight?" queried Paul. "I thought there were nine murders committed by Kevin."

"There *were* nine, but the last one has already been avenged by the killing of the murderer. It is very obvious to me that the Conlon clan killed their son's murderer and therefore I don't feel it is appropriate to make recompense to them. Furthermore, they have plenty of money, not that that is the only criterion for the need for recompense. But I do feel that they have had their revenge. Also, if I made contact with them, even anonymously, they would know it was me because they know who killed their son and I value my safety far too much to risk any contact with them. I couldn't be sure that they wouldn't go gloating to Michael or his mother and I'm afraid that somehow or other they would be able to trace my whereabouts. At least with the other eight victims being Protestant, the risk of feedback crossing the 'religious divide' back to the Bradys is greatly reduced."

"Valid point," mused Patrick. "But go on with your plan. I think I can see where you're headed but please give us more details. This sounds quite interesting so far."

"Well, I thought that if I could raise some substantial money on the sale of the icon - and it would have to be equally divisible by eight - then I would write a letter to each of the families. Don't forget that I have all their names and addresses in that horrible black book. Then I would need to call upon your services to get the money distributed so that there could be no trace back to me or to you. The very last thing I would want to do is endanger you in any way."

"Could the money not simply be delivered to each family without any letter?" asked Paul.

"No. I must write to them all. I feel a very deep need to apologise to each of them. I want them to know that this is a gesture from the heart. I need to ask for their forgiveness even if I will never know if they will forgive or not."

"But surely, it isn't you that is in need of forgiveness. The crimes were not of your doing."

"True. But I really feel that this is necessary, that in some way I am vicariously making a peace offering, a gesture of reconciliation. I don't fully know why, but it is burning away inside me, nagging at me and won't let go no matter how hard I try to rationalise it away. Can you understand?" she implored.

"I think I can, Beth," Patrick replied gently. "The fact that this will not leave you alone, that it is a persistent, almost passionate need in you tells me that this is what the Lord requires of you. He will use your desire-thoughts to accomplish we know not what. The material sacrifice that you are offering will mirror your deep and abiding desire to recompense these families. There is power in desire-thought as there is great power in prayer - in fact, there is precious little difference between the two, to my way of thinking. So do what you must, child, with love and blessing in your heart and you will be giving the Lord the wherewithal to fulfil your desire.

"You may never know first hand what the outcome of your actions will be, how the various recipients will react and how their thoughts and feelings may be affected, but you can be assured that if the Lord has a hand in this - and I can't see how He wouldn't have - then major changes in many hearts will be accomplished, pray God, all to the good."

Patrick reached over and took Beth's hand in his, gently squeezing it.

"You've a beautiful, generous nature, young Beth, and I'm mightily proud of you. You've chosen to do a very gracious and magnanimous thing. No, no!" he raised his hand against her protest. "'Tis true what I've said, for there's many a soul who wouldn't even think to make such a gesture. But you're to do no more about it tonight. For one thing, I know for a fact that Dermot will be dropping in to see to your stitches and to indulge in a glass of 'milk of amnesia' - he telephoned earlier to say that he's had a dreadful time of it of late, what with this 'flu epidemic and all and is in desperate need of a heart-starter!

"For another, for once, there is a good film on the telly tonight and I vote we all just sit and goggle at the box for a change. A little relaxation goes a very long way. Tomorrow I'll telephone John - no, in fact I think I'll call him this evening and maybe he'll be able to drop in on his way home from Dublin. I'm sure that he wouldn't mind doing a roundabout journey back to Donegal. Something tells me that he would be more than happy to stop by again so soon and it's not just the prospect of a good sale in the offing!" He grinned with delight at the bright blush that flamed into Beth's cheeks.

"You are a shocking old man!" she cried.

"True! But you love me anyway."

"Don't be so sure!"

"Ah, you do and you know it!"

"Don't tell me there's more bickering going on in here. Sure, I can't leave you boys alone for five minutes and you're causing mischief of some sort." Susan's sudden appearance caught them all by surprise. "Now, stop your nonsense and come away for your supper or it'll be outside the door for the dogs!"

"We don't have any dogs and well you know it," laughed Patrick.

"No, but next door does and well you know that!"

"Look to it, my friends! She means business!"

Laughing uproariously, they all trooped down the hallway to the kitchen where the delicious aroma of roast chicken mingled with the tangy smell of freshly baked apple pie. They all eagerly sat at the table awaiting their first course of fresh vegetable soup and hot, crusty bread rolls, straight from the oven.

"Ah, Susan, Susan," sighed Patrick. "Where would we all be without you? You're a joy to my old heart, so you are."

"Away with you flannel and eat your soup, you old goat," Susan snapped, her blushing cheeks and bright eyes belying her sharp tongue.

Beth caught Paul's eye and began to giggle, her giggle rapidly turning into helpless laughter. The others, including Susan, joined in, the sound of their merriment echoing through the big house.

"Oh, I do love you people," Beth gasped when she was able to speak.

"And we love you, too, Miss Beth," Susan relied. "We love you, too."

"Hear! Hear!" boomed the men in unison. "Hear! Hear!"

2

Beth stood under the steaming shower, luxuriating in the drumming of the water on her skin. To her surprise, she found that she was singing! Something she hadn't done in months. Her spirits lifted even further, the louder she sang. Song after song flowed from her as she soaped and lathered her body, shampooed and conditioned her hair. Finally, she ended her watery recital with a deep, sweeping curtsey, turned off the taps and stepped out of the shower, laughing delightedly at her own exuberance. What a joy it was to be alive! She hadn't felt this good since she knew not when.

Vigorously rubbing herself dry, she decided resolutely that she would no longer be a downtrodden, namby-pamby little mouse. She hadn't been brought up that way and it was only the circumstances of the last few months of her life that had brought her to such a cowed state of being. No-one is going to put you down any longer, young lady, she told herself firmly, as she zipped up her trousers and pulled on a warm chenille sweater.

As she towelled her hair dry, Beth studied her face in the mirror - something she had avoided at all costs during the last week. To her delight, she saw that the bruises were fading rapidly and the cuts were dramatically improved now that Dermot had removed all the stitches. It seemed to her that now she was so much better on the inside, the outer wreckage of her face was healing with astonishing speed and her skin was recovering its normal healthy glow once more. Even she could tell that she looked positively radiant.

With a new lightness in her heart and a new determination in her step, she skipped down the stairs and along the hallway to the kitchen.

"Good morning, everybody!" she called out as she entered the room and hurried over to where Susan was pouring coffee. She gave the older woman a quick hug and then joined Patrick and Paul at the kitchen table, planting a kiss firmly on each of their cheeks before taking her place. The men exchanged a quick look of astonished delight.

"Good morning to you, Beth," said Paul, when she was seated. "I trust you slept well?"

"Like the proverbial baby!"

"Obviously not one with teething troubles, then," joked Patrick. "I must say that you are looking particularly well this morning and to my mind, it's not just as a result of getting rid of all that stitchery from your face, either. You look altogether different. There's a definite glow about you that we've not seen before."

"That's because I haven't *felt* it before. And I feel so different, more in charge of myself, more in control. I feel as if I can actually cope with my life now. It's as if, having made the decision to do something about his victims, I have taken up the reins of my life again, but in a much more positive way. It seems as if the very act of making that decision has been a catalyst in some way. Does that sound crazy to you?"

"Not in the least," replied Paul. "It makes perfect sense to me. It strikes me that what you are now experiencing is the realisation that by allowing the Lord to have control of your life and every aspect of it, you now have much more freedom because you are no longer tied down by the worries of what to do and how to do it. Is *this* right, is *that* right; do I go *here*, do I go *there*? For there is great freedom in surrendering our will to the Lord and desiring His will in our lives - 'Thy will, Lord, not mine'. He knows what is best for us and by accepting His will as our guiding force, we can then embark upon the exciting journey of discovering just what that entails for each of us individually.

"We still have to do the detailed work of discovery ourselves, but we have the constant assurance of His permanent, never-failing guidance, His ever-present and absolute, unconditional love. If we stumble and fall, then we have the certain surety that He is there to pick us up, comfort us and set us upon the right path again. So we never have to fear our stumbles and failures because we can learn from them, we will grow from them, stronger and stronger, more confident with each forward step."

"You make it sound so exciting," said Beth. "You really make it sound like it is an adventure."

"And so it is," replied Patrick. "It is life's greatest adventure - the discovery of ourselves in Christ and of Him in us. No ascent of Everest or journey on foot across the Sahara or to the poles can ever equal the joy of coming to know the Lord, *personally*, one-to-one. I promise you, there is no greater pleasure, no greater thrill, no greater challenge, no greater or more rewarding prize. It is the absolute ultimate."

"*Wow*!" said Beth, with a little laugh. "*Oh, wow*! How could anyone resist such a challenge when you describe it like that? I can't wait to get started!"

"My dear, you have already begun, believe me. The first steps lie behind you, the future lies before, the adventure is now."

Beth sat back in her chair with a big grin on her face.

"Let's get going then," she said, raising her empty coffee cup high in the air. "Onwards and upwards!"

"Actually, just as far as the study," laughed Patrick. "Paul and I are just off there now to have our morning devotions. Susan has already been in to early Mass - fortunately missing most of the parish gossips by going so early - but obviously I can't be seen in church as I am still supposed to be seriously indisposed and Paul, being an unbeliever, can't anyway."

"Unbeliever, indeed! Speak for yourself, you old heathen!" Paul retorted. "I'll have you know that ...."

"No, you won't," interrupted Susan. "I'll have no ecumenical disputations in my kitchen, so I won't. Now behave yourselves, the pair of you, for each is as bad as the other and I couldn't choose between the worst of you. Get away down that hall and say a prayer for me while you're about it as I've already prayed for the lot of you, may it do you some good."

"Come on, Beth," said Patrick as he hauled himself up out of his chair. "If you would like to join us, I'll explain all in the study."

"Thank you, I'd really like to," she answered, as she rose from the table, tucking her chair neatly underneath.

"Let's just sit by the fire for a few moments while I fill you in on the procedure, Beth." Patrick led the way over to the fireplace and as they sat down, Beth looked quickly about the room and noticed that Patrick's little prie-dieu had been opened out so that it formed a small altar, complete with a large wooden cross and several candles. She was aware of the faint scent of incense which lightly permeated the room, creating an atmosphere of quietness and devotion.

They were all affected by the different mood in the study, the jollity of the kitchen quieted. Not that they were all pious and sober, but there was a general feeling of stillness and peace that flowed around and through Beth and she breathed it deeply into herself.

"Before going much further, I feel I should tell you a bit about our little service. When I'm not able, for whatever reason, to take Mass in the church then I have my own service in here. Often I prefer to 'enter alone into my closet' and meet with the Lord in private, one to one, and so I have my little altar table in this room where I can be alone. When Paul visits, and often when John does, then we share a communion service together.

"You will find it somewhat different from Mass as you know it but it is all scripturally based and spiritually sound, I assure you. We follow a simple order of devotional prayers and scripture readings, along with a few verses of various hymns, all leading up to the partaking of Holy Communion. After that, in place of a sermon, we have a quiet time alone with the Lord.

"This time of quiet is our opportunity to listen to the 'still, small voice' within us, to commune with Him on a deep and personal level, to hear whatever He may have to say for us. For as He said long ago, 'When two or three are gathered together in My name, there will I be also, in the midst.' He longs to commune with us as much and more than we long - and *need* - to commune with Him. Denomination plays no part in this service. Communion, after all, means sharing fellowship between people of like mind and commitment and our commitment is solely to the Lord and in that we are most definitely of like mind.

"There are plenty of pens and paper to hand if you should wish to write down any thoughts, impressions, pictures that come to mind that have relevance for you. It is all very simple and non-threatening, so you have nothing to fear. If you would just like to sit quietly and follow along as we go through the service and join in if you know any of the hymns, you would be most welcome. We can always benefit greatly from someone else's singing. Ours leaves somewhat to be desired, I can promise you, although I'm certain that the Lord hears the singing of our hearts rather than that of our gravelly old voices.

"Then, after we have finished, we have a light snack while we share amongst ourselves anything of significance that we have experienced. So if you are ready, we'll move to the other side of the room and begin our service."

"Does Susan usually join you at these times?" asked Beth.

"Often, yes, she does. But today, as I've already said, she attended early Mass so that she can get on with the preparations for Sunday lunch. John is hoping to get here for lunchtime so we shall be having a veritable feast for I swear Susan thinks he starves himself silly up there in Donegal and it is her bounden duty to feed him fit to bust so as to last him until his next visit. And as far as I'm concerned, he can come here any day of the week, for sure, I never eat as well as I do when he comes!

"Away now! Enough chat. We'll have plenty of time later to do all the chatting we desire."

They had moved over to where three upright chairs were placed before the little altar.

"Beth, if you would like to sit here in the middle. Perhaps there you won't feel quite so 'on the outside looking in', as it were. Paul, could I ask you to lead us in a short prayer to prepare us for meeting with the Lord?"

Later, Beth could remember little about the order the service took. More, she recalled the beautiful peace and stillness and especially the exquisite warmth and tranquillity that she felt during the 'silence'. It washed over and over her, leaving her tingling from head to toe, both without and within. She didn't want it ever to stop and felt that she could have sat there forever, suffused in that glorious sensation. The only way she could describe the feeling to herself was as if her inmost being, her soul, had been caressed, causing waves of the most tender, delicate ecstasy to ripple through her.

Later, she tried battling through her embarrassment to relate the experience to Patrick and Paul, who both beamed with delight at the telling.

"That, my dear," said Patrick, "is the Lord's gift to you today, His message of love for you. For that was the merest glimpse, the tiniest of tasters, of the depth of His personal love for you. And if that was just a taster, try to imagine what the full force would be like! There is nothing on this earth or in our imaginations to compare with His love."

3

There was a general buzz of anticipation in the air as each member of the household eagerly awaited the arrival of John. Susan hummed to herself as she busied around the kitchen, putting the final touches to the meal she had so lovingly prepared for them all, but particularly for John.

Patrick, Paul and Beth were in the study, listening to a concert on the radio, but each taking surreptitious peeks at the clock on the mantelshelf and keeping an ear open for the ring of the doorbell. When it finally came, they all jumped in surprise, almost as if by having listened for it for so long, they really didn't think it would ever ring.

Susan hurried along the corridor and flung the door wide open, a huge smile splitting her wrinkled face from side to side. John swung her up into a huge hug and having executed an almost perfect pirouette, he placed her, breathless, back on the floor and gave her a big kiss.

"It does the heart good to come here, Susan," he laughed. "For there could never be a welcome as warm as that which I receive in this house."

"Sure, there's nowhere else you could be more welcome, John. Of that I can promise you. Come away in now and join the others in the study. They'll be having me up for kidnap, keeping you away from them like this. But sure, they can't run the risk of being seen at the front of the house even still. Away now and I'll bring you a cup of coffee to warm you after your long journey."

When he entered the study, John found three beaming faces ready to greet him. He hugged each in turn, keeping Beth to last and holding on to her for considerably longer than he had the men. Still with his hands on her waist, he smiled down into her upturned face.

"You are looking lovely, if I may say so," he said shyly. "It's a joy to see you without that facial embroidery. All appears to be healing nicely, to my untrained eye at any rate." Oh Lord, he said to himself, I hope she doesn't think I'm prattling on too much. But the look in her eyes quickly dispelled his misgivings.

"It's lovely to see you again, too, John," Beth replied, her voice soft and warm. "And so much sooner than we had expected."

"Well, I almost left straight away last night when I got Unc's phone call, but then I thought better of it, considering how late it would be before I got here. So I left as soon as I could reasonably get away this morning and here I am!"

"And here are we, too!" put in Patrick. "Remember us, old man?"

John and Beth stepped apart from each other abruptly, both blushing profusely.

"Sorry, you two," John stumbled over his words in his embarrassment. "It's just good to see Beth looking so much better and well, just so good to be here and everything." His voice petered out and he looked so little-boy-lost and sheepish that they all laughed.

"I shouldn't tease you, John. I certainly didn't mean to," Patrick said, as he wiped his eyes. "Here," he added, "have a wee heart-starter with us before lunch. You know what Susan's cooking is like. We all need a large apéritif to work up sufficient appetite to face one of her meals."

He had raised his voice as the study door opened and Susan entered bearing a tray of coffees. She placed the tray on the table by Beth's chair and turned to Patrick with a look of mock reproach.

"Just you remember next door's dog, young man," she said tartly, wagging her finger at him. "He's particularly partial to a nice roast leg of lamb, so I've been told. At least, the part that the others don't eat, because you'll be on bread and water again. That's if you're lucky enough to be given anything at all."

"You're a hard woman, Susan!" Patrick called after her as she swept from the room.

"Harder than you suspect," came her rejoinder from the hallway. "So be very careful!"

When they were seated with their drinks and coffee and all the laughter had subsided, Patrick reached for the flat box on the table beside him and handed it to John.

"Down to business," he said. "I imagine you're keen to see just what it is that I've called you all the way back here for."

John set his whiskey glass down on the table and took the

box from his uncle. All eyes were on him as he undid the latch and lifted the lid. Beth held her breath as he unfolded the velvet and looked at the icon for the first time. She knew its worth but also knew that for her there was a larger, intrinsic value to it as well. So she hoped and prayed that her estimate of its real, commercial value would not be distorted by its sentimental one. She so desperately wanted to achieve a substantial amount from its sale. So much depended on John finding the right buyer and that wouldn't necessarily be easy, even taking into account the quality of the work and its rarity. Pieces of this calibre were hard to come by but, sometimes, equally hard to place with new owners.

Beth visibly relaxed as she heard John's sharp intake of breath. He rose from his chair and carried it over to the window to see it more clearly in the daylight, his concentration intense. He studied it from every conceivable angle, turning it over and over in his hands, gently, almost reverently. Finally he looked up, his eyes searching out Beth's from across the room.

"Whoever gave this to you must have thought the world of you," he said quietly.

She heard the question in his tone of voice and her chin lifted defensively.

"He was a lovely old man who also happened to be my boss when I lived in Boston," she replied sharply.

"I wasn't implying anything untoward, Beth, honestly. It's just so rare to find something of this value and in such an unexpected way. I'm sorry if I caused you any offence. Truly I am." His eyes pleaded his cause as his face flushed deep crimson.

Beth sighed deeply. "I accept your apology willingly," she said. "Please also accept mine. I didn't mean to be so defensive. I guess I'm a little sensitive about the icon, especially as I really do need to sell it and for as much as I can possibly get."

John had moved across the room while Beth was talking and now he reached for her hand. He smiled at her with such tenderness that she felt a lurch deep in her stomach and knew that she, too, was blushing furiously.

"I understand completely," John said gently. "I promise I will do all I possibly can to find the right buyer at the very best price. I do have one or two leads I can follow up. Who knows, they, or at least one of them, just might turn out to be the answer to all your troubles."

"Well, at least to this one," Beth replied. She withdrew her hand from his and sat down abruptly, a mixture of emotions surging through her. She was so relieved at John's reaction on seeing the icon and at his news that he might already have a buyer in mind. But she was cross with herself - no, *more* than cross! - that she had reacted so strongly, almost passionately, to him. She had gone positively weak at the knees when he took her hand and smiled at her as he had done.

What was the *matter* with her? Here she was, widowed little more than a week ago, having gone through the most appalling travesty of a marriage and a dreadful, violent beating and now she was going all weak-kneed and girlie at the first man who smiled at her! Was she turning into some sort of nymphomaniac? Angrily, she picked up her sherry glass and drained it in one swallow, unaware that the three men were all looking at her with decidedly perplexed expressions. Patrick sought out the other two with his eyes and shook his head very slightly to warn them not to say anything.

"Tell me, John," he said, as though nothing was amiss. "What are your plans now that you have seen the icon?"

"Well, if I may use your phone later - and I will pay for the calls, for I need to phone overseas - then I will know more. But if all goes as I hope, then I will fly out of here as soon as I can get a flight. With any luck, I shouldn't be gone for more than a week. I would really like to have this all sown up before Christmas, if at all possible. But as I said, I'll know more when I've made a couple of phone calls."

And while you're gone, I'll get myself back together like a normal person, Beth chastised herself sharply. Enough silliness, my girl. You're in danger of becoming positively flighty and then just think what dear old Aunt Mildred would have to say about *that*! 'Just as I always predicted, Douglas. The girl is as frivolous and unreliable as that dreadful mother of hers. You know what they say about the sins of the father. What about the sins of the *mother*?'

4

Beth found that her black mood soon vanished in the warmth of the kitchen, a warmth resulting not just from the huge Aga with its hot ovens but from the conviviality of those with whom she sat at the table. The delicious food and a particularly fine wine certainly made their contributions to the restoration of her equilibrium. She was a little annoyed at letting herself be so affected by negative thoughts and feelings - not that what she had felt for John was in any way negative. But she had allowed thoughts of Aunt Mildred get to her just when she thought that they had all been dealt with successfully. She must always remember what Patrick and Paul had told her about the enemy not wasting a single opportunity to have a go at her and to undermine her new-found peace of mind.

So, offering up a quick prayer for protection, forgiveness and of thanks, she gave herself a shake and joined in wholeheartedly with the conversation that had been going on around her. Patrick noticed her little shake and the straightening of her spine as she sat more upright and, catching her eye, he gave her a wink and a smile of encouragement as if he knew in some way of the battle that had been going on inside her. Her answering smile was warm with appreciation for his observance and his concern and she experienced a further lightening of her spirits as a result.

The two older men, Beth and Susan stayed at the kitchen table, enjoying a leisurely post-prandial coffee while John took his cup with him to the study so that he could make his phone calls in peace. The conversation in the kitchen revolved around the Christmas preparations of the household, especially as the day itself was only two weeks away. It was decided that as Beth was to be their guest this year, then the honour of decorating the Christmas tree was to be hers. Patrick reasoned that as she was an artist, then she surely would have much more of an eye than he himself and that this year they might have a tree that looked considerably better than any in the past. For the tree decorating had always been his responsibility up until now as Susan was far too busy in the kitchen with all the other preparations and so they usually ended up with a very lopsided-looking tree, with baubles placed hither and thither at random just because they had to be put somewhere. This year, theirs would be the pride of the neighbourhood, except that the neighbourhood would not be seeing anything of it because of the need for Beth's safety. However, *they* would enjoy it to the full!

John hurried back into the kitchen in a state of some considerable excitement. He shook his head as Susan offered him another cup of coffee.

"Thank you, Susan, but I really don't have time. I'm afraid I shall have to love you and leave you all now. I must dash home and collect my passport and then get back for an early morning flight out of here. It seems that I may just be on to a successful resolution to your problem, Beth. My contact has passed on to me a name of a potential buyer. I've just spoken with him and he is willing to see me just as soon as I can get there."

"You're being very mysterious about all this, John," remarked Patrick. "Aren't you even going to tell us where it is that you are going in such a hurry?"

"Well, actually, my first port of call is Donegal so that I can get my things together and collect my passport."

"Clever clogs! You know what I mean."

"Sorry, Unc. But I have actually been sworn to secrecy. I'm used to dealing confidentially with clients but this person is insisting upon absolute secrecy. So I can say no more other than the fact that he is extremely interested in what I have to offer for sale and he will be ready to make a rapid transaction if the icon is the one he thinks it is. He seems to know his stuff and is in the market for just the right thing for which he is prepared to pay a very good price."

"It seems that I'm putting you to a great deal of trouble, with your having to rush here and there on my behalf," Beth said apologetically.

John's eyes were so bright that their usual cornflower blue had become a brilliant sapphire blue and they danced with excitement as he smiled down at her.

"Dear Beth, please don't even *think* such things. Believe me, this is a real *joy* for me, not just that I am able to help you - and that I do with the greatest of pleasure - but I get such a thrill out of this sort of thing. Opportunities like this are few and far between and all the more enjoyable for their rarity. In some ways it's almost like detective work, although this time, things have happened with incredible speed. So you have no need to apologise to me. This is a real delight, not an inconvenience in any way at all."

"There is one more thing I would like to ask you," said Beth. "As you know, there are eight families that I need this money for. Do you think you could possibly work it so that the sum you get for the icon is equally divisible by eight, after you have taken out your expenses and usual commission, of course. I do want everything to be fair."

"That would be no trouble at all and we won't even think about my expenses or commission."

"But you must be paid!"

"Hush! Don't upset yourself. All I meant was that I don't want you worrying about incidentals. Minor details can be tidied up once this is all completed. What is important is getting you the very best possible price."

Beth smiled her thanks at him and then added, a little sheepishly, "There is actually one *more* favour that I would like to ask of you because I really don't know who else to ask."

"Ask away," John replied, an anticipatory grin on his face.

"Well, I have some jewellery that I no longer want. Actually, there is rather a lot and all quite valuable and, I believe, easily traceable. Some of it was bought in the States but most of it here in Belfast. I don't know how to go about selling it without questions being asked and I am rather in need of some money for myself as I don't have any at all."

John felt a surge of tenderness at the look on Beth's face. She was trying so very hard to hide her shame. He knew just how she felt about the jewellery because Pat had already told him about her whole situation and once again the desire to lash out violently arose within him. But lash out at what? The perpetrator of her predicament was well and truly - and deservedly - dead. Besides, nothing would be gained by even more violence. So all he could do was to help her in any and every way possible and if that meant flying halfway around the world and back again, then he would do it gladly.

Hoping that the inner turmoil of his emotions wasn't emblazoned across his face, John reached out and placed his hands on Beth's shoulders.

"I'll be very happy to do what I can for you," he said, grateful that his voice sounded steady and friendly, not all quivery as he felt within. "You can be assured that I will do the very best I can. But now I really must leave as there is a lot I have to do to get ready for tomorrow and it's a bit of a haul over to Donegal from here. So if you would run upstairs and get me your jewellery case, then I shall make tracks. I'd like to be away before it gets too dark."

Resisting the urge to throw her arms around him, Beth turned and ran from the room, the sound of her feet pounding up the stairs carrying into the kitchen.

Patrick looked long and hard at his nephew and then decided against saying anything about his observations just then. There would be time for a man-to-man whenever John returned from wherever it was that he was going.

Farewells were said in the kitchen as only Susan could accompany John to the front door as he took his leave.

"With any luck I shall be back before the end of the week or at least by the beginning of next," he said. "If I am, and if it is all right with you, I would like to come here early for Christmas. There would be no point in my going all the way home to Donegal only to turn around and come back a day or so later."

"You're more than welcome, lad. You know that," Patrick answered warmly. "We'll look forward to seeing you just as soon as you can get here and for as long as you like. Besides, that will give us plenty of opportunity to discuss what is to be done with this little lady once Christmas is over." He smiled down at Beth standing at his side.

"Well, you could always put me out for the refuse men to take away with the defunct Christmas tree," she retorted.

"Would we do such a thing?" Patrick answered laughingly. "But you have given me an idea. We might just put you on top of the tree as our Christmas fairy. Sure, you're a lot prettier than the poor old tatty thing that we've got at the present!"

Beth threw back her head and roared with laughter.

"You are a shocking tease!" she cried. "Christmas fairy, indeed!"

The sight of her sparkling eyes and laughing mouth was

almost more than John could bear. He abruptly turned toward Paul and shook his hand.

"I really must be on my way now," he said, rather more abruptly than he wished it had sounded.

Paul shook John's hand warmly in return.

"Safe journey, my boy. We shall be praying for you, both for your wellbeing and for the success of your mission. Hurry home."

"God bless you and go with you, lad," Patrick said as he hugged him warmly. "Give us a call if you can, just to let us know how you are getting on."

"At the very least, I shall call you from the airport to let you know when I'll be back," John replied.

Turning to Beth, he took her hands in his, his heart lurching as he saw what looked decidedly like tears in her eyes.

"I shall do the very best I can, I promise you," he said gently. "The *very* best."

"I know you will," she whispered.

Unable to stop himself, he lowered his head and kissed her gently on the lips. Then he released her hands and was gone. Turning from the front door for one last look before Susan opened the door, he saw that Beth was standing in the kitchen doorway, her hand raised to her mouth, her fingers lightly caressing her lips where his own had been just seconds before. Then she slipped out of sight behind the door and he reluctantly turned away, said his final farewell to Susan and moved down the pathway to his car and the long journey ahead.

5

The days of John's absence passed pleasantly for the occupants of the priest's house. Susan was busy, as always, in the kitchen, cooking and baking, tantalising smells filling the whole house, much to Patrick's distress as most of the results of Susan's hard work were being stored in fridges, freezers, cake boxes and other hiding places and were not for his immediate consumption.

"You're worse than any wee boy," Susan countered his numerous complaints. "If I let you have anything now, there would be none left for Christmas and besides, you'd be that sick by then that you'd not be able to enjoy anything that might be left. So you'll not be having any goodies just now. You'll just have to make do with the normal fare of the house, as the rest are happy to do, without all your complaints."

"I'll say it again, you're a hard woman, Susan," Patrick replied. He gave her an affectionate hug, helping himself to a sausage roll from the counter behind her back at the same time. He popped it into his mouth as he turned to leave the room and almost spat it out immediately as it burnt his tongue, for it was straight from the oven.

"You'll get no sympathy for me!" was Susan's retort. "You got just what you deserved and no more. Now, away out of my kitchen or you'll be getting a lot more than you bargained for, for I'm handier with a rolling pin than you might think."

So Patrick retreated to his study where Paul was engaged in teaching Beth to play cribbage. He had already talked her through the rudiments of the game as they played the first hand. Now they were well into a proper game and much to Paul's consternation, he was in serious danger of being skunked! He, who was the self-proclaimed champion of cribbage, at least in Patrick's house, for his only real competition there was Dermot and he always beat him comfortably. And now here was this slip of a girl, just a novice, having a run of cards such as he himself had not had in a very long time!

"Beginners luck," Paul said, not unkindly, as the game came to its foregone conclusion.

"Just desserts, more likely," Patrick replied with glee. "Well done, Beth. Well done, indeed. It takes a rare person to beat this man at his own game. I'm proud of you, my girl. Another hand, old man. I must see this girl in full action. It does the heart good to see someone get their comeuppance."

"Pure sour grapes, you old goat!" said Paul. "You only say that because you never could win against me and eventually gave up trying. The biggest sore loser there could ever be! But we will have one more hand at least, before lunch, just to give Beth a little more practise."

So, after a quick shuffle of the cards, he dealt another hand and the game commenced. This was a longer game but one Beth played to perfection and which she again won with ease.

"I take my hat off to you, Beth," Paul said magnanimously. "You seem to have a feel for this game. I think I shall enjoy playing more often with you. It will really keep me on my toes. I must have become complacent over the years, for Isobel and Dermot have been such easy conquests but you are making me rethink my capabilities. I don't think I would like to teach you to play chess. You just might beat me at that, too."

"Perhaps we'll leave that pleasure to John when he's here for Christmas," said Patrick. "That's very much his game and it appears to me, young lady, that you have just the right reasoning and thoughtful mind for chess. It would be a joy, I might add, to see you beat John for he is a seriously good player and really puts me to the test every time we play."

"And every time he invariably wins, too," added Paul. "Pat seldom wins against John, just as he never wins cribbage against me, so he loves to see others beat his own victors."

"You make poor Father Patrick sound like an also-ran," Beth said, giving Patrick a smile of sympathy. "But you're not an also-ran to me. To me you are a real hero. You both are and I'm deeply indebted to you both."

"Now, now," Patrick blustered. "You'll have us blushing again in a minute and then Susan will accuse us of over-indulgence and we haven't had a drop to drink today. Which reminds me, shall we have a wee drop before lunch, do you think?"

"Just a small one, Paddy," answered Paul.

"Nothing for me, thank you," said Beth. "For one thing, I

want to keep a clear head as I hope to work on the letter this afternoon. I really want to get it written today if I can and it has to be just so. I don't want it to sound maudlin or patronising or anything negative. It's not going to be easy for me at all so I really need my wits about me."

"I do understand, Beth," Patrick said as he handed Paul his glass of whiskey. "Remember to ask the Lord to guide you. He knows what is in your heart and He will help you to get it all down on paper, to find the right words and phrasing. But you must ask Him for His help. He's only too willing to help but, as I've already explained, He won't force Himself upon us - indeed, He can't - and so we must ask Him. *Then* we can receive.

"By the way," Patrick continued, as he made his way across to his chair and flopped down into the comfy seat. "I've been giving a little thought to the matter of the distribution of your letters and the money. I don't know whether you have had any ideas yourself"

"None whatever," Beth answered. "I just wouldn't know where to begin. Obviously I have the all addresses but I can hardly walk up to the front doors and hand over the packages and then just walk away again. Good grief, I can't even step outside the house! I must admit that I would rather not entrust them to the mail, either."

"Quite so, and with the extra burdens on the post office at this time of year, anything could happen to them - casting no aspersions on our admirable postal services, of course! So if I may make a suggestion, I have a very dear and very discreet friend who just happens to be a senior R.U.C. officer."

"R.U.C.?"

"The Royal Ulster Constabulary, the police!"

"Ah."

"The very man we need. James will be more than happy to do each of the deliveries himself. He's a well-known and well respected man and he will ask no questions of me and I shall tell him nothing that he does not need to know. So, if you have no objections then I shall give him a call and set the whole thing up when you are ready for me to do so."

"I can't find the words to thank you, Father Patrick. I really don't know how I would have coped without you. You seem to have all the answers to my problems and I'm so very grateful. I can hardly wait for the whole thing to be over and done with. I'm more than a little nervous about it all."

"I'm sure that all will be just fine, my dear. Don't you worry about a thing. Your heart is full of goodness, your motives are of the very highest kind, so all will be well."

"Thank you for your confidence in me. I really need it and I really appreciate it."

"Well, it's fully merited, I assure you," Patrick said. "Fully merited."

Beth spent the whole afternoon in her bedroom working on her letter, the pile of discarded paper beside her chair growing higher and higher, wider and wider. Try as hard as she may not to, she found herself growing more and more agitated, more and more dejected. The words simply would not flow and everything she wrote sounded forced or trite, exactly the opposite of what she wanted!

Angry with herself, Beth dropped her notepad on the floor and started pacing around the room. She walked over to the window that looked out onto the back garden. The dull, lowering sky and a steady drizzle did nothing to lift her own dejected mood. Turning abruptly from the window, she found herself facing the painting that had so caught her attention a few days ago. She stood for some time, allowing the beauty of the scene to soak into her and slowly her feelings of anger and frustration began to subside.

Then she moved across the room to study the picture more closely. It was a fine piece of work and the artist, J. Harrison, - whoever that might be - had captured the essence of the day and of the scene with great skill. It had been a day of bright sunlight when the painting had been done, for there was scarcely a cloud in the deep cerulean sky and the quality of the light on the hillside and the sea was really first-class. The artist was obviously very accomplished and, Beth felt, had a genuine love for wherever was the location of the painting. As a fellow artist, she felt that this was a real place of some considerable meaning to the artist for that feeling emanated from every brush stroke. This really was a work of love. Beth felt a great yearning, almost a painful tugging at her heart, to visit this unknown place.

She turned away suddenly, feeling that her emotions were

getting out of control, and returned to her chair. At least her mood of dejection was gone. Perhaps now she could get down to actually writing this letter. Picking up her notepad and pen once more, she sat back in the chair for a few moments and closed her eyes to compose herself. Not making much progress, she opened her eyes and looked quickly about the room. Her gaze immediately fell upon the Bible beside her bed and she almost kicked herself as she realised that she should have asked for help. *When* would she learn that help was always there for the asking?

Once more Beth closed her eyes and this time spent a few minutes in quiet prayer, asking the Lord to guide her in her task, to give her the words that He would have her use and to give her His peace. When she finally started writing she found that this time the words did flow, just as she had hoped - and now, finally, prayed - they would. At last she was finished and as she re-read the words on the page, she felt a sense of relief, of release and of great satisfaction.

Dear ____________________,

You do not know me and for reasons that will become clear, I cannot reveal my identity, but I have a very great need to write to you.

I have recently discovered that some months ago your son was murdered. The reason I did not know before is that I have been living abroad and only returned here with my husband a short while ago. My husband is now dead and in going through his papers after his death I discovered, to my horror, that it was he who was responsible for your son's death. This occurred before I met my husband and I had absolutely no knowledge of his activities before he himself died.

I cannot find adequate words to express my abhorrence and revulsion at the things my husband did. My loss is nothing compared with yours for I feel that my husband's death was fully justified - he, too, was murdered and I believe was made fully aware of the reasons for his murder before he died. However, this does not release him from his guilt or the need for recompense. Therefore, I feel it is only just that I, in some small way, attempt to make amends on his behalf and that of his family.

I truly wish that I could meet with you to express my feelings but my own life is in considerable danger. It is not for my own safety alone that I must remain anonymous but for that of the very dear people who are keeping me in hiding. They are putting their lives at risk every day for me and I cannot endanger them any further by making my whereabouts known. Those who have 'put a price on my head' are powerful people and would, I feel sure, be able to trace this letter and contents if they were to become public knowledge. And so I ask that you keep this to yourself or, at the most, within your immediate family.

As a Christian, I firmly believe that my husband will have to make retribution for his actions, according to God's law. However, I feel that you and your family are deserving of recompense and so I pray that you will accept the enclosed with my most sincere apologies and heartfelt sorrow for your suffering. I assure you that the money is not from my husband or his family but is from the sale of personal items of my own. I know that in no way can this repay you for the loss of your son but I sincerely hope that it will go some way to alleviating your burden.

Please believe that this comes to you with true Christian love and caring and I pray earnestly that you will come to the place where you will be able to forgive. I know that I need your forgiveness.

Beth silently handed the letter first to Patrick and when he had finished reading it, she took it over to where Paul was seated at the table on which the cribbage board was still set up from the morning's play.

"I promise I'm not sulking," he said to her ruefully as he took the paper from her hand. "Just contemplating my ignominious defeats!"

When he had read the letter, Paul laid the page on the table beside him.

"As far as I can see, this is a very good letter but it does end somewhat abruptly, doesn't it?"

"To be honest, Paul, I don't know how else to end it. I can hardly sign off with a flourish and I certainly can't put my name to it. I really didn't know how else to finish it or what else to say. I do need their forgiveness even if I will never know if it is given nor if I can ever be aware of receiving it. So I decided just to leave it as it is."

"May I see the letter again, please?" asked Patrick, holding out his hand. "I'd like one more look at it before I comment. I trust you're looking for our comments, by the way, or you wouldn't have shown it to us."

"Absolutely," replied Beth. "I wouldn't dream of sending this to anyone without your constructive criticism. It wasn't easy to write because there was so much I wanted to say and just couldn't. I didn't want it to be all slushy and sentimental. That would be insulting to the recipient, anyway. And I didn't want it to sound all sanctimonious and pious. That would be even worse. I just hope that they will all be able to tell that it really does come from my heart, that it is a genuine message of reconciliation."

Patrick took the letter once more from Beth and sat quietly studying it for some minutes. Beth paced the room anxiously, stopping to gaze out of the window at the dreary winter rain flattening what remained of the plants into the quagmire of mud that had once been the summer flower beds. She felt quite exhausted after the effort she had put into the letter and at the same time she was tense, taut with anxiety. She so desperately wanted the letter to be received in the same spirit in which it was sent and she would never know if it was. The not knowing seemed to be the most difficult aspect of this whole exercise, so difficult that she almost felt like not going through with it. But there was no alternative, not if she was to have some peace of mind and quietness of heart.

She jumped at the sound of Patrick's voice and turned from the window to face him, her face white and rigid with apprehension.

"Don't look so terrified," Patrick said kindly. "This really is a very good letter, as Paul has already said. I know that it must have been terribly difficult for you to write but I do honestly believe that your sincerity does come through. You have just the right tone, not over-emotional or mawkish and not unctuous or self-righteous. I can see why you stopped where you did. There really is no other way to finish it off and I think that will be obvious to the various recipients. Actually, it adds to the sincerity of the letter. It really does seem as though you were at a genuine loss as to what more to say. I think you have done well, my dear. Very well indeed, especially considering the most difficult of circumstances."

Beth sank into her chair with a deep sigh of relief. She looked absolutely drained and felt as though she had been put through a mangle.

"Thank you," she whispered. "I need your votes of confidence, truly I do."

"Well, the worst part is over. You can now start to relax and enjoy your further recovery. John will be back in a few days and then - pray God that his trip has been successful - you can organise the distribution of the money and the letters and then put the whole thing behind you and really look forward to Christmas and to your new future. I have a feeling that this will be a particularly happy Christmas for us all.

"But for now, I suggest that we find Susan and rustle up a cup of tea. What say you?"

"Delicious!" Beth answered.

"You stay where you are," said Paul as Beth started to rise from her chair. "You've done all the hard work. Now you should rest. It's long past time I reminded my legs what they were created for in the first place. I could do with the exercise."

"Good Lord!" laughed Patrick as Paul headed for the door. "Anyone would think he was off to climb Everest, not just toddle down the hall to the kitchen!"

"Enough of your sarcasm or it will be tea for two!"

Beth laughed along with the men and felt the laughter seeping into her muscles as she relaxed back deeper into her chair. A lovely warm glow seemed to be encircling her heart. Was it just relief or was it much more than that?

Much, much more, she decided, for there was a very distinct aura of love in the room, a love that positively bounced off the walls. It was enveloping, comforting, uplifting, deeply satisfying, a love such as she had never known before.

6

John's return was much sooner than any of them had anticipated. He telephoned from the airport on Wednesday evening to say to expect him early afternoon the following day. Susan bustled about the house, singing merrily as she changed his bed, dusted and polished his room and cooked up yet another storm in the kitchen.

Patrick and Paul were both bouncier and more cheerful than ever, jokes flying thick and fast between them, laughter echoing around the old house.

Beth was the only one not entirely enthusiastic about John's imminent appearance. She was actually in quite a turmoil, her thoughts and emotions all over the place. Naturally, she felt very nervous and anxious about the outcome of his trip for he had given nothing away on the phone. She didn't even know if he had sold the icon, let alone the jewellery, although the latter was of far less importance.

Coupled with this was her apprehension at seeing John again on a personal level. For, much to her annoyance and her confusion, she found that she had genuinely missed him and was longing to see him once more. She was annoyed with herself for feeling such a deep attraction to him and yet it was a very real attraction. She had never met anyone like him before. He was so very different from any of the Americans or Canadians she had known. He was so gentle and compassionate and at the same time, so strong and unassumingly sure of himself. When she thought of him, she had an almost overwhelming desire to just lean against him and feel his arms about her, holding her close and safe. Yes, *safe*! She really felt that with him she would be safe.

Good heavens! What *was* she thinking? Come on, girl, she told herself sharply. Get your act together! Once you leave here, wherever it is you will be going, it's most unlikely you will ever see him again. So, stop fantasising!

When John came into the kitchen where she was drying the lunch dishes, Beth had to stop herself from rushing across the room to throw her arms about him. Very carefully and deliberately, she placed the glass she was drying on the counter and put the tea towel down beside it. When she looked up, John was standing right beside her, his hands outstretched. She placed her own in his and he drew her gently towards him, pulling her arms around his waist and then, releasing her hands, he put his own arms around her and laid his cheek on top of her head.

"Oh, Beth." His voice was muffled in her hair. "Dear Beth. I've missed you so very much. I got home as quickly as I could because I just couldn't wait to see you again."

He raised his head and leaned back slightly from her. She lifted her face to look at him as he gently stroked the side of her cheek. Then he lowered his head and kissed her so very, very gently, so tenderly that she felt tears spring to her eyes. She was falling, drowning, spinning, flying. Surely her heart was going to come crashing out through her rib cage!

Shocked, thrilled, excited, frightened, she pulled back suddenly from their embrace. Seeing the look in John's eyes, a sob escaped from her throat and she was once more crushed against his chest as her tears fell.

"Oh Beth. Beth!" he murmured, his voice breaking with emotion. "I'm so sorry! My timing is lousy, I know, but I can't help myself. I love you so much it hurts! I hadn't meant to say anything yet but just seeing you sent all my resolve out the window. Please forgive me if I have frightened or upset you. I really didn't mean to but I just can't help it. I do love you so!"

After some moments, John relaxed his hold on Beth and, placing his fingers under her chin, he lifted her face up towards him. Gently, he wiped away her tears and then he laid one finger against her lips as she started to speak.

"Say nothing yet. I don't think I could bear to hear what you might say just now. I know I've said far too much and far too soon but I do want you to know how very much I love you. I don't know if you could ever feel anything for me - I hardly dare think that you might - but whatever, please know that I will always be here for you. If all you ever want is friendship, then I will be the truest friend possible. But if you should ever want more than that, then I shall be the happiest man alive.

"Please, don't feel threatened. I am asking for nothing. I have no right to ask for anything from you. But I will ask one thing only and that is that you forgive me for speaking out when I really shouldn't have."

Beth could actually *feel* the sincerity of John's words, so very different from the rash, braggadocio verbiage and promises that had been made to her so short a time ago. *This* was a man whom she could trust implicitly. *This* was a man who would not use and abuse her and then cast her aside. *This* was a man in whom she could have faith, a man of honesty, sincerity and dependability - a man she knew she already loved. But she was still frightened, still nervous, still bruised, although the pain of her past relationship had eased dramatically. She would need time before she was ready to make a commitment again but she knew with a certainty that she would only ever want to make a commitment to John. They had time, though, she was confident of that. John would not push her if she was not ready; he would make no demands of her that she could not happily and wholeheartedly fulfil.

"Of course I forgive you," Beth said. "And I thank you for your love, John. It means more to me than I can say right now. I treasure your friendship and always will, but for now, that is all that I can say." The sweetness of her smile almost took his breath away.

"My darling, it is more than I could have hoped for and more than I deserve."

"No, not more than you deserve, for you deserve the very best, John, I promise you. I have never met a finer man than you."

"Tosh! Now you'll get me blushing again and I don't want to look like a beetroot when we join Unc in his study. He'll put two and two together and make eighty-five!"

"I love it when you blush," Beth laughed. "You positively glow! I think it's really charming and also enlightening. You could never be anything other than honest because it would show all over your face if you weren't."

"Honesty matters a great deal to you, doesn't it, Beth," John said.

"Of course it does!"

"And so it should. I can see that you've been badly hurt by other people's dishonesty. One thing I can promise you, darling Beth, is that I will never knowingly be dishonest with you. I would never let you down in that way or, I pray, any other way if I can possibly help it."

"I know, John, and I'm grateful for your reassurances. I do know that I could always trust you implicitly. That is a great comfort, believe me."

"And I'm grateful for your confidence in me. But now we must join the others in the study. I have much to tell and I think you will be mightily pleased!"

"Goodness! I'd forgotten all about your trip. How awful of me not even to ask how you got on!"

"That was hardly your fault. I didn't give you much chance to speak, did I?"

"This is a true fact, to pinch one of Paul's expressions!" Beth laughed. "John, could I ask you something before we join the others?"

"Of course, darling. Ask me anything at all."

Beth hesitated and then took a deep breath.

"Would you please kiss me again?" she asked shyly.

"Oh Beth!" John moaned as his mouth came down on hers.

7

Three expectant faces greeted Beth and John as they entered the study. While the two young people crossed the room and took their places beside Susan on the sofa, Patrick and Paul exchanged knowing looks and a wink. John was not the only one whose face glowed. Beth was positively radiant!

"Well, young man," said Patrick. "And what have you been up to?"

"What?" John started and flushed even more.

"Come on. Don't keep us in suspense any longer. How was your trip?"

"Oh!" John replied with a great sigh of relief. Beth nudged his arm lightly with her elbow. He glanced down at her but she was staring straight ahead, her face absolutely controlled but her shoulders were shaking with stifled laughter. John elbowed her back sharply and she peeked up at him with an impish grin.

"I'll deal with you later," he hissed.

"Oh goody!" whispered Beth.

This exchange did not go unnoticed by the others and Susan, in particular, beamed with satisfaction.

John cleared his throat several times before speaking, giving himself time to recover his composure.

"Well, now," he said. "Where to begin? First of all, I can tell you that I've been out to the States, but that's all that I'm at liberty to say. The man I had arranged to see was delighted with the icon. It was the one he wanted and he paid handsomely for it. In my case over there," he nodded towards where his cases were sitting, just inside the door, "I have two hundred thousand pounds in cash."

"*How much*?" stammered Beth, her eyes wide with incredulity. The others were sitting, mouths agape in astonishment.

"He really did want it and made a substantial offer at first. After some discussion, however, he willingly and graciously increased his original offer to two hundred thousand. So that will give each of your people twenty-five thousand, Beth. I hope that is acceptable to you."

"*Acceptable*! John, I can scarcely *believe* it! I never dreamed that it would fetch that much. That must be as close as possible to its maximum value. Whoever he is, that man must really have wanted it to pay that price. Oh, John, I hardly know how to thank you. Oh, grief, I think I'm going to cry."

John slipped his arm around her shoulders and drew her to him, secretly thankful for the opportunity to hold her again. He kissed the top of her head and then reached his other hand out to the box of tissues that Paul was holding out to him.

"I knew we were right not to put the tissues away yet," Paul joked.

"I know I'm a real cry-baby," Beth said as she blew her nose. "But I'm so overjoyed. I can hardly believe this!"

When she had finished with her tissues, she looked up at John with a radiant smile.

"Thank you. Thank you! *Thank you*!" she said and she stretched up to kiss his cheek. He squeezed her shoulders tightly and then reluctantly withdrew his arm.

"Tell me," Beth continued. "Have you taken your travel expenses and commission yet?"

"Don't you worry your pretty little head about things like that. All is taken care of, I promise you."

"You are a dear man for saying so but I'm not the least bit pretty."

"I beg to differ," countered John. "You are extremely pretty. In fact, you are very beautiful."

"Now you're being silly," Beth replied. "I am *not* beautiful."

"You are *gorgeous*!" John retorted.

"Ahem!" Patrick coughed. "If you two are quite finished, perhaps you could continue your tale, John."

Beth and John both went absolutely scarlet and everyone burst out laughing. Beth nudged John again.

"And I'll deal with you later," she whispered under the sound of the laughter.

"I can hardly wait!" John whispered back.

"No more whispering in here!" Patrick called. "We've serious business to discuss!"

"Well, actually, Unc," John said. "There's not a lot more I can tell you. I was able, however, to sell all your jewellery, Beth.

The same chap bought the lot for fifty thousand pounds cash. I have that for you, as well."

"*How much*?" shrieked Beth. "You are kidding me. You're having me on!"

"No, my dear. I promise you. He bought everything and was more than happy to pay the price. He was the most obliging person possible. Mind you, not being a jeweller myself but knowing more than a little about artefacts, I would say that he got a good deal. I don't for a minute think that you would have got a better price anywhere else, probably considerably less, in fact. But I think he did well for himself."

He looked down at Beth, his eyes twinkling.

"You're not displeased, I take it?"

"*Displeased*! John, you are a miracle worker! You are an absolute wonder!" This time she reached up and kissed him properly, full on the lips. "And I don't care who sees!" she retorted.

"Just how pleased are you?" John laughed against her lips.

"I think she's pleased enough for the moment, if you don't mind," Patrick said, a huge Cheshire cat grin on his face. "Just think of poor innocent Susan while you're busy ravishing that young thing, will you? Not forgetting her blood pressure, of course."

"My blood pressure, my eye!" retorted Susan. "You're just a jealous old goat and you know you are!"

"Enough of the old, woman. But you could well be right about the jealousy bit, not that I'm the least jealous of you, young man. Ah, but it's been many a long year since I had a wee young thing who was that enamoured of me."

"Dream on!" cried Paul. "You've never for one minute had the girls drooling over you and well you know it. Sure, if one did, you'd have run a mile."

"Don't be beastly!" Beth interrupted. "Father Patrick, you are positively adorable and I should think any number of young girls would have fallen for you when you were a young man. Further more, you are still a very attractive man and if I were considerably older and you weren't a priest and if you didn't have such a delicious nephew, considering I'm not considerably older ...."

"Enough! Enough!" cried Patrick, his hands in the air. "I've got the message! At least I think I have; that is, if there was one to get in the first place. Now, if you've said all you're going to, John, about your mysterious but oh-so-successful trip, then I shall see to pouring us all a drink. That is if you lot deserve one and I have my serious doubts about it."

"Pax. Peace. We forgive you," said Paul.

"You forgive me? Hah, some friend you are. Get off your backside and help me with the drinks or I'll send Susan up to pack your bags for you."

"And who would you play chess with this evening if you sent me home?"

"John!"

"Oops! Who would like what to drink?"

Beth took another tissue from John to wipe her tears of laughter. She leaned happily against him, feeling his love diffusing into her. She laid her face against his arm, feeling the rough tweed of his jacket scratch against her skin. Time would tell, as they say, she thought to herself, but she was going to enjoy getting to know this man. She had no idea what her future held in store for her, where she would live, how she would live, but now she knew that, come what may, John would very definitely be a part of that future. Of this, she was absolutely certain.

8

Beth laid down her pen and sat back wearily in her chair. She had just finished writing out the eighth letter and was now thoroughly drained. It surprised her just how exhausting it had been to copy out the letter so many times - emotionally exhausting. Getting the names and addresses from the little black book had been bad enough, surely the worst part, to her mind. But actually writing the letters, addressing them to a particular person, took on a whole new significance. They became personal, intimate and decidedly painful, no one more so or less so than any of the others. She wept with the writing of each one, her sorrow in no way diminished for the repetitiveness of the task.

But now they were completed. The money had been sorted into equal piles and each letter was ready for its envelope, then to be placed inside the padded bags that John had so thoughtfully brought home with him. Paul had commented earlier on her desire, her insistence, that the money be equally divisible by eight. She had tried to explain that to her it was very important that each family should be given a round figure sum of money. She didn't want any ones or twos or uneven bits. That, she felt, would be almost insulting, as if the money had been cobbled together any old how without real thought and consideration. She wasn't sure if Patrick and Paul understood her thinking. She wasn't entirely sure if she did herself, but for some reason it was very important to her that this whole operation be handled in the best possible way, as neatly as could be. After all, it was a very delicate and sensitive thing she was undertaking and even if she would never meet the recipients or know of their reactions, she could not bear to think that she would give offence in any way. It was more of an instinctive feeling than a readily explainable action. All she knew for certain was that doing this her way made sense to her and had a degree of comfort about it.

Wearily, she closed her eyes and tried to pray but found it very difficult. She was so wrung out that it was impossible to focus her thoughts on anything. So she just sat and let her mind drift and eventually she fell asleep.

Feeling something pressed against her forehead, she awoke with a start and, opening her eyes, found herself looking up into John's face. He was leaning over her, one hand on each arm of her chair, smiling gently down at her.

"Hello, sweetheart," he said softly. "I'm sorry if I woke you. I've brought you up some tea and I did knock but didn't get any answer. So I just popped my head in to see if you were all right and you looked so adorable that I couldn't resist taking a closer look at you. I've never seen you sleeping before and then I couldn't resist giving you a little kiss and that's when you woke up."

Beth reached up her hand and stroked his cheek, running her fingers lightly over his lips.

"I'm glad you woke me," she said. "I was just dreaming about you and now here you are." She slipped her hand behind his neck, drawing his head down towards her and a deep, heart-stopping kiss. John pushed himself upright, grabbing Beth's hands on the way so that she was almost jerked out of her chair and into his arms. He crushed her to him and it was difficult to tell whose heart was pounding the loudest.

"Oh, it's a good thing I left your bedroom door open when I came in or I might not be responsible for my actions," he said huskily. "Always assuming, of course, that you find me equally irresistible," he added with a nervous laugh.

"Don't tempt me, John. Please, not yet. It scares me how deeply attracted to you I am. Good grief, I've been widowed for less than two weeks and here I am, falling in love with you!"

"Are you really, Beth? Are you really falling in love with me?" John's voice was incredulous.

"Oh, my darling, I don't really know but I think so. I've never felt anything like this in my life before. It's as if I've finally come alive after an endless, drugged sleep. I don't really know how to describe how I feel but I do know that with you I feel real, alive, safe, happy in a way I've never before experienced.

"But, John, I've already had one whirlwind so-called romance and look where it landed me."

"Here in my arms," John joked. "But seriously, Beth, can you honestly compare the two? Am I so like your former husband? Is what you felt for him anything like what you feel for me?"

Beth looked deeply into John's eyes as if she were searching into the depths of his soul.

"Dear John," she finally said. "The only resemblance between you is that you both have two arms and legs and you are not female. I find it difficult to refer to him as a man; in fact, to refer to him at all. He swept me off my feet and into a living hell in which I was totally powerless. I never want to experience anything like that ever again. It was so frightening, so soul-destroying, that I lost all awareness of myself as a person.

"I'm not one of these feminist types but I do like to feel that I am a real person, an individual with thoughts and feelings and the right to those thoughts and feelings. In that relationship I rapidly, within days, found that I was a nonentity, a nothing. I was treated with absolute contempt by the whole family. I wasn't even allowed to leave the house on my own. It was as if 'Beth' had never existed. The sense of dislocation was really scary and it's only in the last week that I've started to regain my own identity.

"But this new me, the *real* me - my new creation, as Paul calls it - feels a passion for you that I didn't know I was capable of. More than anything, I want to be with you, to have you hold me, to hold you, to talk with you, to laugh with you and one day, to love with you. But I need to take things slowly, John. *Please* understand. I have to be sure, absolutely certain, that what I'm feeling now is not merely a reaction against all I've been through. That it isn't just a longing for the opposite of all I've experienced up 'til now. I want it to be real more than anything else.

"I love you. I *know* that I love you but I need to know that it's *real*. That sounds crazy, I know, but can you understand? Can you please give me time?"

John studied her face intently, his heart touched by the pleading in her eyes, the little crease that always appeared between her brows when she was in earnest about something and she most certainly was in earnest about this. Her sincerity was palpable, almost tangible and he felt an even deeper love for her surge within him, powered by the thought that she just might love him, really want him in her life forever. What did time matter when he had that promise, that hope to look forward to?

"Beth, my sweet Beth," he said softly. "Take all the time you need. Please don't feel pressured by me. You know how much I love you and want you but don't let that frighten you. I want you to take comfort from that knowledge, feel safe within it. You know how much I want you in my life but I only want you to come to me wholeheartedly, freely, when you are ready. Oh, but we shall be so very happy, I know that with all my heart and I am content to wait until you have that same surety and confidence. I promise you that I shall be gentle and patient with you but I shall seriously enjoy wooing you, none the less!"

"*Wooing*! What a lovely word," exclaimed Beth. "So delightfully old-fashioned."

"And so delightfully enjoyable, I assure you!"

"I have a feeling that I shall have as much enjoyment as you will!" Beth laughed. "I do want to thank you, quite seriously, for being so understanding, John. It means so much to me, knowing that I won't be pressured, that you are giving me this time and space to get myself turned around and my emotions sorted out. They've been through the wars, somewhat, of late but I really believe that I am well on the road to my emotional recovery and it's a real comfort to me to know that you will be taking a major part in that recovery."

"Be assured that I will. I want your complete recovery, your wholeness, not just for myself, but for you, too. If I were wholly altruistic, then I would say for you above all else, but I have to be honest and admit my deep personal interest and acknowledge a very selfish motive. I want you to be emotionally free so that we can enjoy a glorious life together! If that isn't selfish, then I don't what know is."

"I think it is *romantic*! Utterly, utterly romantic. Keep it up and I might just get better sooner than I expected!"

"The sooner, the better! But before you make any further progress I shall have to progress myself out that door while I am still able to. Your tea is well and truly cold, unlike me! So, I'll go and make you some more and then leave you in peace. Uncle Pat will be seriously wondering about us if I don't put in an appearance in a minute. He's wanting a talk with me and I said that I'd only be a minute or two with your tea. I'll be getting you a bad reputation at this rate!"

"I tell you what," said Beth. "You go and see your uncle and I'll get my own tea. Then I must really get on with some work." She nodded her head in the direction of her easel that was turned to face the window.

"*Ah*," John exclaimed. "You're painting! May I see?"

"You most certainly may *not*! At least not yet," Beth added. "All shall be revealed in due course, but not just now. I don't like anyone seeing things that aren't finished. That makes me feel very vulnerable as if I'm exposing myself in some way. Silly, but there we are.

"Now," she said, pushing John before her towards the door. "Out of here so I can get on."

John laughingly allowed himself to be propelled over to the door where he suddenly stopped and Beth crashed into him. He pulled her into his arms, gazing down into her eyes in wonderment.

"You are so beautiful," he murmured. "So very beautiful. I love you so dearly."

"I love you, too," whispered Beth as John's mouth came down to meet hers. "Now go downstairs!" she added emphatically as she pushed playfully against his chest. "While you still are able."

"Did I hear you correctly?" he asked cheekily.

"Downstairs! *Now*!"

"Okay, okay, I'm going! But one of these days I just might not!"

"*Go*!"

Beth chased him downstairs and then dodged past him towards the kitchen while he carried on into the study where his uncle sat, looking towards the door, one eyebrow raised dramatically.

"Just a minute or two, I believe you said. Was that right? Or is my hearing failing fast?"

"Unfeeling beast," John laughed as he flopped into his chair.

9

"Well, young man, and what kept you?" Patrick asked, after they heard Beth's retreating footsteps up the stairs and the closing of her bedroom door.

"We were just talking," John answered, a little defensively.

"*Just* talking, eh?" Patrick emphasised the 'just', noting, with suppressed glee, his nephew's rising colour.

"Well, mostly, just talking," John stumbled over his words. "Oh, but Unc, she's so gorgeous and I must confess that I really have fallen helplessly in love with her."

"Is that an official confession to me in my role as a priest, by chance?" Patrick teased.

John laughed.

"You really can be a rotter when you want to be, Uncle Pat. No, it wasn't 'official' because I have nothing 'official' to confess. Believe me, there is nothing immoral, illegal or fattening about my feelings for Beth. I am quite simply in love. What more can I say?"

"And how does *she* feel? Bearing in mind her circumstances, of course."

"I'm only too aware of them, I assure you. They tend to complicate things somewhat but they're not insurmountable. I know that she needs time to get over the unbelievable emotional battering she has had recently and whatever else I may be, I'm not insensitive!"

"No-one could ever suggest you are, lad. I am, however, concerned that you might get hurt if you rush at things too quickly. I fear that Beth might just run in the opposite direction if you press her too hard or too soon."

"I realise that, only too well. We've talked things over fairly extensively and I think we've arrived at a mutually acceptable decision. I've agreed to give Beth all the time she needs. She knows how much I love her and she also knows that she has my absolute support, that I'm not going to push her into anything for which she is not ready. I'm content to wait for her, to be her friend, to be her confidant."

"And just what will you get out of all this, other than no

small degree of frustration? Bearing in mind, also, that we don't yet know where she will be after Christmas. We all know that she can't stay here indefinitely, as much as we would enjoy having her here. I have commitments that simply can't be fulfilled all the while Beth is here and in danger of her life."

"Actually, Uncle, I've been giving that a lot of thought, especially while I was travelling to and from the States. You know that I have my cottage up on the coast of Donegal. At the moment it is vacant and I've made no commitments to lease it out in the New Year. So it is sitting empty - a perfectly nice house, warm, cosy, well furnished and appointed. I believe that it would be an ideal place for Beth to live. No-one would know who she is. She would be absolutely safe and she could get on with her painting, as well, for, as you know, I usually let it out to artists because of its setting and the big, picture windows which are perfect for the light that they require.

"In fact, I don't think it could be more perfect for her. The neighbours are more than used to having strangers living there for varying periods of time, mostly artists and so Beth would be just one more as far as they were concerned. Also, I would be less than an hour away in Donegal town itself and I could keep an eye on her with no trouble at all. As you know, I have a flat above the gallery in the town, in which I live when I'm there, so that would give her the space she needs but at the same time give me the opportunity to hopefully advance my cause!"

Patrick sat for some minutes in silent contemplation of all that his nephew had told him. John, for his part, could hardly keep still and so he got up from his chair and walked about the room, agitatedly jingling the coins in his pocket and making clicking noises with his tongue against his teeth.

"Do come and sit down and stop fidgeting!" Patrick implored. "You're driving me *crazy* with that noise."

John came over and threw himself into his chair with such a look of dejection on his face that Patrick smiled in sympathy.

"Don't look so hard done by," the old priest said kindly. "Actually, I've been trying to find the flaws - any flaws - in your proposal and can honestly find none. It strikes me that you just might have the perfect solution to Beth's predicament. At least to the question of her immediate safety. We'll say nothing more just yet about any future developments. I leave that in the hands of the Lord - and so should you both!

"I must admit that I would feel far happier, knowing that Beth was within easy reach of someone absolutely trustworthy. And I know that Susan would approve, too. She has taken quite a shine to that young woman - as have we all - and simply wouldn't allow her to go off just anywhere. None of us would, of course, but Paul and I have been most concerned about what to do with the poor girl. Your solution is positively inspired. And I'm sure will be of great benefit to you both!"

"I pray so, Uncle Pat. I really do. Nothing would give me greater delight than to share my life with Beth. I could think of nothing more wonderful. Between you and me," he added shyly, "she has already told me that she does love me and that she would want to spend her life with no-one else, but she needs time to be certain that her present feelings are not just a reaction against what she has been through. So I really do think there is hope for me - for us."

"My boy, *nothing* could make me happier! I respect your confidence absolutely. But do let me know as soon as I can tell Susan and Paul. And when the time comes, I will be honoured beyond measure to perform the ceremony for you!"

"*Now* who's jumping the gun! I haven't even told Beth about Donegal yet, let alone moved her up there. A little decorum, if you don't mind, Uncle. After all, you are supposed to be a priest!"

"Ah yes, but I'm a doting uncle, too."

"Well, you'll have to find something else to dote on for a while yet!"

"How about doting on a glass of whiskey with me? Just to celebrate."

"By the way, what's happened to Paul?" John asked when he had taken the proffered glass from Patrick and the older man was comfortably seated once more in his chair.

"Oh, he decided to wander over to visit Dermot and thrash him again at cribbage into the bargain, I shouldn't wonder. I think he was in need of some fresh air. We all are, in fact, but the situation with Beth makes it difficult. Fortunately, the weather has been so appalling lately that no-one has really wanted to go out anyway.

For once in our lives, we can actually be grateful for the awful Irish weather!"

"It must be difficult for you all to be cooped up in here day after day. I guess Susan is the only one who can come and go with any degree of ease."

"Yes, you're right, although Paul does get out occasionally, usually to take Susan shopping. But the most important thing is Beth's safety and we are all more than happy to make whatever sacrifices are necessary for her sake. Still, I shall be more than a little relieved to be able to move about more freely after you two have departed. I must say that I'm quite looking forward to your departure."

"Thank you very much!" exclaimed John.

"No, no, no. Please don't take that the wrong way. I merely meant that I will be so glad to think that Beth will at last have a chance to get on with her life in a more normal fashion. This has been a terribly difficult time for her and not just her stay here in this house. I mean the whole time she has been in Ireland. I'd love her to get to know *real* Irish people, the *good* people that you and I were brought up with and have known all our lives. Not the low-life types she married into in such tragic innocence. That young lady deserves some *real* happiness now."

"I know, Uncle Pat, and if it is at all within my power, I shall make sure that she is as happy as it's possible to be."

"And I have every confidence in you, old son. Sure, you'll make a fine couple when the time is right and I have little doubt that the time will not be all that far away. I have a very good feeling about you two. But enough of that subject for the time being; there's not a lot to be gained by dwelling on it unnecessarily. Tell me, I've been wanting to know, are you able to fill me in on any of the details of your trip at all? I'm most curious, I can tell you."

John took a sip of his drink and then put his glass on the table beside him. He stood up and moved over to the fireplace where he busied himself, placing more logs on the fire. Then he returned to his chair and picked up his glass again.

"Well, Unc," he said after a few moments. "I must admit that I would like to talk about it, but only to you. It's not that I don't trust Paul or Susan. It's nothing like that but I was sworn to secrecy, mostly to protect Beth from the knowledge of who her benefactor really is. It is all rather intriguing. And with you being a priest, at least I feel I can talk to you about it without breaching my oath of secrecy.

"My contact within the trade gave me the name of a man in Boston who was most anxious to see the icon as soon as he heard it was available. It seems the two men know each other reasonably well and the American had let my contact know a few months ago that if an icon should ever become available for sale here in Ireland, then he wanted first sight and refusal. It's almost as if he was anticipating such an occurrence.

"As you can imagine, my curiosity was pretty intense by the time I met this man at his gallery in Boston. He gave absolutely nothing away until he had opened the box in which I had the icon. Then his face virtually crumpled and I really thought he was going to cry. My first reaction was astonishment, if not embarrassment. I couldn't believe that he could want the icon that badly, even if it *is* particularly lovely.

"He looked up at me and his eyes were filled with tears and all he said was, 'How *is* she? Tell me, how is the poor wee girl?' Then he did start to cry. Well, I almost fell over in surprise. Anyway, without going into too much detail, it transpires that the chap was Beth's old boss!"

"You mean that Sean fellow that she's talked about? It was *him* that you were seeing?"

"So it would appear. She was right when she said that he had given it to her in case she should ever be in great need. The fact that it was on the market so soon after he had given it to her had got him into a terrible state. He knew that the only reason it was for sale was because Beth must be in serious trouble. He would tell me nothing more until I had assured him absolutely that she was well and safe."

"Hang on a minute, old son," said Patrick, as he rose from his chair and picked up John's glass. "I have a feeling that we are both in need of a refill. I get the distinct impression that this is not going to be a pretty tale." He went over to the drinks cabinet and poured them both a large whiskey with just the merest dash of soda.

John took his glass from his uncle and took a large sip.

"I'll not disillusion you on that point, Unc. It is very far from pretty. It appears that Kevin Brady was in Boston on a fund raising mission for the IRA. but unbeknownst to them, he pocketed a considerable amount of the money for himself. It was supposed to be going into a secret account for use at the most opportune moment to mount an election campaign for the Brady's chosen candidate in some future election or other. All very nonspecific and all very dodgy, if you ask me. Sean O'Grady was genuinely convinced that the money he gave to this secret fund was really to do good for the Irish people, to rescue them from the wicked English - it's amazing what a distorted view so many Americans have of the real situation here.

"Anyway, Sean had reservations about Kevin as a person. But despite that, he was very generous in his donations over the years. When Kevin came to the shop and met Beth, quite by accident, Sean was deeply concerned, if not alarmed, for he knew what a charmer Kevin was and how very vulnerable and innocent was Beth. Just as he feared, Kevin swept Beth off her feet and we know the sorry outcome of that.

"It seems that Sean knows the family of old and guessed, rightly so, that Beth would be made most unwelcome by Kevin's mother. Furthermore, he couldn't see the marriage lasting if Beth ever discovered the secrets of that family, despite her faith and her determination to live up to her marriage vows. That was really the reason he gave her the icon. So that she would have some financial security of her own if ever it was needed.

"What he never imagined was that she would have such need so soon and for the reasons she does. He was absolutely devastated when I told him the facts that I know about her. He literally sobbed when I told him what Michael had done to her."

"You told him everything, then?" queried Patrick.

"He wanted to know so I told him all that Beth had told me."

"You didn't tell him where she is, did you?"

"Good gracious, no! I didn't even tell him my name, so there is no chance of a trace, if that is your concern."

"It most definitely *is*!"

"Well, I can promise you that I took every possible precaution so as to maintain our anonymity and Beth's safety. That was absolutely paramount in my dealings with Sean. It was practically all I could do to stop him from coming back here with me to see for himself that Beth was really safe and well, but when I explained to him that he would be putting her life in even greater danger if he did, he backed down. I think it was just panic and genuine concern for her that made him react as he did. But he gradually saw sense and I was able to calm him down somewhat.

"I have every confidence in Sean's agreement to absolute secrecy in this deal. His very real concern for Beth is our guarantee of his silence. Also, he would bring the wrath of the Brady clan down very heavily upon himself if they knew of his underhand dealings with Kevin. The secret account was known only to him and to Kevin!

"He was adamant that he wanted to do something for her, personally, himself - he knew that the money from the icon is to be used for the victims' families - so I asked him if he could find a buyer for Beth's jewellery. He practically had my hand off my arm in his eagerness to get at it and instantly said that he would buy the whole lot himself. He paid cash for everything, then and there. I dread to think what other business he is really involved in because he unlocked a door that is hidden behind a cabinet in his private office, went in and returned with the cash, *in Sterling*! He must have his own private bank in there. He even has a counterfeit testing device and made me check every single note as I counted them, just to prove that he was really above board. It was decidedly eerie, I can tell you. But I was hardly going to argue with the man, not when he was paying out that sort of money.

"By the way, he even paid all my expenses, on top of everything else. But I get the feeling, somehow, that despite all his very real grief about Beth, he still had an eye to the main chance over this deal. I was able to bump him up on the price of the icon - and I do feel we got a fair price on that - but, as I've already said, I think he did well for himself with the jewellery. That Brady guy had a good eye for quality stuff and certainly didn't stint himself. I wonder how much of the money he used to buy it all was really blood money?"

Patrick shot forward in his chair, a look of horror on his face.

"Don't *ever* say that to Beth!" he exclaimed. "Sure, the girl would have heart failure, at the very least!"

John very nearly snapped at his uncle in annoyance at the suggestion that he might do such a thing but managed to bite back the words before they were uttered. Patrick's concern for Beth was no less than his own, perhaps even more so really, as he had seen her through so much trauma and pain, whereas he, himself, had come in at the end of it all. So, he took a deep breath and smiled warmly at the old priest.

"Dear Uncle Patrick, what we have discussed here, in this room, this afternoon, stays *here* between you and me and no-one else will ever know of it. That is a solemn promise. It's only because of the strangeness and the distinctly shady goings-on of my trip that I needed to share them with you - to talk them through. Now I feel greatly relieved, unburdened, and I can leave all the uncomfortable feelings behind me. They won't be able to come between me and Beth now that I have shared them with you."

Patrick sat back and drank deeply from his glass, his expression somewhat relieved but still a little wary.

"I'm very glad to hear it, John. I must confess that I don't like the sound of a lot that you have told me. There are all manner of things I could ask you about your trip but I think I would prefer not to know the answers now. So, if you have finished unburdening yourself, may I suggest that we leave the subject altogether?"

"Fine by me! Believe me, it is an episode that I trust I will never have to repeat. Shady dealings are definitely not my style. I just don't have the stomach for them. Thank the Lord!"

"Just so! And that's what we should do. I think you and I should spend a few minutes in prayer, thanking the Lord for the successful outcome of your trip, but even more important, asking Him to cleanse away all unpleasantness or even ungodliness and to keep you and Beth safe from any possible future repercussions as a result of all this."

10

The following morning, Paul bade farewell to all in Patrick's house. Now that Beth was so well on the way to her recovery and now that her future was settled, at least for the interim - even though she as yet did not know it - there was no call for him to stay in Belfast any longer. Also, his sister was becoming decidedly agitated at his continued absence and was starting to nag him into returning home.

After shaking hands with Patrick and John and sharing a big hug with Susan, Paul turned to Beth, who was standing shyly to one side. He opened his arms and she stepped into his embrace, turning her face against his chest, partly to hide her tears. They stood for a few moments in silence, each vividly aware of a great deal of emotion. Finally Paul broke the silence.

"I shall miss you, young lady," he said. "It has been a joy to know you and a joy to be of help to you."

"And I shall miss you, too, Paul. More than I can possibly say. I can't put into words what your help has meant to me - and your love and prayers.

"Oh, by the way, I've been meaning to ask you something for days now. When you were praying during my counselling sessions I noticed that you often used a foreign language. Was it Hebrew by any chance?"

"No, my dear," he replied, "that was what is known as praying in tongues - one of the gifts of the Holy Spirit. It is not a discernible, earthly language as such but it can be particularly useful when it is difficult to find the right words to pray for someone or some need, or yet again when words aren't really necessary - the Spirit takes over in a sense. Our friend, Hugh, refers to it as 'turbo-charge' prayer. If you wish to know more about it I'm sure Pat will be only too happy to explain further.

"In the meantime, I'm deeply gratified that my input has been beneficial. I hope and pray that you will continue to go forward in your healing, getting stronger each day and I look forward to seeing a big change in you when we next meet. When you're settled in your new home, wherever that may be, Pat will let me know your address and I shall be coming to visit just as soon as you'll have me."

"What a lovely thought! You'll be welcome at my home any time at all. That will really give me something to look forward to."

"And now, my dear, I really must be going," Paul said, as he bent to kiss her cheek. "Pat will keep me informed of your progress and any time you should wish to write to me, I shall be delighted to receive your letters."

"And if you're lucky, you might even get an answer to them," put in Patrick. "There's nothing he loves more than to receive letters but he's far from the world's greatest at answering them!"

"Well, we'll just have to use the telephone then, won't we, Paul?" Beth replied. "I'm not so sure that I'm such a great correspondent myself. I've never really had much opportunity to find out. And anyway, it will do me good to hear your voice."

Paul detached himself from their embrace and reached down to pick up his overnight bag. He looked lovingly from one face to the other.

"My friends, God bless you all," he said, heartily. "May you have a joyous Christmas. You will all be in my prayers and in my thoughts as we raise our glasses to absent friends. May the time pass quickly until we are together again.

"Susan, my dear, your hospitality and care have been beyond compare as always. Bless you for your kindness and your most delicious food!

"John, the Lord be with you and bless you for your contribution to our work with Beth. Your help has been invaluable. Take good care of this lovely young lady. And that's an order!

"Patrick, my very dear friend. What can I say? Once again you have made me most welcome and once again it has been a joy and a delight to work with you."

"God bless you, Paul," Patrick replied. "As always, I couldn't have done this on my own. We make quite a team, you and I, especially with the Lord as the boss-man!

"And now, if you don't get going, Isobel will be on the phone, berating me again for keeping you from your rightful place at home and I don't happen to have a spare two hours for chastisement today, much as I love your sister. Furthermore, if you stop any longer, Susan will be having to get out her mop to clear up all the tears from this young lady and you wouldn't be wanting to create yet more work for the poor old dear, now, would you?"

"I'll 'poor old dear' you, in a minute!" retorted Susan. "You just leave the lovely man alone. Sure, he's no trouble in all the world to look after, not like some as I could mention.

"But you must be on your way now," she added to Paul. "The rain is a little easier just now but the forecast is for another gale a bit later on and I would hate to think of you caught in that bad weather now. Give my very best regards to your sister and make sure you have a lovely Christmas. For all your moaning, you love to have your family about you and well you know it. Come back any time and you'll be as welcome as you always are."

"Bless you, Susan. You're a very special lady and make no mistake about it. And I hear what you say - I shall be away now before the weather closes in. Goodbye, one and all. Susan will see me to the door."

As Paul went to leave the study, Beth slipped an envelope in his hand.

"What's this?" he asked.

"It's not for now. You'll see when you get home," she answered, blushing slightly. "God Bless you and thank you so much, once again." She reached up and kissed his cheek and then pushed him gently towards the door.

At the door, Paul turned to look once more at Patrick, John and Beth, a big smile creasing his face. He raised his hand in silent salute and left the room, pulling the door to behind him.

Susan returned to the study a few minutes later, bearing a tray of coffee and cakes. Leaving the others to enjoy their 'elevenses', she went about her housework, humming happily to herself, having yet again refused Beth's offer of help.

"Susan never ceases to amaze me," Beth said, as she sipped her coffee. "Nor Bridie, for that matter. They are so alike, those two, and they never seem to be happier than when they are busying about cooking or cleaning or generally looking after someone."

"You're right there," answered Patrick. "Those two are very special ladies. I know I tease the daylights out of both of them - sure, it's one of my greatest delights to 'wind them up', as the saying goes - but I never for one second underestimate the value of their devotion, which they see, and rightly so, as their service to the Lord. I truly don't know what I would do without Susan. She is a true God-send, bless her."

"She certainly is and I shall miss her dearly when I leave here, if I ever find anywhere to go, that is."

"Funny you should say that," John interrupted. "I do believe that I may have the answer to your problem. I've already discussed it with Uncle Pat and Uncle Paul to get their opinions and their approval. They are in full agreement with what I have in mind. Please don't be offended that I spoke with them first without mentioning it to you but, under the circumstances, I felt it best to seek their acceptance before presenting the plan to you.

"Have you, by chance, noticed the painting in your room upstairs?"

"Of course. It's beautiful."

"You like it, then?"

"Absolutely! I really *love* it, not just the artistic skill but particularly the scene itself. I've been meaning to ask if anyone knows where the location is. I'd really love to visit that place someday."

"Perfect!" exclaimed John. Beth gave him a quizzical look. "The location is a small village - well, actually a hamlet - up the coast from Donegal town, in the republic of Ireland, and one of those little cottages depicted in the picture is owned by me. I usually rent it out to visiting artists. Young Jack Harrison, a lad from New Zealand, had stayed several times; he was perpetually short of money and so one year he painted the picture upstairs for me in lieu of rent. The cottage is warm, comfortable, cosy, quiet and, most important right now, empty.

"What do you say to making that your new home? You can live there for as long as you like. The neighbours, I know, will make you most welcome and will not ask any awkward questions as they are well used to people - artists in particular - coming and going from the cottage. I live less than an hour away in Donegal town so will always be on hand should you need anything at all, even if it's just some company on a cold winter's evening."

Beth sat forward in her chair, her hands clasped together, her eyes bright with excitement.

"Oh, John," she exclaimed softly. "Do you *mean* it? *Really*?

That picture is where you live?"

"Well, I own one of the cottages, as I've said, but I actually live in a flat above my gallery in Donegal, itself. And yes, I do mean it. You're most welcome to live in the cottage for as long as you like. That is, if you do like, of course."

Beth clapped her hands together and scrunched up her shoulders in glee.

"*Oh, I like*. I really do like! I shall take it sight unseen!"

"Well, if I may suggest, I think it would be a good idea if you first came to stay at my flat. I've plenty of room," he added hurriedly. "And I promise to behave! But seriously, the cottage has been empty for a few months now and so it will need a good cleaning and airing and then a thorough warming up. You might not be aware that it is on the west side of the country and there's not a lot of anything between it and Labrador and this time of year it can get seriously cold, believe me. I would want to be absolutely sure that the place was fully habitable and warm before you moved in but that shouldn't take too long."

"It sounds wonderful! And don't forget that I'm used to pretty cold winters. I grew up in the interior of Ontario, after all, and then spent time in Boston."

"Yes, but you also had pretty efficient central heating, I'm sure. The cottage relies mainly on wood-burning stoves and an old Aga in the kitchen. They're plenty adequate for the size of the cottage, but you'll probably be needing more winter woollies than you've been used to 'back home'."

Patrick sat comfortably in his chair, observing the interchange between his nephew and Beth with a great deal of satisfaction. He was more than content that the move to Donegal would be just what Beth needed; indeed, what they both needed. It was a most beautiful place, he knew from his own experience, and would afford Beth the space and the time to fully grow into her healing, to 'walk out her healing', as his friend, Hugh, had described the process. He could certainly see the hand of the Lord at work in all this. They had all prayed for a resolution to Beth's dilemma and here was what appeared to be the perfect answer.

Added to his satisfaction was the scene being enacted before his eyes, although the 'players' were not play-acting; theirs was a *genuine* 'performance'. It gave him such joy to see the interaction between the two, to hear their animated conversation as they made their plans, discussed their future. Patrick had never seen Beth look so beautiful and alive; she sparkled with vitality and exuberance. And John, his beloved John, glowed with happiness and love; his face was radiant and his eyes had turned that special deep cornflower blue that was always the indicator of the depth of his emotions.

Patrick felt a twinge, almost of pain, in his chest as he realised just how much he was going to miss Beth when she finally left his house. Even the thought that there was every likelihood that she would, at some time in the future, become part of his family did little to lessen his sudden heartache. With a determined effort of will, he turned his mind away from such depressing thoughts and back to the scene taking place before him. He drank in the atmosphere, the ambience, the warmth of their emotions, storing them away to be recalled in the times of quietness and aloneness that often beset a man with so much love inside and so few with whom to share it.

11

The following morning there was an unexpected visit from Bridie, who lumbered into the kitchen behind Susan, lugging several great heavy shopping bags with her.

"Bridie!" called Patrick. "What a delightful surprise! This is not your usual visiting day, so it must be something momentous that brings you all the way down here, and in such weather, too."

"Well, it's nothing to worry yourself about," Bridie answered quickly, as she saw the look of concern that flooded Beth's face. "In truth, I've a little surprise for you. The postman was late today, being that close to Christmas and him being inundated with all the extra letters and things and themselves up at the house had already left to go about God alone knows what evil deeds."

"Bridie!" Patrick admonished gently.

"Well, to be sure, I don't know and I don't wish to know what that evil pair get up to but you can guarantee that it will do no good to any decent living soul and that's the truth. Anyway, as I was saying before himself over there interrupted me as usual, the postman was late - thanks be to God, for it must have been Himself that organised it, for otherwise those two would have been there and would have got at the post before I had a chance to sort through it myself. But for once, they had taken themselves away out of the house, the pair of them, and I was about my own business, polishing the hall table when the doorbell rang, which in itself is a rare occurrence these days, I can tell you.

"Do you know, it's almost as if that young one's murder has been like a death-knell in that house, for no-one ever comes near them now, except that nauseating priest of hers and her stupid doctor. God, it's like a bloody morgue up at that place, so it is - begging your pardon, Father.

"As I was saying, the postman was late this morning..."

"We know that much already, Bridie, but not a lot of anything else," Patrick interrupted.

"If you'll be quiet and let me get on with my story instead of interrupting me every two seconds then I'll be able to tell you what it is I have to tell you," Bridie answered with some acerbity.

"We're waiting patiently and in silence," Patrick said. "And getting greyer by the minute, into the bargain."

"Don't you be rude! As I was saying, the postman was late this morning and," she rushed on, heedless of Patrick's attempts to interrupt yet again. "And he left a large parcel. All the way from America it is and it's not for any of them up at the big house, that's for certain." She winked at Beth and then bent to struggle with a large carrier bag at her feet.

John leapt to his feet and lifted the bag onto the kitchen table, pushing the morning papers to one side to make room for it. He held the carrier bag steady as Bridie withdrew from it a large parcel, wrapped in brown paper, which she ceremoniously handed to Beth. Silently, Beth took the parcel and looked at the return address. As she had suspected, it was from the Sinclair, family and as she read the address, she burst into tears.

"Oh, my Lord!" cried Bridie, in dismay. "If I'd known it was going to cause you such upset, sure I would never have brought it all the way down here, so I wouldn't!"

"Oh, Bridie," sniffed Beth. "It's not your fault. You've done nothing to upset me, honestly you haven't. It's just that it's suddenly come home to me that I can't even send my best friend a Christmas card. I can't tell her anything that is going on in my life and I need her now like I've never needed a friend before," she sobbed.

"Father, what have I done?" Bridie implored, as she turned to Patrick, her face a picture of grief. "I'd not do a thing to hurt the wee lady, so I wouldn't, you know that."

"Of course, we all know that, Bridie," Patrick answered. He moved over to the old lady and placed a friendly arm around her shoulders, drawing her to him. "And you've done not a thing wrong, I assure you. It's just that this is a difficult time for Beth, being so far away from her friends. It must be hard enough at this time of year, under the best of circumstances, but for her, it must be nearly impossible. You know what a loving person she is and it must hurt her deeply not to be able to communicate with her close friends at this time. So don't you worry yourself now. We don't want our beloved Bridie all upset now, do we?"

"Ah, Father," said Bridie, drawing in a shuddering breath. "You're a comfort, so you are. I've always said you are and you always will be and that's a fact. Bless you, Father."

"And bless you, Bridie," he answered, giving her a final squeeze before releasing his arm from around her scrawny shoulders.

Meanwhile, at the first sign of Beth's tears, John had dropped to his haunches beside her chair and put his arms around her. She laid her head against his shoulders and wept and wept, too heartsick to be embarrassed at crying, yet again, in front of everyone. John gently rocked her to and fro, making little crooning noises, allowing her to cry out her sadness. Susan quietly put on the kettle and got everything ready to make a large pot of tea.

While Bridie was taking out her handkerchief to give her nose a good blow, she glanced over at Beth and was astonished to see John's loving, solicitous embrace. She glanced up at Father Patrick, giving him a most quizzical look, arching her eyebrow in such a comical fashion that the priest almost guffawed out loud. Instead, he smiled knowingly and tapped his forefinger against his lips. Interpreting the situation accurately, Bridie scrunched up her shoulders with glee, grinning hugely and gave Patrick such a sharp jab in the ribs with her bony elbow that he caught his breath in a loud gasp.

Hearing his uncle's sharp intake of breath, John raised his head to look at him, which in turn disturbed Beth. She lifted her head from his shoulder, took a loud, deep breath and reached gratefully for John's proffered handkerchief. When she was thoroughly mopped and blown, she looked with a rueful expression, at the others.

"I'm so sorry," Beth said at last. "I didn't mean to be such a cry-baby. I've tried so hard not to even think of Cathy and her family that just the sight of their name on the package, and especially Cathy's handwriting, was almost too much. I didn't realise just how much I miss them all. Not that I think any the less of all of you," she added hastily. "I don't know what I'd have done without you these last few weeks - months, in your case, Bridie. I love you all so much and you have all become like a family to me, but I still miss my other friends terribly."

"And what sort of a person would you be if you didn't?" put in Susan. "Not the Beth that we all know and love, and that's a true fact."

"Agreed most heartily," added John. "And if I'm not very much mistaken, I do believe that I can smell tea brewing in the pot."

"There never was another like you for being able to smell tea!" Susan answered. "I think you can smell just the idea of it. Sure, and how many times have you arrived at my door just as I've put on the kettle?"

"Your tea is worth travelling miles for. There's none better in all Ireland."

"*Flannel*! Pure flannel!" exclaimed Susan as she got the milk out of the refrigerator and poured it into a jug. "Everyone up to the table that wants tea before himself here has it all."

Beth laughed along with the others, grateful for the banter between John and Susan which gave her time to recover her equilibrium. She was more than a little certain that they had actually been putting on a bit of an act, just for that purpose and her heart surged with love for them both - for them all, Patrick and Bridie included. What friends they all were to her and how she loved them all.

As they had their tea, Bridie filled them in on the goings-on up at the Brady house. It appeared that Christmas would not be celebrated in their household this year. Kevin's death precluded any form of celebration or jollity for them and they were not so committed in their religious faith that they would celebrate the true meaning of Christmas anyway. Theirs was a 'faith' of outer show and public display, having next to nothing to do with their hearts.

"Sure, it's like a bloody morgue up there - begging your pardon, Father," said Bridie, gloomily. "And as for Mairead, sure, I don't know what goes through her poor wee mind most of the time, but lately she's been acting awful queer. Anytime the old battle-axe or her evil spawn come into the room, she starts to laugh, very quietly, but just enough to drive them out again. It sounds more like a cackle than a proper laugh. I think meself that she is having a real go at them in her own funny way. It's driving them crazy and the more they shout at her, so the more she does it. I haven't seen her so interested in anything for years, so I haven't. I think she's really enjoying herself."

"She's a very sad lady," Patrick said. "Make no mistake about it and it's all the doing of the people in that house - excluding your good self and your good husband, of course, Bridie - so they've no one to blame but themselves if they don't like her behaviour. I must confess that I can't hold it in my heart to chastise the poor woman in any way. What she has suffered over the years, the Lord alone knows. And thankfully he does, for in His own time and His own way, He will compensate her for all her wretchedness.

"Tell me, Bridie. If they are not wanting to celebrate the Holy Day, will you and Joseph be able to come along to us, for we shall celebrate in style, I've no doubt?"

"Ah, thank you, Father. You're kindness itself. Sure, thinking that we'd be welcome here, I already asked the battle-axe if we could have the day off to come here. Well, you can imagine her response to that! *Give me the day off*! The day that hell freezes over she'll have me serving drinks to the spectators and himself will be counting the money they've made from selling tickets! Still, the doctor says that my ears should be healed in time for Easter, when I'll ask again for the day off. Mind, he said he'd never seen ears so badly chewed in all his days."

Laughter burst forth from all around the table, aching sides held together with one hand as the other was used to wipe their eyes.

"Bridie! *Bridie*!" wheezed Patrick, as he tried manfully to catch his breath. "You'll finish me off, woman, so you will!"

When the laughter had died down, Bridie pushed herself away from the table and rose laboriously from her chair.

"Well, if there's no more tea in the pot and no more cake in the tin, then I might as well be on my way. Besides, if herself comes back while I'm out, they'll be hell to pay when I get home - begging your pardon, Father."

"Don't go just yet, Bridie," Beth said, as she jumped up from the table and ran from the room.

Very soon, she hurried back into the kitchen and handed Bridie an envelope.

"This is for you and Joseph," she said shyly.

"What is this?" the old woman said, as she tore at the envelope. "Is it a Christmas card then?"

"Well, it's more of a present, really," Beth answered quickly, reaching out her hands in vain attempt to stop Bridie from removing the contents there and then.

"Ah well, if we're not going to be having a proper Christmas up the road then I might as well have it now, so as I can thank you properly, that is," Bridie said greedily, as the last of the envelope hit the floor. She pulled out what appeared to be a card, looked at it for a moment or two and then threw herself into Beth's arms.

"Oh, Miss Beth, *Miss Beth*," she cried. "You've done it yourself, so you have, haven't you! Look! *Look*!" she exclaimed, handing her gift around to the others.

The card was, in fact, a watercolour of a small vase of wild flowers, the brilliant blue of the forget-me-nots on the vase itself so like the colour of Bridie's eyes. The posy of flowers was made up of clover, columbines and daisies, all so delicately and loving painted as to be almost real.

"So this is what you've been up to in your room," said John, as he took the card from Susan. He studied it carefully for some minutes.

"You are good," he said, his voice filled with admiration. "I really didn't know that you were this talented. I'd like to see more of your work. If this is anything to go by, then I'd say that you could make yourself a very comfortable living from your painting. I am seriously impressed."

Beth felt herself growing red. The warmth in his voice and the look of admiration on his face were so genuine that she had to believe him. She knew that she was gifted as a painter, but to receive such assurance from someone very much in the know was deeply gratifying. She hoped that he would be as impressed with the woodland scene she had done for his present!

"Oh, Miss Beth!" Bridie's words cut through Beth's thoughts. "I've never in all my life had anything as beautiful as this. Sure, I'd love to be able to show it to everybody but I know that I must keep it well out of sight up at the house for I couldn't explain it away to save my life. And my life wouldn't be worth saving if that evil pair knew anything about this. So, I'll show it to Joseph and then we'll put it safely away where their snooping eyes will never find it. But, oh, the joy it will give me, knowing that you've done this, just for me and himself. Aw, lass, I don't know how to thank you, sure I don't!" The old lady's eyes were brim full of tears.

"Dear Bridie," Beth said, holding out her arms to her again.

"You've thanked me already - more than adequately, really you have. Just give me a hug, that's all I ask. I miss your hugs."

"Not half as much as I miss yours, I can tell you!" responded Bridie, as she threw her arms around Beth.

"And now I must be away," she said, as she pulled herself reluctantly from Beth's hug, "or I'll be in hot water for sure. Bless you all. Have a wonderful, peaceful Christmas. Joseph and I will be thinking of you all and we'll do our best to get along to Mass, Father, that is if the old witch lets us out of the house!"

"Away with you, Bridie. You're a wicked woman, so you are. But I love you just the same."

Christmas passed more pleasantly than Beth could have hoped for a few weeks ago. Father Patrick and Susan put in an appearance at the midnight mass, with Patrick bundled up as though he really was ill. He was able to assure his parishioners that all would soon be well and he would back be in full control again in the new year. He was careful to tell no untruths but still managed to give the impression that it was ill health that was keeping him from his duties - which, of course, was the truth. It just wasn't his own personal ill-health!

Beth and John crept up to the 'peep-hole' room, as Susan called it and were able to enjoy the ages-old beauty of that most special service. They had also spent part of the afternoon up there, observing the children's nativity play that traditionally was held each year in the church. Very softly, they joined in with the singing of the carols, their hearts filling with joy at the sound of the children's sweet voices.

"I don't think there is a lovelier sound on earth than children singing," whispered Beth. "Especially when they are singing hymns or carols. There is such innocence in their voices and they really sound as though they mean every word they're singing. They sound positively angelic from up here. I wonder what they sound like in Heaven?"

"I bet you anything that right now the Lord is grinning all over His face in sheer delight! I wonder, though, what effect the sound is having in Heaven? It must be quite something, you know."

"Well, I can't honestly think that they are enjoying it 'up there' any more than I am right here," Beth replied, as she snuggled closer to John. His arm tightened around her shoulders and he rubbed his chin lightly over the top of her hair.

"I love you, Miss Morgan," he whispered.

Beth caught her breath at the sound of her name and her heart surged with love for him at the realisation that he thought of her as her real self, not the aberration of her self that had been, for such a short but horrific time, the wife of another man. She knew within herself that that period of her life would never be a barrier between her and John, would never be the cause of dissension or negativity in any future relationship they would share. A feeling of deep contentment and comfortableness filled her and she raised her face, radiant with love, to him.

"I love you, too," she whispered as he gently kissed her.

12

Two nights later it was a tearful, yet excited Beth who bade an almost heartbreaking farewell to Patrick and Susan. Earlier in the day, John had taken his uncle's old car along to the garage for some much needed repairs. This then left the garage at the house free for John to park his own car, affording complete privacy as they loaded the boot with all Beth's possessions. Then Beth climbed into the front seat and tucked herself down into the foot-well. By leaving at night, there was little chance of her being seen, especially if John took the motorway out of the city rather than driving through the built up areas.

Once they had been on the motorway for some minutes, John said that it was safe for Beth to sit up on the seat beside him.

"There's next to no traffic about, as I had hoped," he said. "It's a good thing you are so tiny. It couldn't have been very pleasant for you down there but it really was for the best. We just can't take any chances with your safety and we simply don't know who is watching from where at any time."

Beth shuddered.

"In that respect, I shall be more than glad to get away from here and to complete anonymity. At least no-one up in Donegal will know anything about me, not even my name."

John slowed slightly, allowing the car behind him to overtake. He had been surreptitiously keeping an eye on it in his rear-view mirror, hoping not to alert Beth to its presence. It had been sitting on his tail for some while now and he was getting more than a little nervous. However, as it passed, he could see that the occupants were several teenage girls, passing a bottle between them.

"That lot there are well away to the races," he said, nodding towards the car in front. "I think I'll pass them myself and get as far ahead as possible. I don't trust them in the least. They are an accident just waiting to happen and the last thing we want is to be caught up in someone else's stupidity." So he pulled out and accelerated fast to pass the car, relieved that the girls were indeed too drunk to be of any threat to them, other than as a potential road accident. He, too, would be more than glad to get back to

Donegal and normality. All this cloak and dagger stuff was all very well to watch on television or read about in some thriller, but to experience it first hand was not pleasant.

"Actually, I've been giving some thought to your name," he added when they were safely past the other car. "Uncle Pat mentioned it last night after you had gone up to bed and I tend to agree with him that if at all possible, you shouldn't use the name Beth Morgan while you're up in Donegal. I have no doubt whatsoever that you will be completely safe there, but one never knows who knows whom. Can you think of any other name that you would be comfortable with and that would be easily remembered?"

Beth was silent for some time, looking out through the window onto the dark countryside, feeling almost as empty as the blackness that greeted her gaze. Would her life ever be 'normal' again, whatever *normal* was these days? And she was seriously beginning to wonder about that. Everything had been so upside down for so long now that she was feeling very disorientated. Four months ago she had simply been Beth Morgan, then suddenly she was Beth Brady and just recently she had begun to think of herself again as Beth Morgan and now John and Pat thought she should change her name to something completely different. Would she ever have any sense of identity again?

Come on, girl, she told herself. Pull yourself together. Perhaps it is just leaving the safety of Patrick's place that is making you feel all vulnerable and down. So no more feeling sorry for yourself! A new life is ahead of you - *right now*! And John is the key to that life so just be thankful that he thinks enough of you to risk his own safety to make sure that you're safe yourself.

She took a deep breath and straightened her shoulders. John glanced down at her, noting the determination in the line of her chin, thrust forward with great resolve.

"You okay?" he asked.

"Yes. I guess I am really. Just feeling a bit wibbly."

"Wibbly?"

"Yes, *wibbly*! You know what I mean - a bit wobbly, but all inside. But I shall be all right, don't worry. Now to the subject of my name or at least which one I'm going to use for the next chapter of my life!"

"You don't sound all that happy about this. Are you sure you're going to be all right?"

"Don't mind me. I'm just being a bit sensitive about it all. I just hope that I don't lose all sense of my own identity with so many different name changes."

"Well, don't try for anything too drastically different from you real name. I'm sure it would help you to become accustomed to it if it had some ring of familiarity about it. Is there a family name that you could use - a favourite aunt's, perhaps?"

"I will *not* be called Mildred even though my life does depend on it!" Beth said with considerable force.

"*Hah*!" John hooted with laughter. "Mildred you will not be, under any circumstances! There's no way I'm calling you Mildred. Oh blast! I almost missed our exit, what with all that laughter. Mildred, indeed." He turned off the motorway onto the road that led to Ballyclare and Larne.

"Seriously, though," Beth continued. "I've just been giving this some thought and think I might have the answer. When I was very little, my father used to call me Libby. It was his pet name for me that no-one else ever used. My mother's maiden name was Cunningham and none of my married, so-called relations would know that. So I guess I could be known as Libby Cunningham, couldn't I?"

"Libby Cunningham. Hmm, sounds good to me. Libby. Libby," John mused. "I think I really do like that name. It suits you, *I* think even more than Beth does. Somehow it's softer, more gentle, just like you."

"Dope!" Beth said as she smacked his leg. He grabbed her hand and held it as close to him as possible.

"I mean it," he said, smiling over at her. "You are a very soft and gentle sort of person. That's one of the many things I love so much about you."

"Now you're being soppy. Concentrate on your driving," Beth grinned. "Which reminds me, just where are you taking me at this time of night?"

John brought Beth's hand up to his mouth and kissed it before releasing his hold.

"Well, little Beth. *Oops*! Libby, I should say, or should it be Libby-Beth?"

"Libby will do just fine, thank you very much!"

"Okay, *Libby*. We are going to some friends of mine who have a small farm between Ballyclare and Larne. Ellie is the farmer; well, actually, she's mainly a cheese producer and her husband, Kees, is a potter. They have a farm shop where they sell her cheeses and his pots."

"*Case*?" Beth said, quizzically. "That's a weird name."

"It sounds like 'Case' but it's spelt K-e-e-s; it's a shortening for Cornelius. He's a Dutchman who came over here some years ago, fell in love with Ellie's laughing Irish eyes and never went home. They've become good friends of mine over the years and I sell some of Kees's pottery in my shop in Donegal and also in Dublin. I think you'll really like his work - and Kees and Ellie, too. They're good people.

"I haven't told them anything about you, about why you're with me. The least said about that to anyone outside the family, as it were, the better. I shall simply introduce you as my friend Libby, from Canada, who is going to stay for a while in Donegal to do some painting. All very truthful and all very safe. It'll be a good practise-run for us both!"

"I'm so very glad I have you," Beth said as the car slowed and turned into a farm entrance.

"And I'm very glad that I have you," John answered as he stopped the car and leaned over to give her a kiss.

Just as John had foretold, Ellie and Kees were delightful people, most welcoming and totally unsuspecting of Beth - *Libby*, as she must now start to think of herself. A hot drink, a long, friendly conversation and a warm, cosy bed were the perfect ending to what had been a somewhat traumatic day.

The gale that had been raging for most of the night finally blew itself out and they awoke to a bright blue sky, brilliant sunshine and cold, crisp air - a perfect day. Having said their farewells, John and Libby took their leave, laden with several cheeses, two delightful coffee mugs for Libby's new cottage and several jars of home-made jam.

The scenery up the Antrim coast was breathtakingly beautiful. Libby was entranced with all she saw. They took a quick detour through the Glens of Antrim and then back to the coast road, stopping for a pub lunch at Ballycastle.

"I've a little treat for you this afternoon," John said as they drove away from the pub. "I thought it would be nice for you to see the Giant's Causeway as we have to drive right past. It'll mean another overnight stop before we reach Donegal but I think you'll be happy with tonight's accommodation, too."

"More friends of yours, I suppose?"

"Now that would be telling! That shall remain a surprise, I promise you."

"Tease!"

"But you love me anyway!"

"What makes you so sure?"

"I see it in your eyes; I hear it in your voice."

"You old romantic!"

"Enough of the 'old'! I'm only thirty-three - just."

"And I'm only twenty-four - far too young to be associating with old-age pensioners!"

"Would you like to get out and walk?"

"You wouldn't dare put me out on the road!"

"Oh, wouldn't I?" John pulled the car off the road into a farm gate. "Out you get, you hussy!"

"Suit yourself!" Libby answered and went to open the door.

"Oh no, you don't!" John reached across and grabbed her, pulling her to him. "Just you come here. I see that I shall have to teach you some manners, young lady, if you are to become the sort of lady a man of my standing would wish to associate with!"

"You rotten beast!" Libby retorted.

"But you love me really!"

"It strikes me that this is where this conversation started and I'm not going through it again. Now behave yourself!"

"Not a chance!" said John, his face coming down closer and closer to hers. "Not a chance!"

Some minutes later, he turned the car fan on to full power to demist the windows.

"Reluctantly I must release you and let you go, in the words of some awful song or other, otherwise it will be dark before we even reach the Giant's Causeway, let alone get a chance to see it."

Libby reached up and stroked his cheek.

"You *are* right, though, you know. I do love you."

"Temptress!" he hissed as he kissed her once more. "I love you, too."

The wind was very cold as they walked down the winding road to the Causeway and John took full advantage of it by keeping his arm tightly around Libby's shoulders. He was tempted several times to stop and kiss her but the voices of the Americans following them down the path kept him walking. He wasn't that much of a lovesick teenager, he told himself, although he really wasn't entirely convinced!

"Oh my goodness!" Libby exclaimed when they rounded the final bend and could see the Causeway at last. "This can't be for real!"

Up in the exhibition centre, they had read about how the extraordinary hexagonal basalt columns had been created by volcanic activity. Libby had also been fascinated by the legend of Finn McCool who was said to have built the causeway to bring his lady-love from her home on Staffa in the Hebrides. The romance of the story appealed to her sense of the mysterious.

She and John clambered out as far as they dare on the columns, for the wind was blowing the sea water over them and making them very slippery. Also, the tops of some of the columns were convex and some were concave, as if one had fallen off the other and landed right beside it, which was absolutely impossible for they were so tightly packed together. Libby was sure that if they could be picked up, then one would fit perfectly on top of another when inverted. It truly was a phenomenal feat of nature and Libby was overawed by the experience of being out there, amongst it all.

Turning to face the sea, she raised her arms in the air, trying to keep her balance against the wind.

"I votes for Finn McCool!" she shouted against the wind.

"You're crazy!" John said as he came up behind her and slipped his arms around her waist.

Just then a deep-voiced American accent boomed out from behind them. It was one of the men who had followed them down the path and he was having some difficulty maintaining his balance.

"*My God*!" he exploded to his friends. "You'd think when they built this thing, they would have had the decency to level off the tops!"

Libby shrieked with laughter and John spun her around and buried her face against his coat. He, too, was shaking with suppressed laughter.

"Behave yourself, child!" he hissed in her ear. "You'll have us both over and into the sea! *Oh, grief,*" he added. "How can some people be so appallingly ignorant? This is a story to keep for our grandchildren."

Libby raised her head and looked up into his face.

"Grandchildren?" she said quietly.

John caught his breath at the look on her face.

"Time to go," he said, giving her a little kiss and then dropping his arms, releasing her. "It'll soon be dark and we are expected for tea."

Libby took a quick breath and shook her head, as if to clear it.

"Expected where?" she asked.

"That's all part of the surprise!"

The journey to their destination did not take too long and try as she may, Libby could not get John to tell her a thing about where they were going. Finally, they pulled up outside a pleasant house in a quiet suburban street in an unknown town - unknown to Libby, that is. John got out of the car and came around to open her door, offering her his hand to help her out. Ignoring her plea to tell her where they were, he took her elbow and guided her up the pathway to the front door, which opened before he had a chance to ring the bell. Libby could scarcely believe her eyes for it was Paul who opened the door.

"Come in, my dears. *Come in*!" he boomed. "How delightful to see you!"

Libby stumbled across the doorstep and into his arms.

"Oh, Paul," she cried. "What a *surprise*! John wouldn't give me even the tiniest hint where we were going. I had no idea at all that you lived up this way, least of all that we would be coming to see you."

"That's my boy!" laughed Paul, as he shook hands with John. "He's good at keeping secrets, this one. We wanted it to be a complete surprise for you. Now, young man, you run and fetch your bags while I show this little lady up to your rooms."

"We're staying *here*?" Libby asked in surprise.

"Well, you don't really think that I would let you stay in an hotel on my own doorstep, would you, when there are two spare bedrooms right here in this house?"

"I just had no idea," Libby said as she followed Paul upstairs and into a room overlooking the back garden. She went to the window and looked out.

"What a lovely garden you have," she said. "Even in the depths of winter, it looks so lovely."

"Ah, that's all down to Isobel, I'm afraid to admit. I'm a little too lazy to do much more than cut the grass but my sister is a real green-fingers."

Libby turned from the window and looked around the room. A comfortable looking double bed was flanked either side by rosewood cabinets topped with lamps with frilly shades. The pink floral bedding matched the curtains at the windows and several prints on the walls continued the very feminine theme. It wasn't really to her taste but it all looked very clean and comfortable.

"I hope you will be comfortable in here," Paul said with one eyebrow slightly raised. "My sister is also the interior decorator in the family. She has very decided views on most things, you'll find, but she really does have a heart of gold. At the moment she is visiting old Mrs Johnson across the road who had a fall before Christmas and is now home from hospital. Isobel was over there like a shot as soon as the ambulance brought her home. Mrs Johnson will have enough broth and junket to keep her going for weeks, I'm sure.

"Ah, there you are, John," he added as John appeared at the doorway with Libby's case. "I was just telling Beth that Isobel is out visiting the halt and the maimed but will be back any moment now, especially if she saw you draw up."

"Perhaps before she does get here I should tell you that Beth is no longer Beth," said John, putting down Libby's case beside the bed.

"*Pardon*? Did I miss something?" asked Paul.

"It's been mutually decided that it really wouldn't be such a good idea for her to continue to use the name Beth Morgan and certainly not Brady, just in case. So, on the way here, we've come up with the name Libby Cunningham - at least Libby has. Libby was her father's pet name for her as a child - and I must say that I really like it - and Cunningham was her mother's maiden name, so it's not all that foreign to her."

"Well, it'll take some getting used to for me, I can tell you," Paul said. "But, yes, I can see the logic in your decision. And how about you, child?" he said, turning to Libby.

"It'll take some getting used to for me as well," she answered. "But at least Libby is a name I know and love and one that I can respond to comfortably."

"Then that's all that really matters. If you're comfortable with it then who am I to complain? It might take a little explaining to Isobel. She can be a bit funny at times but I'm sure we'll manage somehow. By the way, she has no idea what you have been through down in Belfast. I never discuss any of my dealings with Patrick with her. Not that I have anything to hide, but it's all a matter of confidentiality. She knows that you have been staying at Pat's house and that John is taking you up to Donegal for a holiday and that is all."

"Thank you, Paul," Libby said gratefully. "The fewer people who know, the more comfortable I shall feel. I'm sure I would find it very difficult to relax, knowing that people might be looking at me and imagining all sorts of horrible things."

"Comfort is a wonderful thing, child, and the Lord most definitely wants us to be comfortable. Now let's go back downstairs and I'll put on the kettle. That's bound to bring Isobel running. She has a sixth sense about her kitchen. She can't bear for me to go in there and start messing it about. Drives the poor woman to distraction!

"By the way," he added, "the bathroom is right beside your room. You'll have to share that one with John. Isobel and I have another at the front of the house."

The front door opened just as they reached the hallway and a woman entered who could be no-one other than Paul's sister. She was shorter than Paul and was slender whereas he was decidedly portly, but there all dissimilarity ended. With her hair pulled back tightly in a bun, even their hairstyles looked similar. Their facial features were so alike that they could have been twins.

"Ah, Isobel," said Paul. "You're just in time. I was just going through to make some tea for our guests."

"You stay out of my kitchen!" Isobel said sharply, wagging her finger at him. "John," she said, holding out her hand. "How lovely to see you again. And you must be Beth," she added, extending her hand also to Libby.

"Actually, her name is Libby, Isobel," Paul said quickly.

"But you told me her name was Beth."

"Anno Domini, my dear. Anno Domini. Elizabeth, Beth, Libby, all much the same to an old fogey like me." He winked at Libby.

"You get worse with age, Paul Hopkins, you really do. I shall soon be worrying every time you go out, just in case you can't remember how to get home."

"Oh, come, I'm not *that* bad," Paul retorted.

"Well, that remains to be seen, doesn't it. And now, you take John and Libby through to the drawing room - if you can remember the way - while I go and make tea for us all."

The very substantial tea was followed later by an enormous dinner, then a good night's sleep. John and Libby left shortly after breakfast the next morning, promising to keep in touch.

They drove straight into Londonderry, across the river and out the other side. John was anxious to get across the border and into Donegal as quickly as possible.

As they left the city behind, John reached over to take Libby's hand and give it a reassuring squeeze.

"Just up the road here we'll have to go through a check point," he said. "It's best if you don't say anything at all unless you are spoken to directly, which would be unlikely anyway. I shall have to show my papers as I'm driving but you won't be asked for any, so whatever you do, don't worry. And try not to *look* worried, either. Everything really will be fine."

"I wish I felt as confident as you sound," whispered Libby. "I'm absolutely *terrified*. What if they start questioning me and won't let me into the country? They might take me back to Belfast and hand me over to the Brady's." Her voice rose slightly with her fear.

"Don't even *think* such things!" John said sharply. "I've already said that they will only want my papers. They probably won't even look in your direction. If they do, just smile naturally and all will be well. Mind you, you'll probably knock them off their feet with that beautiful smile of yours," he added more gently.

"No time to worry any longer. Here we are." He slowed the car down, headed between the barriers and stopped in front of the red light. He wound down the window and handed his papers to the policeman who was waiting to take them. The officer glanced at them and then ducked his head down to look into the car.

"Morning, ma'am," he said to Libby. "Cold day, isn't it? Still, it's better than all that rain we've been having."

"Yes," Libby answered weakly, hoping beyond hope that he wouldn't speak to her again, for she was certain that her voice would pack up on her altogether but he was only being polite and had already turned to John to ask him some questions.

"Where are you going, sir?"

"Home to Donegal."

"And where have you been?"

"Visiting my uncle in Belfast. We were down there for Christmas."

"What's your uncle's name?"

"Father Patrick Delaney."

"A priest, is he? Well, have a safe journey home." He handed John's papers back and walked off towards the car waiting behind them.

"Say nothing yet," John said softly and he closed the window and drove off. A few hundred yards down the road and they were safely across the border into Donegal and John finally released his breath in a huge sigh.

"Am I glad *that* is over!" he said.

"I don't think I have ever been so terrified in all my life," Libby answered with a croak. "I feel like a criminal and can hardly believe that I haven't been caught and arrested."

"Look, there's a nice restaurant and bar just up the road here. What say you we stop and have ourselves a heart-starter, as dear old Unc would say? I for one could use a drink right now."

"So could I! *Most* defiantly!"

John laughed.

"You're getting as bad as Unc at messing up words. I think it's going to be a lot of fun, getting to know you, little Miss Libby Cunningham."

The rest of the journey was uneventful. John drove home through the west, taking minor roads through the mountains so that Libby could see as much of the spectacular Donegal scenery as possible. She was silent for most of the way, happy to sit and watch the scenery through the window, overawed at its majestic beauty.

"I've never seen anything like this in my life," she whispered every now and then.

John exulted in her delight, seeing the familiar countryside with new eyes, the places to which he had become so accustomed taking on a whole new meaning through Libby's enthralment. Finally they reached Donegal town and John pulled up his car behind his gallery. He helped Libby out of the car and led the way to the back door, which he unlocked and then preceded her upstairs. Leading her into the sitting room, turning on lights as he went, he stopped in the middle of the room and took her in his arms. He looked down into her eyes and then lowered his head towards hers.

"Welcome to my home," he said as he kissed her warm lips.

13

Libby stayed with John for two weeks whilst the cottage was being cleaned and prepared for her. It was a quiet time of the year for the gallery, right after Christmas, and so he was able to take plenty of time off and he used the time to the fullest. He and Libby spent the days exploring the Donegal countryside, walking in the mountains on the few days that the weather permitted; driving along the dramatic coastline, clambering down to the seashore wherever possible to walk along the beaches, often buffeted by fierce winds, heedless of driving rain.

They spent a couple of days wandering through Yeats country in County Sligo, roaming the heavily wooded mountains, so very different from those in Donegal and yet no less beautiful.

Libby fell in love with Donegal town with its lovely 'diamond', rather than the more traditional town square - though to her mind it looked much more like a triangle than a diamond! - surrounded by delightful shops of all descriptions. Using some of the money from the sale of her jewellery, she stocked up on clothes - sweaters, skirts, trousers - delighting in the fine wools and tweeds, the colours of which - rusts, greens, browns, heathers - were so reminiscent of the colours of the hillsides and mountains round about the town. Gradually she would replace all the clothes that had been given to her upon her marriage - clothes befitting the life style of a lady of leisure, or the 'wife of a gentleman of substance', as her poor, sad husband had so pathetically put it.

Libby settled into the cottage with ease, feeling that she had really 'come home'. Indeed, she hadn't felt so at home anywhere since the early years of her life with her parents. The cottage was small - a large sitting room with a small kitchenette at one end and a bedroom and bathroom across the hall - but the upstairs was fully given over to a studio with huge double-glazed windows and wonderful views out towards the sea.

There were no more than a dozen or so other cottages scattered around the inlet so her neighbours weren't plentiful; nor were they intrusive. Perhaps they were used to having temporary residents, all of an artistic bent, in John's house and so kept their distance a little. But they weren't unfriendly in the least and were only too happy to help Libby out in any way.

Her immediate neighbours were the local postman, Taig Bonner, his wife, Ailene, and their two young children, Ronan and Niamh. Shortly after Libby moved in, young Ronan paid her a visit, carrying in his arms a huge gangling puppy. His dog, an Irish wolf hound named Murna (apparently in honour of Finn McCool's mother!), had had a litter some while ago and this was the last puppy not yet to have found a home. Ronan had asked his Mam and Daddy if he could offer it to the new lady because she might be lonely, all by herself in the cottage.

Libby was not the least bit sure that she wanted a dog just then but the puppy had other ideas. When Ronan put him on the floor, he walked quietly over to Libby, stood on his back legs, placed his paws against her chest and looked long and deep into her eyes. Then his great tongue flashed out of his mouth and licked her face enthusiastically. And so began the enduring love affair between Libby and Jake.

Jake became her constant companion as she roamed the hills above the inlet, searching for inspiration for her painting, for places to be alone with the Lord. Jake always seemed to sense when she needed peace and quiet - and also when she was ready for a game of chase-the-ball or remove-the-arm-from-the-shoulder-socket under the guise of wrestling a stick from her hand!

As the dog grew, in great leaps and bounds, so did Libby's love for him. She had never had a pet of any description before and was astounded at her fierce devotion to him. John was equally besotted with Jake, often taking him for long walks while Libby was busy painting, for John was a frequent visitor to the cottage. He telephoned her every evening and often sent her little notes of love and encouragement, for there were still times when she felt fragile and weak, even frightened.

It seemed that the new year had brought no lessening in Michael's determination to locate his missing sister-in-law and he had begun to suspect Patrick of having had some involvement in her disappearance. But as she was nowhere to be seen and Patrick was back in full command at his church, being 'fully restored to health', there was little for Michael to go on. But Patrick had no illusions about the man and knew that he still had to take great care. He never spoke on the telephone to John about Libby, just in case his phone was tapped, and sent all his letters with pleas to the Lord for protection, to be on the safe side. One simply did not know, in this day and age, who knew whom and just what they were capable of doing.

Gradually, as the weeks became months, Libby grew stronger within herself, more confident in her relationship with the Lord, more certain of her feelings for John. The raw pain of her time in Belfast was fading with increasing rapidity and the deep heartache had become a sort of gentle sadness. She found that she was able to look back at those times far more rationally, without the violence of emotions that had plagued her for so long. If the truth be told, she was quietly rather proud of herself (and daily gave thanks to the Lord), that she had come so far from the place where she had been. She was beginning to believe that she really was a 'new creation', as Paul had described it; beginning to experience the reality of it. There was no doubting that the Lord had transformed her life and in ways of which she could never have dreamed.

Another benefit of Libby's new self-assurance was a major upturn in her painting. There was a quality to it that had never before existed. John was delighted with her work and had sold several pieces privately, wishing that he was able to stage an exhibition but cognisant that the publicity could be dangerous for Libby. He could hardly launch a new artist sight-unseen, with no publicity photographs or public appearances! Especially as the art world had never heard of Libby Cunningham, they would most definitely want to see what the artist looked like and very likely do interviews and such like. So, for now, he had to be content with his private sales.

One Wednesday morning, early in June, Jake's wild, excited barking brought Libby down from her studio to see what all the commotion was about. John was standing outside the front door and Libby marvelled yet again that he, the owner of the cottage, had never once entered it uninvited. She held out her arms in welcome but dropped them immediately at the sight of his serious expression. Realising that something was amiss, she stepped back into the room, allowing him to follow her indoors.

Libby stepped over to the window, nervously and unnecessarily rearranging some wild flowers that were in a vase on the sill. Something really must be wrong, she thought. It was unlike John not to greet her with affection and he was here in the morning on a work day. Even Jake was subdued and he always went berserk when John arrived.

John came up behind her, placed his hands gently on her shoulders and turned her to face him. His eyes, darkened to almost navy blue with concern, studied her face for a few moments.

"Libby," he said very gently. "I have some news for you that may, well, I don't know what it may be. It's pretty shocking and yet, could well be a relief for you as well."

"*Please*, John. Just *tell* me!" Libby pleaded, her voice shaking with fright.

"Oh baby, please don't be frightened! I'm sorry that I'm not handling this better but I hardly know where to begin."

"At the beginning, maybe?"

"Sweetheart, Uncle Pat phoned me this morning. Bridie had been on the phone to him first thing and he called me as soon as he had all the details from her. It seems that Mairead had finally had enough of the Bradys. This morning, just as Bridie was serving breakfast, Mairead got up and left the room. She must have gone into Michael's study for she came back a few minutes later carrying a gun that he apparently kept in his desk. She went and stood beside Michael and placed the gun against his temple. Then she said, 'I hate you!' and pulled the trigger."

"She *killed* him?" Libby gasped in horror.

"Obviously. And then she turned the gun on Clementine, who was sitting motionless as though rooted into her chair, said to her, 'I hope you rot in hell!' and pulled the trigger again. A single shot through the forehead."

"Oh my God, *my God*!" cried Libby, her eyes wide with shock, tears running down her cheeks. "Oh poor, *poor* Mairead! What on earth will they *do* with her?"

"They won't have to, sweetheart. She's already done it."

"What do you *mean*?"

"After she had killed the old lady, she turned to Bridie, who was standing, open-mouthed at the other end of the table..."

"*Oh, no!*" screamed Libby.

"Shh! Bridie's okay." John placed his fingertips against her lips. "She phoned Uncle Pat, remember?"

Libby almost collapsed with relief, her body sagging heavily against John.

"What happened next?" she whispered.

"According to Bridie, Mairead said, 'Thank you, Bridie, for your every kindness. I'm so very sorry.' Then she put the gun to her own temple and fired. She's dead, too, sweetheart. And I'm so very, very sorry for I know that you had great compassion for Mairead."

His arms tightened around Libby as she started to sob. He held her, gently rocking to and fro, as she wept deep, sorrowing tears for her sister-in-law who could have been her friend if so many things had been so very different. Gradually her weeping subsided and Libby drew away from John, accepting his handkerchief.

"Shall I make us some coffee?" he asked.

"Please. I could do with some warmth inside me right now."

"I think a drop of brandy is needed, too, despite the hour of the day. You sit down and I'll bring things through."

Libby tucked herself in one corner of the sofa, drawing her knees up under her chin, wrapping her arms around her legs. Over and over, John's shocking words ran through her mind. What on earth had driven that poor soul to do such a thing? *What, indeed*! As if anyone need ask, she thought angrily. Hadn't she herself lived in that house long enough for it to drive *her* almost insane. Poor Mairead had been there for years and under far worse circumstances than her own. It was a wonder she hadn't done something like this before. But, oh, *why* did she have to kill herself? Libby felt tears start to well up in her eyes again. She gently knocked her head against her knees, willing the tears to stop but to no avail.

A large, very cold, very wet nose was placed in her ear. She raised her head and looked into Jake's big, mournful eyes. Releasing her grasp of her legs, she threw her arms around his neck and buried her face in his rough coat.

"Oh, Jake. Why does life have to be so horribly cruel to some people?" she sobbed. "She didn't deserve that sort of life! I know she didn't. And I couldn't do anything to help her at all! That's what *really* hurts. I couldn't do a *single thing*! I made no difference to her life."

Jake whimpered as Libby cried but did not make any attempt to pull away from her. When she had stopped, he gently licked away her tears, nuzzling his face against hers.

"Oh, Jake! I do love you so much," she said. "You're such a comfort to me. Why couldn't I have been a comfort for *her*?"

"Now, now! We'll have none of that," John said firmly, as he handed her a mug of steaming coffee. She hadn't heard him come back from the kitchenette or put the tray of drinks on the table beside the sofa. "Self-pity never did anyone any good at all. Besides," he continued as he sat down at the other end of the sofa, "from what you've told me, there was not a lot you or anyone *could* do for the poor woman. I gather she was pretty far gone when you went there to live."

"You're right, I know you are," said Libby, reaching for a glass of brandy from the tray and taking a large sip, relishing its heat, burning down through her chest. "I wonder why we so often feel sorry for *ourselves* when we hear bad news about others? How perverse we humans are!"

She and John sat quietly for some time, sipping their coffee and brandy, busy with their own thoughts.

"I've just realised something," Libby said, breaking the silence. "She *spoke*. She actually *spoke* to each of them. I understood that she hadn't uttered a word for years. I know that *I* never heard her speak and believed that she was virtually beyond the ability for speech. Perhaps her lack of communication was self-imposed, a means of self-preservation, maybe."

"It's possible," answered John. "There's also something else to be considered, my love. You realise that you are now the sole Brady heir. Uncle Pat said that it was common knowledge that the old lady had left everything to Michael and now with him gone, too, you are the only surviving Brady. So everything will come to you, I guess, other than personal bequests."

Libby jerked violently as if she had been stung by a wasp.

"I want *nothing* of theirs!" she exploded. "*Nothing*!"

"Okay, sweetheart. That's fine," said John calmly. "But you will have to decide, at some time, what you want to do with it all -

how you want to dispose of it. The tax man will want his share and won't wait forever for it so there are decisions that you will just have to make, sooner or later."

Libby stood up abruptly.

"John, I'm sorry but I need to be on my own. Please stay here, but I'm going out for a walk. Come on, Jake." She turned and left the cottage, not bothering to close the front door. She climbed the steep hill behind the cottage, walking hard and fast, her heart pounding with exertion and emotion. She was angry - with John for saying the things he had said about her apparent inheritance and with herself for reacting in such a negative manner.

She reached the top of the hill before Jake did and flung herself on the spongy heather, her breath coming in deep, wrenching gasps, her blood thundering in her ears. She lay there motionless, thoughtless, mindless, unaware of Jake standing sentinel, his eyes full of bewilderment, his heart aching with some unknown, uncomprehending concern.

After some time Libby pulled herself to her feet, walked to the cliff edge and stood facing the sea, feeling the cool breeze blowing through her hair. Her thoughts, when she found herself able to start thinking once more, were in turmoil, flying helter-skelter all over the place. Her emotions flew with them, like the seagulls before her, reeling, diving, rising above the waves.

Jake nudged her hand with his nose and she bent down to lay her cheek against the top of his head. She could feel his love and devotion for her as he pressed himself against her side. His presence had a calming, settling effect upon her and she moved over to a rocky outcrop where she could sit and where there was room for Jake to curl up beside her. It was a place that had become very special to them both and they had spent many long hours up here while Libby reflected on the events of the past months and on her progress. Grateful for Jake's undemanding, silent vigil, Libby turned her thoughts to the Lord, asking for His peace, His guiding so that she would know what was right for her to do.

A couple of hours later Libby felt, sensed, rather than heard, John's footsteps as he came across the headland towards her. She turned to look at him and seeing that he looked rather apprehensive, she held out her hand towards him.

"Come and sit with me," she said.

"Are you okay now?" he asked tentatively as he sat beside her on the rocks, warmed by the early summer sun.

"Yes. Yes, I am," she answered with a smile. "I must admit that I was pretty shaken up earlier and was probably not very nice to you - and I'm really sorry - but I've been doing a lot thinking up here. I've got things pretty well sorted out in my head now and if I may, I'd like to talk them through with you."

"Time to play sounding board again, is it?" he chuckled.

"You're the best one I've got."

"I'm the *only* one you've got!"

"True! But it really does help me so much to get things straight in my head if I can talk them through with you. Somehow you make me see things so much more clearly and then I can get them properly into perspective. So let's see what sense I can make of the news you brought me this morning.

"First of all, Michael and Clementine. I am shocked by their deaths, but not the least bit surprised. My feelings, I think, are really of nothingness. There's no sense of grief or sadness. I think the best thing I can do is simply commit them to the Lord and let Him take care of them. I'm just so grateful that nothing more is expected of me.

"As for Mairead, I'm deeply moved with compassion for her. My heart really aches when I think of what she has been through, but I realise that she is probably in the best possible place now and I commit her to Him, too. At least she won't be suffering any more; she won't be ridiculed or abused or humiliated any longer. I know that the Lord loves her and will take good care of her."

"He loves the other two, as well," John said gently.

"Oh, I *know* He does but I don't feel ready to think about that!" Libby paused for a while, looking out to sea, watching the sunlight dancing on the waves.

"I guess if I'm to be truthful," she said at last, "what I really feel for them both is a deep pity, a real sadness that they were so totally wrapped up in the acquisition of all their wealth and power that they lost all sight of the real meaning of life, of love and kindness, of true friendship, goodwill and giving. They must have been so lonely with only their fear of other people's greed to keep them company. They were so suspicious all the time, so bitter and friendless, so empty, I now realise. Yes, they are to be pitied.

"I also have to admit that I am glad that they are gone, if for no other reason than that their threat to me and mine has gone with them."

"That is very true and for that I'm deeply thankful, too."

Libby looked up at John with a smile of such warmth that he couldn't resist giving her a kiss, to which she responded with considerable enthusiasm. He slipped his arm around her shoulder, drawing her closer to him, grateful to have her back from the dark place of her anger and pain.

"Obviously I do not want anything to do with their business activities, whatever they might have been," Libby continued, once they had drawn apart. "Whatever may come to me I shall sell off immediately and then worry about what to do with the money! It will have to be given to some cause that is really worthwhile and where it will do the greatest possible good.

"Which brings me rather neatly to the house itself. I've decided that the best possible arrangement will be not to sell it but to give it away. I don't know whether you've ever seen it - somehow I think not; they're hardly the sort of people you would associate with! - but it really is huge and has lovely, large grounds. I thought that perhaps Patrick and Paul might like to have it for a healing centre."

"Are you *serious*?" exclaimed John.

"Yes, I am. Absolutely. Patrick mentioned several times when I was staying with him that his real dream was to have a place of his own where people in need could come to stay and receive counselling and prayer ministry; somewhere he and Paul would be able to help people openly, not behind closed doors and in secret as they have had to up 'til now. And now that Paul is virtually retired he would be more than willing to move to such a place so that they could get on with their 'real work', as he put it.

"I can think of nowhere better, can you? A large, beautiful house, completely secluded from the neighbours and with a built-in housekeeper and handyman."

"A what?"

"Bridie and Joseph, of course! They'll need somewhere to live and a job to do now. This way they won't even need to pack! And of course, Susan could join them! What do you think?"

"Well, I've never seen the house but I do know the area it is in and there are some amazing properties up there. So I'm sure that it would be more than adequate for your plans. As to what Uncle and Paul would say, well I'm sure their feet wouldn't touch the ground for many months after hearing such news. Of course, you realise that it would take quite a sum of money to set up and run an establishment like you envisage."

"You're right, as always."

"Naturally!"

Libby nudged him in the ribs.

"Chauvinist!"

"But you love it!"

"Be quiet and let me speak! You're distracting me again. As I was saying, money. Yes, now I guess that's where the businesses come in. As I've already said, I have no idea what they are or what they're worth - I just hope they are legitimate! - but with luck and the Lord's blessing I will be able to realise enough on their sale to fund the whole operation or at least a substantial part of it. Anyway, there's no point in trying to work it all out now because we just don't know what is involved but at least I feel so much better about being the sole heir - if that's true."

"Perhaps by doing what I would like to do, it will in some way balance the scales. So much of that family's activities brought so much grief to others. Now, maybe, the rewards of their wrong-doings will be put to beneficial use. Good coming from evil and all that. I know it would make me feel a whole lot better about things."

"You're a very special lady, Miss Libby Cunningham, and I'm very proud to know you."

"Nonsense!" Libby retorted, blushing most becomingly, he thought.

"It isn't nonsense. It's the truth. You're such a loving and generous person and I admire that enormously. There's nothing avaricious or self-seeking in you whatever. You're one of the most selfless people I've ever known."

"Well, I think you're pretty wonderful, too, and I'm very proud to count you as my dearest friend, in some ways even dearer than Cathy," Libby added with a smile. She suddenly caught her breath and clapped her hands together, her eyes dancing with excitement and delight.

"*Hey! I've just realised something*! I can write to Cathy at last!!

She must think that I've fallen off the face of the earth but if I had let her know even the slightest detail of what was going on, you can bet your life that her brother, Steve, would have been over on the first available flight, blundering around as only he can - bless him - and causing no end of trouble as a result.

"It's been so hard not being able to be in touch with her all this time but with the contacts the Bradys have in Boston, I couldn't be sure that they wouldn't be able to get at Cathy and her family somehow and that they might be able to trace me here. It's probably a bit far-fetched to think like that but Father Patrick was pretty adamant that I didn't write to Cathy, just to be on the safe side. But it will be *so* good to write to her again, maybe even talk to her but how I would explain all this over the phone, heaven only knows!"

"Why over the phone? Why not in person? We could go and pay her a visit."

"*Oh, no*! I'm not risking taking you over to Boston. Cathy is far too beautiful and besides, she'd eat you alive! You're just her sort of man."

"Am I *your* sort of man, Libby?"

"What a question! *Of course* you are."

"Seriously?"

"Seriously."

"How seriously?"

"What do you mean?"

John paused for a moment. Then, gathering up Libby's hands in his, he looked deeply into her eyes.

"Will you marry me, Libby?"

Libby felt a deep love-surge within her and she smiled a smile of such exquisite tenderness and love that John thought his heart would stop at the sight of it.

"Oh, John," she whispered. "Do you *really* need to ask?"

Jake got up and wandered along the cliff top, chasing in his mind the birds flying above the waves that he could not chase in reality, not minding that he couldn't catch them. It was safe to leave her alone. She would come to no harm with *him*. And when they finally went back down to the cottage there would be a meal ready for him, and another game, just like always.